CW01020248

# YURI GERMAN

## A NOVEL

Translated by *Olga Shartse*

**RADUGA PUBLISHERS**

MOSCOW

Translated from the Russian

Edited by *Robert Daglish*

Designed by *Inna Borisova*

**Ю. Герман**

ДЕЛО, КОТОРОМУ ТЫ СЛУЖИШЬ

*На английском языке*

First printing 1961
Second printing 1974
Third printing 1989

*Printed in the Union of Soviet Socialist Republics*

$$\Gamma \ \frac{4702010200\text{-}339}{031(01)\text{-}89} \ 005\text{-}89$$

**ISBN 5-05-002436-6**

## CONTENTS

Chapter One

    Natural Sciences . . . . . . . . . . . . . . . . 7

    Father Is Back . . . . . . . . . . . . . . . . . 13

    No Skeletons for Sale . . . . . . . . . . . . . . 16

    Man Can Do Anything . . . . . . . . . . . . . 21

Chapter Two

    Typhus . . . . . . . . . . . . . . . . . . . . 29

    Man and Wife . . . . . . . . . . . . . . . . . 34

    The Daughter . . . . . . . . . . . . . . . . . 41

Chapter Three

    Mushrooms . . . . . . . . . . . . . . . . . . 45

    Fathers and Sons . . . . . . . . . . . . . . . . 48

    The Student . . . . . . . . . . . . . . . . . . 55

Chapter Four

    Gifts . . . . . . . . . . . . . . . . . . . . . 60

    Grandfather . . . . . . . . . . . . . . . . . . 65

    After the Theatre . . . . . . . . . . . . . . . . 68

Chapter Five

    Polunin . . . . . . . . . . . . . . . . . . . . 72

    Arguments and Discord . . . . . . . . . . . . . 82

    Time Flies Unchecked . . . . . . . . . . . . . 87

Chapter Six

    Divorce . . . . . . . . . . . . . . . . . . . . 94

    We, Red Army Soldiers . . . . . . . . . . . . . 98

    Old Man Pych . . . . . . . . . . . . . . . . . 101

Chapter Seven

    First Aid . . . . . . . . . . . . . . . . . . . 108

    Professor Zhovtyak Himself! . . . . . . . . . . . 113

    Postnikov . . . . . . . . . . . . . . . . . . . 117

    We Have Different Roads . . . . . . . . . . . . 122

    I Drink! . . . . . . . . . . . . . . . . . . . . 128

Chapter Eight

    A Nocturnal Conversation . . . . . . . . . . . . 134

    To the "Aeroplane" You Go! . . . . . . . . . . . 149

Roulades . . . . . . . . . . . . . . . 157
Anthrax . . . . . . . . . . . . . . . 163
Chapter Nine
    "My Colleague" . . . . . . . . . . . . 172
    Sweet Life! . . . . . . . . . . . . . . 178
    What Is Happiness? . . . . . . . . . . . 183
Chapter Ten
    Dodik and Wife . . . . . . . . . . . . . 195
    Father Is Dead . . . . . . . . . . . . . 205
    The Rigorist and Tormentor . . . . . . . . 209
    I'm Sick and Tired of You . . . . . . . . . 214
Chapter Eleven
    The Trumpet Soundeth . . . . . . . . . . 217
    Certain Changes . . . . . . . . . . . . 227
    You People Are Amazing! . . . . . . . . . 237
Chapter Twelve
    The Oath . . . . . . . . . . . . . . . 243
    The First Job . . . . . . . . . . . . . 247
    Good-Bye, Varya . . . . . . . . . . . . 252
    Abroad . . . . . . . . . . . . . . . 257
Chapter Thirteen
    The Road to Khara . . . . . . . . . . . 260
    The Great Doctor . . . . . . . . . . . . 264
    Things Are Bad for the Great Doctor . . . . . . 272
Chapter Fourteen
    How Are Your Herds? . . . . . . . . . . 277
    So This Is the Way to Work! . . . . . . . . 287
    Alone Again . . . . . . . . . . . . . . 296
Chapter Fitfeen
    The Sorcerer . . . . . . . . . . . . . 303
    What Is the Purpose of Life? . . . . . . . . 312
    Black Death . . . . . . . . . . . . . . 319
    The Cause You Serve . . . . . . . . . . . 326

Dedicated to the memory
of Yevgeny Lvovich Schwarts

And never ending battle!
Tranquillity is but a dream...

*Alexander Blok*

### Chapter One

## NATURAL SCIENCES

It happened to him when he was in the ninth form. All at once Volodya lost interest in everything, even in the chess circle, which instantly fell apart without him, even in his form-master Smorodin, who had always considered Volodya Ustimenko his best pupil, and even in Varya Stepanova, with whom till only a little while ago, during the November holidays, in fact, he used to enjoy watching the slowly flowing Uncha from the edge of its high, steep bank. Life, so jolly and amusing, so busy and noisy, so fascinating in all things, big and small, suddenly seemed to stop, and everything around Volodya stood still, listening apprehensively, on the alert, as much as to say: let's see what's going to happen to you next, youngster!

And yet, nothing had happened really.

He and Varya had gone to the cinema. There had been the usual autumn drizzle that night. Varya talked her usual nonsense about the "art of the theatre" (she was the star actress of her school drama circle) and some smug-looking hens of a special breed flapped about the screen. And then Volodya became all attention and started breathing loudly through his nose.

"Shut up," he said to Varya.

"What's the matter with you?" she asked, surprised.

"*Will* you shut up?" he hissed.

A scientist had appeared on the screen and was filling a syringe with some sort of liquid. The man had a prominent forehead, thin lips and a haggard face. There was nothing very pleasant or, as Varya's mother liked to say, "charming" about this great scientist. And he was not doing his work so very skilfully either. Probably he was annoyed because they were taking pictures of him for the news. People of his sort hate being photographed at all, and now he was surrounded by cameramen!

Varya was all sympathy for the doomed guinea pig.

"The poor little dear," she said with a frightened glance at Volodya.

He did not so much as hiss at her now. He seemed to glow inwardly as he listened to the man in the white cap and smock earnestly telling the audience the story of the wise old Aesculapius and his daughter Panacea.

"I don't understand a thing," Varya complained in a whisper. "Not a single thing. Do you, Volodya?"

He nodded. And afterwards, when the feature came on, he just sat there glumly, biting his nails and thinking. And he did not smile once, although it was a funny film. He had a way of suddenly removing himself from everyone, of leaving the world of small talk for one of meditation, of withdrawing into some secret retreat of his own. That night, too, though he took Varya home after the show, he was not with her, but quite by himself, alone.

"A penny for your thoughts," Varya said.

"I have none," he muttered ungraciously, absorbed in those thoughts.

"What fun to be with you!" Varya said. "Such tremendous fun! I'm afraid I'll split my sides laughing."

"What?" he asked.

And so they had parted for about three months. Varya was touchy and proud and he had suddenly entered a strange world of seeking and mental strife, discoveries of long discovered truths, a world of sleepless nights, a world of infinite knowledge in which he was nothing, a trifle, a speck of dust caught in a storm. He was tossed and whirled about amid words which he had to keep looking up in the *Encyclopaedia*; he tore his way through books in which he understood next to nothing; there were hours when he all but wept from the sense of his own impotence, but then there were moments when he fancied that he understood, that he was grasping it, that he was almost at home, if only in that one particular chapter, that one page, and all he wanted now was to dig into it deeper and then everything would go splendidly. But again he would be plunged into gloom for, after all, he was still only a "silly goose" as his Aunt Aglaya was wont to say.

"What's that?" she asked one very cold night coming into Volodya's "den", as his slit of a room had long been called.

"Where?" Volodya asked, tearing himself away from his book with an effort.

"Why, there! Have you taken to buying pictures?"

"That's not pictures, that's a copy of *Lesson in Anatomy of Doctor Tulp* by Rembrandt."

"Oh, I see," Aglaya nodded. "But what d'you want this *Lesson in Anatomy* for, you silly goose?"

"The reason why I want this *Lesson in Anatomy*, dear Aglaya Petrovna, is because I'm going to be a doctor," Volodya declared, stretching himself luxuriously and yawning with relish. "That's what I've decided."

"For the time being, you mean," Aglaya suggested. "At your age, decisions are altered pretty often. I remember very well that you were going to be a flyer first, then a detective."

Volodya said nothing and smiled. Yes, he could recall something of the kind.

"Was this Tulp man a good doctor?" Aglaya asked.

"He was a Dutchman," Volodya said, peering at the faded reproduction. "Van Tulp. He was a doctor of the poor and a professor of anatomy in Amsterdam. He is usually portrayed carrying a candle and the doctor's motto: A light to others, I burn myself out."

"That's beautiful," Aglaya said with a sigh. "To think of the things you've learnt. And all these books you've cluttered your den with..."

She opened an anatomical atlas Volodya had borrowed from the library and shuddered.

"Ugh, what horrors! Let's go and have tea, it's late. Come along, you future Tulp."

By the time the winter holidays came round, Volodya had so many bad marks in his report that he was quite surprised himself. He had to talk to someone. He walked to Proletarskaya Street to see Varya, striding angrily over the crisp snow and thinking in perplexity: "A light to others..." It was just stupid the way that phrase had stuck.

"Oh, she's out, she's at a rehearsal," said Yevgeny, Varya's half-brother, a round-faced youth with a languid manner. He was wearing a hair-net. (Yevgeny was very particular about his appearance, he liked a sleek head of hair and went to no end of trouble to keep it so.) He was lying back comfortably on the sofa, reading his science. There was a cloying smell of vanilla biscuits in the flat; Mme. Lisse, a friend of Yevgeny's mother, was playing the piano in the next room. Two voices were talking there, one in the weary tones of Yevgeny's mother, the other in the rumbling baritone of Dodik, the well-known motorcycle and automobile man. He was also a tennis player and chief umpire for the town and the region.

9

"Want to buy a car?" Yevgeny asked. "Dodik's selling one. A Hispano Suiza, 1914 model, in running order. He's sold two already and got himself a new one. He's a fast worker, a really smart chap. I envy the man."

Volodya said nothing.

"This is a dog's life," Yevgeny went on in a bored voice. "Cramming and cramming, but what's the use? However, study we must." He changed to a briskly business-like tone. "Which is what I do. But you, people say, are making no effort at all."

"I'm not," Volodya admitted indifferently.

"There, you see! It's bad, you know. Take me, now. There are some subjects I can scarcely master at all, it's a terrific strain. And, mind you, I've had TB."

"Huh, you a consumptive!" Volodya said with a smirk, looking at Yevgeny's healthy flush.

"Looks are extremely deceptive," Yevgeny replied peevishly. "By and large, TB should not be regarded as..." "By and large" was a favourite expression of his.

He dwelt at length on the subject of TB and on how he had been rescued from the clutches of that dread disease when it was almost all up with him. Yes, literally rescued, they had tried everything including aloes cooked with honey and lard.

"A mother's love can move mountains!" Yevgeny proclaimed emotionally. He liked to indulge in a bit of pathos occasionally. However, Volodya's long yawn made him cut short his TB tale and he now proceeded to criticise him.

"You have also broken away from the collective." Yevgeny's tone was well-meaning. "By and large, you're all wrapped up in yourself. That's bad. You ought to show more enthusiasm, vigour and cheerfulness in the true Komsomol spirit. You and I, don't forget, are studying at good Soviet schools, workers' schools, not at some bourgeois college."

"How d'you know my school is good?" Volodya asked.

"By and large, all our schools are better than bourgeois colleges." Yevgeny suddenly winked as much as to say: "Fend that one off!"

Volodya found nothing to say quickly enough, and Yevgeny continued:

"If you're in difficulties, the collective of pupils and teachers will help you. Haven't you got a close-knit collective? Of course, you have. And so it will help. Why, you have Vovka Sukharevich in your form, he's an ass, of course, but an ass full of noble impulses. I've heard he's always helping the backward. Ask him, he'll give you a leg up."

In the next room, Dodik gave a loud chortle. Yevgeny got up, shuffled to the door in his bedroom slippers and shut it tight.

"I honestly don't know what to do," he said looking worried. "He practically lives here, this comrade dealer in cars and motorcycles. And what does my dear mama see in him anyway? Fun will be had by all when the Terror of the Seas comes home."

Volodya sat blinking vacantly. He supposed that "Terror of the Seas" was Yevgeny's name for his stepfather. Volodya's eyes felt full of sand and the back of his head ached from the nights he had spent without sleep, poring over books that had nothing to do with his school subjects.

"But why fun for all?" he asked.

"Can't you guess?"

"No."

"Husbands, I imagine, take exception to situations of this kind."

Yevgeny nodded at the door. Now it was Mme. Lisse who was laughing. Still Volodya understood nothing.

"All right, but what am I to do anyway?" he said.

"By and large, I'd say take yourself in hand," Yevgeny said. "To be quite honest, as man to man, you're a lot cleverer than I am, but you can't stick to one thing at a time. It's a damned bore, of course, but we've got to finish school. We have our paters behind us today, but tomorrow we may have to face our destiny single-handed. After all, we don't want to end up as porters or something like that..."

Yevgeny flung his science book on the sofa and started giving Volodya some instruction. He was as well-meaning as ever, but his preachings made Volodya feel as if he had eaten too much toffee. Yevgeny was right, of course, but not really right somehow, there was something twisted and shameless about his rightness. Staring in front of him with his transparent eyes, Yevgeny spoke in an affected drawl:

"Take school activities. It's your own affair but it *is* nice for the school to have a good drama circle and be able to put on good shows. It's a point in your favour at teachers' meetings. Or take the wall newspaper. I've been the editor for over a year. I couldn't care less about it really, but *they* need it. I suppose you think it takes up too much time, but I have it all worked out. All the teachers know that I'm the editor, and they simply can't help making allowances for my public spiritedness. And then the teachers have human frailties too. It tickles them to read

11

something flattering about themselves in the paper, whether it's thanks or just good wishes. Now, you're keen on natural sciences. Fine. The school loves such things, but within the limits of the school, my dear friend, within school limits, mind you. What you ought to do is get a group together and go and see the teacher. Dear teacher, we pupils have come to earnestly beg you to take charge of our natural science circle. You and you alone. Do you see?"

Yevgeny took a cigarette out of his bedside table, lit it and inhaled.

"Clear enough?"

"You're no fool, you know," Volodya replied.

"Such is our stand," Yevgeny quoted resignedly. "Are you going to wait for Varya?"

Volodya started back home feeling low. The smell of vanilla biscuits and the sound of Yevgeny's bored voice haunted him for many blocks. Turning the corner where the monument to Radishchev was, he saw Varya. She was walking along in a crowd of boys. She waved to him. The cocky voice of Sevka Shapiro, their chief producer, carried clearly in the crisp, frosty air:

"I support the principles of biomechanics, and am wholly opposed to the doctrines of Stanislavsky. With all due respect..."

"The young fools," Volodya reflected with senile condescension. The thought startled him, for it was not so very long ago that he himself had thought it all such fun.

High in the sky a bell began to toll. It was Saturday and they were ringing for evening service at the cathedral. Boom! went the bell again.

> *Away with all the clergy,*
> *Away with all the monks,*
> *We'll climb into the heavens*
> *And drive out all the gods...*

A group of boys and girls from the school atheist club were coming down the street and singing. Volodya stopped and said to Galya Anokhina, their leader:

"You and your songs! What good does propaganda like that do? You ought to hear a talk on the Inquisition instead."

The youngsters crowded round Volodya and Galya, but they were enjoying themselves too much to listen to the sad story of Giordano Bruno, or Bruno the Nolanese, as Volodya called the great man. Nor did they want to hear just then about Michael Servetus, who had been burnt at the stake twice, first his effigy and then himself, burnt alive together with all the books he had written. But, Volodya persisted, there was the father of the chair of anatomy too, Andreas Vesalius. He had also been murdered by those confounded zealots of the Inquisition. They had sent him on a pilgrimage to the Holy Land, but the boat that was taking him there sank.

"A clear case of sabotage," Boris Gubin, a friend of Volodya's, said. "It was all fixed beforehand."

"And as for Galileo," Volodya went on, "he got cold feet. He put his hand on their Bible and made a statement that he honoured the Most Reverend Grand Inquisitor and swore to believe in all that the holy church preached and recognised as right. Of course, he was only a feeble old man by then."

"Boo-m! Boo-m! Boo-m!" came from the belfry.

"All right, let's get going," said Galya. "By the way, Ustimenko, it wouldn't do you any harm to give a talk on the subject yourself."

They all went off together, vaguely disturbed by Volodya's erudition, the angry gleam in his eyes and his haggard face.

"Him and his lectures," Galya said resentfully. "What does he think he is, a lecturer or something?"

"Don't say that," Boris Gubin put in. "He really is a thinking and reading chap."

### FATHER IS BACK

The moment he came in, and even before he had switched on the hall light, Volodya knew by the faint smell of tobacco and leather that his father was back. Still in his overcoat, he rushed yelling into his father's room. Afanasy Petrovich was sitting at the table, very erect as always, reading a newspaper. He wore a well-pressed, smartly fitting tunic with an airman's collar straps and gold chevrons on his sleeve. His belt hung on the back of the chair, which meant that he would stay the night and was not leaving right away. They greeted each other with their usual handshake. The father wrinkled his eyes a little and drew his son towards him, but they did not kiss; they were strange to the habit. Instead Afanasy Petrovich gave the boy's shoulders a squeeze or two, and told him to take off his overcoat and sit down to eat. Aunt Aglaya appeared from the kitchen with a platter of Siberian fish pies. Her face was glowing and her eyes twinkled merrily with happiness. She loved her brother to distraction, took pride in him, and invariably turned his visits home into great holidays.

"Tell me everything," he said after he had taken a glass of chilled vodka.

Volodya told him everything, concealing nothing. Afanasy Petrovich held a pie in his big hands and looked steadily at his son.

"He's making it all up!" Aglaya cried. "It can't be true. He was always bright, he was nearly top of the school."

"Reasons?" Afanasy Petrovich asked, taking no notice of his sister's interruption.

"I'll come to that later," Volodya said. "But to put it briefly, the thing is that I'm definitely set on becoming a scientist."

His father did not permit himself even a faint smile.

"He studies all night long," Aunt Aglaya broke in again. "The number of books he's fetched home is simply staggering, and now this surprise. It's all rubbish, rubbish!"

Later on, when Aunt Aglaya had fallen asleep worn out by her own hospitality, the two Ustimenkos sat side by side, and Volodya listened to his father talk.

"It's difficult for me to judge," Afanasy Petrovich said. "I'm not a learned man, I'm an air force pilot, but I imagine that every science must have a foundation. Take my job, for instance, the air. It sounds simple enough — lever forward, lever back — and yet..."

They were sitting side by side and Volodya could not follow the direction of his father's eyes, but he could feel his calm, stern gaze just as surely as he felt his father's powerful muscles with his own boyishly skinny shoulder. And he was happy, securely and completely happy. This man with the rugged profile and lined, weather-beaten face, this tough and daring flyer was his father, and to be able to talk to him as an equal, to meditate on the right words to say and say them, was a sensation comparable with nothing in the world.

"And yet, my boy, that simplicity is not really so simple," Afanasy Petrovich went on pensively. "Nothing much is required of you, of course, if all you want is to keep up with the next man, but you do need a pretty firm foundation if you want to push aviation ahead just one short step, or a couple of steps, perhaps. Bluster won't get you anywhere. Take my word for it: I've lived a long time, and you're only just starting out on your journey through life."

Afterwards they went into Volodya's den and there, among the scattered books, magazines and notes, with Rembrandt's *Lesson in Anatomy* on the wall above them, the son began to tell his father about the natural sciences. Afanasy Petrovich sat on Volodya's bed looking closely and searchingly into the boy's drawn, flushed face, and listening to his feverish discourse on the strides made in medicine, on what a true innovator was, on the quest for artificial proteins, and a way of operating on the human heart.

"Now that's laying it on a bit thick, son," said Afanasy Petrovich. "Operating on the human heart, that's an exaggeration."

"An exaggeration!" Volodya shouted. "An exaggeration, you say! I'm sorry, Father, but your words make me think of the people who laughed at Filippov, the Russian surgeon who sutured the hearts of animals in the eighties of the last century. And Ludwig Rehn, a German, stitched up a heart wound in 1896 and the patient lived. Conservatives in science..."

"All right, innovator," his father grunted peaceably. "Tell us another one. Are you going to sew people's heads back on to the necks too?"

"That wasn't funny," Volodya said in a huff. "Incidentally you're a flyer and the dreams of a flying man..."

"All right, all right," Afanasy Petrovich broke in. "I get you, but there are such things as wars..."

"What about wars?" Volodya asked, missing the connection.

"You do read the newspapers, I suppose?"

"I do, but not very regularly."

"Make it regular. And you've got to realise just what Hitler, Goebbels and Himmler are, and that swine Goering, too, who calls himself a flyer. And also Krupp von Bohlen. We had a commissar down to see us a little while ago, a very clever man. He gave us a real analysis — not for jabbering about, of course — specially for us, for the military. So you see, son, if the trouble starts, I'm afraid it will hold up all those artificial proteins."

"Will it?" Volodya asked sadly.

"Sure to. If it wasn't for imperialists in all the countries, science would certainly leap forward."

He undid the collar of his tunic, grew thoughtful for a moment, and then said with a smile that was at once sad and a little embarrassed:

"Our breed is on the upgrade. Your grandfather was a drayman in Kharkov, myself now, I'm a fighter, a flyer, commander of a regiment, and my son is going to brew artificial protein, going to be a scientist. Too bad your mother's not living,

15

that would have made her happy. All right, come on, tell me more."

After midnight Volodya got really extravagant in his over-statements. Mere dreams he passed off as scientific routine, and the very, very distant future appeared reality to him. His father gasped and sighed, but his eyes were merry.

"We have a chap like that, an engineer, Pronin by name," he cut in abruptly. "A good chap, knows his job, but it's dangerous listening to him too long."

"Why?" Volodya asked.

"Why, because he doesn't look underfoot. Only ahead. But there can be ruts in a path, and other stuff too ... your boots need wiping if you step into it. It's time you went to bed, son."

He saw Volodya's disappointed look and added:

"Still, it's better to look far ahead than always keeping your nose to the ground. But you have to do that as well."

In the morning Volodya discovered a note from his father and some money. The note told him to buy all the books and anything else he needed for the "speediest production of artificial protein". It was signed formally: "A. Ustimenko" and a P. S. said: "In the meantime do a good job of work for your country at school. I honestly believe you will."


### NO SKELETONS FOR SALE

It was quite a lot of money — a packet of thirties and two packets of smaller denomination, a regular windfall in fact. Volodya decided to go out at once and buy the thing he had long been dreaming of.

A school appliances shop had opened recently near the town market, not far from the skating-rink. And here Volodya saw Varya standing beside a pedlar of hot pies. She was eating two at once, a meat pie and a cabbage pie squashed tightly together. Her boots and skates hung by their laces on her arm. A brass band was playing behind the tall skating-rink fence.

"Want a pie?" Varya asked as casually as if they had only seen each other the day before. "They're good! I like the fried ones better than the baked, specially for eating two at a time."

Large, heavy snowflakes fell on Varya's cap, her pies and the sleeve of her coat.

"The ice will go all squashy again, won't it, Volodya?

What a rotten winter this is." She stared at him. "Gosh, aren't you skinny!"

Tum-tum-tum went the kettle-drums behind the fence. Tum-tum-tum!

"Done your skating?" Volodya asked.

"Yes!" Varya lied, just in case, and thought with beating heart: "Oh, I *am* so terribly in love with him! It's not even nice."

"Let's go and buy a skeleton," Volodya said.

"A what?"

"A human skeleton. At the school appliances shop. They've got one in the show-window. I've seen it."

"For the school?"

"For what school?" Volodya snapped. "For myself personally."

"You mean for you?" Varya pointed her finger at him.

They started off. However, when they got to the shop they found that it was all very different from what Volodya had expected it would be. A bald, very unpleasant man with a mouthful of gold teeth told him that skeletons, both human and animal, were sold exclusively to educational establishments, only on application in writing and not for cash. No skeletons whatsoever could be sold to a private individual.

"What if he's a scientist?" said Varya with a nod at Volodya. She always had a ready tongue.

"Scientists acquire theirs through their scientific institutions."

"But what if he doesn't belong to any scientific institution?"

"In that case he is classed as a private individual," said the salesman with a gleam of gold teeth.

"D'you think we're going to make money on your silly old skeleton or what?" Varya said angrily. "What if a person needs it, what if a person had dedicated himself to science..."

Volodya left the shop, he felt ashamed. Oh that Varya girl, she was always kicking up rows! He waited and waited, but she did not follow him out. Some twenty minutes later Volodya went back into the shop: there was Varya writing something in the "Book of Complaints" in her large, still childish hand. Volodya glanced over her shoulder and read: "Refusal to sell a skeleton for cash may be called stupid bungling..."

"Varya, stop it!" he whispered.

"Don't be spineless," she snapped at him.

"Stupid bungling or something worst..." Varya wrote on.

17

"Worse," Volodya corrected in a whisper.

"They'll know!" Varya said. "And anyway, go away, Volodya, let me carry this business through to its logical conclusion."

Her cheeks were flaming. A sweet little curl was dangling over her tiny ear, which had a blue stone in the lobe.

And so the attempt to buy a skeleton fell through. Instead, Volodya bought an anatomical atlas, a 1900 edition, fairly clean and rather cheap, at a second-hand bookstore in Tenth October Square, near the cathedral. Varya walked beside him, her skates clinking, her cap pushed back, her face flushed with anger as she talked about the red tape that was still so much in evidence, and the ruthless struggle that had to be waged against those damned survivals of the past.

"Has your father written?" Volodya asked.

"There was a letter last Sunday," Varya replied and, dropping the subject of red tape, told Volodya that maybe she would get hold of a couple of tickets for the Moscow Art Theatre's guest performance of *Uncle Vanya*.

"They've already arrived, they've all put up at the Moscow Hotel," Varya said. "Zina Kryukova saw two of them. She can't tell for sure just who they were, but they may have been Comrade Kachalov and Comrade Livanov. They were both wearing fur-lined coats. Have you got something on your mind again?"

"There really is something psychopatic in this theatre craze of yours," he said. "Seriously, Varya, what's the sense in this sort of art? It's stupid, a sheer waste of time, a senseless squandering of nerve cells, pure and simple imbecility."

This had the beginnings of a quarrel, but it did not come to a head. That Sunday Varya noticed something that had so far escaped the understanding of older, intelligent and educated people: she realised that he was an outstanding personality. With a thrill of wonder she entered Volodya's "den", in which she had not been for such a long time, sat down on the rickety chair, and listened open-mouthed to his ideas on Pasteur and Koch, on Pavlov and Mechnikov, on Pirogov and Zakharyin, on the chances of combating malignant tumours, and, of course, on making artificial proteins. She stayed to have dinner with Volodya.

"D'you know, Volodya, I'm quite dizzy," she said over the soup.

"Why?"

"You've been talking for three solid hours without a break."

"Aha!" cried Aunt Aglaya not without malice. "You're here and gone, but what about me? I come home from work, dead-beat, tired out, my head splitting, and off he goes about his bacteria!"

Still, Volodya did go with Varya to see *Uncle Vanya*. The guest performance by the Moscow Art Theatre had caused such a stir in the town that they actually had to fight their way through the crowd gathered in front of the new House of Culture. While they were still streets away, they were waylaid by people with worried faces and voices that were hoarse from asking if anyone had a ticket to spare. The two felt particularly sorry for an elderly man in uniform who told them with genuine despair that he was "begging" not for himself but for his daughter.

"This is mass psychosis," Volodya said. "The famous Kraepelin has written something to that effect."

Varya thought with a long-suffering sigh: "So we're on to Kraepelin now, are we!"

They had good front-row seats in the balcony. Volodya bought a programme, handed it to Varya without glancing at it, and cast a superior eye over the stalls and the crowded boxes.

At last, the curtain parted with a faint rustle, and the miracle began. On the face of it, what business was it of his, an airman's son, that all that was happening to Sonya, Uncle Vanya, Doctor Astrov, and those other people from a different age, a different world which neither Volodya, nor Varya, nor their fathers, nor even their grandfathers had ever known? Volodya tried so hard not to disgrace himself in front of Varya! He counted up to ten, clenching his teeth till they hurt, and thinking of other things, but those damned, stupid, senseless tears of his kept trickling down his nose, and one actually fell on Varya's hand when she stretched it out for the programme. The last act shattered Volodya's poise completely. He no longer counted or gritted his teeth, he strained his whole body forward and watched human suffering with anger, vowing to do something, clenching his perspiring hands and brushing away the tears that kept welling up in his eyes.

The last act was nearly over when suddenly the elderly woman in rustling silk who sat next to Volodya gave a little cry and started muttering something in a swooning voice. Volodya motioned her to be quiet, but she would not stop muttering and began to get up. Others hissed at her and she uttered a cry. Luckily the play was over. Through a veil of tears Volodya saw the woman's ashen face and her twisted mouth about to scream.

"Mice! Mice! Mice!" wheezed another woman in green.

"What's so exciting about it?" Volodya said, picking his tame white mouse off his neighbour's lap. "What's so frightening? There's no danger of anything like *that*. I hardly fed it today. It just felt lonely and came out."

He was escorted to the militia just the same. Art had not softened the hearts of the people who sat next to Volodya in the front row of the balcony at the House of Culture. After weeping through *Uncle Vanya* they now proceeded to drum it into the elderly militiaman in voices of steel that the young man in question had committed an act of hooliganism with malicious intent. The militiaman took down their statements. Varya sat in a corner and gave Volodya encouraging winks. She had a feeling that she was guilty of something.

When the people had filed their complaints and gone, the officer asked Volodya to show him the mouse.

"Here it is."

"I say! A white one!" the man marvelled.

"I've got lots," Volodya told him. "For my experiments. But I'm sorry for them. You get used to them, you know. They're clever, and this one's tame. Here, take it in your hands."

The officer held the mouse on his ruddy palm for a moment, asked Volodya what he fed his mice on, and let him go in peace.

"Thank you, comrade officer," Varya said. "It upset everything, you know. The play was so wonderful, and suddenly — bang — off you're taken to the militia!"

The officer was studying Varya's face with a hard, cold stare, and when she stopped speaking he asked:

"Now, why does your face seem familiar to me, can you tell me?"

"Why, the fight — remember?"

"I can't be expected to remember all the fights," he answered. "In a job like mine..."

"Why, there was a fight at your skating-rink yesterday. Only yesterday. Surely, you can't have forgotten yesterday's fight?"

Flushing slightly, she told them about the fight between some small boys at the skating-rink the day before. As no one attempted to pull them apart she had butted in herself and received a few knocks too. Undaunted, she had tried again, setting up a screech, which brought help soon enough.

"I see... Stepanova is the name," the officer said stiffly. "Stepanova. Very well, you may go."

Walking home, Varya brought up her pet subject — the theatre. In her opinion, the Moscow Art Theatre was on the way out. But then Vsevolod Meyerhold was giving up a bit too. For instance, his *La Dame aux camélias* was nothing like his *Final Conflict*.

"I didn't know you'd seen these plays," Volodya said.

"I haven't seen them, I read about them," Varya said enthusiastically. "I do follow the magazines, you know, and I read all the reviews. And besides, we discuss lots of things in our drama circle."

It was a queer sort of night. They did not agree on anything, yet they could not part. They walked, sat talking on a bench, shivered with the cold, and all the while they felt that they simply could not do without each other. Why? They did not know...

## MAN CAN DO ANYTHING

In spite of everything, Volodya Ustimenko went up into the tenth form. A great deal was said about him at the next teachers' meeting. Smorodin was particularly resentful: the old man felt he had been betrayed. "Imagine," he cried. "Just imagine the question that callow youth asked me. What use is literature to anyone? It demagnetises one, if you please! And then he gave me a whole theory about *Uncle Vanya*, which he had deigned to go and see."

The other teachers also spoke of Volodya in outraged tones. He could have been the pride of the school, but had gone downhill instead. But the worst thing was his attitude, his indifference. Why? What was causing it?

Little old Anna Filippovna stood up for him: Volodya Ustimenko was not as bad as all that, he had many good points, it wasn't right to dismiss all the boy's virtues. But on the whole (Anna Filippovna glanced apprehensively at Tatyana Yefimovna, the director of the curriculum department, who was showing her annoyance), on the whole, Ustimenko had really got out of hand, he had become most undisciplined, and urgent measures were called for.

"They say he's engrossed in natural sciences," said the science master Yegor Adamovich, whom the pupils generally called Adam. "I call it sheer rubbish. A boy who is really keen on science will not go jumping out of schoolroom windows and will not, moreover, incite his friends to such acts of hooliganism. Just consider this: with a shout 'Chapayev's men, after me!' the overgrown idiot leaps on to the windowsill and..."

Tatyana Yefimovna rapped the table with her pencil. She did not want the meeting's attention to be focused on the window-jumping episode because her own son had also jumped, and, remembering how tactless Adam always was, she decided to say something in Volodya's defence.

"The boy has no mother to look after him, and no father if it comes to that," she said. "His aunt holds a responsible post and cannot devote much of her time to his upbringing. Naturally, as his teacher of mathematics, I cannot say I am satisfied with him but..."

The voice of injured pride spoke in every one of them. And not one stopped to think, as teachers too often forget to do, that the boy was on the brink of something, that he was in a muddle, and not the kind of muddle dull-witted idlers get into but the kind that sometimes entangles the gifted.

The meeting decided to send a note to Ustimenko's father asking him to come and talk the matter over. In the event of his being away, the invitation was extended to Volodya's aunt, Aglaya Petrovna.

Aglaya Petrovna came the very next day. The forbidding Tatyana Yefimovna gave Volodya's aunt a cool reception. Tatyana Yefimovna spoke with a twang and kept blowing her nose. She had a touch of flu, which she preferred to call "my influenza".

"I shan't deny that your nephew has a certain amount of ability," she was saying. "So much the worse for him. Granted, he *is* engrossed in his natural sciences. Very good! But he is not the only one. Today thousands and thousands of young citizens inhabiting our vast country are busy assembling their own radio sets or making flying models; nevertheless they still do all they can to improve their minds..."

Suddenly Aunt Aglaya yawned. Tatyana Yefimovna saw it and took umbrage.

"Of course, you work in public education yourself, but you only started recently, very recently. And the Workers' and Peasants' Inspection where you used to work has its own peculiar features as, incidentally, have the schools for peasant youth of which you are now in charge..."

"I quite agree," Aglaya Petrovna said indifferently. "But the schools for peasant youth are Soviet schools all the same."

"And we are not running a tsarist gymnasium or an ecclesiastical seminary, either. This is a Soviet school par excellence..."

"Oh, I know all that!" Aunt Aglaya cried in exasperation. "And let's not waste time on generalities. You have called me in on an urgent matter, I understand."

"I have called you in to inform you of something most unpleasant," Tatyana Yefimovna said, now in a perfect fury. "Unless your nephew takes himself in hand or rather you take him in hand, unless Ustimenko begins to show some genuine concern for the honour of his school, unless he comes to realise that we are bringing up not individual geniuses but..."

"Tatyana Yefimovna, that's not what you called me in for, you know," Aunt Aglaya interrupted her. "Volodya told me himself that it was about something else. If I am not mistaken, it was the boys jumping out of the window after a science lesson."

Tatyana Yefimovna dropped her eyes. She had never thought Ustimenko would tell the whole story to his aunt. And there was her own boy in this, too.

"Jumping out of the window, that's just naughtiness," she said, trying to keep calm. "It may be shocking, but it is just naughtiness. Yet when I questioned him about the person responsible for the naughtiness in the first place, Aglaya Petrovna, your nephew quite flatly and even rudely refused to name the instigator!"

"I'm sorry he was rude, but it's good that he is no sneak," said Aglaya Petrovna looking hard into the other woman's eyes. "I think that a person who is a telltale in school can never be relied upon in battle."

"Oh, you do!"

"Yes, I do," Aunt Aglaya said brusquely. "However, opinions differ on that score. More's the pity."

She got up, a thickset, rosy-cheeked woman, a mocking gleam in her narrow black eyes.

"Do you imply that to be frank with his teacher..." Tatyana Yefimovna began, but Aunt Aglaya cut her short:

"To be frank is one thing, to be a sneak is another. Informing, sneaking, bringing tales are loathsome habits. What you should strive for is getting your pupils to speak the truth fearlessly to each other's face instead of telling you things here privately in your office, bringing scraps of information for your ears alone. Good-bye."

Tatyana Yefimovna made no reply, and Aunt Aglaya thought: "Oh, I am good at making enemies!"

Once outside, she muttered furiously, "In charge of the curriculum department too, is she! The humbug!"

Volodya was at home. He was drinking milk and reading about the thyroid gland. He had completely forgotten that his aunt had been called to the school. There was a glow of exultation in his eyes.

"You know, Aunt Aglaya, the thyroid gland is really terrific!" he said. "Just you listen to this! Why, it's amazing."

His pink lips were framed in milky whiskers, a soft and happy light shone in his eyes, and altogether he was still sort of lop-eared, gawky and raw. Aglaya went up close, pulled his head down and kissed the back of his neck. She permitted herself to be so demonstrative about once or twice a year, no more.

"See there's no more of this next year," she said as sternly as she could. "D'you hear me, Volodya?"

"What's that?" he asked absently.

"I mean those leaps out of schoolroom windows and the rotten marks. Promise?"

"Promise," Volodya replied, still in the clouds. "But look, you're not listening about the thyroid."

"Yes, I am. But I am not listening properly, I have to go to work. There are people waiting for me, you know."

"All right, go."

"Thanks for the permission," Aunt Aglaya said with a wistful smile. "It wouldn't occur to you to ask me, who are the people that are waiting for you, what's new with you, Aunt Aglaya, why do you look careworn today and yet you were carefree yesterday? Oh no, that's too much to expect from you. Mind I don't fall in love in my old age, and go and marry someone and leave you all alone."

"What's the matter with her anyway?" Volodya wondered momentarily, but returned immediately to his books and his reflections on what he had just read, lost to the world.

Summer was nearly in. The wind had blown away the clouds, and the maples at the open window were whispering exciting secrets to one another. Hours had gone by unnoticed again. Volodya did not feel like warming up his dinner, so he ate some bread and drank a little milk that had gone rather sour. He was surprised to find it was nearly dark and the light had to be switched on. Somewhat later Yevgeny Stepanov came in looking worried. He played a bit with the white mice, rocked

24

for a moment in the broken rocking-chair, and then said plaintively:

"I'm in the soup, old chap."

"In what sense?"

"The pater has honoured me with a letter. His advice is that I go into the naval academy."

"Rodion Mefodiyevich, you mean?"

"None other."

"Well then, go ahead."

"But it's difficult, don't you see?"

Volodya shrugged his shoulders.

"There's even some poetry in the letter," Yevgeny said pulling a crumpled envelope out of his pocket. "When the Terror of the Seas gets going he's a menace."

Yevgeny unfolded the pages with a rustle and read:

> *Your foes you forgave neither blood nor offences,*
> *You carried the banner of battle for long,*
> *The Baltic Sea waters and shores of Taurida*
> *Will leave your descendants a wonderful song.*

"What's wrong with that?" Volodya asked.

"I don't want to inherit any wonderful songs. Got that?" Yevgeny replied with a bright smile.

He put the letter back into the envelope neatly, sighed in vexation and added:

"What banner of battle? The revolution has been carried through, hasn't it? What more does he want?"

How Volodya wished Yevgeny would go! Why did he have to go dropping in on people? Did he find his own company so dull? He showed no intention of leaving, however. He sat there rocking himself and nagging.

"I have no interests, you see. I haven't found myself yet."

"You will."

"What will I find?"

"Whatever it is you haven't found. I'm simply telling you you will."

Yevgeny minded that but not for long.

"I came to you as to a friend, and you're not even listening," he said. "It's myself I haven't found."

"Oh, I see," Volodya said vaguely and almost began praying to himself: "Go away, Yevgeny, go away, there's a good chap!"

But Yevgeny did not go. As a matter of fact, he had nowhere to go. He had already tried out all the ways of amusing himself he could think of that day. He had seen two films, he had been to the Zoo to take a look at the new giraffe, he had eaten several ice-cream cones and taken a few shots in the shooting gallery.

"Varya tells me you're all set on becoming a great man. Is it true?"

"How do you mean?"

"Having a grab at science, eh?"

"You must be mad! What do you mean — grab? I find it interesting, that's all."

"Interesting, my foot!" Yevgeny drawled. "What's so interesting about it? They'll teach you all that later at the medical schools, and you'll have to learn it." Suddenly a gleam came into his eyes and he said, "Look, why shouldn't I have a go at medicine too? What d'you say? You have to specialise in something there as well, I suppose, like surgery, therapy, pediatrics and what have you, but there *are* doctors who are taught to manage the show, aren't there?"

"I don't get you," Volodya said.

"Why, you don't necessarily have to do everything yourself, like chopping up the stiffs, mucking about with their insides, treating the sick, and peering into a microscope. After all, someone has to direct the show generally."

"I suppose so, experienced doctors and professors," Volodya said. "Who else should do the directing but the people who know most?"

"You think so?" Yevgeny asked doubtfully. He scratched behind his ear, thought for a moment, and said, "Perhaps you're right. Mother had her appendix removed by Professor Zhovtyak, the most famous surgeon here. He still drops in sometimes. What he says is that being a doctor doesn't amount to much. The main thing comes afterwards: maintaining theses or degrees, I don't remember exactly which. What it boils down to is this: if you're merely a qualified doctor you travel second class, but if you get your M. D. you'll go by de luxe express. Pretty tough, actually. But why shouldn't I made the grade? Comrade Zhovtyak is no great brain, yet he's pushed his way in among the big shots. And he's in command, too. Or is he a good professor?"

Yevgeny stood up, planted his short legs firmly, pulled down his coat, which had been made to order by Dodik's tailor, assumed a stern expression and pronounced loudly:

"Doctor Yevgeny Rodionovich Stepanov."

After a pause he said, "Perhaps, Professor Stepanov. Because if a doctor you must be, let it be in the grand style. A professorship, no less. What do you say?"

Yevgeny's transparent eyes sparkled with mockery and Volodya felt a fool, as he often did in Yevgeny's company. Not a downright fool exactly, but sort of oafish.

Aunt Aglaya came home from work and got angry right away.

"Honestly, what the devil! He can't even warm up his dinner. And why do you stay indoors all the time, you misery of mine?"

Volodya smiled guiltily. She loved that smile of his, just as she had loved him ever since the day when as a three-month-old baby he had been left to her care. And here he was, a grown person already.

"You giraffe," she said" "That's what you are. All neck."

Yevgeny stayed for dinner, and went on with his complaints as he ate.

"It's rather nightmarish at home. Dodik has his own way all the time. Varya wants to leave her hearth and home... It's one row after another."

"I wish you wouldn't gossip," Aunt Aglaya said.

"I'm just sharing my troubles with you as friends," Yevgeny said with a sigh. "It's not easy on me either, you know, Aglaya Petrovna. I'm at the crossroads just now. Father's writing grim letters full of educational maxims. Varya's busy singing — songs with her Komsomol boys, and now she's going away for the whole summer to a Young Pioneers' camp as troop leader, and here I am — left to straighten out the mess."

"Go to a Young Pioneers' camp too," Aunt Aglaya suggested with a little smile.

"Who, me?"

"Yes, you."

"No thanks. I haven't Varya's health, I'm made of different clay."

"Don't we know it," Aunt Aglaya said, leaving the table. "You're blue-blooded of course."

Yevgeny did not take offence. He had a way of letting unpleasant remarks go unheard. Besides, he never took what Aglaya Petrovna or his stepfather said quite seriously, as if he were the wiser in years.

"Incidentally, while we're on the subject of blood," he said. "Volodya and I have been putting our heads together, and I believe I have decided to dedicate my life to medicine as well."

"What luck for medicine!" Aunt Aglaya sneered.

"Why not? Professor Zhovtyak is a friend of Mother's, I know him, too. He has weight, he'll help if necessary."

"Listen, Yevgeny, this is rather disgusting!" Aunt Aglaya suddenly flared up. "Surely you know it yourself?"

"Good Lord! But life is life, after all!" he said quite candidly. "It's different with Volodya since he's so terribly gifted. But what about me? Virtue alone won't get you far, everyone knows that."

And he went on to explain why he could not go into the navy.

"I'm sure to be seasick. I'm even sick on the river. By and large, the sea is not my cup of tea at all. Storms, hurricanes and things. In this respect the pater's an idealist. Now, look here..."

At long last Yevgeny left. Aunt Aglaya went to bed and Volodya was left in peace. In the middle of the night the lamp bulb in his room began to hiss ominously, and Volodya was afraid the light would go out before he got to the end of the chapter. The hissing continued but the bulb did not burn out, and Volodya read on, his hands clenched tight, jumping up now and again to pace the floor and whisper rapturously:

"Isn't it splendid, wonderful, beautiful! Intellect can do anything, anything!"

"And then this man," Volodya read on, "their lonely seeker, arousing rabid hatred in some and transports of joy and admiration in others, freed medicine at last from the fetters of tradition: medicine which had once been the glory of science, and which with the years was becoming its disgrace."

Volodya's face was burning, a shiver ran down his spine. He understood much more of what he read now, this boy Ustimenko who had been discussed with such dislike at the teachers' meeting. He understood more, but still it was far from everything...

It was four in the morning when he heard the door open with a creak and saw Aunt Aglaya come in looking sleepy, with her hair hanging down her back in plaits.

"I'll turn you out of the house," she said. "How dare you make a wreck of yourself! Look what a sight you are. Will there never be an end to this?"

"Never!" Volodya replied unsmiling. "Never, Aunt Aglaya. Please don't be angry. Let's go and eat something instead. I'm so hungry I feel sick."

In silence he ate six fried eggs, a huge slice of bread and butter and a dish of sour milk, then looked around for more.

"Enough. You'll burst."

"Man can do anything," he said, continuing with his own thoughts.

"Eating, you mean?" Aunt Aglaya asked with a smile.

Volodya gave her a startled look.

### Chapter Two

### TYPHUS

In February 1919, Rodion Stepanov, a former able seaman second class of the dreadnought *Petropavlovsk*, was to his surprise appointed assistant chief of the Petrograd railway junction, and a few days later — the chief. Until March, he put up with sleeping on the desk in his office, but suddenly he felt terribly worn out and demanded a "bit of hammock space" to be made available to him where he could get some decent sleep. The moment he received the order, made out on a grey piece of paper endorsed with an illegible signature and a blind rubber stamp, he set out for the address in Furshtadtskaya Street. He banged hard on the oakwood door with his tattooed silor's fist, and with not so much as a glance at the woman who admitted him, marched straight into his room, a large one with heavy draperies at the tall windows and a huge red leather sofa.

The luggage he brought with him comprised a couple of undershirts, very good ones, of best Holland cloth, that had been issued by order to the railway staff, a ration of soggy bread, six Havana cigars, a revolver, a half-pound of yellow unrefined sugar, and an old army haversack.

The moment Rodion Stepanov entered the room, which though cold seemed nonetheless strangely cosy after what he had been used to in recent months, he collapsed on the sofa and with a low gasp fainted away. The condition he had taken for exhaustion was, in fact, the onset of typhus.

Alevtina, the Gogolevs' maid, or Alya as Mr. Gogolev, a barrister, used to call her, who had remained in the house with her five-month-old baby after her master and mistress had fled the country, listened to "that blessed commissar" groaning for a long time without doing anything about it until the thought of being held responsible if something should happen to him made her timidly enter his room.

"Water!" growled the sailor.

Apparently he had been asking for water all that time and not groaning.

Alevtina fetched some water and squeamishly gave the sailor a drink out of a delicate porcelain cup that belonged to a Chinese tea service. And then, with little Yevgeny in her arms, she ran up the stairs to the floor above to call Doctor von Pappe, a very fashionable Petersburg gynecologist who resided there. Von Pappe was enjoying a cup of real coffee, and at first he flatly refused to treat the commissar. On second thoughts, however, he agreed to go down to the Gogolevs' flat because that bitch Alevtina might inform against him if he did not.

"It's typhus," he said in his thin womanish voice. "Mind he doesn't infect the place with lice, Alevtina, or that'll be the end of you and your Yevgeny."

The former lady's maid looked at the doctor sadly. To be on the safe side and soften the harshness of his verdict, von Pappe poked the baby in the tummy, fluttered his fingers in the air, and added:

"Our poor long-suffering people have so much to endure!"

At that moment the doctor's eye fell on the cigars.

"I'll take care of these," he said hurriedly. "They're of no earthly use to commissars."

"They are!" Stepanov said in a weak but implacable voice. "But a bloody bourgeois like you is definitely not!"

The commissar turned to Alevtina and ordered curtly: "Lady, throw him out."

Perhaps because he was not thinking very clearly he added a few spicy epithets, on hearing which von Pappe fled in confusion. Stepanov told Alevtina to go to his railway office to collect the food ration that was due to him, and got them to send a "proper doctor" and what help they could. "Why the hell die, anyway, for no good reason?"

"It's inexpedient from the point of view of the world revolution," the commissar said in a low but determined voice. "Just tell them so, lady, say it's inexpedient. Get me?"

Still, Alevtina made no move.

"Is this sabotage?" Stepanov demanded. "Get this into your nut: if I croak, you'll have to answer."

"I'm going," Alevtina replied. "But will you be all right alone?"

"Just listen to this poem about our bunch," said the commissar with a grin.

Crushed by the man's personality, Alevtina timorously sat down on the edge of a chair and listened to him recite:

> *You roving heroes, men of the sea*
> *Who feasted on every gale that blew,*

*Sailors, oh sailors, as the albatros free,*
*My song shall shine like sapphires for you.*

"Got it clear now, lady?" he asked.

There was laughter in his eyes.

Carrying her baby in her arms Alevtina started on the long walk to the railway office. A couple of hours later a regular delegation of grimy, exhausted but strangely cheerful people arrived to see the commissar. And in spite of the fact that they all used expressions which Alevtina had grown unaccustomed to hearing while in the Gogolevs' service, she had a sense of belonging to them and thought they were all very nice, especially the elderly woman with the lined face and gnarled working woman's hands, who wore a nurse's white kerchief on her head.

"Widowed, are you?" the woman asked her.

Alevtina dropped her eyes.

"It's even harder on you then," the elderly woman said. "But don't you weep, comrade. Those days are over, you'll have popular support now."

Everything was so queer, so strange and unexpected. The promise of popular support for something that had seemed so shameful and mortifying before, the old woman calling her "comrade", the people Alevtina used to think of as "roughs" and Mr. Gogolev called "rabble" treating her so politely and actually inviting her to share their meal with them, a soup of horseflesh and millet. All this put life in quite a different focus for Alevtina. Her step became firmer, she no longer dropped her eyes or felt ashamed that she had no husband and had never had one.

The commissar was fast getting well.

Alevtina unlocked a secret storeroom and got out some bedsheets; she also sold an antique porcelain chandelier and with the money bought provisions that included even a lump of pork fat! When Stepanov's beard began to overrun his face, Alevtina, after a moment's hesitation, opened her runaway master's English leather dressing-case, and produced seven beautiful razors, each marked with the day of the week: Monday, Tuesday, Wednesday, and so on.

"What did the bastard want seven razors for?" Stepanov asked in astonishment.

"Metal has to be given a rest," Alevtina primly repeated Mr. Gogolev's words. "That's why there's a razor for every day of the week."

"The cunning bastards, eh!" the commissar swore good-naturedly.

He kept the razor marked "Sunday", and made presents of the other six to his pals.

"You mustn't do that!" Alevtina shrilled. "They're not yours to give away. Mr. Gogolev will show you when he comes back!"

"Why should he come back?" Stepanov asked, unruffled.

"They're his razors!"

"True, we could have left him one, but seven is too many," Stepanov reasoned. "Lady, all this belongs to the people now. So it's no use kicking up a row."

"Mr. Gogolev will show you just the same."

"Maybe I'll show him?"

And again there was laughter in his eyes.

There was a song he often sang under his breath while busy with his own thoughts.

> *Down the passage flickers faintly*
> *Candlelight in lantern high,*
> *And the sentry, bored with living,*
> *Clinks his spurs as he goes by...*

"So you've even been kept in prison?" Alevtina asked him one day.

"No, I've never been kept in prison, unless you mean the prison of peoples called the Russian Empire."

Alevtina did not understand, but she heaved a sigh of sympathy to be on the safe side. Some bearded, scruffy and very talkative gentlemen had been in the habit of coming to see her master at one time, and her mistress had spoken of them as "martyrs for the people". Later, those martyrs had all put on service jackets and leggings, started driving about in motorcars, and finally vanished together with Mr. Gogolev. Everything was such a puzzle. Alevtina found herself studying her commissar with keener and longer looks, she talked to him more often and listened with growing attention to his curt stories. She noticed sometimes that he, too, was looking hard at her.

No sooner was he up and about than he ordered Alevtina to open up all the Gogolevs' secret storerooms. Alevtina burst into tears, and the baby joined his wails to hers.

"I don't want it," Stepanov said somberly. "I'm trying to safeguard it from myself and from you. The stuff ought to be requisitioned and not sold on the quiet bit by bit."

Alevtina sobbed the louder. She had learned the art of sobbing like this from her mistress. Yevgeny seconded his mother with all his baby might and produced some very piercing notes indeed. Undeterred, Stepanov carried the requisitioning through according to the rules. He made out a list of "bourgeois surplus requisitioned from former citizen Gogolev" with an indelible pencil which he kept wetting with his tongue, and after that, using Gogolev's own sealing wax and seal, secured all the gentleman's chests, trunks, wardrobes, closets and secret storerooms.

"You're a lunatic, that's what you are," Alevtina uttered between sobs. "And it was ours to use and use!"

"I'm not a lunatic, I'm a revolutionary sailor," Rodion Stepanov said instructively. "We didn't overthrow your precious Nicholas just to grab stuff ourselves on the quiet. We overthrew him for the good of the whole people... That chandelier, by the way, I've put it down as sold to aid my recovery from typhus fever."

The requisitioning and Alevtina's wails tired Stepanov out, and he lay down. That evening, for some reason, she chose to tell him her life story. He listened in silence, lying on the sofa with his powerful arms folded under his head. His eyes were half closed.

"She just went and slapped your face?" Rodion asked abruptly.

"She did," Alevtina nodded, biting her lips.

"But how old were you then?"

"Not quite sixteen."

"The bitches, the vermin, God damn their souls," he said.

"Why are you cursing?"

"I'm sorry for you, that's why."

After a while he asked:

"Who's the kid's father?"

"A fellow used to come here, a non-commissioned officer, he was so sweet..." Alevtina started whimpering again.

"Don't cry. What happened to him?"

"How should I know?"

"Stop crying, I said. Life is different now. You ought to study. You can rise to any position on your own."

"But I'm almost illiterate."

"And what d'you think I am?"

"That you shall remain — an ignorant sailor."

Rodion ignored the jibe and, smiling in the gathering dusk, said:

"That's where you're wrong, Alevtina. The revolution of the proletariat has no use for ignorant sailors. I'm going to start on my education just as soon as we've exterminated the scum."

Alevtina stole a look at Stepanov and marvelled at the compelling, unassailable confidence that emanated from the man. He went on speaking thoughtfully, his eyes on the moulded ceiling of Mr. Gogolev's study.

"Yes, I was an ignorant bumpkin when I first joined the navy. I came all the way from the Voznesensk forests, ever heard of them? My father couldn't read or write a word. Well, I worked my way up to be a torpedoman, and then I got demoted to able seaman second class on the *Petropavlovsk*. I knew what was what though. I was on the *Aurora* when she fired on the Winter Palace."

"You fired on the Winter Palace?" Alevtina gasped.

"Other gun-crews did. We fired once, but it was only a blank. I didn't have that great honour," he said with a smile. "Still, I did serve on the *Aurora*."

And he took Alevtina's hand in his.

She leaned towards him, submissive and gentle. He turned away and said:

"Move away, Alevtina. It won't be much fun if you catch typhus off me."

But Alevtina was smiling softly. Now she'd be a commissar's wife! A calf like him was easy to rope. He was one of the soft-hearted kind. He had actually winced when she told him about her beatings. As a matter of fact, it hadn't been anything really: she had simply broken a scent bottle and got what was coming.

"Teach me the song you're always singing," she said.

"What song?"

"About the little light, and the sentry bored with living."

"All right," Stepanov said, and very softly sang:

> *Take your chance, the night is gloomy,*
> *But the wall is high and long,*
> *And the gate before us looming*
> *Is secured with twin-locks strong...*

## MAN AND WIFE

A month later, they began to live as man and wife. Yevgeny now had a surname — Stepanov, and Alevtina was the wife of a commissar, no longer a housemaid, a servant of

Mr. and Mrs. Gogolev, but a mistress in her own right, a woman commanding respect. In her desire to wipe out her hateful past altogether, she begged Rodion to move to another part of the town, to Vasilyevsky Island, or at least to the Vyborgskaya Side.

"Why 'at least'?" Rodion asked with a dark scowl. "What foul notion is this?"

"No one lives on the Vyborgskaya Side except factory workers. No one but roughs," Alevtina explained.

"You *are* a fool," he said bluntly. "What about yourself, what noble family do you come from?"

"I don't come from a noble family, but I am the wife of an outstanding man," she murmured with downcast eyes.

They moved to Vasilyevsky Island. Spring came and famine. Stepanov practically lived at the railway junction working all day and night; when he managed to come home, he tumbled into bed beside Alevtina and in his sleep gritted his teeth and shouted terrible words:

"Saboteurs! I'll get you shot, you dirty sharks, it'll be too late then."

Behind the curtainless windows the white nights sped on, dangerous, uneasy nights. Alevtina would peer into her husband's young, hollow-eyed and utterly exhausted face, at his parched lips, and weave her fervent dreams, wishing so hard for them to come true that it hurt. He would climb the ladder, to the very top, and stand alone above all the rest, and everyone would be afraid of him, and then she, Alevtina, would take a ride through the town in a red, powerful car with great big headlights, the kind of car that once used to be brought to the door for Mrs. Gogolev, the barrister's wife. She was eaten up with ambition, tortured by it. Only to live till her ship came in, and then she'd show them, she'd let them all see! In the meantime she welcomed her husband home at night, read as many novels as she liked about the doings of princes, barons and marquises, dressed her child like a little gentleman, the way the Gogolevs used to dress their offspring, in velvet suits, lace collars, and foppish little berets and caps, and served tea, or rather a carrot brew, in exquisite Dresden china cups.

In the autumn, Stepanov was drafted to the Revolutionary Military Council of the Astrakhan fleet, and left town. Occasionally friends of his called on Alevtina, brought her her rations and advised her to get a job. She gave them a cool, tight-lipped reception, and discouraged lengthy conversations.

She got all that was due to her husband and some that was not at the stripped Petrograd warehouses. She was also quick to pick up the way of talking she thought was essential to success.

"So you're sitting pretty, you sharks!" she would say, holding up her fat-faced baby, dressed in poor clothes specially for the occasion. "And a commissar's wife can just go and starve, eh? Never mind, I'll go to the Cheka and everybody'll get it hot. They'll give you a good shaking up, you bourgeois bastards. They'll put a couple of you up against the wall, then I'll get my jam quick enough."

She would get her jam, but still life was very hard. The car with the huge headlights remained a dream, and thoughts of silks and black straw hats occurred to no one. But Alevtina waited, she waited stubbornly, with bitter, even frantic impatience. She'd make "her man" do everything she wanted, oh yes, she would. She wouldn't stand for any nonsense, she wasn't that kind. And a beautiful world of things — costly, wonderful, different things — appeared to her in her empty room: carved wardrobes ornamented with brass and filled with lovely, scented gowns, Chippendale chairs — she remembered the name, scent bottles, boas, sable capes, gloves, love seats, peignoirs, carpets, a bathroom all in blue like the one the Baron Rosenau had in Furshtadtskaya Street, nose veils, boxes of powder, tea and dinner services, tea waggons... She had seen all those things before, and now she wanted them for her own, she wanted to walk through a suite of rooms, flinging open the connecting doors, and be the lady of the house, the mistress, the owner.

"A suite of rooms!" with dry lips she whispered words that sounded beautiful to her. "North Express!" Or: "Julie, put the screen in front of the fire!"

Or the thought of chocolates in huge boxes.

Never mind, she'd wait!

She would wait as long as she had to, but she'd have her day.

Rodion Stepanov, meanwhile, was scouring the Ukraine, for Nestor Makhno. The anarchist robber ataman Makhno led Stepanov's detachment a three-thousand-verst dance without accepting battle and wearing his pursuers out. Somewhere, just ahead, the machine-gun carts were racing along the country roads through the steppe; Makhno's men left jeering messages behind at the wealthy farmsteads; all Stepanov's men were treated to by the surly, grey-haired farmers was a drink of water from the well. And on those hot summer nights, thunder rumbled peaceably, even cosily, overhead, and warm, copious rains poured down.

Together with a representative of the Revolutionary Military Council and four other Cheka men Stepanov was sent to Makhno to conclude a truce and do propaganda work among the ataman's detachments. None of the six Communists, picked for the job by Frunze, Commander of the Southern Front, entertained any hope of coming back alive when they left the commander's train after receiving their orders.

At Starobelsk, in a low-ceilinged cottage drenched in perfume, Nestor Makhno sprawled picturesquely on a feather bed, a sweaty, pock-marked individual with jaundiced eyes. His henchmen, their astrakhan caps right on the back of their heads, stood or sat around him.

"Maybe we'll chat without weapons?" the ataman asked and tossed his long hair. "I don't like weapons, I'm a kindly, peaceful man."

"You're kindly alright," Stepanov said and kept his revolver on him.

He hardly slept in the next three months. Makhno might finish the six of them off at any moment, and besides they were all billeted in different units. But their slow, painstaking work gradually bore fruit. Makhno's men got more and more shaky in their allegiance to the ataman, and spoke with growing determination about making peace with the Bolsheviks. And after the Soviet Government had issued the decree allotting the land to the peasants for nine years, Rodion Stepanov no longer had reason to think that Makhno's men would cut his throat.

Certain mementos of that period remained with him for the rest of his life: a white scar above the wrist where a Browning bullet had found its mark, a shell-splinter lodged in the shoulder-blade, and a wound below the shin which ached with a dull pain for a long, long time.

...One quiet night, the division with Stepanov, a former sailor of the Baltic fleet as commissar, reached the shore of the Sea of Azov. The men plunged into the water to wash themselves. Stepanov suddenly felt homesick, he knew he must serve in the navy, that without the sea he might as well be dead, and that it was time he went back to his real job.

And from then on life became so difficult that, in comparison, the years of the Civil War seemed child's play. He entered school. He had to master algebra, geometry, trigonometry, make drawings, learn to read and write in English and German, and know what's what in history. He had to study so that in due course rather than stand on the captain's bridge beside a so-called navy specialist, an officer of the old school, he could himself take command of a battle cruiser, or a destroyer, a formation of ships or even a battleship.

The foppishly refined and sneering instructors with their imperturbable expressions put the former sailors through their paces far more stiffly than they had the noblemen's sons. The working lads, one-time sailors, gunners and mine men who had gone through all the hell of the Civil War and had not yet caught up on the sleep they had missed in those years, stood at attention, listening to the edifying sermons of men, some of whom had only just deigned to recognise Soviet power. And often, too often, Stepanov heard the icy words:

"Why do you not understand? Because, my good men, you lack general development. And it does not come at once. One imbibes it with one's mother's milk. And the culture that is so essential to a naval commander cannot be acquired by cramming either. You will forgive me, I am not a Marxist, but it is a birthright..."

The student Rodion Stepanov paled with fury but kept silent. "Like hell it is," he thought. "Like hell it is, you stinking survival. Watch us in ten or twenty years from now. You'll wake up with a jolt, but too late: we'll make smarter intellectuals than you and your whole wobbly breed!"

He slept four hours a day, no more. But he was particular about his daily shave, using the old razor marked "Sunday". His knowledge of English now went farther than the special naval terms and expressions required of him; with the help of the dictionary he could read articles describing experiences in the navy, which he thought might come in useful to him. He also tried to do as much talking as possible with his friends — officers of the Baltic, Black Sea, and Sea of Azov fleets — in English and in what they believed to be the manner of English sea lords conversing at their Admiralty, drawling, smoking and taking their time. In that period, too, higher mathematics assumed a peculiar radiance for Stepanov, becoming a source of enjoyment and not merely of terror. The foppish and extremely refined instructor who but a short while ago had explained to Stepanov that perceptivity was an essentially inherited quality, happened to say in passing: "Stepanov's a clever brute, you know."

Stepanov overheard the words and they were perhaps the highest praise he could have wished for in those years: the enemy had admitted himself beaten, and that was worth something.

Alevtina was always complaining that she was tired and bored. She led a perfectly idle existence; she often went out visiting other "ladies" or entertained them herself. With their little fingers sticking out genteelly they drank tea out of translucent cups, fondled young Yevgeny, and talked in a languid, drowsy manner. Their conversations were queer and the words unfamiliar to Stepanov. Their hairdos they called "bobs", little Yevgeny, they said, looked like the "infant in exile", some chairs were "modern", others were "rococo", and they talked of a club where people were making fortunes "on hard currencies". Somehow they procured imported perfume — a bottle of Chanel, say, between the lot of them.

They seldom spoke to Stepanov, but when they did their tone was jocularly deferential. They had a way of calling him "our future Nelson", or Marat, or "who has been naught shall be all". When thus addressed, Rodion felt like cursing in his old pre-revolutionary fashion, or picking up one of those pieces which Alevtina called "old Sèvres" and smashing it to smithereens on the floor. He did nothing of the sort, of course; he just scowled and retreated to his rickety desk, finding relief in his books, notes and drawings.

Varya was still a baby. Alevtina had much less love for her than she had for Yevgeny. The boy always stirred a chord of pity in her heart, and Rodion was often hurt to hear her whispering over the sleeping child:

"You poor little orphan, you poor little stepchild, my silly darling mite, mother will protect you, mother won't let anyone bully you, have no fear, my orphaned baby..."

"Who's bullying him anyway?" Rodion said in exasperation one night. "Why talk such rot? He's the one who'll do the bullying, there's no managing him already. He smashed a bottle of Indian ink this afternoon and when I threatened to box his ears..."

"If he was your own child you wouldn't have threatened him," said Alevtina. "You wouldn't lay a finger on Varya, I'm sure."

"But have I ever touched him?" Rodion said aghast.

Alevtina ignored the question and went on whispering over her son. Rodion shrugged and went back to his drawings. He was surrounded by quiet homely sounds: the ticking of the clock on the wall, Varya's deep breathing, the tiny rustle of paper as Alevtina turned the pages of her novel. A family, wasn't it? But just what was a family?

Rodion could not indulge in reflection. He was always pressed for time. Time was hurrying, the country was hurrying, and he could not lag behind. He was interested in everything: newspapers, books, conferences, meetings, talks, lectures. He wanted to miss none of it. It annoyed him to hear Alevtina complain in the words of her former mistress that she was "bored to extinction", but he just blinked and refused to be provoked.

"Alevtina, I'm not a circus to provide amusement for you," Rodion flared up one day. "I've told you a hundred times: find something to do. There are no doors closed to you today. Go and study. You can even aim at a people's commissar's job, if you like."

"I've done my share of work!" Alevtina cried furiously. "I've drudged since I was sixteen. No, even fifteen. And I have a perfect right to relax now and live like a human being. Oh, but there's not much hope of that with you, since you can't even hire a servant for me."

"A servant? For you?" Rodion was dismayed. "And where did you get this servant stuff from anyway? A domestic worker we say nowadays, there are no menials."

"All right, hire a domestic worker then," Alevtina smirked. "I don't care what you call them, but I'm not obliged, after the Revolution, to..."

"You're a fool," Rodion swore wearily.

"You're the fool, not I," she came back. "A revolutionary sailor! What did you get for your wounds? A position in society? Did you get even a poky five-room flat? No. You're turning grey, but you're still cramming like a schoolboy. We barely manage from one payday to the next, and if it wasn't for my business deals..."

"What business deals?" he asked, turning livid. "What business deals are you up to?"

Frightened, she made no reply.

Soon after that, Yevgeny fell ill with TB. The doctors said that he must not stay in Petrograd. Alevtina was alarmed. She remembered the Voznesensk forests her husband used to tell her about, and cross-examined him about the sort of town they had there. The doctors unanimously approved of the forests, the climate, and the Uncha River. In May 1923,

Rodion Stepanov took his family to the town where he had once been conscripted to serve his tsar and his country.

He had an old friend in that town, Afanasy Ustimenko, an air force man. Afanasy's sister, Aglaya found a flat for the Stepanovs in Proletarskaya Street. Once the family was settled, the two friends — Afanasy, a widower, and Rodion, now a grass widower — started back for Petrograd to continue their respective studies. In the slowly moving train, they drank some vodka, ate some cold chicken, and eagerly plunged into recollections of the Civil War, of Afanasy flying his Sopwith, dropping on the Whiteguards pennants inscribed with proclamations, and getting shot down in 1920.

"Thinking of getting married again?" Rodion asked.

"Frankly — no. A look at your Valentina decided me, nothing doing!"

"What Valentina? You mean Alevtina."

"She told me to call her Valentina," Afanasy said and yawned. "She told me to forget the name Alevtina. Shall we have another?"

They had another glass each and ate some pickled apples.

"You've a nice kid, I liked him," Rodion said.

"Volodya? He's all right, a bit naughty."

### THE DAUGHTER

...The ex-Alevtina, now known as Valentina Andreyevna, refused to return to Leningrad, but then Rodion did not insist. For the most part he lived on his ship or in Kronstadt, where he rented a room from an old boatswain's widow. All his spare time, of which he had very little, he spent reading. He was almost thirty when he first read *War and Peace, The Past and Musings, The Cossacks, Ward No. 6*, and *A Hero of Our Time*. He did not love his wife; that was as obvious to him as the fact that she did not love him. But he wanted to love, he wanted to read aloud to a woman and not to Mikhalyuk, the senior officer, about Natasha Rostova singing at her uncle's, he wanted to walk one white night to Peter the Great's monument with a woman he loved, and not with Mikhalyuk again, he wanted to look forward to letters, to write letters himself.

And then his life changed suddenly and strangely for the better.

Valentina wrote to him that she could not manage Varya.

The child was rude, impertinent and disobedient, and had to be taken in hand. It would be a good idea if her father came and did something about it.

After some reflection, Rodion wrote back and told Valentina to send the child to Kronstadt.

He met Varya's train in Leningrad.

Without quite understanding what was happening to him, he picked her up in his arms and kissed her freckled forehead, her tight little plaits, her neck, and her frail shoulders. With soft little squeals Varya clung to her father's stiff white linen tunic.

He discovered the happiness of being a father.

"A person can't live without love," he mused in those days. "He can't and shouldn't. Oh well, I had no luck in marriage, but I am lucky in my daughter. She's a lovable kid, I can be happy loving her."

The boatswain's widow tied Varya's hair with pretty blue ribbons, Rodion put her little feet into a pair of new patent-leather shoes and, leading her by the hand, took her to his ship. The day was windy, dusty and hot, with a briny moist smell coming from the sea; he was taking Varya to his real home, to people he could really call his own. His chin, which he had cut shaving that morning, was not quite so firm as usual. All the way there, father and daughter talked to one another like two grown-ups. Varya, walking slightly pigeon-toed, marvelled at the sea-gulls, at "all that water", at the "too blue" sky. And he wanted to know why she did not listen to Mummy, why she was rude and cheeky.

"Oh Daddy, why do you?" Varya said. "Everything was so nice, and there you go, just like Mummy."

She was neither rude nor cheeky. She was independent, free in spirit, and had a very generous nature. The legend that Varya was impertinent was born the day she first went to school. In the middle of the second lesson, the little Stepanova girl neatly packed her books in her bag and started for the door. The teacher called her back indignantly. Varya replied, when she was already on the other side of the door, "I'm hungry."

The small, sturdy, frowning girl with the short pigtail had simply left school and gone home. "Yevgeny would never have done that!" his mother cried. And Yevgeny agreed that the whole story was monstrous.

After that, Varya gave her new pinafore to the girl next door because, she said, she had two pinafores and the girl had

42

none. A belt of Yevgeny's she presented to Sasha the plasterer, because Yevgeny had many leather belts and Uncle Sasha had to keep his trousers up with a bit of rope. Valentina gave Varya a whipping. The child did not cry, but she never cuddled up to her mother again.

"A proper tomboy," the crew called Varya, and everyone came to love her. They spoiled her outrageously in the mess, at the forecastle, the quarter-deck, and wherever she flitted in her red and polka-dot frock. She never cried, sulked or whined, she always obeyed with alacrity, and the look in her shining wide-open eyes was ever one of happy surprise.

That winter Varya attended the Kronstadt school, and it was a happy time for her father. They spent their evenings at the cinema, or going up to Leningrad to see a play, or else he helped Varya's girl friends with their decimal fractions, and together with them did sums about basins and trains. After that Varya would preside at the samovar and pour out the tea, while her father would be thinking proudly and all but aloud: "What a daughter, what a girl! Varya Stepanova, my daughter! Find another like her in the world!"

In the early spring the boatswain's widow died, and Stepanov got his sailing orders. The whole crew to a man came to see Varya off. Her face swollen with tears and her legs shaky with misery, she threw her slender little arms round the necks of all the sailors and officers in turn, touched their rough, chapped cheeks with her soft childish lips, and said:

"Come and stay with us, Uncle Misha, we've got a good river too."

"Come and stay with us, Uncle Petya, I mean it on my honour!"

"The moment you're demobbed, come and stay with us for good, Uncle Kostya."

In the winter, Stepanov went to see his family. He entered the house a stranger. Yevgeny, a hairnet on his head, was lying on the sofa reading a thick illustrated book. The next room was as thick with perfume as Nestor Makhno's cottage had been. Valentina was at the theatre, Varya at her girl friend's. Yevgeny stretched himself and asked:

"Well, what's new, Dad?"

"Nothing in particular," Stepanov replied. "What's that book you're reading?"

"The *Niva* for 1894," Yevgeny said. "A frightful bore."

"Why read it if it's a frightful bore?"

"But what's there to do?"

A little later Valentina came home, looking flushed and prettier, than before in her fur coat.

"Oh, the great mariner has honoured us! What joy!" she said sarcastically.

She had learned to use sarcasm now.

Tea was served in a special sort of teapot, the cheese was sliced very thin, the sausage was almost transparent, and no one thought of asking Rodion if he would rather have a regular meal, a glass of vodka after the long, cold journey, or a nice big omelette.

"By the way," his wife said, "I didn't write to you about it because you choose to show all my letters to Varya, but she has become quite impossible. She spends all her days with her Young Pioneers, sings coarse songs, pays no heed to any crici ... cricitism..."

"Criticism, you mean?"

"Precisely!" Valentina said irritably. "And altogether she's too, too Soviet."

Rodion scowled, purple spots stood out on his cheekbones.

"What do you imply by that?"

"Just what I said."

"Be more explicit then."

"She's just dumb, and thinks too much of herself," Yevgeny said, rocking in his chair.

Instead of the planned fortnight, Rodion stayed only three days. He spent them with Varya, going to the skating-rink with her, to the Ustimenkos — Aglaya Petrovna and Volodya — and to the theatre. He even went to a meeting of the Young Pioneers and gave a talk about the Soviet Navy. Varya did not think much of the talk.

"You put it too popularly, Dad," she said. "Our boys and girls are pretty bright, they don't want it served up on a plate for them."

Her father turned a bright red.

"A person lives for years and years, and still gets treated like a child," Varya said with a sigh.

"D'you know what?" she suggested. "Let's not go home to dinner, there's an eating place near here, the salad is wonderful there, and they sometimes have good hamburgers too."

Varya swept the bread crumbs off the oilcloth-covered table and said without looking at her father:

"Tell me, Dad, when did you fall in love for the first time? You were a bit on the old side, weren't you?"

"Oh, not really," he said in confusion.

"But I do know some people fall in love very young sometimes, and very hard too," Varya said, turning away. "Yes, yes, very hard, terribly hard."

Her father wore a lost smile. So he was to be deprived of his last joy, all he had left to him. No, no, she was too young!

"Don't be in a hurry to fall in love, there's plenty of time," he pleaded softly.

But Varya did not hear him. Perhaps she wasn't listening. That night he left.

### Chapter Three

### MUSHROOMS

One Sunday in August, Varya, Volodya and Volodya's friend Boris Gubin went mushrooming in Gorelishchi. At first they picked all kinds, and then only the best. The day was greyish and warm, there was a fine rain, they got wet, or rather very damp and not really wet. They started a fire and sat around it baking potatoes while Volodya talked.

"One should not invent, not fabricate, but search into what Nature does and brings with it, that is, what Francis Bacon said. There's even a shorter formula: Nature is conquered by those who obey it. But you must agree that this sort of reasoning won't get you far. It's all put very cleverly, but at the same time much too passively. On the other hand..."

Varya turned away, and fell into a doze. Boris Gubin, a considerate soul, kept awake, but suddenly gave a howling yawn that brought tears to his gentle eyes. This made Volodya angry and he pounced on Boris; leaves and pine needles flew. Boris stuck his foot into the smouldering fire and yelled. Varya was startled awake. The boys wrestled, kicking up the forest mould and yelling because life was good, because they were strong, young and healthy.

"Me too, me too, me too!" Varya shouted. "The more the merrier!!"

She flopped down on top of the two boys, and suddenly all three felt shy. A look of bewilderment came into Varya's eyes.

"Silly fools!" she said, almost in tears.

She pulled down her skirt and drew up her legs. Volodya and Boris avoided each other's eyes.

"Next time don't butt in," Volodya said after a while. "Two can fight, but three's a riot... What's happened to my penknife, Boris?"

45

The two boys made a great show of looking for the knife.

It was all so embarrassing that Boris even started a song, but he got muddled and went on with words of his own composition:

> Autumn's here, it rains and pours,
> The farmer spends more time indoors,
> Down the street a song is ringing,
> We walk into a fine new building...

"Oh Boris, must you!" Volodya begged.

They started back for the station. It was still drizzling. Their baskets, heavy with mushrooms, creaked softly as they walked. It was already evening when the three cross and weary youngsters reached the railway clearing and saw the crowd. A shepherd boy of about fourteen was lying beside the track, writhing and wheezing horribly. He was still conscious. There was blood everywhere, on the rails, the sleepers and the oily ballast. A short distance from the boy lay a leg in a footcloth and an old rubber shoe; an old woman was wailing, and the peasants stood about in glum silence not knowing what to do. Nearby, a sheep that had also been run over was in its death throes.

Volodya pushed his way through the crowd, tore off his shirt and, grey-faced with horror, began to put a tourniquet on the stump with hasty, inexperienced hands. Someone helped him; it only occurred to him later that it had been Varya. A peasant in a battered straw hat obligingly handed Volodya the severed limb. Volodya swore at him savagely. Boris ran off to the station, and some twenty minutes later a trolley came up bringing a doctor and stretchers.

"Who applied the tourniquet?" the old railway doctor wanted to know.

The peasant in the straw hat pointed to Volodya.

"Are you a student?"

Volodya made no reply.

"They're all drunk, the devils," the doctor said vexedly. "It's a church holiday today. What are you howling about anyway?" he shouted at the dark-faced, old woman. "Sorry for the sheep?"

He indicated the trolley with a nod and told Volodya to come along.

In the small first-aid room at the station, the doctor called for a white smock for Volodya and proceeded to give the shepherd an injection of anti-tetanus serum. For a moment Volodya felt faint. He heard the doctor's crusty voice as though in a dream.

"Good for you, I must say. Not bad for a first-year student. You've got your wits about you, that's the main thing. Why are you so pale? Nurse, give him a sniff of ammonia. Let him go out for some air."

Varya and Boris were sitting on the bench outside.

"Where's your basket?" Boris asked.

Volodya shrugged. He felt sick. "I'll never make a doctor, never, never," he was thinking in anguish.

The loss of the basket hurt too. It wasn't losing the mushrooms that he minded, to hell with them anyway. He simply felt a bit ashamed.

Two days later Volodya saw an article in the regional paper about the modest Soviet student who, having demonstrated resourcefulness and courage, to say nothing of sound knowledge, vanished without giving his name. In conclusion the moral was drawn that such nameless heroes were only possible in our country. Boris Gubin told the story to everyone, and when Volodya came to school on the first day of the autumn term he was given a regular ovation.

"Well, nameless hero, tell me all about it. I'm curious," his aunt said that evening.

"Did Varya sneak?"

"Maybe."

"You see, I bought a course of lectures on field-hospital surgery."

"Go on."

"I got it out of that. But I'll never make a doctor. I'm ashamed to admit it, but everything went round and round."

"Things go round and round with everyone at first," Aunt Aglaya said, looking at her nephew with glistening eyes. "If you only knew what I, a former laundress, felt like when I first came to school!"

After the accident Varya turned perfectly meek and crossed Volodya in nothing. Yevgeny was the only one to speak of the matter ironically.

"They pinched your mushrooms, didn't they?" he asked in a deliberately nasty voice. "And after that you're supposed to sow the seeds of kindness, mercy and wisdom."

"Would you like to have your face pushed in?" Volodya asked.

"That's puerile!" Yevgeny said sternly.

"There are cases when it's senseless to argue," Volodya

replied. "A good punch — and the whole thing is settled."

"What about the law? Think I wouldn't sue you for assault? And you'd land in a corrective labour camp, my fine friend, I'd see to that," Yevgeny said in a level voice.

Volodya glanced at him and was surprised to see that Yevgeny was not joking. He looked calm and collected, a model of uprightness in his smartly fitting tunic and shoulder belt, the type of young man one saw on posters. "Maybe I should really give him one?" Volodya wondered. But all at once he felt bored, and left.

### FATHERS AND SONS

While still at school, Volodya began to live the life of the Sechenov Medical Institute. He had learned from Boris Gubin that some of the departments ran student circles offering free admission, and he had been punctually attending the pathoanatomists' class ever since. Professor Ganichev, short, fat and absolutely bald, was quick to single out the new young man with the long neck, and although he demanded no answers from him he often seemed to be delivering his lecture to Volodya alone. At school, matters were going well enough with Volodya, but the teachers were on their guard with him, and some were hostile. At teachers' meetings they referred to him as their "child prodigy", and Tatyana Yefimovna stated quite flatly on several occasions that Ustimenko was an individualist with a blurred outlook, and that she expected no good to come of this presumptuous youth. Not all the teachers shared her view, but arguing with her meant quarrelling, and no one felt like quarrelling. The teachers' displeasure with Volodya increased as time went on. They were irritated by his silent preoccupation which alternated with boyishly rowdy high spirits; by his cold aloofness, by his attachment to an inner world in which he lived independently of the school pattern, it irritated them that he was self-sufficient and was for ever seeking instead of being satisfied with the inviolable truths set out in textbooks.

"If only I could get into medicine sooner! That's where you've got real accuracy and clarity, it's the only real thing!" Thus ran Volodya's fervent thoughts at night.

And yet Ganichev told his pupils with a smile that was not encouraging:

"Think a hundred times before you come to us. Hippocrates insisted that physicians should always try to be pleasing to their patients in their appearance, and that, if you come to think of it, is not as simple as it sounds. And it's sometimes a blow to one's vanity to follow some further advice given by Hippocrates: if a physician finds himself at a loss, he must fearlessly call in other physicians to explain to him the patient's condition and indicate the necessary treatment."

Ganichev also said:

"Read Goethe, dear friends. Some very bitter truths are uttered by Mephistopheles, truths that have not lost their meaning to this day. And don't imagine you've heard them all in Gounod's opera. Read and think, reflect, seek, and ask yourselves: will I have sufficient strength in practice not to succumb to the greatest temptation of all which is to drift into the thoughtless execution of duty..."

Tapping his brightly polished shoe with its dangling shoe-lace, he recited in German, making his own translation as he went along:

> *The spirit of medicine is not hard to understand:*
> *You carefully study the great and the small world,*
> *Only to leave everything to God's will*
> *When all is said and done...*

He told them, harshly and angrily, of the practice of departmentalism in the history of medicine, of the pompous and stupid old men who stifled the thought of gifted young men merely because their ideas were disturbing; he read by heart the pledge sworn by those who in days long past graduated from the celebrated University of Bologna.

"You must swear," Ganichev pronounced solemnly and even haughtily, with an angry gleam in his eyes, "you must swear to uphold the science that is publicly preached at Bologna University and other celebrated schools according to the authors *already acclaimed* through so many centuries, to uphold the sciences expounded and set forth by the doctors of the university and the professors themselves. You will never permit anyone in your presence to refute or belittle Aristotle, Galen, Hippocrates and others, their tenets or their conclusions...

"That, if you please, is what was once invented and drawn up as an oath and pledge: a noose on the neck of science. A noose! Because anything original or new most certainly entailed reviewing something established earlier, and to review the conclusions of the great Aristotle, Galen and Hippocrates, to say nothing of those *others* — the devil knows what *others* —

49

led to His Holiness the Grand Inquisitor and thence to the stake. It was only natural that many of the gifted in those days, instead of getting down to work, made all the use they could out of the words of our father of medicine, Hippocrates: 'Life is short and Art is long; the Crisis is fleeting; *Experiment risky; Decision difficult.*' Giordano Bruno chose a different road that was quite unlike the beaten tracks taken by the diploma'ed dullards of his day. 'I am an Academician of a non-existent Academy,' the great Bruno said about himself. 'And I have no colleagues among the holy fathers of ignorance.' As you know, it ended tragically..."

The plump little professor preached doubt, he wanted to relieve the institute beforehand of crammers to whom a top mark was an aim in itself, of mother's little darlings, of bored young men who had not yet made up their minds where to apply their talents. Never stop seeking, he told them, and intimated that no doctor's manuals, textbooks or conscientiously noted lectures would help the future "Children of Aesculapius", as he liked to call them, if they themselves did not seek perpetually.

"Textbooks still haven't been abolished, have they?" Misha Shervud, a fair, rosy-cheeked, lobster-eyed boy who sat next to Volodya, once asked Ganichev.

"Textbooks differ," Ganichev replied pensively. "In my time, for instance, we were recommended to prescribe the so-called 'neutral' drugs, placebos, to humour the sufferer as well as his family and to uphold the honour of medical science. In my time, pharmacology introduced us to a vast variety of drugs that were known to be ineffective. Textbooks also taught generations of doctors to diagnose a disease on the basis of what drug helped. Do you understand? *'Ex-juvantibus'.*"

"Sounds queer!" said Shervud.

"In ancient times," Ganichev went on, "people were treated with everything under the sun, spells and astrology included. Frog liver was supposed to be good for gout and rheumatism, an image of a lion on a golden background cured renal diseases, jaundice was treated with an infusion of swallowwort simply because it was yellow in colour. It was also believed that the human brain changed in size in conformity with the phases of the moon, and that the movement of blood was influenced by the ebb and flow of the sea. Molière was absolutely right to make his Bèralde say that the magnificence of the art of such doctoring lay in its nonsensical solemnity and scholarly gibberish which substituted words for sense and promises for results."

"Do things like that happen nowadays too?" the lobster-eyed young man persisted.

"Textbooks are written by people, and the people who teach medical sciences are also human," Ganichev went on, as though he had not heard the young man's question. "And even the great doctors were human. There is a dangerous tendency, I should even venture to say a harmful, mean and rotten tendency to proclaim the great physicians of the past beyond the pale of human judgement, so to say, and to overlook the mistakes they made and the nonsense they wrote. It hampers the progress of science. Our prominent contemporary scientists naturally make mistakes too, and occasionally talk a lot of rot. These mistakes are stuffed into people's heads because the people who make them are very, very highly esteemed, and some are even honoured academicians. But you've got to use your own brains, or else you'll never make real doctors but only the kind Molière wrote about: 'They will tell you in Latin that your daughter is ill.'"

"The old cynic," the lobster-eyed Misha Shervud whispered to Volodya.

"And you're a young ass," Volodya whispered back.

"Look here!" Shervud burst out.

"Did you want to ask something?" Ganichev asked.

Volodya said nothing.

By the end of the autumn term in school Volodya rid himself completely of the habit of asking the teachers questions that not all of them could answer. As for answering *their* questions, he could not do it the way they wanted it because of his crude, inborn honesty. And so every time Ustimcnko was called to the blackboard the class was treated to a free show. He naturally knew less than the teacher, his knowledge was certainly more superficial, but he invariably showed that his scope was wider and often said things that were a revelation to the teacher, and were not in the textbook of course. Often, Volodya's answers stimulated the whole class to deeper thought, and then everyone would listen in delight to the verbal duel between him and the teacher.

"That's pure and simple idealism, it's mysticism, it's religious superstition!" Adam, the science master, once shouted.

"A Marxist is supposed to examine any fact that emerges from the experimental stage, and not simply condemn the fact itself," Volodya said calmly and firmly. "I have given you a fact, and you object."

He calmly went back to his seat, while Adam first put a "poor" against Ustimenko's name with a shaky hand, and then changed it into an "excellent". For all his limitations, he was an honest man. Volodya's friends furtively stuck up their thumbs for him and slipped notes to one another, such as: "He showed him, didn't he!" "Our pride and glory!" or "Wonder what'll come of him?" But Volodya noticed none of this, he saw and heard nothing. He was already sitting at his desk engrossed in a new book on blood circulation which he could only keep till the following night when the medical circle held a class. In the sixteenth century the Spaniard, Michael Servetus, had almost solved the riddle of blood circulation, but he ended his life at the stake. Oh, the fiends!

"What's that you're mumbling?" asked the boy who sat next to Volodya.

"Was I?" Volodya said, startled.

And yet, Volodya only got into the Medical Institute by the skin of his teeth. Choosing Turgenev's *Fathers and Sons* for the theme of his essay, he concentrated entirely on Bazarov, calling him, in his impassioned, almost fanatical way, a "trailblazer of new, as yet untravelled paths in Russian science", and poor Turgenev "an idle nobleman, who wrote for the sole purpose of asserting art for art's sake or, more likely still, to while away the time when he was not listening to Pauline Viardot-Garcia's coloraturas". Volodya liked this elaborate sentence so much that he even underlined it with a wavy line, never thinking, of course, that it was precisely this sentence that would make the examiner, a sensitive soul, reach for her heart drops. Excerpts from Volodya's essay were read at the meeting of the selection committee, evoking general laughter and disparaging comments. Ganichev alone did not laugh. And because he enjoyed everyone's respect at the institute, respect tinged with awe, those present at the meeting took careful note of *how* he did not laugh.

"Admittedly the young man has blundered," Ganichev said meditatively and regretfully. "He has blundered badly and rather grossly. But he wrote what he honestly thinks is true. The point is, dear friends, that he was not trying to pass his examination or win our favour; he was not trying to show himself to us in the most advantageous light, he was simply defending Bazarov. Ustimenko is too young to know, or simply hasn't found out yet, that he isn't  the first person in Russia

to stand up for Bazarov. He conducted his defence overzealous-
ly. But, dear colleagues, consider the very fact of this vehe-
ment intercession. A young man, a mere boy in fact, has stood
up in defence of Russian science. There is genuine pain in the
essay, in Bazarov the boy discerned the features of Sechenov
and Mechnikov and Pirogov. Permit me to voice a certain blasphemous thought: if Turgenev were alive today and had read
that essay he would not have minded. He would have laughed a
little, but certainly he would not have minded, and perhaps
he would have been touched as well. Because if you sweep away
all that has been rashly misstated here, you will see plenty
of civic courage. Don't you agree? In so far as our institute,
our alma mater, is concerned, I must say that the style adopted by our applicant reveals to me a personality that will
make an active doctor, a fighter, a warrior, you will forgive me this high-flown speech, an intolerant personality of
course, but one of originality, single-mindedness and dis-
tinction. And our need of people like that is dire, considering moreover the disastrous state of affairs arising from the
desire of young people of a certain type to enrol in an institute, any institute, so long as they are registered as students. There is no denying that we do sometimes graduate perfect young ladies with a higher education but not doctors
in the true sense of the word. Sometimes we graduate very nice
and amiable doctors too, but..."

Ganichev smiled wryly and made a gesture of dismissal.

"As for Ustimenko, I know him from our study circle.
And I mean it when I say that, whatever anyone else may think,
I personally should very much like to have him not merely as
a pupil but also a successor, provided, of course, that the
crazy young cucumber would devote himself to pathoanatomy.
One sometimes wishes, you know, to be able to pass on one's
chair not to a stranger, but to... However, if my colleagues
are in two minds about admitting Ustimenko, we could interview
him."

The colleagues were in two minds about it, and the interview was arranged for 2 p. m. that day. Volodya came two hours
early and paced the long, dusky corridor. Making an about turn
he saw Yevgeny. His manner was as affected as ever but now he
looked wide-awake and happy.

"What are you doing here?" Volodya asked, surprised.

"Enrolling, what else?" Yevgeny seemed surprised at Volodya's question. "I asked your advice about it, you know. The
pater, by the way, is pleased, he thinks a lot of you for some

inexplicable reason, and so he's glad we'll be studying together. I've made friends with the third-year students already, and I've heard their torch-song, quite a cute little song, in fact."

"What torch-song?" Volodya did not understand.

"I'll sing it for you. It's called 'To My Prosecutor Friend'."

Yevgeny sat down on the window-sill, opened his pink mouth and sang rather pleasantly. He often sang at home, at school parties and even in amateur art shows.

> *When all earthly ties are broken,*
> *And I'm laid on the slab, I implore,*
> *Take care of my heart, don't drop it*
> *In haste on the hard stone floor...*

His singing has attracted a small audience, and now Yevgeny was explaining to his future fellow students:

"The most curious thing about it is that the words were written by Garshin, who, incidentally, was a pathoanatomist. It's cute, don't you think? Would you like me to sing you another song, an old medicos' song? It's about the dissecting room where we're fated to spend quite a bit of our time."

There were two examiners coming down the corridor. Yevgeny watched them out of sight and then sang in almost a whisper:

> *That fellow's a marvel, his fun he would seek*
> *Down in the morgue, that abode of reek.*
> *He goes there, of course, more knowledge to gain*
> *Only to err again and again...*

Yevgeny's appeal was amazing. A couple of songs sung in the corridor had made him friends already. He was walking up and down with them now, laughing, slapping shoulders, and calling everyone by name.

"Hey you, the future Pirogov-Sklifosovsky-Burdenko all rolled in one, come and join us," Yevgeny called out to Volodya. "Meet the crowd: Nyussia Yelkina, Svetlana, and this is Ogurtsov."

Interviewed by the selection committee, Volodya — a frowning, lanky, long-armed youth with sharp cheekbones and tufty eyebrows — looked straight into the eyes of anyone who asked him a question and answered discreetly, briefly and even charily, but so forceful was his own, personal attitude to the subject he had chosen for his lifework, that nearly all the judges found themselves exchanging delighted looks and sometimes meaningful winks. Only one man eyed Volodya with animosity. This was Gennady Tarasovich Zhovtyak, a typical professor to look at: bald-headed, beard neatly trimmed, and rings on his fingers. There was something about Volodya that irritated him: perhaps it was his lack of deference. Still, everything ended well. Pulling out his watch on its decorative chain hung with charms Zhovtyak glanced at it and left to attend a consultation. Volodya was dismissed with kindness.

### THE STUDENT

"Yes, a pleasure indeed," said the dean of the faculty. "It's a pleasure to meet such a boy. I was sitting and thinking that we had never had an Ustimenko at Novorossiisk University, not in my class anyway. Incidentally, there's another lad I thought rather likable, a very young, apple-cheeked boy. No genius, of course, but an extremely pleasant young man. Makes a good impression ... now, what is his name..."

Yevgeny Stepanov's name appeared to have slipped the dean's memory, but since it was known to some of the teachers that Yevgeny was a friend of the family and, what was more, often sang his romances in the dean's drawing room and was rather more than just liked by Iraida, the dean's daughter, they supplied the name obligingly.

"Yes, yes. I believe the name is Stepanov," the dean nodded. "Very nice lad and good-hearted, no doubt about that. Jolly good fellows, we used to call them in my day. Something truly Russian in him, something of the steppes, generous and dashing."

Feeling that he had gone a bit too far, the dean returned to the subject of Ustimenko and called him a "model of the future Soviet doctor".

"That's better!" Ganichev said with ominous approval. "He's not one of your smart all-rounders with bright rosy cheeks. He knows what he's after. The expression is not a fashionable one but it's apt in the present case: he is a high-principled young man. Needless to say, he'll give trouble, but it will be worthwhile. He *is* conceited though, shamelessly so..."

It was not clear from the way he said it whether he approved of Volodya's conceit or not. It rather seemed that he did.

"And he won't grow into another Zhovtyak," Ganichev added. "Not under any circumstances, I vouch for that. Far be it from me to deny our highly esteemed Professor Zhovtyak a certain amount of charm, like Gogol's 'altogether charming lady' or his Shponka, another very pleasant little gentleman, I believe."

The day Volodya became a medical student his father arrived, flying a funny, small, green plane. The airfield was on the bank of the Uncha; Afanasy Petrovich climbed down from the cockpit and began to stretch his legs as if he had been sitting a long time in a horse-drawn cart. He wore no helmet and had nothing glamorous about him at all. The men who were sitting about on the grass jumped to attention and it was clear from their faces that they knew and respected Volodya's father. A feeling of pride in his father brought a flush to Volodya's face; he was proud of his outward ordinariness and simplicity, of the laughter wrinkles around his eyes, of the strength he deliberately seemed to hide, and of the generosity of his nature.

"Hasn't Rodion reported yet?"

"No, he hasn't reported," Volodya replied smiling.

True to military tradition, his father never said "came", it was always "reported", and never "I'm going to bed", but "I'll be turning in".

"You rascal, laughing at an old man!" Afanasy Petrovich said and gave Volodya a mighty push.

Volodya swayed but did not fall down. The airmen were talking about something. Must be about my father, Volodya thought.

Aunt Aglaya had a meeting to attend, and was not home till dinner-time, to serve the gala dinner she had spent the evening before and the early hours of the morning getting ready. Yevgeny also came to dinner, or rather to "taste the bait" as he called the prospect of some good food at his friends'. He had also been admitted to the Sechenov Medical Institute, true not without Iraida bringing some pressure to bear on her mother, who then used her influence with her husband, the dean. Even so, Yevgeny's squeezing into the institute had not been managed too smoothly: his name had at first been left out of the list and was only "appended" to it after some lengthy negotiations. At the moment Yevgeny felt like a man who had safely jumped on board a moving tram after a hard race but had not yet quite recovered his breath. Nevertheless, his mood was excellent, not to say triumphant. As a matter of fact, no one except the dean of the faculty knew how the whole thing had been fixed, so why worry, it was no use letting *him* see that Yevgeny was grateful, much indebted, and all the rest of it.

Yevgeny's stepfather was overjoyed. Surely it showed that there was some good in the lad, if in spite of being pampered by his mother and having no outstanding gifts, he had managed to make the grade. It must be all aboveboard because you had to pass the competitive exams; there couldn't have been any monkey business about it.

"When my machine runs down, you'll fix me up, eh?" he told Yevgeny.

Rodion came to the Ustimenkos in civilian clothes and only his deep sunburn and his rolling, springy walk betrayed the sailor in him. He would not let Varya or Volodya, for that matter, leave his side for a minute. After drinking a glass of vodka he grunted with relish and recited the words of an old drinking song:

> *Drink up, fellows, while you're here,*
> *In the next world there's no beer,*
> *But if there is and not too dear*
> *We'll drink it there and drink it here...*

Rodion's father, Mefody Stepanov, came later. He was fresh from the bath-house and wore a waistcoat over his long silk shirt. There was an air of great contentment about him.

"Sit down, root and stock of our family!" Rodion said to his father. "And rejoice: you've lived to see your grandson a medical student. And Volodya too. That calls for the biggest glasses!"

"A surveyor would've been better," the old man declared.

He had an opinion entirely his own about everything.

"What are you doing without your uniform?" he asked his son. "You're a high-ranking officer, so wear it for people to see. When I came back from the Japanese war I kept my shoulder-straps for a long time, it gives you dignity, it does. Once I took them off, I was a nobody all over again."

Then he turned to Aglaya.

"What did you pay for the herring?"

"Money!" Aglaya replied.

"And the mutton?"

"Oh, drop it, Dad. What does it matter to you?" Rodion said.

"I was just making conversation," the old man replied.

Varya clung to her father and whispered:

"Stay with us a while, Daddy, please stay. Take a long furlough and let your boats go hang."

"Ships, not boats," her father corrected her. "There're only three of you that need me here, but there's a whole crowd back there. Think what you're saying, daughter!"

"Yevgeny's sort of funny," Varya said. "I just can't understand him."

"We'll look into that."

Afanasy Ustimenko fetched a guitar, adorned with a large bow, and gently plucking the strings began to sing:

> *Ah, you gloomy night!*
> *Autumn night so dark!*
> *Why so deep a frown,*
> *Not a star looks down...*

Aglaya's strong contralto picked up the last line:

> *Not a star looks down...*

Everyone felt strangely melancholy. Old Mefody alone tried to keep the party spirit going a little longer, but then he too grew quiet.

"What's the matter?" Aglaya said. "Why did you give up half-way through?"

Rodion was looking worried; Afanasy had put the guitar down on the sofa and was contemplating his son. Yevgeny was whispering to Volodya that he must slip away at once: the crowd was having a barbecue on the bank of the river, Iraida and Misha Shervud would be there, and perhaps the dean himself would do them the honour. Follow me?

"I follow," Volodya replied curtly.

Varya's future came up for discussion when twilight fell. Volodya suggested the medical institute, Afanasy Petrovich spoke highly of the technological, while Aunt Aglaya smiled and suggested nothing. Varya said with a metallic ring in her voice and a stubborn line between her eyebrows:

"I am going to work in art."

"Where's that?" old Mefody, slightly tipsy by now, wanted to know.

"Well ... the theatre, for instance," Varya said in a louder voice and rather disagreeably.

"Some work that!" the old man brought out on a yawn.

"But have you the gift for it?" Varya's father asked gently.

"Look, Varya dear, I'm not saying this to hurt you, but you haven't got a very good ear, for one thing. And your build, too, you're like a little turnip ... nice and robust, but I don't remember ever seeing an actress like that."

"I'll grow taller," Varya promised sullenly. "And I must eat less starchy stuff. As for my singing, I'm not going into the opera for one thing, and for another voices can be developed."

Volodya looked at her pityingly. Varya stuck her tongue out at him and turned away.

Later that night, Afanasy Petrovich made himself comfortable on the sofa with his feet up on the bolster to read a slim volume in a bright cover. He puffed leisurely at his cigarette and expressed his wonder aloud.

"Listen to this! The eagle is the only bird in the world that can look straight at the sun. Well, well. That's where the expression 'eagle-eyed' comes from. Did you know it, Volodya?"

"No, I didn't."

"They're handsome devils," his father went on. "I used to admire them back in the days when I was piloting a Sopwith. They'd come straight at you and make you swerve. Brave birds."

Aglaya listened to her brother with a dreamy smile and a soft light in her dark eyes. The samovar on the table hummed quietly to itself, and it seemed that they had always been like that, the three of them together, and that they would always be together, always...

But at dawn, Volodya's father left. He forbade them to see him off.

"Long farewells mean more tears," he said cheerfully. He finished his tea, gave his son a punch in the shoulder the way he had done at greeting, hugged his sister, and walked out.

Volodya leaned far out of the window to watch his father go.

He was standing on the doorstep and looking up at the greying sky. "Eagle-eyed", the words came back to Volodya. His father was holding his cap in his hand, and the porch light shone down on his uncovered head. So Volodya saw his father for the last time in his life, and so he was to remember him always: a man standing on the doorstep, scanning the sky — his flyer's road.

### Chapter Four

## GIFTS

Day had already broken when Afanasy Ustimenko reached the airfield. Rodion Stepanov was there in his white navy tunic, walking up and down the river bank.

"I told you not to," Afanasy said glumly. "Why go short of sleep?"

"I couldn't sleep," Rodion replied. "I'm not bothering you, am I? Go ahead and take off. I shan't hang on to the tail."

The soldier on duty came up and held a brief conversation with Ustimenko. Two other men approached him. Ustimenko listened to the sound of the motor, and then took a smoke with Rodion.

"When do we meet again?" Rodion asked.

"Not too soon, I think."

"Where will you spend your furlough?"

"I want to take a mud cure," Ustimenko replied. "It's an old wound but it's bothering me. Why the sad look, sailor man?"

"I'm all right," Rodion's sigh belied the words.

The motor roared, died down and roared again as the mechanics did their checking. Afanasy shook Rodion's hand with his own strong, hard one, pulled on his gloves and with a boy's nimbleness climbed into the cockpit. He shifted about before he was snugly settled, shouted down his flyer's orders, and the plane began to skip and hop along the runway. In a matter of minutes the black dot faded away in the blue.

"How am I to live now anyway?" Rodion mused. "Surely it can't go on? Or can it? Perhaps, other people live like this, too, but simply don't think about it, don't let it worry them?"

Anyhow it was not the time to think about it when he was in a state of unreasonable annoyance, and he was indeed annoyed just then. It was not easy to keep his temper where Yevgeny was involved, nor could he ever talk quite calmly to Alevtina. He could never be calm or reasonable with them, or so he believed, for he was his own sternest judge. And once again, for the thousandth time, he saw her face, the elaborate hairdo, and the look she had given him on his arrival the day before, a look of resigned hatred.

"I'm going away into the country," she had told him the moment he came in. "One can't live in this dust and heat all the summer. As it is, I'm quite exhausted with all these exams."

"What exams?"

"Why, Yevgeny's of course."

"Did *you* coach him?" Rodion had not been able to refrain from saying.

"I made him comfortable," she had said. "You're still such a poor provider for your family that I can't even afford one servant."

"Back to where we started, eh?" Rodion had asked, turning pale with fury. "Or perhaps it pleases you to call things by the names used in the days when you were..."

"Shut up!" she had shrieked.

There was nothing she dreaded more than her past becoming known; she might have been a thief or a murderess at least.

Such had been the reunion of husband and wife.

She wanted him to go, and so did Yevgeny, but he decided to stay. There was Varya, and, besides, he had nowhere to go now that his ship had been put in dock. Leave had practically been forced on him and he had no booking at a holiday home. Let Alevtina go to the country and stay there with her friend; he'd remain here. It was a restful place, there were some poplars and birches outside his window, he could take a shower and lie down with a book, go to the park to hear the band in the afternoons, and when Varya was through with school they could take a pleasure cruise, or do a hundred other wonderful things.

Let everyone do what they liked, so long as they were happy.

After all, Yevgeny had been admitted to the medical institute. Maybe he really was unfair to the lad; maybe it was all because of his being only a stepson. He must change all that, he must make this day a happy one for everybody. For Volodya and Aglaya, for his old father, for Yevgeny and Varya. He had been unfair to Yevgeny, he knew that. He had had Varya alone to stay with him in Kronstadt, while Yevgeny had remained with Alevtina. And had he ever had a real talk with his stepson? He made up his mind to straighten matters out here and now, he simply had to find a key to Yevgeny's heart, Yevgeny the future doctor!

Busy with these thoughts he shaved and took a shower while the household was still asleep, put plenty of money in his pocket, and went out shopping. At a commission store he bought a camera; the delicatessen store he left loaded down with pastries, cakes, sardines, strawberries, bottles of wine, and other delicious and expensive things. Rodion Stepanov had never been a spendthrift, his half-starved, difficult childhood had taught him the value of money at an early age, but on that memorable morning he cheerfully squandered his money with a lavish hand, and was actually happy to do it. He bought Varya a red sweater, and his father a pair of shoes. For Volodya he got a splendid leather-bound collection of Herzen. He also bought tickets for all of them to hear *Faust* that night. It was a guest performance by a Moscow opera company, and the tickets were all sold out. He had gone in to see the stout, very imposing theatre manager and, with much embarrassed hemming and hawing, told him that he was a naval officer on furlough, and would like...

"That's what everyone would like," the man had replied insolently. "Our House of Culture, I regret, doesn't stretch..."

Still, Rodion had managed to secure six seats in the eighteenth row. Mopping his perspiring face after the ordeal he got into the waiting taxi, piled high with his parcels.

Varya had already left the house when he arrived, and Yevgeny was talking listlessly into the telephone:

"They make me sick, but it's a must. After all he is the dean, you never know how your life will shape. Don't spit in the well, my child, you may want to drink out of it one day."

"I've heard it put differently," Rodion said harshly, striding into the dining-room. "Don't drink out of the well, you may want to spit into it."

Yevgeny put his hand over the receiver and glanced obliquely at his stepfather.

"Witty but impractical," he said. "Life, my darling papa, is not such a simple thing."

He took an armchair and settled down for a long, insipid chat with some friend of his. He was wearing his confounded hairnet; he yawned and stretched all the time he talked. Animosity surged up in Rodion, but he stifled it. He told himself once more that children are never to blame, it is the parents who are to blame for everything. Rodion was one of those people who blame themselves harshly even when they know they are entirely innocent, and even more so, of course, if the fault is indirectly theirs. And again, though artificially now, he began to work up the mood he had known early that morning and, while Yevgeny chatted on the phone, arranged the presents on the dining-room table, placing the theatre tickets on top.

Yevgeny put down the receiver, took another stretch, and sauntered lazily over to the table.

"It's a good camera," his stepfather said. "A good thing to own. Our optics are first-class, and it's nice to be able to take a picture yourself sometimes."

It was an effort to force the words out. The sentence was inane and long-winded, and there was something like blandishment in the tone of his voice.

"The new reflex cameras are handier, I think," Yevgeny said. "Iraida, our dean's daughter, has a Zeiss camera. Beautiful job, looks quite posh. And this damned thing here wants a tripod. It's rather unwieldy, don't you think?"

"I did get a tripod," his father said eagerly, too eagerly. "A tripod, yes, you're quite right, you can't do much photography without a tripod. But to start with, a camera like this one is very good, Yevgeny, my boy. We had a chap at school, his name was Yevgeny, too, by the way. He was quite an artist: he took a picture of a bee once, a bee feeding on a buckwheat flower. It looked so true to life, with all its fluff showing, they had the photo reproduced in the newspaper in fact, there was a photographers' competition, and his camera wasn't half so good as yours."

"But I never said it was bad. The camera's all right. It's unwieldy that's all, and none of our chaps use that kind any more."

"Who are these — chaps?"

"Why, you know that as well as I do, there's Kirilov, Boris, Semyakin, we often get together and do things."

Rodion nodded at every name, though he had no idea who they were.

"Why don't you mention Volodya?" he asked, thrusting his chin forward. "Where does Volodya come in? Isn't he good enough for your crowd?"

Yevgeny turned slightly pale. An expression of resigned hatred appeared in his eyes.

"You know, Dad," Yevgeny said, standing a good distance away from the older man, "you know, I can never understand what it is you want of me, I honestly can't. Your precious Volodya is a fanatic, a maniac, and we're just ordinary chaps. I'm not sure, maybe he'll really turn out a great man. I'm not saying he won't, but if you want to know we're young and we enjoy taking all the jolly things life has to offer."

"All right. Clear enough," Rodion nodded.

"After all, Soviet power is Soviet power," Yevgeny continued, his spirits lifting somewhat and his manner more amiable, even confiding. "Surely you don't want your children to miss all the jolly things in life and happiness generally after the struggle you all waged, and the hardships you and Mummy endured for years."

"Clear enough," his stepfather cut him short.

Rodion felt he would choke. He flung the window open and drank some lukewarm water out of the carafe on the table. "I mustn't quarrel, I mustn't quarrel," he told himself. "I must see it straight. It's Alevtina who's implanted all this rot in Yevgeny's mind. It's all her doing, it's she who is ruining the boy." To change the subject, he asked Yevgeny how his mother was getting on in the country.

"It's killingly dull there," Yevgeny replied, putting his foot on a chair and tying his shoe-lace. "Her dressmaker Lucie lives next door, you know."

"A Frenchwoman or something?"

"No, why? She's Russian. She's a pal of Mother's but they quarrel pretty violently too. The other day Lucie ruined Mother's organdie."

"Ruined what?"

"Mother's organdie — a stiff, patterned fabric."

"I get you," Rodion said, not getting anything. "One more question: what's that new picture you've got over there?"

He was looking at a picture that had just caught the rays of the morning sun. It depicted a gaunt reddish plain dotted with plants that seemed to be covered with prickly warts.

"Oh, cactuses," Yevgeny answered casually. "Mother's latest fad. She and Lucie grow them."

"Cactuses, you say?"

"Yep."

"Do they make jam from them or what?"

"No jam or anything," Yevgeny said with a smile. "They're beautiful, see? They're simply decorative."

"What's happened to the fish-bowl? It doesn't seem to be here."

"The fish-bowl's been taken out of the house. The fish got sick and passed away. They *passed away*, make a note of that. Mother gets angry if you put it any other way."

"They passed away!" Rodion repeated. "All right, clear enough. Now the cactuses, I still don't understand: do they blossom beautifully or is it their pleasant smell?"

"Neither. They're just green and prickly. It's the fashion, understand? It's the fashion to exclaim: Heavens, aren't they sweet! That's all there is to it."

"All right, no use talking about them. You know what we'll do, as soon as Varya comes, we'll have a slap-up meal with Aglaya and Volodya, and then we'll push on to the theatre. What d'you say?"

Yevgeny said nothing.

"It's *Faust* by Gounod, it's an opera," Rodion added after a while. "Sverlikhin is singing Mephistopheles, his voice is the real thing."

"Sverlikhin or no Sverlikhin, I'm afraid I can't do it, Dad," Yevgeny said slowly. "I have an invitation for tonight and I can't very well get out of it. And this afternoon we're all going to watch a football match. The Uncha team is playing 'Torpedo', that's no joke. So you'll just have to manage without me."

"Clear enough," Rodion said for the hundredth time. "I get you."

And, with drooping head, he walked out of the room.

### GRANDFATHER

Varya was still out, and the stuffy, futile day dragged on senselessly.

At last old Mefody turned up. He brought in a bunch of green onions, some radishes wrapped in a newspaper, and a can of kvass. The old man rarely came to stay with his son except when Alevtina was away; he did not dare remain long with her in the house. It maddened her that he went about in his bare feet and wore a long, beltless shirt, that after drinking a glass of vodka he invariably sang in a reedy, sentimental warble: "Ah, you poor little seamstress, you were only sixteen at the time," or suddenly began to press food on her guests saying, "It's all right, we've plenty more." After staying with her a while the old man's manner would become flustered and frightened, he would begin to blink very rapidly, bow much lower than necessary, talk less and less and, finally, start back for his village, back to his little cottage with its smell of feathers and ashes.

When Alevtina, now Valentina Andreyevna, or Devilina Andreyevna, as old Mefody called her, was away, he walked on firmer ground, smoked his pipe in the kitchen and the corridor, and imparted his recollections to Varya in a loud voice. But when Yevgeny's friends called, the old man grew silent and kept out of the way, saying with a wily little smile that "he'd do just as well where he was, while the young gentlemen were enjoying themselves". Rodion had once heard a guest of Yevgeny's telling the old man to go out and buy him some cigarettes.

It made him sick in the pit of his stomach to see the meek old man growing meeker still, but Alevtina blushed in such embarrassment when he appeared before her guests that Rodion, unable to decide who was more deserving of pity — his father or his wife — would see the old man to the station with mixed feelings of regret and relief, and thrust an extra bit of money into his pocket "in case of emergency".

And so, after waiting for Varya vainly they had dinner alone. The bearded old man was wearing a jacket that was much too long for him, his small light-coloured eyes, which were like his son's, held a look of unsmiling deference, and the way he said "Rodion" gave this form of address all the formality of a name and patronymic. He refused both pastries and sardines from sheer politeness; instead, he stuffed his mouth full of green onions, observing as he chewed that onions must certainly be plentiful that year since they were so cheap. In this roundabout way, the father gave the son to understand that he wasn't one to throw money away, and that he was piously watching over the interests of Rodion's home.

Together they washed the dishes.

"Look here, Dad, what about the two of us going to the theatre tonight?" Rodion asked. "Would you like it? I don't think you've ever been anywhere except the circus, have you?"

"Let it be the theatre then," his father said, picking his teeth with a match. "I've nothing against it. I can go if other people do, why not!"

There was anxiety in his eyes, however, and he was blinking very quickly, as if something had frightened him.

At long last Varya and Volodya came in. Her father had been waiting for her all day and where had she been? At the tailor's with Volodya to see him try on his first "real" suit, a student's trousers and jacket.

"Student's trousers — what are they?" Rodion asked testily.

"Oh, she's just talking rot," Volodya replied. "They're altering my father's uniform for me. Of course, Varya must have her say."

He sat down on the sofa, picked up a book and was immediately lost to the world. Varya, gasping with delight, bolted cakes and meat pastries, eating them together, washed the green onions down with kvass, then stuck her finger in the salt, licked it and said, "Gorgeous!"

The moment tea was over, old Mefody began to get ready for the theatre; he cleaned his boots in the kitchen, then started wandering aimlessly from room to room in his underwear. Blinking worriedly as he pulled on his trousers, he first tucked them into his tall boots, then let them come down over the boots. Rodion sat smoking and thinking that in all these years he had never found the time nor the money to buy his father a decent suit. "Organdie, fish-bowl, cactuses!" he repeated the irritating words in his mind.

"Here, put on my civilian suit," he said. "You're not tall, it'll just fit you nicely. I want you to look your best, don't disgrace me."

The words "don't disgrace me" decided the old man, and he arrayed himself in his son's blue serge suit and white tennis shirt, and then, standing in front of the looking-glass, he made a terrible face and said:

"My, my! Well, I'll be damned!"

They called for Aglaya on the way. She was waiting for them on her doorstep, dressed in white, her dark eyes shining and her cheeks very pink.

During the performance the old man kept pointing at the stage and asking questions with complete disregard for the people hissing at him.

"What's that? What's ailing him? Which on is his wife?"

Or again he would say with an angry snort:

"The fool! A fool, that's what he is. Selling his soul, imagine that! My, my!"

The people around them giggled, Rodion smiled and exchanged looks with Aglaya. It was wonderful what companionship there was in her silence and smile.

Walking about the foyer during the interval, Grandfather endeavoured to get in front of a mirror whenever he could and, making a wrathful, forbidding face, muttered under his breath, "Well, I'll be damned!"

The old man liked Mephistopheles best.

"That's a sly one," he said. "A real devil he is. He got what he was after. Better not to get mixed up with his sort if you can help it. Am I right, Varya?"

# AFTER THE THEATRE

They had supper at home. Yevgeny was not back yet. Varya and Volodya were whispering together about something, and to Rodion it seemed that she was striking attitudes. Grandfather regretfully took off the blue serge suit, drank a glass of vodka, and went to bed. Aglaya and Rodion sat by the window; she told him, without making a grievance of it, how tiring her job was. The most wearing part of it was the poor roads and the need to drive all over the region; also, the idiotic, formalistic attitude of some of the education officers.

"I'm not so young as I was," she said, "and no longer as tough. I know I make mountains of molehills sometimes, and let fly at people..."

Folding her small, sunburnt hands in her lap, she sat looking down at them, then she glanced straight into Rodion's eyes and said:

"You have your troubles too, Rodion. I can see it, your temples are turning grey."

He smiled guiltily and poured himself some wine.

"I've no complaints about the navy, Aglaya dear, it's here that it's... It hasn't worked, it didn't come off. Look at Yevgeny..."

"What about Yevgeny?"

"I can't understand him," Rodion said ruefully. "There's no making him out."

"Volodya, for one, understands him all right. And rather thoroughly too. I say, Volodya, tell Rodion Mefodyevich what we were saying about Yevgeny this morning."

Volodya shook his head, unwilling to talk about it.

"Tell me," Rodion said. "It's all one now."

"It'll be tough," Volodya said, getting up from the sofa. "I don't know how to be tactful."

"I'm not asking you to be tactful," Rodion said with an attempt at smiling.

"I don't know who's to blame in this, I wouldn't venture to judge," Volodya said. "But your Yevgeny will rather follow a sidetrack than a straight path, if you know what I mean. I said this to him in a private talk we had the other day, so I'm free to repeat it to you."

Volodya jerked up his chin, thought for a moment, and began to speak. His voice was harsh and steady.

"I told him what I thought, and for that he called me a preacher, a prig and many other nice things. He all but called me a climber. But I don't care, it's what I think and I can't think differently. Every man in our country must live by the fruits of his own labour, only his own, and not his father's or grandfather's. Am I right, Rodion Mefodyevich?"

"Yes, carry on," he said, ungraciously for some reason.

"Well, Varya and I were talking about the hammer and sickle the other day. No better emblem could have been invented than the hammer and sickle. They symbolise our social system, and there's a deeper meaning to the symbol than just the working class and peasantry. The law that governs our life is embodied in that symbol, the cardinal law, am I right, Rodion Mefodyevich?"

"Not everyone sees it that way yet, I'm sorry to say," Rodion replied now more sad than angry. "There's Varya, too, there's no knowing what she's about, whether it's to be geology, or the theatre, but as for being useful to society..."

"Now, you're on to me!" Varya said sulkily. "Can't a person have a bit of trouble choosing his career?"

"Why should he?" Volodya broke in harshly. "You've been having too much trouble with it. But we're not talking about you. Rodion Mefodyevich, I hate to say it but Yevgeny lives a separate existence, he lives not by his own merits but by yours, at least, with their help, and he keeps his life entirely separate from the symbol I've just spoken about. It's not that he uses your name as a lever, no, he does nothing of the sort, but he does look upon you as a reserve — just in case. And his philosophy is all wrong too: he believes that because you and Valentina Andreyevna have known hardship and difficulty in life you owe it to him and Varya to make their life beautiful and easy. He and his friends — I know some of them — are convinced that the Revolution was made for them personally, so that they could enjoy a life of ease and contentment. That's all wrong, and you're wrong as well with your all-for-the-children policy, but I shan't say more because you'll get angry."

"I thought it was something like that," Rodion said. "Yes, something like that, but how can a person make you out? You're a damn queer lot."

With his hands behind his back, he paced the length of the dining-room with firm steps. He looked confused, there was misery in his face.

"Yevgeny is a time-server," Volodya said quietly but very firmly. "A young one, but a perfect specimen. And already fully ripe."

Rodion winced.

"Are you quite sure?" he asked.

Volodya shrugged and said nothing.

"We are sometimes apt to overcomplicate things," Aglaya said. "Life is a complicated business, of course, but take this, for example. Isn't a boy who is a telltale in school, an informer and sneak, a character to reckon with already? I'll say this to you, Rodion, plainly and bluntly: I never could stand your Yevgeny and I think you ought to not simply try and reform him, but actually fight him with whatever means there are."

"What means precisely?" Rodion inquired with a bitter smile. "Don't you realise that my rights as regards Yevgeny are not just limited but non-existent? I have my duties but no rights. Oh well, what's the use of talking..."

Grandfather came in in his underwear and a black navy top-coat.

"Is there any kvass in this place?" he asked. "I drank three dippers of water and it didn't help. And it isn't as if I'd eaten anything."

He looked at all of them in turn, then suddenly noticing that the strings of his pants were trailing retreated in embarrassment to look for kvass elsewhere.

"That's that!" Rodion said. "A nice jolly evening. Well, I hope you'll excuse me."

When the guests had gone, he kissed Varya and, seeing pity in her eyes, said that he would go straight to bed. If there was one thing he could not stand, it was pity. He heard Varya splashing about in the bath for a long time, then she, too, settled down to sleep and all grew still. He came back into the dining-room, poured himself a cup of cold tea, and started pacing the room again.

Yevgeny came home late, he opened the front door with his own latchkey and walked into the dining-room. His stepfather was still pacing up and down, a cigarette between his fingers.

"Good evening," Yevgeny said.

"Good evening," Rodion replied and added that Yevgeny might have come home earlier. It was said without anger, though. He felt it was a stranger who had dropped in uninvited.

That stranger now sat down at the table and began to eat. Speaking rather too hastily, he described the game of the right wing, and how, after the match, they had all gone to Shilin's place in the country, where they had drunk iced lemonade, taken a swim and generally enjoyed themselves. Rodion listened in silence. Perhaps, if he just went on listening and saying nothing he would find the lost key. After all, there had been a time when he had rocked the sick, snivelling little boy in his arms for hours on end, a time when he had procured sugar for him in hunger-ravaged Petrograd at the cost of his pride. There had been a time when he had taught Yevgeny his ABC. Was it possible? A time-server? Someone utterly alien. A person who lived for no one but himself.

And once again, for the hundredth time, Rodion asked himself the same question: when, how and why did it happen?

Suddenly he knew why.

It was like a revelation. The reason was because Alevtina's entire life had once been centred on Yevgeny. He was her all, everything was done for him alone, all was permitted him. When Rodion came home dead tired in the evening, could he have sent the boy to the corner store to buy something for him? No, the boy was to know nothing but joy; as an alternative to pleasure, he could study. According to Alevtina, childhood years were the happiest. And if Rodion started an argument with her she said:

"You're saying that because he's not your own flesh and blood. He's an orphan, so naturally... But remember this: I shan't let anyone bully him. Just remember that."

One day at dinner about five years ago Yevgeny had been abominably rude to him. Like all kind-hearted men Rodion was quick-tempered. Blind with rage, he had picked up a stack of dishes and flung them on the floor. Alevtina had shrieked, little Varya had hung on his arm, and Yevgeny had said calmly, with pale lips:

"The raving lunatic!"

Rodion had left the dining-room. From the next room he had heard Alevtina saying something nervously and meekly to Yevgeny, who put in from time to time, "Oh to hell with him, the old fool."

After that he had heard Yevgeny walking up and down the corridor, stamping his feet and singing with bravado. He sang from the awareness of his own strength, his power, he sang because he realised how helpless his stepfather was. But why shouldn't Yevgeny sing? He was a highly strung child, while his stepfather came of the "rough lot", the yokels, the rabble. That last epithet, borrowed from Mr. Gogolev's vocabulary, struck firm root in Alevtina.

And so Yevgeny had grown up a stranger.

There he sat now, eating the pies, the sardines and the

strawberries, and drinking tea. And, strangely, his eyes held warmth and tenderness. It was a very different look from the kind he used to have for his stepfather. Oh, how well he knew this look! It was Alevtina's look when she wanted peace restored in the house after wearing her husband's patience thin with her perpetual nagging. Yevgeny, too, wanted peace in the house, he wanted to be on good terms with his stepfather, to adapt himself to him, it was that and nothing more, Rodion realised.

He scanned the face of the young stranger with grim curiosity. There was nothing wrong with him: the face was sunburnt and unblemished, the eyes clear, the hair soft and the teeth white. The look in the eyes was open and straight. Rodion was a skilled judge of character; he had known thousands of men, he could instantly, at a glance, tell baseness and caddishness from the real thing, he was seldom wrong, almost never.

"Oh, and another thing, Dad," Yevgeny said. "I've a favour to ask you. Our dean is a very nice old fogey, not too brilliant, but he's very good to me personally. His daughter is a friend of mine, it's her birthday tomorrow, and you and I are invited."

"But where do I come in?"

"Why, you'll tell them some of your experiences, surely with your glamorous past you can find something to tell. Well, say about Nestor Makhno. Or perhaps your Cheka work. You've got some amusing stories to tell, haven't you? They want you very much, do come, please."

"I'll think about it," Rodion brought the words out with an effort.

He went through all his pockets looking for the cigarettes which were there before him on the table.

### Chapter Five

### POLUNIN

Study was a painful process with Volodya.

In his first year he read Pirogov's famous *Annals of a Surgical Clinic*, in which the author questioned a number of truths that were indisputable in his day, and Volodya, too, began to have his doubts on certain matters. The self-confidence of some of the teaching staff put him on his guard, while his ever suspicious look irritated the staff. The Sechenov Medical Institute took all the strength he had. He could not understand how one could take down a lecture idly but accurately in order to learn it by heart afterwards, the way Yevgeny did it — Yevgeny, that model of efficiency, respectfulness to professors, and such a "jolly good fellow". Neither could Volodya cram hysterically for his exams. He listened to the lectures attentively and retained in his memory all that was important, essential and useful; anything that struck him as conventional generalities he made a mental note of, with a view to finding the objection to these inviolable general truths and proving them unsound when he had the time. Nevertheless, he always knew what he was expected to know, in fact he knew more, but in his own peculiar way. Ganichev, whom Volodya loved, would often say to him:

"A certain wise French pathoanatomist despised academic degrees but held that it was more convenient to despise from the top of that damned ladder than standing at its foot and looking up. Remember that, Ustimenko. A man who stands at the foot of the ladder may be suspected of dullness and envy."

In his third year Volodya took a great liking to Professor Polunin, a close friend of Ganichev's, a giant of a man, always a little short of breath. Prov Yakovlevich Polunin had carrot-red cheeks, a thick neck, and frizzy flaxen hair. He spoke in a deep, frightening growl, showed disrespect for what other members of the staff mentioned with a catch of admiration in their voices, and occasionally told the class some pretty queer stories, which seemed utterly irrelevant.

"Take Fyodor Ivanowich Inozemtsev," he told them once, "he's quite a bright personality in the history of our medicine, a gifted man with a powerful intellect, I should even say a penetrating intellect in many respects. Naturally he was an excellent diagnostician, a super diagnostician is the expression nowadays, I believe. And, of course, he was quite a fashionable practitioner in his day. I trust you do know what private practice is?"

"We do," rumbled the whole class, whose knowledge of private practice had been gleaned in the main from Chekhov's *Ionych*.

"This private practice got on well with Inozemtsev and he got on well with it. He liked his peace of mind to be safeguarded by a sizable bank balance, and since he could not manage his numerous patients alone he was forced to maintain a regular staff of assistants, popularly known as the 'Nikitsky braves', in honour of the mansion owned by Inozemtsev in Nikitskaya Street of our much revered city of Moscow. In that period of his 'practical' eminence, he was very keen on ammonia as a panacea for a number of diseases and for a catarrhal condition in general. Now, this pet ammonia theory of his was no worse, my friends, than many others practised in Inozemtsev's time. The curious thing, however, is that whereas other fantastic, trumped up theories soon fell into oblivion, the ammonia theory thrived. Do you know why?"

Polunin ran a shrewd eye over his audience expecting an answer, but none was forthcoming. With a despondent sigh, he resumed his narrative.

"Because the 'Nikitsky braves', all of them sly customers, men of experience diligently solicitous for their own welfare, whether young, middle-aged or advanced in years, only provided their chief with information on cases where a miraculous cure had been achieved with that confounded ammonia. By playing up to Inozemtsev's wishful thinking, they ruined the reputation of this truly splendid doctor among his students, who were already treating the ammonia cure as a great joke. Yet Inozemtsev was by no means niggardly in sharing out the bread to his braves, or rather his flunkey quacks, he gave them bread and butter and jam. In their gratitude and lest they disappoint their chief and patron they deceived him shamelessly. According to Pirogov, they 'fed on fat, slept on down, and swaggered tipsily in the hour of national calamities'. As for Inozemtsev, he naturally lost none of the honour due to him for his great services to science, but he did make a fool of himself before his contemporaries, and since contemporaries inevitably have chroniclers in their midst, nothing can remain a secret for long. I did not tell you this story to belittle Inozemtsev, far be it from me. I have simply cited this glaring example to warn you, sons of Aesculapius, never let your discoveries be put to the test by people who depend on you for their daily bread, people subordinate to you and connected with you in a hierarchy. A snigger is a very nasty thing. It will stick tenaciously to the most talented of men should he blunder. Safeguard yourself and your colleagues from that danger very carefully, and for their own sakes, in the name of friendship and the honour of your medical profession, tell them the truth, only the truth, and always the truth."

Polunin began to single Volodya out from the rest more and more obviously as time went on, and sometimes the two of them enjoyed long conversations in the quiet institute garden. Polunin found it relaxing after his work in the therapeutic clinic; he would sit smoking his thick cigarettes, which he rolled himself, glancing up at the sky, and discoursing. He would open the conversation without preamble as though he were picking up the threads of an interrupted discussion.

"If one could write a book about the mistakes made by the great doctors! I suggested it to a certain clever fellow the other day; you can't imagine how angry he got, and what big words he brought into play. It would be discrediting, demoralising, it would undermine the scientific world outlook — he got ever so angry, that clever fellow, amazingly so. Ah, our air is still thick with clannishness, at times it's pretty hard to breathe it. They're all most venerable, all highly esteemed, they're all hoping to get in among the great, by fair means or foul. But it's not so easily done. And so they defend themselves in advance, so that the cup may pass from them. They needn't worry, it will! It's the mistakes of the great that are of interest, not theirs. But no, they won't even listen. Pirogov was so great that he was not afraid of writing about his mistakes himself. And it proved highly instructive for generations to come. But no, they say, that's not the same thing. Naturally, it isn't. And yet the material I've collected is excellent. This clever fellow of mine glanced through some of it and reminded me of the reception our clan gave to Veresayev's *A Practitioner's Notes*. That, he says, is mere blossoms, we'd like to show you the fruit and how it grows."

One day, coming across Volodya in the street, Polunin showed him the book he was carrying: an elegant volume, leather-bound, gilt-edged and stamped in gold.

"The baseness of it!" Polunin said indignantly. "The title of this volume, if you please, is *The Plague in Odessa*, a research with portraits, plans, drafts and drawings attached. First and foremost we see the portrait of the Duc de Richelieu, next Vorontsov in full regalia, bloated with the sense of his own superiority over the little people of this world, after that come Baron Meyendorff and other conquerors of the Odessa epidemic. But, I beg you to note, there is not a single doctor. There is a picture of a rat; the spleen of a black plague-infected rat got into this volume, together with the bubo of a black rat, but there was no room for the doctors. They were unworthy of the honour. This resignation of theirs was modesty verging on baseness! I bought it at the bookstore, glanced through it and lost my temper. Why should all these dukes, counts and barons in their epaulettes, aiguillettes and decorations be represented there, and the honour be denied our Gamaleya — that wonderful, fearless and pure-hearted doctor? However, good-day."

Another time, sitting on his favourite garden seat with Volodya, he told him:

"We all know that our great Botkin fought hard and valiantly against foreign dominance in Russian medicine, and his struggle was justified historically because, for example, the chief medical inspector under the Empress Maria, Ruhl the physician in ordinary, actually *wrote* and not merely said that while he was the medical inspector of the Empress Maria's institutions no *Russian* doctor would ever become so much as an intern at a hospital of which he was in charge, to say nothing of becoming a head physician. And that, mind you, was written in Russia and approved by the ruling family, who incidentally knew no Russian. Botkin's fury was quite understandable, of course, but then why should he, he of all people, behave as he did? Instead of rising above Ruhl he *descended* to Ruhl's own level. In his anger and indignation, absolutely beside himself, Botkin committed acts so foolish that they were a disgrace to his own and his country's reputation; he went so far in his antics as to indulge in spreading stories, indecent because chauvinism or nationalism in any form is disgusting, you must agree. Granted Ruhl was a scoundrel and a flunkey, but why use his methods? And yet that was precisely what our great Botkin did, and he carried things so far that when he had to select his interns from among the available candidates he only considered those whose surnames ended with the Russian 'ov' or 'in'. I'll tell you a story more sad than amusing in this connection. Botkin rejected a most gifted young man by the name of Dolgikh. Too busy with his consultations, reception hours and calls to give the matter much thought, our great Botkin decided that this young man from Siberia was a German like all the Münnichs, Libichs, Rüttichs and other 'ichs' that he hated. I shall not dwell on the disgrace of selecting interns according to this principle of Botkin's, but let me say that in this matter, too, the honest men ought to have put up a fight against Botkin's excesses. Instead, they preferred to *let it go* and efface themselves, thereby putting the name and the greatness of our Botkin under fire both in his lifetime and afterwards. Was it necessary?"

In the course of a lecture, he once said:

"What didn't they do to Russian science, oh what didn't they do! They chose to appoint Sergei Petrovich Botkin, the greatest teacher of a whole generation of Russian doctors, physician in ordinary to that ageing bitch, the Empress Maria, thus forcing him to leave the Academy for a considerable length of time. But the Academy was his life, and the meaning of life was his work. Botkin's genius was at its zenith, it was the very time for him to work his hardest, and instead he had to stroll about in Livadia or Cannes or San Remo or Mentone and inquire: 'Has Your Majesty slept well?' Abominable!"

Polunin walked up and down in front of the class and, with his eyes wrinkled in a kindly smile, told them about the brilliant doctors of the past, of whom he knew so much and in such minute detail that he might have been personally acquainted with them. Volodya noticed that in spite of his critical turn of mind Polunin enjoyed speaking well of people, marvelling at the brilliance, depth and force of their thoughts, at their capacity for work and at the way they "gave all they had to their job", as he put it.

"The history of medicine makes their life-stories sound very flat," he said. "All our dear doctors are very nice and sleek, they might all be wearing halos, they never ate a square meal, fell in love or lost their tempers. But they were human beings like Pushkin or any other men of genius. And another thing I want you to note is that we are much too niggardly when it comes to putting a medical man in true perspective, that is, giving him his full due for his brains and the energy with which he worked. Our medical writers are niggardly on this score, they are afraid to overpraise the dead. Evidently, one of the reasons is that every one of them must have made some mistake in elaborating his theories, and that being so it is best to be on the safe side. One idiot I know wrote an article actually criticising Zakharyin, that most amazing of geniuses, for not knowing his microbiology. What I'd like to know is what that charming idiot would have done in Zakharyin's day, and how he would have acquitted himself personally in that turbulent epoch of the development of microbiology? Stepanov, why the sardonic look, have I been saying anything preposterous? I am telling you all this as a preventive measure, to put you, my pupils, on your guard against any upstarts that may have a say in science."

The audience listened spellbound. Yevgeny scrupulously took down everything including the "upstarts". He feared and hated Polunin, sensing that he was despised.

Volodya sat with his chin cupped in his hands, certain that something interesting was coming.

"Let's talk about Botkin, it's good for us. Incidentally, his colleague at the Academy of Medical Surgery, a professor of botany, Merklin by name, had once been a gardener to the

Grand Duchess Yelena Pavlovna. This highly esteemed scholar actually *read* his lectures, and this is what he read: 'A plant is made of cells, just as a stone wall is made of bricks.' But after all he was a gardener in the service of the Grand Duchess herself, so why not take a leap into the professorate? Bogdanovsky, a gifted man, adamant in his beliefs and actively opposed to Lister's theory, also taught at the Academy at the time. He performed his operations in his everyday clothes, and to protect his frock-coat from being soiled wore a black oil cloth apron over it. His ligatures were hung on the window latch, and whenever he wanted one the assistant wetted it in his mouth to make it stronger, pronouncing with dignity as he handed it to his general: 'Here's a reliable one, Your Excellency.' Not a drop of carbolic acid, sublimate or anything else was used of course. And at the same time, Professor Pelekhin, who was an ardent admirer of Lister, was so carried away that for the sake of hygiene he shaved off not just his moustache and beard but also his eyebrows."

The audience laughed.

"There's nothing funny in it, comrades, our future doctors," Polunin said touchily. "Progress in science goes hand in hand with tragedy. Pelekhin believed — can you understand this? — he believed and tormented himself and others with his belief that this was the only way of saving human lives. I realise, Comrade Stepanov, that Pelekhin appears ridiculous to you, but I — and I'm not ashamed to admit it — I wept when I heard the story of our dear Pelekhin shaving off his eyebrows and facing his family and, what is worse, the Academy looking like a freak."

Polunin delved into his briefcase, found the piece of paper he wanted, waved it and said:

"Listen. This is what Professor Snegirev said in his speech at the opening of the first congress of obstetricians and gynecologists in Russia. The congress took place in 1904, not so very long ago for that matter, it was in our day and age.

"'It horrifies me to recall that the abdomen remained open for an hour, two hours, three hours. The patient, the surgeon and his assistants were kept under an uninterrupted spray of a 5% solution of carbolic acid. You know what a spray is, don't you. Everyone who was there acquired a sweetish taste in his or her mouth from carbolic acid and a dryness of the mucous membrane, while both doctors and patient showed a plentiful amount of carbolic acid in their urine. We were poisoning ourselves, and poisoning our patients, because we believed (*believed!*) that we were poisoning the infection in the patient's organism and in the surrounding air. May we be forgiven that craze of ours! Matters became more appalling still when sublimate took the place of carbolic acid. We washed our hands and our gauze swabs in the solution, we lost our teeth, and the patients lost their lives.'"

Polunin's large face wrinkled up and he said, thrusting the paper back into his briefcase:

"And that was how Lister's great teaching was first put into practice. Funny? No, it isn't funny. A splendid Russian surgeon, Troyanov, died of nephritis caused by carbolic acid poisoning. And that is not funny either. Let us go back to Botkin. Botkin, the flower of our medical science, blossomed forth at a very difficult time for science. And yet he created his own school, he started a powerful movement in medicine and though no orator he *always* drew at least four hundred and sometimes five hundred listeners to his lectures. In diagnostics he stood head and shoulders above *all* his contemporaries, he knew how to auscultate, to reason, to size up the symptoms and the patient comprehensively, and solve the problem strategically. His powers as a diagnostician are confirmed by numerous facts of which we have already spoken, but I wish to mention another. One day a middle-aged woman was brought to the clinic. The anamnesis yielded no useful information, but the patient herself told the doctors that after eating some pike soup eight days or so before she had felt sick, lost her appetite and taken to her bed. The symptoms were: coughing, cyanosis of the face, cold limbs, aversion to food, and drowsiness. Doctors of experience diagnosed it as bronchopneumonia. And then in came Botkin and after thoughtfully auscultating the patient he thought for a moment and then said, 'During the autopsy on the *body* tomorrow, look for an abscess in the rear mediastinum near the alimentary tract.'

"Imagine the faces of all those most highly esteemed doctors, serious scholars, of course, but not brilliant. And here was a genius!

"Well, there was an autopsy and the conclusion was: suppurative inflammation of the wall of the alimentary tract, its prolapse and subsequent formation of an abscess in the rear mediastinum and putrefactive blood poisoning.

"The whole thing was clear. A fish bone had stuck in the alimentary tract and caused suppurative mediastinitis with all the ensuing consequences.

"Comrade students, I did not use the word genius accidentally. Botkin was a genius in that he could see and hear what was invisible and inaudible to others, he knew how to focus a clinical analysis on the cause of the pain and the innermost processes, and what was most important — he knew how to find the 'crux' of the illness. But much of what he himself felt and sensed he could not explain. No one else would detect a change in the sounds of a heart, but he would insist that he could hear a 'slight accent', and a little later he would catch a murmur. And only when the illness was coming to its tragic climax would the other professors begin to hear what Botkin had assured them of from the outset. 'I see a greyish-purple tint,' he would say, holding a pince-nez in front of his spectacles. His sight was weak, yet he saw things that others failed to see. 'I can clearly feel a slight swelling here,' he would say, before anyone else could detect it. And therefore Botkin's authority was always and absolutely indisputable."

Polunin paused to scan the tense faces of his students. And all of them knew that they were about to hear the most important thing of all, the thing for the sake of which the name of Botkin had been brought up so frequently of late.

"Indisputability, however, holds a peculiar tragic element of its own, and my purpose in telling you this small episode is not to besmirch the memory of a great doctor, but to enable you, the future doctors, to draw the necessary conclusions from it. During the academic year in question, Botkin took a particular interest in typhoid cases, and it so happened that the object of study and clinical analysis conducted by Botkin for the benefit of his students was a certain chemist's assistant. The patient recovered, but he went on complaining of a headache. Since headaches did not fit in with Botkin's scheme of things, the chemist's assistant was out down — officially, mind you — as a malingerer who refused to abide by the clinic director's formula: 'Fit to work'. And the doctors at the clinic who *were of a different opinion from Botkin's did not speak up*! As for that young sixteen-year-old boy he died, yes, he just went and died. Professor Rudnev said to the students before starting on the autopsy, 'We are about to learn from this body the meaning of malingering as a disease that causes sudden death.'

"The patient had died of an abscess in the brain.

"In this case the indisputability of a truly brilliant doctor's authority brought about disaster. A collective decision is imperative, my future doctors, in solving difficult problems, even if there is a professor of Botkin's stature present. And if you see an eminent scientist making a mistake, you are in honour bound to speak up."

Polunin remained lost in thought for a minute or two, and then asked abruptly:

"Tell me what you know of our contemporary, Professor Klodnitsky, of his assistants and pupils."

The class remained silent.

"But you do know, don't you, that Professor Klodnitsky is our most prominent epidemiologist?"

"And author of several works," Misha Shervud said, "well-known works."

"If a man is a prominent scientist he is also, in all probability, an author of several works," Polunin said with distaste. "You are right as usual, Shervud."

He did not resume at once.

"By a strange association, I have remembered something about death and autopsy I'd like to tell you. If I remember correctly, on October 2, 1912, a Russian doctor, Deminsky by name, who was Professor Klodnitsky's friend and assistant, first isolated the culture of bacillus pestis from a spontaneously afflicted suslik. This took place in the Astrakhan Gubernia, where a series of plague outbreaks had been registered. Well then, Deminsky contracted pneumonic plague, he made an analysis of his own phlegm, and sent a telegram to Klodnitsky in Djanybek. I suggest, my future doctors, that you take down the wording of that telegram so you will remember it always."

Walking up and down with measured step, Polunin dictated it in a voice that was steady and seemingly calm:

"'I have contracted pneumonic plague from susliks. Come and get the culture I have obtained. All my records are in order. The rest you will learn from the laboratory. Dissect my body and study it as an experimental case of a man being infected by susliks. Good-bye. Deminsky.' Got it down?"

"Yes," Pych replied.

"Yes," Ogurtsov echoed.

"Klodnitsky came, of course," Polunin continued. "He came and executed the last will of the deceased, dissecting his body in the graveyard, in the wind, thus exposing himself to the danger of infection. Those are the sort of men I advise you to learn from."

It was quiet in the lecture hall, quiet and tense.

And again Polunin spoke of Botkin, but this time in connection with plague epidemics.

81

"A doctor, my young comrades, must never get trapped in his own scheme of things, for if he does he may run into all kinds of unpleasantness. Late in the 1880s, our excellent Botkin, a man of intelligence and marvellous gifts, seriously expected the plague that had broken out in the Volga region to come to St. Petersburg. In the history of medicine that particular epidemic is recorded as the 'Vetlyanskaya'. Well then! In expectation of the plague, Botkin kept an eye on the swelling of lymphatic glands in his patients and made a surmise that the quantitative development of such swellings formed a pathological basis for the plague epidemic spreading to St. Petersburg. And then a certain yard sweeper, Naum Prokofiev, turned up and fitted into that well-prepared pattern. There was a swelling of glands all over his body; he was isolated and put under the strictest observation, while a diagnosis was pronounced peremptorily in the presence of the medical students: the plague! Botkin himself had said: the plague. The great Botkin himself. And since none of the doubters (and there *were* some) dared to object in this particular case either, there was havoc. The Petersburg of functionaries and bureaucrats fled. Carriages sped away from the royal city, and overcrowded trains rumbled off; howling with terror, all the privy and state councillors, the retired generals, businessmen and general staff officers took to their heels, fleeing to their country seats to get as far away from the plague as they could. So much for that, Comrade Stepanov!"

## ARGUMENTS AND DISCORD

Yevgeny could not stand either Ganichev or Polunin. He could not understand what they were talking about. During their lectures his face showed his bewilderment; he actually put the matter before a Komsomol meeting, complaining that he was fed up with negative lectures. What he wanted was positive knowledge and not sceptical sneers at the great gains of science. Pych, the oldest student among them, already turning grey and showing a bald spot on his head, a taciturn sort who was always very busy, suddenly flared up and crashed down on Yevgeny like a ton of bricks. And after Pych, all the Party and Komsomol members present advanced on Yevgeny in close order. Yevgeny asked for the floor again to explain what he meant, but was refused. He asked to be allowed to admit his mistake, but that was refused him, too. Old Pych, however, took the floor for the second time.

"Comrades!" he said in a husky cavalryman's voice. "Professors Ganichev and Polunin are teaching us to think. To ratiocinate. Yes, we do find it difficult to subject the simple textbook truths to doubt. But the time will come, when each of us will find himself alone with his patient, without the professors' help, without the clinic — a doctor and a patient alone in a remote cottage. Is it humanly possible to memorise all we may have need of that day? But what we *can* learn to do is think like medical men, like doctors. Have I made myself clear?"

Pych spoke for a long time, and everyone listened to him readily and gladly. It was nice to know that Pych, the "Old Man", whom everyone loved and who put so much effort into his studies, understood Ganichev and Polunin. And since there is no secret in the world that remains a secret for ever, it may be presumed that both Ganichev and Polunin found out about the meeting and the enthusiasm with which their students had spoken of them...

Polunin was the region's leading physician. He lectured at the medical institute, ran the therapeutic clinic, and received patients at the clinic's out-patient department. This giant of a man, who looked bursting with health in his white, crisply starched smock and rolled-up sleeves, though boorish and derisive with his students, was amazingly gentle and meek with the genuinely suffering, extraordinarily patient with the gravely ill, and when with them seemed almost ashamed of his stentorian voice, his good colour, his health and his indestructible strength. He carried out the more intimate and complex examinations of his patients with great tact, he never offended their modesty by bringing in crowds of jabbering students, or upset the patients with long descriptions and demonstrations of their ailments. He told the students all they needed to know in a language he kept specially for use in the clinic, and they understood him perfectly.

Gradually Volodya came to realise that Polunin's life was the clinic. At the clinic Polunin would spare neither time nor effort to analyse a case and try to explain to the students as clearly and precisely as he could all its deviations from the normal. Then he would group the deviations together and, finally, make the diagnosis. At first there was a hesitant, cautious inflection in his rich growl, then his voice would become steady, the questioning "Is that so?" would disappear and the iron logic of his assertions would come into its own. Again and again accidental, trivial facts and observations would crop up obstructing his view; angrily he would deal with these, seeming to sweep them away with his broad palm, and then, gesturing with his huge hands, he would proceed to build the pyramid, the crowning point of which was the diagnosis.

"See that?" he would ask in a triumphant whisper, while the students gazed at him enraptured, as though he were a magician. "One has to think, my young comrades, to think and solve the problem *strategically*. At the moment we have established the position of the enemy's troops, his manpower and his reserves. Now, what do *we* have at *our* disposal?"

Volodya's heart would hammer wildly. The thing that only an hour ago had seemed vague and blurred, obscured in a multitude of symptoms, signs and similarities, assumed form, a clear and perfectly defined shape: the disease had been named. And the disease was not very rare or even rare at all, it was something quite common, which the future doctors were sure to have plenty of dealings with. Polunin did not indulge in a practice that is still, unfortunately, popular with some medical instructors. He did not demonstrate the rarest diseases to the students, because he did not consider them or the exceptionally complicated forms of certain "fascinating cases" so very essential for young practitioners.

"If you're in a quandary, my young friends, you can always call in an ambulance plane. We're not living in the dark ages, this is the Soviet state. Your alma mater must teach you to give mass medical assistance, to be capable and energetic doctors with a broad view of life, and not specialists in a narrow branch of science."

What a pleasure it was to follow the train of Polunin's thought as he proceeded from one question to the next, slowly and cautiously like a blind man tapping his stick before him, as he felt the patient's spleen and liver, studied X-ray photographs and results of laboratory tests, as, armed with weapons from the stockpiles of pathology, anatomy and physiology, he forged ahead, undaunted by obscurity, gaps and contradictions, comparing phenomena and suddenly, instantaneously transforming chaos, absurdity, nonsense and mutually excluding symptoms into one harmonious, finished whole, into the crowning point of his pyramid — the diagnosis.

With trepidation that was almost sacred, fearing for his god, Volodya entered with the other students the grey building of the dissection department, on the pediment of which there was an inscription in Latin: *"Hic locus est ibi mors gaudet*

*sucurrere vitam."* ("Here death gives succour to the living.")
The patient, the hopelessness of whose condition Polunin had
established a month ago, had died. What had caused death? This
they would now learn from Ganichev, the supreme and incorruptible judge.

Polunin took a seat near the dissecting table; the attendant Uncle Sasha, as the students called him, began on the
autopsy. Speaking in a monotone, Ganichev, who never joked
in the dissecting room, or allowed others to, explained to the
students what they had not understood before. It was awe-inspiring and, strange though it may seem, jolly to hear that Polunin had been absolutely right a month ago, that armed with
X-ray photographs and laboratory tests he had seen the invisible. The patient was dead. Science could not yet cope with
that particular disease in that particular stage, but science
was already penetrating into regions that until only a little
while ago had been inaccessible. And science could have saved
the man's life if he had appealed to it earlier, only a little
earlier.

The autopsy was over. Polunin, Ganichev and the students
came out into the garden and found seats. The cold, autumn sun
shone brightly, the yellow leaves of maple and birch spiralled
slowly to the ground. Ganichev lit a cigarette. Polunin, a scowl
on his prominent forehead, sat downcast and glum.

"If we could only learn how to give proper treatment!"
He spoke abruptly and savagely.

Ganichev patted his shoulder gently. Polunin got up and
walked away.

"Is anything the matter?" Volodya asked Ganichev.

"No, nothing," Ganichev replied with a brief sigh. "But
doctors, who think, do sometimes have fits like the one you've
just witnessed."

He heaved another sigh and added:

"Billroth who, incidentally, was not a bad doctor, wrote
that the road to success lies across mountains of corpses.
There are the so-called doctors who reconcile themselves to
this without an effort, and to whom writing 'exitus letalis' becomes a matter of course before they're thirty, but there are the
others, people like Polunin, who blame themselves for every
death. Mostly, however, it's Polunin's sort who push medicine
ahead. Do you understand?"

"Of course, we do," said Nyussia Yelkina, a rosy-faced
girl with a turned-up nose. "But you must agree, Comrade
Professor, that one can't take everything to heart all one's life,

no nerves could stand the strain. After all, composure in a doctor is a very important thing, isn't it?"

"That is perfectly correct," Ganichev agreed much too docilely, and went back into dissecting room.

He returned at once, however; he did not sit down, he stood leaning on his sturdy oak stick.

"Pettenkofer and Emmerich," he said, "took internally *pure cultures* of cholera bacilli, having first neutralised the hydrochloric acid in their stomachs with soda. Our own Mechnikov, Doctor Hasterlik and Doctor Latapi did the same thing. About sixty years ago, three Italians — Borgioni, Rosi and Passigli — implored Pellizzari, a professor of syphilology, to inoculate them — three healthy young men — with syphilis. Pellizzari flatly refused at first, but they finally got their way. And you must know, Comrade Yelkina, that syphilis was treated differently in those days. With mercury! Dr. Lindemann inoculated himself with syphilis every five days for two months. A commission, appointed by the Paris Academy of Medical Science, reported on his condition. I remember the conclusion well. Both his arms, from the shoulders to the wrists, were covered with sores, many of which had merged together and were encircled with acute and painful festers ... well, and all that went with it, of course, to say nothing of the abundance of papules that had broken out all over his body. But even then Dr. Lindemann wanted to go on, he did not want to be treated yet. So much, Comrade Yelkina, for a doctor's composure, which you are already so anxious to safeguard..."

The blood rushed to Ganichev's plump face and he screamed:

"It's not too late yet! Off with you to the sewing circle! To the short-hand class! To your mamas, papas, husbands, to the devil!"

Nyussia complained afterwards:

"He won't let you put a word in! And anyway why drag in the sewing circle and the short-hand class? All professions are honourable in our country, and why should short-hand be so inferior to pathoanatomy, I don't know."

Nyussia's pink cheeks were smeared with tears, and her eyes glittered angrily.

"Why don't you really train for an office job?" Volodya found himself saying impulsively. "Get going, if what's been said is so completely lost on you. You'll find life prettier and less worrying there."

"But on the other hand, you can't expect every doctor to

inoculate himself with syphilis," Yevgeny put in. "It's ridiculous, to say the least."

"Oh, no one does!" Volodya shouted, losing his temper. "That's not the point at all!"

## TIME FLIES UNCHECKED

Varya alone, though not concerned with medicine, understood everything. She had an amazing way of listening and grasping all that was vital to Volodya, that filled his entire life, deprived him of sleep, delighted or saddened him. She did not know Ganichev or Polunin, but she thought them great men. After what Volodya had told her, she greeted Nyussia Yelkina very coldly. She always shared her information on progress in medicine generally, and in surgery in particular, with her friends at the technical school. And she was not merely voicing Volodya's thoughts. No, these were her own thoughts, which came to her as she listened to his inspired, somewhat wild and happily excited talk.

This is what happened. One Sunday the two of them went to the second-hand market to see what books they could unearth there. Good books were to be had there sometimes. While Volodya was busy going through the stack, Varya slipped into the next row of stalls and suddenly stopped short, gasping with joy. She saw a lady sitting on a folding chair in the hot sun with an old rug hung up on display beside her. "She must be a former countess or something," Varya thought. The lady was smoking a cigarette stuck into a long, slim holder, and was selling the most wonderful things: there was a corset, some ostrich feathers, a queer-looking object, which the lady explained was a "boa", two coffee mills, a string of fake pearls, and — most wonderful of all — a skull, a real human skull, a neat, yellow skull.

"How much is that?" Varya asked.

"Mademoiselle is interested in the skull?" the "countess" inquired and rapped the back of the yellow head with the fingers of her mittened hand.

"Actually what I'm interested in is a complete skeleton," Varya said. "You don't happen to have one?"

"Who does Mademoiselle take me for?" the "countess" exclaimed. "A complete skeleton, indeed! Where could you possibly get one, I'd like to know!"

"The school appliances shop has them sometimes, but they will only sell against written order and only to institutions

87

at that," Varya, the genial soul, went on to explain. "And I'm not an institution, I'm a private individual."

"Ah yes, the times are hard on private individuals," the "countess" agreed.

Varya bought the skull. At the base it had a small metal plate with an inscription saying that it was a present from so and so to so and so.

"Maybe Mademoiselle is also interested in ostrich feathers?" the "countess" asked.

"Mademoiselle is interested in neither ostrich feathers, nose rings, nor human scalps!" Volodya said rudely, suddenly appearing from the crowd. "Mademoiselle is not a fragment of what has been smashed and done with, she is a member of the Komsomol. Come along, Varya."

Varya had wrapped the skull in a newspaper, and until they got home Volodya had no inkling of the surprise she had for him. He had books and pamphlets stuffed in all his pockets. A very thin pamphlet he carried in his hand and kept leafing it all the way home. They were dazed and exhausted by the noise and jostle of the market crowd, the dust and the wail of the gramophone that the pedlar of records kept going at full blast. They drank some tap water, made room for the skull on top of the bookshelf, and settled down to read Karl Marx's humorous "Confessions".

"Wait a minute, I'll wipe your face for you, it's all wet," Varya said.

She loved taking care of Volodya. She was glad when he had a button missing or a handkerchief that wanted laundering. "Oh you, men, you're hopeless!" she would say. "You can't do a thing for yourselves." But she invariably added, "All except Father. There's nothing he can't do. Sailors are like that, you know."

"Your shirt collar is dirty too," she said.

"Leave me alone," Volodya said brusquely. His eyes on the page before him, he asked her, "What's your idea of happiness, Comrade Stepanova?"

"A big, eternally mutual love," Varya said blushing, but the words came out promptly and loudly.

"Sit down, you won't do."

She tried to see what the book said, but he pushed her away.

"D'you know, I don't see anything so very humorous in this," Volodya said. "I suppose it just rubbed some hypocrites up the wrong way, so it had to be called humorous. Listen to this and think, that is, if your mental faculties are up to it."

Volodya read and Varya listened with her mouth slightly open — a pink-cheeked, unsophisticated girl with a large bow on the top of her head, little more than a child.

"What is your favourite virtue in people? Simplicity. What is your favourite virtue in men? Strength. In women? Weakness."

"I'm not weak," Varya said. "Not very weak, I mean."

"Who, you?" Volodya said. "That's a laugh, Varya. You who scream at the sight of an ordinary, harmless frog!"

"It doesn't wear a sign that it's harmless, and it's goggle-eyed just the same."

"So you think you're strong! Look at her, the strong woman! It makes me sick to hear you talk."

Suddenly he gasped and cried:

"Listen to this. Just think. The question is: what is your chief characteristic? The answer is: singleness of purpose."

"Colossal!" Varya said.

"It's magnificent, not colossal. Next: what is your idea of happiness? The answer is: to fight. To fight, you see, Varya, it's to fight, that's what happiness means! Next: your idea of misery? Submission."

"Look, I submit to you in lots of things, and I don't see that it's such misery really," Varya said.

"It's a different submission," Volodya replied sternly. "You submit to me intellectually, understand?"

"Idiot!"

"Don't be rude, you nonentity."

Aunt Aglaya shouted from the next room:

"Stop it, Volodya, you'll make her cry again."

They did not hear her, however; they were reading, sitting close together, their shoulders touching.

"The vice you detest most: servility. Your favourite poets: Shakespeare, Aeschylus, Goethe. Your favourite colour: red. Your favourite maxim: I consider nothing alien that is human. Your favourite motto: subject all to doubt."

Aunt Aglaya appeared in the door. She had just taken a shower and her thick black hair had a wet shine.

"There's something terribly, terribly nice in both of you," she said. "But you're silly kids still."

She sat down next to Varya.

"It's easy for you to tackle both Marx and Engels, you're well educated people, but, heavens, how difficult it was for me!" she said regretfully.

After that particular Sunday, Volodya and Varya often thought about things together. Varya read far less than he did, but when he spoke she grasped everything at once, almost before the words were out of his mouth. After Volodya had read *The Holy Family* he gave Varya a talk on the subject; next he plunged into *The Poverty of Philosophy*, which Varya found much more difficult to digest, and then he spent several nights reading *The Eighteenth Brumaire*.

"D'you know that when he wrote that book he had nothing to go out in, all his clothes were in pawn," Aunt Aglaya said.

Volodya glanced at her vacantly, stuffed some bread into his mouth and went on reading. In the early hours of the morning he leafed through Schiller to discover, with happy amazement, more and more gems in the heavy volume.

> *Time flies unchecked. It strives for steadfastness.*
> *Be steadfast too, and you will shackle it...*

Yes, time, damn it! It really did fly, and Volodya got so little done. Everything was interesting, important and essential, even uninteresting things were interesting because they demanded attention. But sometimes he simply longed for a swim in the Uncha. He wanted to drop everything and call Varya with a shrill highwayman's whistle outside the Stepanovs' old house, and then go strolling with her late into the night up and down the river bank, hear her yawning at his dull talk and listen to her nonsense about art. She had already learned some back-stage talk, and said that Galileyev-Presnyak, the town's leading actor, never went on except as a second number. "Actors work on their nerves," she would assert. Volodya would giggle, and she'd hit out at him.

"Hey, not so hard!"

At one time he used to hit back, but now for some reason it was impossible. They had also stopped wrestling. Varya became more and more easily hurt and wept her sweet, quickly pouring tears. Volodya felt terribly sorry for her and ashamed of himself, but he never asked her to forgive him and merely muttered:

"Oh, come on. What's the matter anyway? You misuse a fine poem by wailing it instead of reciting. It's sickening to hear you."

"Idiot, you don't know the first thing about rhythm, and dare to judge. Esther Grigoryevna, our teacher, says..."

"All right, all right, but please stop crying."

He was unmercifully hard on her. She was younger than he was and tried her best, but at times it was more than she could bear.

"At your age, Herzen and Ogaryov..." Volodya would begin.

"But I'm not Herzen or Ogaryov," Varya would whine. "I'm Varya Stepanova, and I don't imagine I'm anything special."

"Last Saturday I gave you *Anti-Dühring* to read. You haven't yet..."

"Oh Volodya, have a heart!"

"I repeat, last Saturday..."

"But last Saturday we had our dress rehearsal!" Varya shouted in exasperation.

"And what day is it today?"

"Saturday."

"So you didn't find time to open the book in a whole week?"

Varya was crushed into silence.

"Sit over there and read what I tell you to read, and let me get on with my work," he ordered. "No more theatres, movies or clubs for you. And why are you wearing scent? Don't you know that scent is mostly used by people who are physically unclean?"

"I'll bite you for that," Varya said, and bit Volodya's ear very hard. She comforted him afterwards by saying:

"It could have been much worse. You know what sharp teeth I have. I could have bitten your rotten dirty ear clean off."

"Aunt Aglaya!" Volodya called. "Take your beloved Varya away, she bites!"

Still, it was good to be together. They enjoyed their long silences when each was busy with his own affairs and paid no attention to the other, and the sudden surge of happiness that came over them at the thought that they were together, within reach: Volodya at his desk, Varya by the window. They always had something to talk about, to quarrel over only to make up at once.

Occasionally, Varya bought "her" books along, that is fiction. If Volodya was disposed to be kind, he graciously permitted her to read aloud to him some of the passages she had marked as exceptionally fine. Blushing a bright red, tugging at a strand of hair and coiling it behind her pink ear, Varya read in a tone of entreaty a passage describing the beauties of Nature.

"It's too drawn out," Volodya said with a deliberate yawn. "Who's interested? The sky was mauve and the wind was a wet towel lashing out at you..."

"It doesn't say that at all! It's not like that at all!"

"Read on."

Varya read on, hastily and defensively.

"Don't act it, read," Volodya interrupted. "What's the good of all these antics? You can't speak the part of a colonel of the hussars anyway."

"But I..."

"Read on."

Suffering tortures, Varya read on. Volodya listened, rapping the table with his pencil and rustling his papers, but sometimes the story carried him away in spite of himself. One never knew just what would stir a chord in him. Gradually Varya came to understand what sort of books he needed. "Needed" was the word, no other fitted so well. Her first understanding of Volodya's taste in books came with her reading Tolstoy's *Sevastopol in December*.

"'You begin to understand the defenders of Sevastopol,'" Varya read nervously with side glances at Volodya. He had let his papers alone and sat motionless, pensive. "'And for some reason you feel conscience stricken in this man's presence. You feel you want to say so much to express your sympathy and admiration, but you cannot find the words, or you find the words that come to your mind inadequate; and you bow your head in silence before this man's mute, unconscious greatness and fortitude, before the embarrassment he displays at his own merits.'"

"That's real!" Volodya suddenly said.

"What's real?"

"That is. The bit about displaying embarrassment at one's own merits. Read on."

She read on. He lay on his narrow bed, with his arms folded under his head. Vague shadows seemed to flit over his face: he scowled one minute and smiled a sudden happy smile the next. Listening, he thought his own thoughts, he was always thinking, always solving some problems known to him alone, problems that were always difficult, almost tormenting.

"'Men cannot endure such awful conditions for the sake of a Cross or a title, or under threat of punishment: some other, more exalted, reason must prompt them. And that reason is a feeling, rarely manifested, shy in the Russian but present deep in the soul of everyone — love for the Motherland.'"

"That's all very well, but what about us?" Volodya asked, suddenly sitting up.

"Us, who?"

"Why, we two Komsomol members, a certain Varya Stepanova and a certain Volodya Ustimenko. How do we live? What for? What were we born for anyway?"

Varya blinked in fright.

"All right, don't blink," Volodya said harshly. But all books without exception must be written for some reason. Understand? All those mauve sunsets and winds like tightly stretched towels..."

"Oh stop it, Volodya!"

"Or take that: there was an exquisite smell of decayed wood in last year's melting snow..."

"You're talking rot."

"It isn't rot. A book should make you envy wonderful people and want to become like them. When you read it you should want to take a more critical view of your own actions, do you understand, Ginger?"

When he felt particularly well-disposed toward Varya he called her Ginger, although her hair was pale brown with no ginger in it at all.

"And poetry?" she asked.

"Poetry's all drivel except Mayakovsky."

"You don't say! And what about Pushkin, and Blok, and Lermontov?"

Volodya frowned and said nothing. And then in a soft voice, hardly above a whisper, Varya recited a line of Blok:

*And never ending battle! Tranquillity is but a dream...*

"What's that?" he asked in surprise.

Varya recited the whole poem. Volodya listened with eyes closed and repeated the words "and never ending battle".

"Isn't it beautiful?" Varya asked.

"It's not that, it's something else I'm thinking of," Volodya said, still reflecting. "If we could only live our lives so that it would really be like that: 'and never ending battle, tranquillity is but a dream'."

"Are you sure you're not insane?" Varya said warily.

"I'm quite sane. And now you may do your reciting alone and I'll get down to work. It's chemistry. Ever heard of it?"

He sat down at his desk, switched on the old lamp with its patched-up green shade, and immediately forgot that Varya was there. And she, gazing at the back of his thin neck and narrow shoulders, thought happily and emotionally: "There sits a great man of the future. And I am his best friend. And maybe I'm much more than a friend, even though we've never kissed yet."

Acting on an impulse, Varya came up to Volodya from behind and, thrusting her hand in front of his face, said, "Kiss."

"Whatever for?" he said, puzzled.

"Kiss my hand this instant!"

"This is something new!"

"Oh no, it isn't," Varya said. "We women gave birth to all you men, and for that you must be eternally grateful to us!"

Volodya glanced up at Varya, grinned wryly, and planted a clumsy kiss on her broad, warm palm.

"That's better," she said complacently.

### Chapter Six

### DIVORCE

Late that autumn, Rodion Stepanov paid a flying visit home. His wife had guests. There were two ladies, both no longer young, both smoked, both were running too fat and enjoyed talking about their moods of depression, their intermittent heartbeats, whatever that meant, and its all being due to "nerves". There was Iraida, the dean's daughter, a tall, lithe, green-eyed girl hung with numberless little chains, charms and medals, as though she had carried off all the prizes at a dog show. There was Mme. Lisse, the town's star dressmaker, on whom everyone was dancing attendance; there was Daniel Polyansky or "Dodik", elegantly smoking a pipe, and another man — his friend Makaveyenko, paunchy and fair-haired, wih merrily insolent eyes that seemed to be popping out. They were also expecting Professor Zhovtyak, but he rang up to say that he could not manage it and was "prostrated with grief". After listening to some records of Vertinsky and Leshchenko, procured on the black market, they had dinner and then settled down to coffee and liqueurs. They talked about events in Spain. Dodik spoke about the prime minister of Spain, José Girál, as though he were a good friend of his. He also had something to say about José Diaz. Rodion listened patiently to the two ladies, to Makaveyenko and to the dean's daughter Iraida. They all voiced their opinions on the situation in Spain and their approval of Mikhail Koltsov, whose dispatches they found interesting and stimulating. Dodik, however, did not share this view.

"It's Spain, you know. Any eyewitness of the events in Spain could write about them more colourfully and vividly than Koltsov is doing. The main thing is to be there, together with the people..."

"And bullfighting, I believe that's in Spain too?" Valentina Andreyevna asked in her habitually languid manner.

"It certainly is," Makaveyenko confirmed. "It's their national sport, like the merry-go-round with us or, say, fist fights. They think very highly of it in Madrid."

Rodion put his unfinished cup of coffee on the tray and left the room. Varya was out, of course. In the kitchen he found Yevgeny eating soup.

"How's everything?" he asked.

"We've been making up the newspaper," Yevgeny said listlessly. "Such a bore. We've no types, the material is dull and superficial, I have to write all the articles for everyone myself, it's enough to make you weep! I'm the editor of the institute paper, Dad."

"Well, don't write for everyone then," Rodion said. "It's a swindle, writing for others."

"Oh, pater, you *are* an idealist," Yevgeny sighed. Rodion walked idly about the rooms, smoking and thinking. He came back into the dining-room and heard his wife talking to Dodik in the hall. He winced with pain.

"The matter has to be decided once and for all," she was saying. "Flatly and finally. I can no longer stand that man coming here, a stranger to me, both in spirit and in everything else. Heavens, can't you see that I am suffocating in this atmosphere..."

"All right, all right, I'm quite willing, but surely not just now," Dodik promised hurriedly.

"I'll tell him today," Valentina threatened.

The front door banged. The woman Stepanov thought was his wife walked into the dining-room. He confronted her with his fists clenched hard, standing very still and pale.

"Tell me *now*," he ordered.

"You've been eavesdropping," Alevtina shrieked. "How very noble! He's taken to eavesdropping on top of everything else!"

"You've got to tell me yourself," Rodion said. "I've

known for a long time, only a blind fool·could have failed to see it, but you've got to give me the final word. Say it."

"What?"

"Do you want a divorce?"

"I want to live like a human being," she screamed. "You owe it to me, but what have I got? Other wives have everything: cars, country-houses, they take rest cures in the South three times a year, and I..."

It was the same old story with tears, heart drops, and then Yevgeny taking her pulse. No, he could not stand it any longer.

"Let us part in peace," he said in a calm but rather husky voice. "You'll go to Dodik..."

"Very noble of you," she said. "I'll move into one poky room, and you'll lord it here. Think again, Comrade Stepanov."

"In other words it's the room that worries you?"

"That and everything else. I refuse to be left a pauper. We've worked for all this together, and we'll share it equally."

Rodion nodded, he could not speak. Ten minutes later, he heard Alevtina ringing up all her lady-friends in turn with brisk and business-like efficiency, sobbing a little as she told them her troubles, and saying emotionally to one of them, "Ah, my dear, you know it as well as I do. One has to be *born* a gentleman."

An end had to be put to all this at once. As soon as Varya came home, Rodion called the family to the dining-room, drank a large tumbler of cold water, and said, biting off the words:

"We have decided to separate. You're both grown up, you'll understand. But there's one thing you must decide for yourselves: will you remain here with me or leave with your mother?"

Varya clutched hard at her father's sleeve and said nothing. Red spots were flaming on her cheeks. Yevgeny, who was wearing a pair of striped pyjamas and his inevitable hairnet, paced the floor between the table and the sideboard.

"Yevgeny!" his mother cried in entreaty. "Yevgeny, how can you hesitate?"

Yevgeny crushed his cigarette in an ashtray, smirked, and said with narrowed eyes:

"You are a funny person, Mother. Surely you don't imagine I'll give up Rodion Mefodyevich for that ... imposing, handsome, elegant, but ... forgive me, that shady character?"

Stepanov stared fixedly at Yevgeny. What did he mean? What was he really thinking just then?

"I shall skip the details and say that I'd like to remain the son of the man to whom I owe everything," Yevgeny declared. "And it'll simplify things for you, too, Mother dear. You'll be free, young, with life beginning anew. Right?"

He gave his mother a hug, kissed her and walked out.

In the morning Dodik drove up in his car. He appeared extremely annoyed, and, greeting Rodion brusquely, went straight into Valentina Andreyevna's room. A little later he knocked on Rodion's door.

"We must have a man-to-man talk," he said taking a seat and pushing down the tobacco in his pipe bowl with his thumb. "We have to make arrangements about the house, the furniture, and so on and so forth. Valentina Andreyevna is worried about it, and you're going away..."

"Yes, I am going away," Stepanov cut him short. "Make all the arrangements with Yevgeny, he has a good head on his shoulders. And that's that."

He turned away to the window.

He heard them leaving the house — his wife and her Dodik, he heard the front door bang and the car drive off. Varya came in quietly.

"D'you want some tea, Dad?" she asked.

"No," he said despondently.

"Shall I make some coffee?"

"No, no coffee either."

"Then, perhaps, you'd like a glass of vodka?"

"Are you trying to comfort me?" he said with a wry smile. "Don't, daughter. I've plenty of staying power."

"Maybe you'd like Yevgeny and me to come and stay with you in Kronstadt?"

He thought for a moment before answering.

"Look, my darling little girl, this is confidential: there's no sense in your moving just now because I myself can't say where I'll be tomorrow."

"What d'you mean?"

"Just this. I may be sent off on a long voyage. Volodya's father has been gone a fortnight already."

Varya clung to her father's shoulder.

"I understand, Dad, I understand," she whispered. "But Volodya doesn't know anything."

"We'll go and see him a little later and then he'll know."

While Varya and her father were away, Yevgeny haggled

with Dodik, gaily and ferociously, over the household utensils, books, furniture, and floor space.

"Listen, are you trying to make a fool of me?" Dodik said touchily. "I'm no child, you know."

"I'm not either," Yevgeny said. "I'm dividing everything into four: three shares are ours, the rest is yours. Ask any lawyer, there's no other way to do it. And anyway it's too funny. You are in love, you are loved, and here you go messing about with this junk. It's indecent, if you ask me. A pretty story for the newspapers..."

"And the grand piano?" Dodik inquired glumly.

"It's a piano, not a grand. What d'you want it for anyway? Mother doesn't play."

"Hard-boiled isn't the word for you!" Dodik flared up.

Stepanov left on the night train.

## WE, RED ARMY SOLDIERS

From that day the friendship between Varya and Volodya became even closer. They now had a secret to share, a secret from everyone. They shared their pride in and their constant anxiety for their fathers, for pilot Afanasy Ustimenko and naval officer Rodion Stepanov. They let no one into the secret, not even Aunt Aglaya. That had been agreed between Volodya and Varya's father the day he left; there was no sense in worrying Aglaya; she had known too much grief in her life as it was, why add to it by this daily and nightly anxiety for her brother's safety? They told her he had been sent on an assignment, destination unknown.

"To Spain?" she had demanded sternly.

"It's not for us to know," Rodion had replied, turning purple for he was a very poor liar.

Aglaya had merely nodded. She was supposed to know nothing. To aid the conspiracy, the map of Spain was kept in Varya's room and not Volodya's. Without telling Volodya, Aglaya bought herself a map too. She studied it at night with the door locked against her nephew. Afanasy was there, she knew it. He had to be there, just as her late husband would certainly have been too. She knew that generation of Bolsheviks well, loud-voiced lads who had gone through fire and water and never said die. Practically illiterate in the years of the Civil War, they were now graduates of academies. There was nothing they couldn't do, those men of steel. In the fiercest cold they fought for Perm, in scorching heat they clashed with *basmachi* bands in Turkestan. Weak with hunger, they sat through *Yevgeny Onegin* for the first time in their lives and loved it; and before they had cooled off properly from their deep raids into the enemy's rear they took their seats in a schoolroom and obediently learned the two English cases — the nominative and the possessive.

She pored over the map for hours in the silence of the night, and in her ears rang the song both Afanasy and Grisha, her husband, had loved so well:

> *We're out to fight the bankers, the landlords and the rest,*
> *We'll seal the doom of kulaks, the damn blood-sucking pests.*
> *We, Red Army soldiers, are fighting for the poor,*
> *To give the people freedom and make their lives secure...*

The raw November wind whistled and blew. Volodya lay on his back, arms folded under his head, and stared into the darkness, roundly cursing the torreros of Seville for giving in to Queipo de Llamo, the insurgent general. And then through a veil of drowsiness he saw the island of Minorca and the Valencian expedition on board the warship *Almirante Miranda*. The warship had stopped its engines and Rodion Stepanov was looking through his binoculars and then seaplanes, led by Volodya's father, soared up into Spain's bright blue sky. All the best flyers, all that was best and truest in the world, be they Italians, Germans, Frenchmen, Bulgarians, all swung round in formation behind their leader, his father...

In his tired brain Latin words got mixed up with the names of Spanish towns. Saragossa suddenly got muddled with *musculus recti abdominis*, the stomach muscle; Bargas with the *quadriceps femoris* — it was a long time since he had dissected a corpse! He must start going to the dissecting room, to Ganichev. And the Iviza landing? What was happening there now? Why didn't the newspapers say anything about it?

Varya now wore a Spanish cap. She looked thinner and more grown up. Letters from "over there" came to her address. To be exact, there were no letters from "over there". Simply a strange comrade regularly sent them their fathers' greetings and informed them that all was well. It could not be done any other way, Volodya and Varya reasoned. It would have been stupid of them to hope for anything else. That would be playing into the fascists' hands.

All the little things of life that had once seemed to matter now receded into the far, far distance. It horrified Varya to think that she had not always been home when her father wanted her there. Her father, who was now fighting for the freedom of the whole world. There, in far-away Spain, strange and wonderful Spain. He could probably speak Spanish now with his dear and funny Volga accent, and he was probably for ever on the look-out for a cup of good strong tea. She did not suppose they drank tea in Spain, or did they? And there was no one to answer her question. Did the Spanish ever drink tea or did they only drink coffee?

When the news appearing in the papers was bad Volodya scowled, when it was good he beamed. It seemed to him that matters could not be bad where his father and his eagles were fighting. He could just see him with his sun-bleached hair and well-scraped chin peering into the sky. There he was, climbing into the cockpit, settling down comfortably and shouting, "Contact!"

What was the Spanish for "contact"? A friend was *amigo*, an enemy was *enemigo*, but what was "contact"? Oh, if he could only see them all together — Enrique Lister, General Lukach, and Father. What did they call him there? What was the Spanish for Afanasy? And Rodion? Did the two — the sailor and the flyer — ever meet?

Volodya now brooded longer and deeper on the purpose of man's existence. He drew further and further away from his fellow students whose ambition stopped at getting the best marks, from those of them who openly discussed ways and means of staying on as postgraduate students rather than working, from those of them — shrewd young people — who were guided in their choice of speciality by the chances it offered of remaining in town as against being assigned to the provinces.

And what about the fond mothers and fathers?

What about those mothers weeping outside the rector's door? Those fathers, military men, officials, scholars, workers, "bringing influence to bear" on the dean, or rather notes from their influential friends asking him to give another chance to a student who had again failed in a subject which it was imperative for a doctor to know!

No one ventured to approach Volodya, who was on the board of the Komsomol organisation, with such requests. In fact, the dean, who was a weak man, sometimes appealed to Volodya for help when the attacks on him became too many and too ominous. Volodya would beat off the attackers rudely, bluntly and mercilessly.

"You're a narrow-minded prude," Nyussia Yelkina told him.

"Ustimenko will be the only graduate of the Sechenov Medical Institute. He thinks no one else is worthy," said Svetlana.

"The most orthodox of the orthodox!" Misha Shervud sneered.

Volodya looked appraisingly into Shervud's pale, protuberant, spiteful eyes. That boy would certainly go far. With absolutely nothing to his credit yet, he was already on the look-out for a good theme to present for his candidate's degree as soon as he graduated. But then who in the world cared for their marks even if they were good, their exams and their dissertations? Who but themselves?

### OLD MAN PYCH

It was during that period that Volodya became especially friendly with Pych, or the Old Man, as the students called Pavel Chirkov, who was already thirty-four when he enrolled.

Pych was reticent, dryish and had a sharp tongue. His small, pale blue eyes would suddenly start boring into someone like a pair of steel drills. He did not absorb knowledge easily, less easily than anyone else, but he was persevering and thorough and knew much more than did many of his more gifted fellows. Volodya often helped him. Pych never thanked him or shook his hand, he merely said with a sigh, "You *are* intelligent, Ustimenko." He said it without a shade of envy, however; rather, with a gruff sort of tenderness. Both were devoted to Ganichev and Polunin, and both were kept back one day by Ganichev after his lecture.

"Look here, my kind pupils," Ganichev said sternly, closing the door. "I have been observing you for some time, and I see that you have become infected, not without my assistance perhaps, with a loathsome and shameful disease called medical nihilism. Such words as 'quackery', 'scientific demagogy', 'Latin cookshop' and others keep flying off your baby lips, you will forgive me, of course. You are little more than ignoramuses yet, and it's not for you, young devils, to scoff at the tragic seekings for truth that have been going on for centuries. Professor Polunin and I want to stimulate your thought, but we are not inviting you to smirk at the state of contemporary science. Seek but do not scoff. Don't ever dare to scoff! A man can listen to the heart and his amazing intellect will tell him, unaided by any instruments, which one of its mitral valves is functioning faultily and the precise nature of the fault: insufficiency or constriction of the valve. And what of anaesthetics? And vaccines?"

Ganichev was thoroughly annoyed; he blew his nose very noisily and said sharply, "Go along! Read Pirogov. And think of what I said."

He handed them a book with some markers in it, and they left.

"We've upset him," Pych said.

"It's my fault," Volodya responded. "Remember when I started that conversation yesterday about quackery in pharmacology how he snapped at me. 'Don't you take pyramidon when you have a headache?'"

That night, they read Pirogov together, sitting on Pych's bed in the hostel.

"Some percentage!" Pych exclaimed, closing his tired, red-rimmed eyes. "Three-quarters of the people operated on dying of purulent poisoning!"

"And that was in Pirogov's day," Volodya said. "See what it says: 'I know of nothing positive to say about this frightening scourge in surgical practice. It is all a mystery: both the origin and the course of development.'"

Volodya found the next marker, and read:

"'When I think of the graveyard where so many of the graves belong to patients infected in hospitals, I do not know what to marvel at more, the stoicism of the surgeons who are still devising new operations, or the trust which society still places in the hospitals.'"

"Your conclusions?" Pych asked.

"Lister."

"Antiseptics."

"Exactly! You're awfully brilliant, Pych," Volodya said. "Why not go on and say that surgeons, the once wretched slaves of purulent poisoning, have become its conquerors, and the whole thing will be in the perfect Ogurtsov style. He loves that kind of talk."

"Why not? A little pathos is good sometimes," Pych said seriously. "We talk and talk, but to make a doctor you've got to be able to believe in a Lister of the future."

"You can't live by faith alone," Volodya said with a sigh. "Remember what the ancient Greeks did? And later too? Chrysippus forbade his feverish patients to eat, Dyocsippus to drink, Sylvius insisted that they sweat, and the venerable old Broussais bled them till they all but fainted, while Carry gave them cold baths."

"All right, we know our Veresayev," Pych said angrily.

"He was a fine doctor."

"Listen, go home," Pych said. "My head is splitting without you to make it worse."

But Volodya did not go. Pych started pulling off his old, battered top-boots, his roommates returned home, but Volodya still went on talking.

"Physiology has given us a lot already, and it's giving us more and more with every day," he said. "I read somewhere that theoretical medicine is, in fact, physiology. And so it's from physiology that you've got to deduce the applications you need, then you'll have practical, applied medicine. As for the cookbook..."

"And in the meantime, sit twiddling our thumbs — is that what you mean?" Sasha Poleshchuk said.

An uproar started in the room. Mechanically, Pych began to pull on his boots again. It was a reflex dating back to the Civil War. Any noise in the room made him put on his boots before he was quite awake.

"You suggest retreating into the celestial regions of pure science?" Ogurtsov, a freckled young man with far-spaced teeth, attacked Volodya. "Speak up, Ustimenko. And anyway, what's all this drivel you're treating us to?"

"Why drivel? Ustimenko's right," Misha Shervud put in. "You may remember that a certain wise Arabian physician once said that an honest man may find delight in the theory of medicine, but his conscience will never permit him to take up the practice of medicine, no matter how great his knowledge."

"What?" Pych cried on a high note.

Shervud repeated it.

"That sums up our argument, it's fine, it's really wise," Pych said, boring into Volodya with his small blue eyes. "We're so honest that we'll only delight in the theory of medicine. We're so damned virtuous and scrupulous, you see, that we'll let the people rot until our theory is elaborated to perfection. Let the women die in childbirth, let the babies perish in hundreds, let our Soviet people be killed by diphtheria, typhus and Spanish flu — we shan't budge from our seats! We shall sit in our labs and sum everything up scientifically, we shall get more and more skilled at subjecting everything to doubt and end up by losing faith in our work entirely, it's less trouble that way."

Pych got up, drank a glass of water, and in the silence that fell over the gathering began to speak with such compelling conviction and passion that Volodya, who had never seen the Old Man like this before, was stunned.

"Our regiment had Zhilin for its commanding officer, a heroic, legendary figure. But one day he was taken ill on the march. There was a raging blizzard, it was terribly cold, we had nothing to eat, and there was the regiment commander in delirium, talking all sorts of rot that we couldn't make head or tail of. The doctor we had with us was an old chap who'd only been to a three-year medical school, Tutochkin his name was, a conscript doctor. Some cavalryman! We had to fix a feather pillow to his saddle, a real joke he was. He had a look at Zhilin and said it was measles. Good old measles. In addition Zhilin's heart was not doing its job properly. And so, for a fabulous sum of money we got some sunflower oil, boiled it up, and our Tutochkin dissolved some camphor in it and proceeded to inject Zhilin with it. He had boils the size of a fist all over him. And yet he did get back into his saddle again and lead the regiment against the Whites. Well? What is it, science? Empiricism? What I say is: let the professors here teach me and train me to be another Tutochkin, so I'd know how to bring a dead man back into the ranks like he brought Zhilin, who later became first a division and then an army commander of legendary fame! Let them, I say. I'm speaking to you as a Communist: we must fully appreciate the complexity and difficulty of our job; I'm saying what Ganichev and Polunin are trying to instil in us — that in approaching each new case we must be fully prepared to encounter some quite unique and unknown disease; we must always seek and not give up the quest, but also we must get on with the job in hand. And all those Arabian theories of Comrade Shervud's are disgusting and have to be squashed. And you too, Ustimenko, I'd advise you to do a little thinking. He doesn't like pathos, if you please. But I do like pathos. And that's that. It's time for bed."

Pych began to remove his boots once again. Volodya slipped out of the room, went down the steps and raised his burning face to meet the icy wind. In the swirling snow the street lamps blinked their round yellow eyes blindly. To make things worse, Shervud followed him out and said in his neat, rather formal manner:

"Do be so good, Ustimenko, and back me up if Pych decides to become unpleasant. I have my own coherent point of view and Pych has his, but then he wants everyone to look at things his way, whereas I..."

"I agree with Pych, absolutely," Volodya said. "And I absolutely disagree with your Arab. Viewpoints like that should be smashed, and smashed without mercy!"

"Oh, is that so?"

"Yes, that is so," Volodya said firmly. "And if you're going to base your candidate's dissertation on that particular viewpoint, you'll get licked to a frazzle!"

"My dissertation will be based on viewpoints that are concordant with our world outlook, and no other! And as for the expression 'get licked to a frazzle', it's rude and vulgar, and doesn't suit you at all."

Shervud hitched up the overcoat he had flung over his shoulders, and turned back into the hostel. Volodya made a dash for the tram, jumped on board as it was moving off, said "swine" and, on the spur of the moment, decided to go to Varya's to make a clean breast of it, to explain how disgusted he was with himself. The Stepanovs now lived in Krasivaya Street. Varya's grandfather opened the door. Her father had told her she was to ask her grandfather to make his home with her, and she was never to let him go, no matter what happened.

"A good guest always comes at mealtime," said the old man not unambiguously, and turned into the kitchen whence came a tantalising smell of frying potatoes.

"Volodya, is that you?" Varya called out.

"Who else would it be!" her grandfather answered from the kitchen. "Varya, call the cat," he shouted. "He's sniffing at the cream!"

Varya went to the door to meet Volodya; she wore a woolly shawl on her shoulders and looked lovely. The cat was rubbing itself against her legs.

"Say what you may, Volodya, but I'll never be a geologist," she said despondently. "My mind's made up, I'm going to make the stage my career. That's flat. What are you gaping at?"

"Varya, do finish technical school first!" Volodya implored.

"What for?"

"Because you... I know you... You won't make a success as an actress."

"Because I've no talent?"

He looked at her sadly through his long eyelashes and said nothing. She pulled her shawl round her and waited. The cat Waxie went on rubbing himself against her strong, slim legs.

"You see, Varya old girl," Volodya said. "Look, Ginger,

we've just had an argument at the hostel. It's hard to explain but the way I see it is that whatever you're doing should be interesting and essential not just for you alone, but for everyone, for society, for the people. And then it will continue to be interesting and essential for ever. But if it's for you alone, it will suddenly become pointless."

"Come in where it's warm, don't stand out there," Grandfather called from the kitchen. "The potatoes are ready. Varya, lay the table. And fetch some pickles from the cellar."

It was a silent meal. Nowadays Grandfather was not to be outdone in conversation and voiced his opinion most emphatically on everything, and so as a rule he spoke alone and to his heart's content. But that night he was out of sorts, and only grumbled about the cat.

"He's a menace, he's so spoiled. Mice he won't catch, he just blinks at them; a rat came in this morning, and he turned tail. Maybe we should chop his tail off, eh?"

"What on earth for?" Varya said, alarmed.

"Because cats with chopped tails are quicker," he said, helping himself to some sauerkraut. "In the land of Siberia, the peasants chop all their cats' tails off. You can see their point — the cold is fierce, and cats are slow coming in, dragging in their long rigid tails. Letting them in and out takes all the warmth out of the house. But a shortened cat, now, takes half the time to come in and out — it's arithmetic. And they're quicker round the house too. They're scared they might get another bit chopped off."

"Grandad, if you shorten Waxie's tail I'll leave home," Varya said. "He's a proper Malyuta Skuratov that grandfather of mine," she told Volodya.

While Varya was doing the dishes, Volodya talked, piling abuse upon himself and praising Pych to the sky. Yevgeny came home and rebuked Volodya.

"Why weren't you at the club?" he demanded. "You're always shirking your social duties. The student body was playing host to Lev Gulin, the well-known writer. We, Soviet students, are supposed to be holding debates on his book, discussing it enthusiastically in a spirit of comradeship, and two-thirds of the chaps just don't bother to put in an appearance. It's a downright insult!"

"But what if I've never read Lev Gulin?" Volodya asked.

"It's a regrettable fact in your biography. Lev Gulin is making a tour of the Soviet Union and holding meetings with his readers."

"All right, put us down with the illiterate," Varya said angrily. "Why don't you leave us alone?"

"It's for your own good," Yevgeny said sulkily. "Honestly, can't you understand that life is life, that you have to be noticed, seen and heard. Nothing but potatoes for supper?" he went on in the same tone. With his mouth full he told them how he had taken the floor and without putting it in so many words had nevertheless given the meeting to understand that in his opinion the author had, willingly or unwillingly, denigrated Soviet students as a whole by portraying Shemyakin, a present-day student, as a time-server, a crafty, unscrupulous character.

"Have you read the book?" Varya asked.

"I glanced through it just before the discussion. I also looked at what the critics had to say about it, so I knew my way about, you needn't worry on my account."

"You'll certainly go far, Yevgeny my pet," Varya said with a sigh.

"I've no intention of stopping anywhere near here, sister dear. I can't afford to because then everyone will see that Yevgeny Stepanov is not too gifted a man. But when I'm farther away and, God willing, a good bit higher up, then..."

"Go away!" Varya screamed at him. "Go away, Yevgeny, please go!"

The following morning Volodya went up to Pych and said that he agreed with him in everything and was going to give up this stupid nihilistic attitude of his. The Old Man accepted the confession so calmly that Volodya felt slightly hurt. Not for long, however. They were soon talking about the so-called "power of breath" cure. Volodya had read about it in the tram on his way to the institute that morning. He told Pych about it. Turkish medicine men as a rule took a long time with their black magic, they hung their patient with charms, muttered spells, burned incense, danced about him, howled, and ended up by blowing hard at the sick person. But it took a *khoja*, a healer with the "power of breath", to really cure the patient. The author of the booklet, an eminent doctor who had made a long and thorough study of Turkish medicine men, assured his readers very emphatically that "power of breath" was indeed instrumental in curing the sick.

Pych thought for a moment, rubbed his tired eyes as he often did, and said:

"Personally, I think it's all a question of the patient having confidence in his doctor. What good will you and I be, Ustimenko, if we make a faultless diagnosis and prescribe the correct treatment but fail to win the patient's soul, so to say? A patient is like a soldier in battle, he must trust his commanding officer implicitly, knowing that he won't fail his men. He must believe that with this man in command they'll make short work of the enemy and come through safe and sound."

"I suppose you're right."

From that day on, Volodya and Pych always studied together; neither suggested it, it simply happened. Pych came to the Ustimenkos at supper-time, had a large dish of borsch, smoked a cigarette of home-grown tobacco, and then the two of them settled down to work. Pych was amazingly persevering, Volodya was brilliant. Pych got badly stuck sometimes; Volodya would be very far ahead, but occasionally the knowledge he gathered was superficial. Pych ploughed through knowledge, turning up thick, heavy layers, Volodya indulged in flights of fancy. They argued themselves hoarse, they quarrelled and cursed, but they could not do without each other.

"I hope they'll assign us to the same hospital after graduation," Volodya once said.

"Can't be done," Pych replied gruffly. "We're too used to being rude to one another, and you know how it is in hospitals: 'I beg your pardon, Pavel Lukich,' — 'Oh no, it's *my* fault, dear Vladimir Afanasyevich'... You have to stand on your doctor's dignity."

And so came spring.

### Chapter Seven

#### FIRST AID

It was a dry summer without a drop of rain, close and dusty with frequently gathering thunderstorms and sudden whirlwinds. The woods were on fire on the opposite bank of the Uncha and smoke crept over the town. In the town itself more fires broke out — the Yamskaya Sloboda and the old warehouses on the river front were burnt to the ground in a thunderstorm.

Volodya worked as an ambulance attendant. The town's first aid had only two cars, two old Renaults with low-slung bodies and snub-nosed radiators. But then there were plenty of spring carriages with red crosses on the sides and rattling windowpanes covered over with white paint. The horses were kept in excellent trim. As a rule, Volodya rode on the box beside the driver, urging him on, afraid that they would be late. He accompanied the doctor to the door, carrying his wooden first-aid case, which also had a red cross painted on it, knocked or rang, and when a voice asked who it was, he answered impatiently, "First aid".

He had already seen death more than once. He had seen terrible, irreversible hemorrhages. He had seen death agony. He had also seen the return of a mortal from "there" as he called it in his thoughts. There was no miracle in such "returns" for the old, very near-sighted Dr. Mikeshin. But Volodya, assisting him energetically, experienced something like reverential bliss. His despair was abysmal when the miracle refused to work, when Mikeshin, pushing up his spectacles with a habitual gesture, cleared his throat and turned to leave the room where "science was powerless".

"The fact of the matter is this," Dr. Mikeshin would say, climbing into the carriage. "We came a little late, Volodya. Had we come an hour or two earlier, perhaps..."

The door would slam shut and the carriage would go clattering over the cobblestones, swaying from side to side. Volodya felt too frightened and ashamed to look back: he seemed to see the bereaved family staring after them with hate-filled eyes, he fancied they were all cursing science, Mikeshin, Ustimenko. But the next call would make him forget his emotions of a few minutes ago.

He saw a man come back to life very quickly after injections of camphor, caffeine and morphia. With his gruelling pain gone, he looked about him in bewilderment. It was the syringe, the ampules, Mikeshin's hands, Mikeshin's experience that had brought him back from "there".

"Well, that's that," Mikeshin said and adjusted his spectacles which was another gesture of his. "Now he just needs a little peace and quiet and everything'll be all right."

"Everything'll be all right, you hear!" Volodya felt like shouting. "You — his wife, his daughter, all of you — can't you understand the man was dead! Now he's asking for something sourish to drink but a moment ago he was dead!"

The carriage clattered over the old cobblestones of Plotnitskaya Sloboda, and the driver Snimshchikov, fondly stroking his rich beard, said:

"There's sure to be umpteen calls today. I can feel it in my bones. There's no much chance of getting a proper steaming in the bathhouse!"

A case that impressed Volodya particularly was rather simple as a matter of fact, but it struck him as a miracle, and the memory remained with him for many years. It happened about the middle of August. They received an urgent call, after midnight, to go and see a certain Belyakov who lived in Kosaya Street, in a detached wing in the yard. In the clean low-ceilinged room, on a wide bed lay a man no longer young, worn out by hours of suffering dying a slow and painful death. His broad chest with its protruding ribs rose and fell unevenly, sweat poured down his forehead, filled his eye sockets and trickled down his cheeks; long spasms of pain made him groan and grit his teeth.

A thin youngster gave hurried explanations to Mikeshin.

"Daddy was restless at first, Doctor. He kept jumping up one minute, then sitting down again, and running in and out of the room, and then he began to shiver. The way he shivered, I've never seen anything like it. And then he said he was hungry. 'Let's have supper, Anatoly,' he said. Anatoly that's me. 'Let's have supper.'"

"What's this?" Mikeshin asked picking up an empty ampule.

"That? He gives himself injections of insulin. He's got diabetes," the boy explained.

Mikeshin nodded. He peered into Belyakov's face for a second or two, and said, "Some sugar. Quick." A spasm so violent seized Belyakov that the bed creaked under him; Mikeshin turned him on his back and started swiftly and deftly sprinkling the sugar into his mouth, ordering Volodya in the meantime to get everything ready for an intravenous injection of glucose. Some twenty minutes later, when the spasms had stopped, Belyakov was given an injection of adrenalin. His expression was now blissful and amazed. The thin youngster was crying in the corner, reliving his fright.

"You gave yourself an overdose of insulin, my dear man," Mikeshin told the patient. "Should you ever feel anything like that again, which God forbid, quickly eat a piece of white bread or two lumps of sugar and do so at once. Be more careful next time. I'll be expecting you at the hospital tomorrow..."

As they were going out through the dark porch, Mikeshin suddenly got very angry. "What the devil!.." he exclaimed. "What d'you think I am, a priest or an archbishop or something?"

He explained his outburst as he climbed into the carriage:

"That brat tried to kiss my hand, if you please!"

Volodya climbed up beside the driver, and said to him in a constrained voice, "There's nothing as magnificent as science,

Comrade Snimshchikov. A minute ago, Dr. Mikeshin literally saved a man from death, from certain death."

"You can't save anyone from certain death," the driver said sternly. "It *can* be done if it's not certain. You've only just started going round with us, but I've been watching this science of yours for twenty odd years. Saved from certain death, that's a good one! Even professors can't do that, let alone our old Mikeshin!"

Snimshchikov had a sceptical turn of mind and not a whit of respect for Dr. Mikeshin, who was far too polite to be anyone of importance, saying "please", "be so kind" and "thank you" all the time. Why, he only had one old overcoat, which he wore the whole year round.

It was after two in the morning. The moon floated over the town, over its dusty squares, over the former Noblemen's Park, the former Merchants' Park, over the cupolas of the cathedral and the wide Uncha. Hungry, ferocious watchdogs barked and tugged at their chains in the backyards. From the other side of the river came the smell of the burning forest. Dr. Mikeshin removed his white cap and said rather huskily:

"Beautiful, isn't it, Volodya!"

"Thank you, Anton Romanovich," Volodya mumbled.

"For what?"

"For ... well, for teaching me, I suppose."

"For teaching you?" Mikeshin said in a genuine amazement.

"Not in that sense. I mean tonight, for instance..." Volodya grew hopelessly confused.

"Ah, tonight!" Mikeshin said sadly. "That Belyakov man, you mean? But that was a simple trick, the most elementary case imaginable."

In Mikeshin's voice Volodya detected a familiar note Polunin's note — slightly mocking, ironical and a little weary.

The timber stores on the other side of the river caught fire. The fire broke out suddenly just before dawn in the barracks where the stevedores slept and no one woke up soon enough. A strong wind blew in gusts scattering red-hot embers and scorching ashes; Snimshchikov's black horses snorted, backed and shied off the road. Their bells clanking, one fire engine after another raced across the bridge; firemen in smouldering overalls pulled the victims out of the flames, and hospital attendants carried them away at a run to their ambulance carriages and cars.

"Treating burns is something we still know nothing about," Mikeshin said when that awful day came to an end.

His eyes were swollen and his lips parched; he had lost his white cap and now his hair stood up like feathers.

In the middle of that gruelling day Volodya saw Varya walking down Lenin Street. She recognised him from afar — sitting in his usual place beside the driver — and raised her hand, but did not dare wave. He looked too exhausted and forbidding.

By the time the autumn term began, Volodya was able to write off many things as past worries. Among these were the symptoms of inflammation, which once had to be learned by heart: *calor, dolor, tumor, rubor et funcziolesa*, meaning heat, pain, swelling, redness and impairment of function. His confidence that the essence of a subject was not so very difficult to grasp was also a thing of the past. So were the arguments about the riddles of medieval medicine and about Paracelsus, who treated hearts with heart-shaped leaves and kidneys with kidney-shaped ones. Long since overcome was the fear inspired in him by the heavy door of the dissecting room with the inscription: "Here death brings succour to the living." He felt self-possessed and almost unaffected in the room now, where death was no longer a mystery but a vile thing that had to be watched and fought daily. But how to fight it?

The sight of a corpse no longer frightened Volodya, but one case made him writhe inwardly. On the dissecting table he saw the body of a nineteen-year-old boy, the body of an athlete, sunburnt and splendid, trained for a long, healthy life. Why such a failure as this? Why had victory gone to the vile thing? And how much longer would doctors go on with their futile blabbing about the powers science possesses but yet knows not.

A great deal was behind him, but how many were the doors that he was still to open, and what awaited him behind them?

With youthful intolerance and finality Volodya now subdivided his professors and teachers into the brilliant and the dull. Pych argued with rather good sense that the reason why mankind needed people like Tolstoy, Tchaikovsky, Mendeleyev, Lomonosov, Mayakovsky and Sholokhov was precisely because they were *the* geniuses, whereas physicians could not always be geniuses, "there wouldn't be enough to go round, you hothead!"

The year had a difficult beginning.

To be "a light to others" was not as simple as it sounded.

To begin with, one had to know how to provide "light" that was of some use. And what was one to do if the highly experienced doctor Mikeshin told Volodya more than once in the course of the summer that "we don't know how to go about it yet, colleague". Or: "The process is irreversible." Or again: "Listen, Volodya, don't torment yourself, we haven't even learnt to treat a cold in the head properly yet."

Polunin, that man of great intelligence, sometimes replied when asked what to prescribe, "Nothing at all. It'll cure itself."

This was what he said in the case of the Polish woman with the blue eyes and ivory skin, whom Volodya was attending in Polunin's clinic.

"It'll cure itself."

"But how?"

"It just will."

"By itself?"

"Oh well, she needs a well-balanced diet, rest, sleep, a chat with you now and again — you're not a dull lad, you know, but much too serious. And in time it will all go. Is there anything you want to say to the contrary?"

No, there was nothing to say.

### PROFESSOR ZHOVTYAK HIMSELF!

Certain curious observations worried Volodya. The more fuss and bother the "treatment" entailed, the greater the variety of cures the patient was subjected to, the more grateful he became. If, on the other hand, little medicine was prescribed, no probe had to be swallowed and laboratory tests were not made all the time, the patients complained that they were given "too little treatment", that it was doing no good and that they were being neglected. Volodya observed, too, that the most popular doctors were the "kind" sort, whether they were skilled, honest and gifted or not. Patients also liked their doctor to look "like a professor" with a nice trim beard and beringed fingers; and they were pleasurably overawed by the regal entrance made by some medical men who knew the value of pomposity in their trade.

"What a worthy man!" Volodya once heard a sick old woman's gasp of admiration for Zhovtyak, a stupid and conceited man, but a popular physician and a professor to boot. "Not the usual kind we get! Him I call a real professor!"

A benevolent smile, a playful "boo" at the baby, a funny little joke, were all weapons of Zhovtyak's, who stopped at nothing to maintain his popularity, and with him the patients were like "flowers lifting their faces to the sun". And yet Postnikov, the austere and glumly reticent surgeon, who, incidentally, had no academic degree, quite often earned dispraise from the very people he rescued from predicaments which Professor Zhovtyak never even attempted to extricate them from, preferring to act through Postnikov where a risk was involved. In the very few, quite hopeless cases when Postnikov "blundered", Professor Zhovtyak would long and reproachfully shake his handsome head with its scented bald patch and scold him in silky tones.

"Ah, that was unwise of you, colleague!" he would say. "What made you operate on the inoperable? Why imperil our *statistics*? He would have passed on as *happily* at home with his near and dear ones about him, but no, there you go crippling my good showings. And what *profit* is it to you anyway? No, my dear man, don't you do it again, don't spoil my record. Consider our prestige; another risky venture of yours and people will start talking about me *personally*, they'll say Professor Zhovtyak was remiss. And I am not the smallest pebble on the beach in either this town or this region, and there's no reason for me to break my neck because of you."

When introducing himself, Zhovtyak, unlike Ganichev or Polunin, invariably stressed the title: *Professor* Zhovtyak.

He operated rarely and clumsily, but he made a great show of it and was very fond of uttering truisms while he worked, "quoting quotations" as Polunin once called it in a moment of anger. Zhovtyak did not risk performing the smallest operation unless Postnikov was there, standing beside him as though the professor were a practising student. And everyone could see that Postnikov was watching him nervously, everyone felt ashamed, even Zhovtyak himself. At least Volodya once heard him say in rather wretched tones while scrubbing his hands after a particularly clumsy operation:

"I must be getting old. I remember..."

"What *do* you remember?" Postnikov asked rudely.

Sometimes he would turn his inscrutable ice-blue eyes in a long, reflective stare on his superior's well-fed face with its Assyrian beard, and no one could tell what he was thinking of then. And Zhovtyak, breezily holding forth and enjoying the sound of his own voice until a moment ago, would wilt at once, blush in confusion, break off his lecture, or rather speech, in mid-sentence, and hurriedly make his exit.

He hated Postnikov but the man was indispensable to

114

him. Postnikov shouldered the entire responsibility for the clinic, he conducted the students' practical studies, and performed the more difficult operations; there was talk that he wrote some of his chief's articles for him as well. Zhovtyak was a terribly busy man. He acted as consultant everywhere (naturally taking the taciturn Postnikov along when a case was too complicated), he went duck shooting with people in authority, assumed an earnest, business-like manner at meetings, indulging in an occasional venomous remark, when it was safe to do so, opened regional and city medical conferences, knew exactly how long one should clap when presiding at a meeting, and began all his speeches in the following manner:

"Dear comrades! To begin with, allow me to salute you on behalf of the scientists of the Sechenov Medical Institute!" (At this, Zhovtyak would begin to clap and then turn the page of his long, narrow writing pad.) "I shall start with figures. In 1911 our entire region had at its disposal only 122 beds..."

"Listen to this!" Polunin would say. "You are about to hear some staggering news. Apparently when old Nick was on the throne, health protection wasn't as good as it is under the Soviets!"

And he was never wrong. Zhovtyak went through all the old truisms over and over again, and mildly criticised the work of officials not higher than the head of the regional finance department — while the rest of the presidium exchanged whispered remarks and notes, and the audience buzzed with a steady, unbroken hum of conversation. Blandly, Zhovtyak talked on and on about the number of hospital beds, multiplied the average number of beds occupied annually by the number of days in the years, gave a breakdown to the total number of beds available in the country, analysed the nomenclature of hospital beds, and at long last, after having his speaking time prolonged thrice, left the platform with head held high.

"Why does he do it?" Volodya once asked Polunin.

"Turpentine has its uses too," Polunin replied enigmatically.

"Why turpentine?"

"You know what Kozma Prutkov* says in the *Fruits of Cogitation*: 'Zeal overcomes everything.' He's got another pithy

---

* The collective penname of Alexei Tolstoy and the Zhemchuzhnikov brothers.— *Tr.*

115

aphorism too: 'Always lead trumps!'" And Polunin turned away
with bitterness in his eyes.

Zhovtyak was indulgent with the students, particularly
with those who were said to be clever. He was indulgent with
Yevgeny Stepanov because he edited the institute newspaper.
He was also indulgent with the unapproachable Pych, just in
case, for it worried Zhovtyak when he sensed disapproval, even
if silent. But with Volodya he was more affectionately indulgent than with all the others because Volodya was spoken of
as a very capable student, and also because Volodya regarded
him with unbearable enmity. Still, for all the affection Zhovtyak lavished on him, Volodya was quick to see through the
loquacious professor and conceived a dislike for him as violent and strong as the affection he felt for the austere and sombre
Postnikov. But perhaps he did not really see through Zhovtyak;
perhaps it was simply that, being observant by nature, Volodya
had noticed the exaggerated politeness amounting to mock courtesy with which Polunin treated the head of the surgical clinic.

Zhovtyak was too obtuse to understand that this courtesy
of Polunin's was reserved for people he deeply despised, but
Volodya, who knew both Ganichev and Polunin well, took note
of the glances they exchanged as they listened to Zhovtyak
hold forth, and once overheard and docketed in his mind a short
conversation between the two in the garden as they sat on their
favourite garden seat.

"The contempt we feel is justified," Ganichev said in a
bored voice. "Contempt is hatred in a state of tranquillity."

"Isn't it too early in the day for us to enter a state of
tranquillity?" Polunin asked with malice. "Aren't we being
a little too unconcerned about this fatuous society pet with
his unscrupulous little tricks?"

"Oh, stop it," Ganichev replied indifferently. "We are doing our job honestly, so what more do you want? Getting involved with him will take up so much time, you know."

Volodya, who was sitting on the garden seat next to
theirs, gave a discreet cough to tell them he was not eavesdropping. Polunin glanced at him indifferently, and said something that Volodya was to remember for a long time afterwards.

"The trouble with us is our inertia. Mine to a lesser degree,
yours to a greater. We know very well a man is a son of a bitch
and we ought to strike him down mercilessly, but what do we
do? We laugh up our sleeves."

Volodya let the thought sink in. "Inertia. It is inertia. Polunin is right. Is it age that makes people so tired out,

or what? But Zhovtyak is a hale and hearty chap. He can probably even bite."

That day marked the dimming of Ganichev's star for Volodya, and the rising of another — Postnikov's. This neat, pedantic, stern man with stiffly upturned grey moustache also noticed Volodya and allowed him not just to be present but also to assist him, performing the work he was teaching him with such excellence that Volodya felt dizzy with envy.

Volodya's fellow students responded in different ways to his praise of Postnikov. "He's the real thing, no doubt about that," Pych said. "But why hasn't he even a candidate degree?" Nyussia Yelkina voiced her doubt. Yevgeny Stepanov drawled, "By and large, your raptures are always so puerile, Volodya. He's not outstanding, of course, just a sound practitioner, no one's denying him that. But Nyussia is quite right. Queer, that he doesn't even have a candidate's degree considering the opportunities for advancement our country offers! Maybe he has some 'white' lapses in his biography?" Svetlana declared that Zhovtyak appealed to her because he was so good-natured, unaffected and polite. Ogurtsov rushed to Postnikov's defence, Sasha Poleshchuk called Svetlana a jelly-fish for some reason, while Misha Shervud thought it safest to say nothing at all. He no longer let his tongue run away with him, and after all it was not Postnikov but Zhovtyak who gave them their marks.

### POSTNIKOV

It all began the day Volodya saw Postnikov come into Polunin's department as a consultant, sit down on a white-painted stool, bend over the patient — a land surveyor, Dobrodomov and proceed with the percussion. The ward with its five patients grew perfectly silent. Polunin had asked them beforehand not to make a sound. Postnikov tapped the patient with his fingers, he did not believe in instruments. Wrinkling his cold eyes, he tapped now strongly and rapidly, and now with a barely perceptible movement of the fingers. No less than thirty minutes went by. The monotonous, dull tapping made one drowsy, and Volodya thought not without resentment: "He's showing off, just trying to impress!"

All at once Postnikov straightened up, took the jar of iodine from the nurse's hands, and painted a square on Dobrodomov's cyanotic skin.

"There's an abscess here. Transfer him to my surgical department."

Postnikov got up, carefully covered up the patient, and holding his head high walked out of the ward.

"Did you see that?" Polunin said enthusiastically to Volodya.

"I did see it," Volodya replied mechanically.

"And just what did you see?"

"It was wonderful!"

Dobrodomov was operated on the following Tuesday, and Postnikov's diagnosis was fully confirmed.

Polunin gave Volodya a piece of advice.

"Now let Postnikov give you a lesson in post-operative care," he said. "In the 16th century Ambroise Paré used to say, 'I performed the operation, now let God heal them.' Take a lesson from God. Postnikov is a strategist, not an empiricist. He's the kind of surgeon who thinks. Learning from him will train you to work in any conditions and you may find that very useful. You never know, there might be a war. You won't find an X-ray machine everywhere. A word of warning though. If Postnikov is rude to you, never mind. He's a man of efficiency and hates anyone getting in his way. And he can't stand idle curiosity. Just learn all you can from him. Drain the cup to the dregs, to put it elegantly, and you'll be grateful ever after."

Volodya repeated what Polunin had said to the class.

"Oh, no, my dear chap, I have no wish to train myself for conditions where there's not even any X-ray," Yevgeny said indignantly. "In fact, I can't quite picture such conditions. By and large, you know, there's rather a whiff about your Polunin's philosophy, something not quite..."

"Again?" Pych demanded menacingly.

"Yes, again!" Yevgeny replied in a bellicose tone. "Yes, again! There's Ganichev, Polunin and now Postnikov, they're not *our* people, that's what! Not *ours*. That's my point of view!"

About a fortnight later Polunin asked Volodya:

"Well, are you draining the cup?"

"Yes, I am."

"And how's it going?"

"Pretty hard."

"No wonder you look so thin."

"I still know so little," Volodya complained. "It's awful how little I know."

Polunin buttoned his mackintosh to the neck, offered Volodya his large, warm hand, and said:

"Good-bye. It doesn't matter about your knowing too little.

Your friend Stepanov knows very much and it's all thoroughly mediocre."

Volodya sighed and trailed wearily back along the maple-lined walk to the squat building of the surgical department. There, in the laboratory, a three-coloured mongrel called Sharik was kept prisoner, a victim of Volodya's.

The door swung back with a bang, Volodya turned on the light and called the dog. Sharik responded from his cramped cage with a weak yelp and wagged his tail feebly. "I do nothing but torture him, and there he goes wagging his tail in welcome!" Volodya thought angrily. Anger was a counterpart of pity with him.

In the silence of the laboratory he could hear the rabbits busily crunching their cabbage-stumps, the white mice running about inside their glass jars, and the dog Misha Shervud was experimenting on heave a sigh. Postnikov was at work in the next room, Volodya heard his "well, well". Postnikov spent not less than two hours a day there, experimenting, reflecting, and experimenting again. "In the clinic under my direction..." Zhovtyak's words came back to Volodya.

Sharik dragged his body to the door of the cage. He kept licking his scars and shivering painfully.

"Come out, you silly," Volodya whispered. "I've got a hamburger for you and some sugar. Here, Sharik, here!"

Volodya was very hungry, and the hamburger sandwich was his own lunch. Since Sharik refused the bread and was the weaker of the two, he got the hamburger and Volodya ate the bread.

"Oh, you don't like it?" Volodya said. "So even a hamburger's not good enough for you now!"

Sharik sniffed at the hamburger indifferently, turned away, and dropping his head on his front paws closed his moist, anguished eyes. Volodya broke off a piece of the hamburger, squashed it with his fingers and thrust it under the dog's lip. Just then Postnikov came in pulling off his rubber gloves.

"Mankin's ill, he's got tonsillitis," he said. (Mankin was the old hospital attendant whose job was to feed the experimental animals.) "The animals weren't fed. Alla and I had a hard job feeding Noah's Arc today."

Alla, a pretty girl, winked at Volodya over Postnikov's shoulder. He got the glove off his left hand at last with a snap, threw it on the table, and rapping his fingernail on the jar containing the mice, said:

"My advice to you, Ustimenko, is take your Sharik home.

You won't get the dog back on his feet here, not after the re-section you did on him. At home, you may succeed perhaps in re-storing the animal's strength. However, it's up to you. Sher-vud, for one, told me his parents dislike dogs."

That evening Volodya brought Sharik home and rang up Varya.

"Look here, Varya," he said brusquely in a voice that was like Postnikov's, "you are to come here at once, it's urgent."

"But I've..." Varya began to say, but he cut her short.

"What you have is your own affair, but come here you must and at once too!"

Aunt Aglaya was out. Volodya put Sharik down on the floor in his "den" on an old folded quilt. The dog kept trembling all over, licking his scar and uttering almost human sounds. Volodya warmed up some milk, stirred in a lit-tle sugar and an egg. Sharik sniffed it and turned away.

"This is apparently where the doctor 'must hand the case over to the gravedigger'," Volodya remembered a sentence out of some old book. He glared balefully at the *Lesson in Anatomy*. Try and be a light to others when you can't even cure a dog, though you know exactly what's wrong with him!

He was still crouching over Sharik and eating cold boiled potatoes when Varya arrived.

"A dog!" she gave a scream of joy. "You've bought me a doggie?"

"Oh, do stop yelling!"

"Is he ill? Are you treating him? Oh, Volodya, do get him well for me!" Varya cried excitedly again. "It's a pure-bred dog, isn't it?"

She squatted down beside Volodya.

"He won't bite me, will he?"

"I removed a large chunk of his intestines," Volodya said glumly. "There was something else I had to do to him besides. And yet he licks my hands and treats me like a friend. He must be the only living creature that takes me for a doctor."

"What about me? Don't I take you for a doctor?"

"Anyhow I've got to get Sharik well. And you will help me. Is that clear?"

"Yes."

"Well then, look after him, I'll be working at the clinic all night. If anything happens, ring me up at the surgical de-partment. Take down the number."

Obediently, Varya took it down. After a bath and a shave and a very strange meal prepared by Varya — it was something cooked on a frying-pan, "Fantasia" she called it — he left, forgetting to say good-bye to her. As a matter of fact he was always forgetting to say hello and good-bye, to ask what was new, to shave and get a haircut; he was always forgetting to do what Varya called "behaving like a human being" and Yevgeny "observing the rules of public hygiene".

The front door banged shut. Varya found a rather old boiled sweet in her pocket, washed it under the tap, and popped it in Sharik's mouth before he knew it. He crunched it between his teeth and wagged his tail. Varya then emptied the whole sugar bowl on the floor close to the patient's whiskered and bearded mouth. Sharik took a tentative lick, and in a matter of seconds the floor was wiped clean.

"Good doggie, nice doggie! Oh, you doggie, doggins dear," Varya cooed the way people do when alone with their pets, in a peculiar idiotic way. "There, doggie-doggins, drink your milk now, Sharik boy, eat like a good boy and you'll grow some nice new intestines. There, my lovely dog, there! Only, you won't be called Sharik any more, you'll be Earnest. All right? My clever, ferocious, beautiful Earnest!"

Volodya was wheeling a trolley out of the dressing room when Alla, the nurse on night duty, called him to the telephone. It was after ten, the patients in Professor Zhovtyak's clinic were already going to sleep, and so he had to keep his voice down to a whisper.

"He's eating!" Varya shouted in his ear. "He's eating! And he had some milk too!"

"Thanks," Volodya said.

"And he's no longer called Sharik, he's Earnest. I'll spell it out, shall I? Should I take him out? Or, perhaps, there's an old pan I found in the kitchen..."

"Thank you very much," Volodya said and hung up.

"Ustimenko, are you going to leave that trolley here?" Alla asked with a flash of her splendid eyes at Volodya. She thought the obsessed young student with the thick eyelashes and the boyishly fresh lips very attractive. "Shall I show you where they're kept?"

She was almost in love with Volodya, but that did not stop her from asking him to relieve her for an hour or two while she had a little snooze. She was one of those people who believe that no matter how hard you try you'll never do all that wants doing in this world, and was quite frank about putting her own comfort first. Volodya regarded all her sort as belonging to Nyussia Yelkina's "armada" and it surprised him that Postnikov failed to realise it. He even gave her grudging praise, though Alla was sham incarnate.

Two, three, four hours went by, but Alla was still asleep. Volodya went to see the patients when they rang, gave one an injection of morphia, helped another to make his operated leg more comfortable, and sat beside a third for a while because the man had a nervous fear of the night. And at 4 a. m. Dr. Lushnikova, the surgeon on duty, a very tall, sharp-nosed woman, rang up Postnikov's home to consult him about an emergency operation she was about to perform. It was Postnikov she rang up, and not Zhovtyak.

Volodya was standing so close to the phone that he heard Postnikov's usual answer: "Good luck."

Alla, looking fresh and rested, flashed her eyes at Volodya once again and whispered:

"I love a snooze."

Volodya turned away.

Postnikov arrived when the operation was under way. The tips of his bristly moustache stuck out rigidly, his milky-blue eyes were calm and as cold as chips of ice. It was his way to come always but never to interfere unless his advice, direction or help became imperative. And if things went well, he left in silence, his step firm and still youthful, his head held high.

That morning he said to Volodya as he was leaving:

"It's Sunday today, so if you have nothing better to do, come to my place at about eight. But don't be later than nine."

"Thanks," Volodya was too stunned to be more articulate.

"Do come," Postnikov nodded.

"He's invited you to his place, has he?" Alla began to pester him the moment Postnikov was out of earshot. "To his flat?"

"Yes."

"Gosh, don't you have all the luck!"

### WE HAVE DIFFERENT ROADS

He got home at 6 a. m. and quietly let himself in. Sharik waddled forward to meet him. Varya, fully dressed, was asleep on Volodya's bed, her face cushioned in her palm. The desk lamp was screened so that the light would not fall on the floor where Sharik was supposed to be lying. Beside the bed of the convalescent "Earnest" stood the old pan daintily covered with a lid of pink cardboard.

"Volodya!" Aunt Aglaya called softly.

He went to her room in his stockinged feet, trying not to make a noise. She was sitting up in bed with the blanket up to her neck. Her slightly slanting eyes regarded him fondly as he entered.

"Dead beat?"

"Nearly."

He told her in whispers of Postnikov's invitation. For a moment he fancied that she, too, had something to tell him, but he forgot to ask because there was so much other student news he wanted to share with her, and when he was finished it was time to go to bed. Sleep always knocked him out the moment his head touched the pillow. Dimly he heard his aunt telling him her news as, bed and all, he sank deep into something soft and cosy. He was fast asleep.

"Well, Sharik, that's that," Aunt Aglaya said, stroking the future Earnest's bristly hair behind the ear. "No one cares about me."

Sharik snorted a little and scratched himself gingerly — he was very careful of his person.

"And I'm interested in everything that concerns him," she said softly, scratching the dog's ear. "Why is it so? Don't whimper now, it doesn't hurt. You are a nervous dog, aren't you?"

Varya stayed for breakfast in spite of her grandfather's irate telephone calls with shouts of: "There's no reason for the girl to sleep at other people's and eat their food! Goodness knows, we're not beggars, we've a home and breakfast aplenty!" Aglaya kept glancing at Volodya with a question in her eyes — would he ask her about her last night's news? — but no, he did not. Varya was teaching the former Sharik, who had cheered up considerably, to hand her his paw. The dog yawned absent-mindedly and turned away.

"Do you think Earnest will get well?" Varya asked Volodya.

"M-m," Volodya replied.

"Why does he keep yawning? It's not oxygen hunger, is it?"

Volodya ignored the question.

"He won't deign to answer!" Varya said to Aunt Aglaya. "The great man, the future luminary!"

"And as absent-minded as all great men," his aunt said.

"But great men don't snub ordinary citizens, do they? And your nephew does."

Varya perched on the edge of Aunt Aglaya's chair, and

the two of them, with their arms about one another, proceeded to discuss Volodya as if he were not there at all.

"He's one of those self-centered characters."

"A pinchbeck celebrity! More conceit than brains."

Volodya glanced absently at his aunt and Varya, asked the time, and delved into his papers once again.

"He may still disappoint us all!" Aunt Aglaya suggested. "To look at, he is science itself, but inside he's hollow."

"Makes you sick to look at him," Varya agreed dejectedly.

"It certainly does," Aunt Aglaya said. "He has no real knowledge to speak of, it's nothing but a pose. Baron von Soap Bubbles was our name for people like that at the workers' school."

"But perhaps he's just a swot, Aglaya Petrovna?"

"More than likely. Narrow-minded, too."

"I say, why're you pitching into me like this?" Volodya asked miserably.

All at once, Aunt Aglaya burst into tears. She cried in her own peculiar way, not as women usually do. She was laughing too, but the tears simply splashed.

"Why, what is it?" Volodya asked, bewildered and confused. Only it was no use asking her now.

She brushed her large teardrops away with her fingers and said nothing. Varya gave her some water. Aunt Aglaya went to the window, flung it open and stood leaning out. Her shoulders were shaking. And then, pulling herself together abruptly, she said:

"Don't mind me, children. I've been feeling the strain lately, you know how it is. You go on and on and suddenly feel tired out. And now it's harder than ever on me. I wonder if I'll manage?"

"Manage what?" Varya asked very softly.

"Everything," Aunt Aglaya replied pensively.

She put on her raincoat and left.

Varya, pretending to be a good girl, washed the dishes while Volodya read the newspaper. Suddenly he knew what it was his aunt had wanted to tell him about last night. There was an article in the newspaper about the conference of Kamenka District teachers held the day before at which one of the speakers had been Aglaya Petrovna Ustimenko, head of the Regional Public Education Department.

"Hear that, Varya? Oh, I *am* a swine. Naturally it's difficult at first, it's a new job, and last night when I came home... Oh, how lousy of me!"

Varya sat down, untied her apron strings, and threw the dish towel on the table.

"Well, say something!" Volodya demanded.

"What?"

"After all, I'm not so terribly in the wrong."

"There's nothing you can do about it," Varya said, sighing. "You're like that. The main thing for you is not here, it's there."

"Where's 'there'? What 'main thing'?"

"Don't be angry," Varya begged sadly. "It may be fine, but it's hard, Volodya. There, at the institute, you're not selfish at all perhaps, but here you're so selfish it's frightening."

It was amazing how clever this girl could be, and how surely she could hit the nail on the head. But in the next breath she said something too silly for words.

"A Gypsy told me my fortune last Sunday, you know. Honestly ... you don't believe me ... word of honour. A horrible old Gypsy hag with a great beak of a nose and huge piercing eyes. She told me that ... well, anyway, it was about you and me. She said you didn't need me. She said we had different roads..."

Volodya was slow to answer. He stood with his back to her, gazing at the red clusters of the rowan-tree just beyond the open window and shivering in the cool autumn wind.

"All right, Varya old girl, I know I'm a beast, but I'm not as bad as all that, honestly," he said wretchedly. "You shall see, I'll change completely. I'll be considerate and, what d'you call it ... all those other saccharine words."

"You won't be able to do it."

"And just supposing?"

"You won't," Varya reiterated, looking straight into his eyes. "Then you won't be you. It'll be someone else. And it's you the way you are I don't want to see taking a different road from me. You!"

"What about yourself?"

"Me?"

"You may choose a different road, too. Your crazy Gypsy told you that *we* had different roads."

He went up to Varya and gripped her arms above the elbows. Though he loved her, he never could bring himself to put it into words. It wasn't that so much as the embarrassing thought that, supposing he said, "I love you," she might reply, "So what?" She certainly was capable of it. And anyhow she knew he loved her.

"Ginger, do you understand?"

"What?" she asked in all simplicity.

He gripped her wrists. It was beyond Volodya to drop such schoolboy stuff as pulling her hair and twisting her arms. But the fun was not there — their horseplay days were over. His pity and tenderness for her were incomparably stronger than his boyish impulses now.

"So you understand nothing?"

"Nothing," Varya said, hiding her face.

"Then, look out!" Volodya said roughly and, hugging Varya clumsily, pressed her back against the windowsill.

The cold wind lashed at his cheek and noisily shook the rowan branches, but he was beyond noticing any of that, he did not even feel Varya freeing her hands and pushing him away; he only began to come back to his senses when he saw Varya's palm thrust at the crucial moment between his mouth and her pink lips.

"There!" she said.

"And very silly too!" Volodya, still panting, blurted out angrily.

"You must tell me of your love properly," Varya said gravely, without a smile, as she fixed her hair. "Understand? You've time enough for your germs, your Pasteur and Koch, but none for poor Varya Stepanova? Don't worry, I won't laugh at you."

"Shall I offer you my heart and my hand in marriage?"

"Your heart — yes, but I'll manage without the hand."

"You mean you won't marry me?"

"That's my business."

"But I thought it was all settled!"

"In what way?" Varya asked, surprised.

"It's simple enough: you and I will marry."

"In your spare time, Volodya dear?"

He blinked rapidly and said nothing: his heart was still hammering hard. Varya was reaching up to fix her grown-up hair-do, coiling her hair on the back of her head.

"I love you so much, Varya old girl!"

"As a pal?" she asked slyly.

"As a pal, too," Volodya said in some embarrassment.

"In your spare time?"

"What is it you want anyway? An ivory tower or what?"

"A tower wouldn't be bad either," she agreed complaisantly. "But a log cabin on a lake would be better still. There'd be just you and me, and later some little white lambs. We'd take Sharik and his new name along, too," she said with a twinkle in her eyes.

"You're awfully scared of being sentimental, Volodya. Just awfully scared. You'd rather die. But it's sad, you know. There *was* some sort of romance in it when you pulled my hair and twisted my arms, but now it's all 'nice and snappy', as our Yevgeny likes to say. 'You will marry me', and that's that. Ah, Volodya, Volodya! At times I feel years older than you."

"I don't understand, am I so bad?"

"Oh, you are not bad. You're good, rather. In your spare time, of course."

Without looking at him, she busily swept the bread crumbs off the table. And once again it struck Volodya how true her perception was and how exactly right her reasoning. Here she was, a mere slip of a girl, but already she could put her finger on what was funniest and shabbiest in a person, she could punish with a word and aim her sting at the sorest spot.

Varya really went for him that day.

All he did was wince.

But later she praised him.

"You'll make quite a decent worker."

"Is that all? Just decent?" he said feeling hurt. "And as for you, you'll make no sort of worker, believe me."

"Not all of us are geniuses in this sinful world."

"That's vulgar."

"But throwing my mediocrity in my face is not?"

"Stop it, I'm fed up," Volodya said sharply.

"Do you know another bad thing about you?" Varya asked as if she had not heard him. "Do you? You are merciless. Oh, you are so merciless! Volodya, you do torture so. I don't know how to explain it properly, but you either hate or adore."

"You, I adore," Volodya muttered ungraciously. "Especially when you are not delivering lengthy speeches."

Sharik came into the kitchen, his nails rapping sharply on the floor, and after a few turns at Volodya's feet, lay down.

Varya read two lines of a verse, inaccurately, as usual:

> *I shall sit by the fire and drink,*
> *A dog would be nice, I think...*

She was in a temper; red spots stood out on her cheeks.

"Do you know what you need me for? Do you?" she demanded after a while. "You need me, Volodya, dear, because I listen to your ravings not when I am interested but when you want to get it out of your system, when you want to be listened to. I know your worth and mine. All *you* have to say is interesting and important, of course. But anything that happens to *me* is of no importance or interest whatsoever to you. All I have to say is sure to be stupid. Will you deny it? And if you want to know, I read something very apt in a book last night and remembered the words: 'Autumn came into their friendship...' That's about you and me."

"Honestly, you're still such a kid," Volodya remarked condescendingly.

It was the worst thing he could have said. Varya left in a huff, she even slammed the door. Volodya was left alone with his sad thoughts and the sick dog. And, to give him his due, he certainly gave himself a good scolding for his indifference, hardness, rudeness, for his cursed selfishness, and finally for his meanness to Aunt Aglaya. The things he said to himself were more cutting by far than anything Varya had said. He swore he would not be a beast again. But was it his fault that while he was calling himself names his thoughts began to work in his mind, quietly, in a stealthy whisper as it were, thoughts that had long been bothering him on the chances of grouping illnesses, on the disorder of the chemistry in the human body, and then — furtively, like a thief, ashamed of his own action — he pulled down a volume of Gamaleya from the shelf to read one very interesting paragraph again, just one paragraph. Just one, to bring back the idea he had, to verify it.

And then it became imperative for him to look up other books, and naturally he did not hear Aunt Aglaya open the front door with her latchkey, come into his den and ask:

"Shall we have dinner, you simple soul?"

"M-mm," he mumbled, leafing through his book.

"Has Varya been gone long?"

"Who?"

And it only struck him on the way to Postnikov's that he had again failed to ask his aunt about her troubles.

## I DRINK!

It was all so strange, so different from what he had expected. He had imagined that even in his private life Postnikov was a rigorous ascetic living in a bleak room with a camp bed, a table and hard chairs, living amid his books which, Volodya fancied, he had stacks of. "He'll offer me tea, of course, but I think I'll refuse," Volodya was thinking on the way there.

The door was opened by Polunin. He was wearing an apron, the most ordinary of aprons, like the one Varya put on when she did the cooking. Ganichev had a towel tied round his waist, and there was another man there Volodya did not know, also wrapped in a dish towel. He was a thick-set, sunburnt man with a slightly Kalmyk cast of features. The hands of all three and Ganichev's face as well were covered with flour. "What's wrong with them?" Volodya actually felt alarmed for a moment, but the next he was sitting with them at a huge kitchen table on which *pelmeni* * were being made. Postnikov, who was busy rolling out the dough, nodded to Volodya, and Polunin said, "Oh, Ustimenko, you don't know Nikolai Yevgenyevich, do you?" The sunburnt man gave Volodya a long keen glance that he almost felt physically and then rapped out:

"Glad to meet you, how d'you do. I'm Bogoslovsky."

The name was familiar. Yes, he remembered now. He had heard it from both Polunin and Postnikov, and it was often mentioned in town as well, for Bogoslovsky was the head physician of the hospital at Chorny Yar and also the chief surgeon there. A lot of interesting things were said about this rather rustic-looking doctor with the clean-shaven head, and now Volodya found himself staring curiously at the "God-anointed doctor" as Polunin, ever stingy with his praises, had once called Bogoslovsky.

In the meantime, the three took up the threads of their interrupted conversation.

"I want to say one more thing, the last," Polunin said. "I shan't make a nuisance of myself after that, or you'll get angry. Well, there is one honest man in the history of medicine, if it comes to that, and his name is Time. You don't agree?"

"That *is* going far!" Bogoslovsky said with an almost imperceptible smile. "One man, he says! How you do get carried away, fancy one alone in the history of medicine!"

"But we're not speaking of subjective honesty; it's honesty of a different kind, objective honesty."

Polunin deftly tossed some neatly made *pelmeni* on to a dish sprinkled with flour, and said:

"Think back and see if it isn't true. The most honest

---

* *Pelmeni* — small round casings of dough filled with highly seasoned chopped meat, cooked and served hot with vinegar, sour cream, etc.— *Ed.*

of the early pioneers defended themselves when they were wrong, and the most honest people, erring too, put up a fight against truths that are today incontestable. All the long years of my life I've been thinking..."

"Years make men old, not wise. So don't brag," Postnikov said. "I know that from experience."

He put aside the rolling-pin, and his long fingers went to work very capably shaping the *pelmeni*. Volodya was hopelessly bad — the thin dough burst, the meat oozed out, and the edges refused to stick together. However, nobody noticed or, at least, they pretended not to notice.

The water for the *pelmeni* came to a boil; Polunin volunteered to lay the table, and invited Volodya into the dining-room.

"The *pelmeni* Postnikov makes are unexcelled," Polunin said as he set out the plates. "There are different ways of having them, but in this house it's art, pure art. No vulgarities, no eclecticism, *pelmeni* without embellishments. Do you drink vodka?"

"I do," Volodya lied a little too eagerly.

"And can you?"

"There's nothing to it, is there?"

"Don't be too sure."

As Volodya fetched the dishes, plates, glasses, knives and forks from the small sideboard he took in the whole room. It must have been a very nice room once, but now everything had a neglected look, the whole room wore a faintly musty, unlived-in air. It was as if the owner took no pleasure in coming here, as if he had just arrived or was about to leave. The rug lay crookedly, a curtain with a torn lining draped only one of the windows, and the tablecloths were kept in a suitcase. Books lay stacked on the floor, on the top of the wardrobe and on the windowsills. There was a table lamp but it did not work. A cat lay stretching languidly on the desk, one of those "garbage-can" cats; evidently its master gave it free run of the place, and it smelled of cat in the room, not man.

"We have a *pelmeni* tradition," Polunin said, lighting a cigarette. "We do it every year on Postnikov's birthday. He is a widower, we come without our wives and have a real stag party. And we always remember Olga."

"Who's Olga?"

"Olga Mikhailovna, his late wife. Here, take a look."

Volodya raised his head and crossed glances, as it were, with a pair of laughing, youthfully eager eyes that belonged to a sweet woman with fluffy and, apparently, very soft hair. Her hair-do was queer, "pre-revolutionary", Volodya thought, and in her hand she held a stethoscope.

"Was she a doctor, too?"

"Yes, and a very good one."

"Why did she die?"

"She caught typhus in a military hospital in 1918," Polunin replied, drawing hard on his thick cigarette. "And she died there."

"Really?" Volodya said.

Suddenly Volodya noticed a photograph of Alla, the Alla who always wanted "to have a snooze". The photograph was in a handsome leather frame with brass corners, and Alla looked out of it defiantly, as if to assert that she was the real mistress there and not the woman who had died in a military hospital in 1918.

"Tell me," Volodya said, looking from the portrait on the wall to the photograph in the leather frame. "Tell me, did Postnikov love his wife?"

"Very much," Polunin replied calmly and convincingly. "He hasn't forgotten her and loves her even now."

"Then what is Alla doing here?" Volodya demanded uncompromisingly. "Her photograph, I mean."

"You've condemned him already?" Polunin smiled wryly. "Didn't take you long, did it? You are developing into a hard specimen, Ustimenko, an extremely hard specimen. Take my advice: be easier on people, especially if they are real people."

Volodya wanted to reply, but he did not have the chance.

The door was kicked open by Postnikov carrying a huge tureen of *pelmeni*. Before getting down to them, they all stood up facing the portrait on the wall and drank full glasses of chilled galingale vodka. No words were spoken by anyone; as a matter of fact no one had known the woman well except Polunin. The *pelmeni* were really delicious, they were fragrant, light and terribly hot; Postnikov gave everyone a "special" sprinkling of pepper. He was a jovial host. Food tastes better, he said, when offered gladly. After the galingale vodka they had some pepper vodka, followed by ashberry vodka flavoured with blackberry leaves, and finally some Gudauty vodka made from wheat, which Postnikov called the "governor-general over all vodkas". Volodya became drunk at once, his face turned red, he gesticulated too freely and dropped his knife on the floor.

"Less vodka and more *pelmeni*," Polunin advised him.

Polunin drank without toasting anyone, a decanter of vodka flavoured with St. John's wort stood at his elbow and he took it out of a heavy green tumbler and not a vodka glass.

"Here's to you, Prov Yakovlevich," Volodya raised his glass.

"You'd better toast me in some *pelmeni*," Polunin suggested.

"I'm not a child!"

"Of course not, no one says you are."

The dinner was jolly, noisy and delicious.

Volodya felt a little ashamed of himself for starting that stupid conversation with Polunin and Alla's photo being there. It was just one of those things, when you came to think of it.

"In my stables..." Bogoslovsky was saying.

"Why stables? Don't you work in a hospital?" Volodya asked.

"I run a small farm to help the hospital," Bogoslovsky replied dryly.

"Goodness, I believe I'm drunk!" Volodya thought with alarm, and made a go at the *pelmeni*. "The main thing is to keep mum."

For a moment the pretty dishes with their blue-painted ladies and gentlemen, houses, windmills, boats and dogs swam before his eyes. He clenched his teeth and the painted dishes came to a standstill. "The main thing is will power," he told himself. The dishes swam again. "Stop, will you!"

Wasn't it all superb! And wasn't their conversation interesting, if only he were in a condition to follow it and not just snatch a word here and there!

"Oh, stop it! After all, every net is made up of holes," Volodya heard Polunin say.

"Jolly well put!" Volodya strained his attention again. "And how true! Every net is made up of holes. Varya will like that. But then she's mad at me."

He made a stupendous effort to thrust himself into their clever conversation, but they were on to surgery now and not nets at all.

"*Spas* * is right," Postnikov, sitting across the table from Volodya, meditated aloud. "*Spas* is right in everything."

"Can he mean Christ?" Volodya thought in drunken amazement before it dawned on him that *Spas* was short for Professor Spasokukotsky.

---

* *Spas* is the Russian for Saviour.— *Tr.*

"You often find that a surgeon can't handle his tools," Postnikov said. "To this day it thrills me to watch a carpenter, a joiner or a tailor at work. How beautifully they wield their chisels, saws or needles, as the case may be, how perfectly calculated their every movement, precise, and never wasteful. But we... You know how boys tease girls about the sissy way they throw stones, well that's what we do sometimes — handle the instruments in the same sissy way. But blast it all! The joiner and the tailor have a piece of wood or a length of cloth to deal with, and we have human lives."

"You're right, I agree absolutely!" Volodya shouted. He thought with jealousy: "Surely he doesn't talk of that to Alla, too?"

"I'm glad to hear that you agree," Postnikov nodded. "Help the young man to some *pelmeni*, will you?" he said to Bogoslovsky.

Volodya ate another plateful. "The young man!" What was Postnikov implying by that?

"By the way, if I remember correctly, Professor Spasokukotsky is the author of the maxim: 'Not a drop of blood on the surgeon's fingers after a herniotomy.' Right?" Volodya declared, articulating carefully to sound sober.

"Right," Bogoslovsky said, looking at Volodya with laughter in his eyes. "But why did you bring that up?"

"I simply asked," Volodya replied, working his mouth hard. "I took the liberty of asking a question. However, I must apologise. I was butting in, I believe. Two more words, or rather one very important, vitally important question about Professor Spasokukotsky's views on research work."

All were silent. The room grew still and frightening. Volodya clenched his teeth again. "So they think I'm drunk? I'll show them whether I'm drunk or not!" Mustering all his faculties, he asked in a loud voice, careful not to slur over the syllables:

"Is it true that it was Professor Spasokukotsky who said that scientific *initiative* is the *sole* token of the abilities of a scientific worker?"

"It is," Postnikov said, studying Volodya seriously with eyes that were not at all icy just then. "Spasokukotsky also constantly warns against *multiplication* of one's scientific works, that is, against bandying words on one and the same subject served with a different dressing."

"Lovely," said Volodya, growing limp again.

The dreaded moment was past. He had stood up to it.

133

And now he could relax on the sofa, as though to reflect.

"Ah, pussy! Hello, pussy!" he said cheerfully to the "garbage-can" cat.

Then he closed his eyes. The cat at once began to purr in his lap. Volodya's reflections were rather protracted; the table had long been cleared and the men were drinking strong, pitch black coffee when he returned to the party.

"Ah yes, *si jeunesse savait, si vieillesse pouvait*," he heard Postnikov say.

"What are you talking about?" Volodya asked Bogoslovsky in a groggy voice.

"Had a little snooze?"

"No, I was thinking..."

"A jolly good fellow, I know the sort, but when you put them to the test the fellows who're so jolly and good at a party prove to be not much good," Polunin said angrily. "And anyway," he turned to Ganichev, "it's all part of that delightful theory that good-hearted people are almost inevitably drinking people, and drinking people are sure to be good-hearted."

Volodya pulled a large cup of coffee towards him and reached out for the cognac bottle.

"Ustimenko, you've had enough!" Polunin told him sharply.

"Do you think I'm drunk?" Volodya asked darkly. "I'll toss off one more and there'll be nothing the matter with me."

"Enough! And behave yourself. You've slept some of it off, I should think."

"Maybe you'd like me to leave?"

"No need to leave, but don't bother the grown-ups."

They were arguing about Zhovtyak again, but with Volodya there they refrained from mentioning his name, presumably for educational reasons. Ganichev lost his temper. There was no arguing with Polunin, he said, and so he gave it up and went next door to borrow a guitar.

"Listen to this," Polunin said to Volodya. "It's *By the River, by the Bridge* in Latin."

He sang softly, accompanying himself on the guitar.

*Propter flumen, propter pontem...*

"I heard it all from him, every word, people like that have no shame," Polunin said a little later. "He was one of those practitioners with a three-year medical school education. A sly devil, a man of rare slyness..."

"He certainly is sly, but he was born a bit late," Bogoslovsky put in, chuckling. "Out of his time."

Ganichev, running his fingers over the strings, uttered wistfully, as if reciting to music:

"It's always their time. The time is always theirs."

"Listen, damn it!" Polunin shouted. "You don't often get to hear anything to beat this! During the war, when they were stationed near Volochisk somewhere, a child was born to the junior captain's wife, née zu Stakkelberg und Waldeck. I remember the name well because our flunkey and lickspittle pronounced all those 'zus' and 'unds' with a loathsome gasp of admiration. Well, she had the child and then she didn't like any of the doctors because they weren't attentive enough to her 'und-zu' infant if you please! That devil of a woman had all the orderlies running in circles; the junior captain himself began to take heart drops. It was then that our fine fellow suggested that they should call him in. 'I'll fix everything in no time, your honour,' he said. 'You'll have no complaints.' So he was called in. A doctor friend of his lent him his tunic and shoulder-straps. And there was our public servant, the champion horse in the stables of the regional medical service, armed with some instruments borrowed from the vet, of a size used on horses, needless to say, and he had also picked up a surveying compass and a tripod from the sappers. Madame zu Stakkelberg und Waldeck was astonished, impressed and moved, and came to believe in medicine once and for all time after that ignoramus and impostor had measured her and her offspring with the horse instruments, levelled the surveying compass at her, and, a couple of hours later, pronounced his diagnosis: 'All is well, but the child is somewhat delicate and needs special care which cannot be provided in front-line conditions.' The lady departed, leaving her junior captain free to carry on his affair with a Red Cross nurse, while our fine fellow received a hundred-ruble tip from madame and another hundred from monsieur. He made up his mind there and then to enrol in the medical institute because he clearly saw that the road to the stars, in spite of what Seneca said, was not so thorny after all. And he made capital of his lowly origin. Try and find out if he really comes from a Donets miner's family, or is it perhaps the crafty merchant class that he belongs to, as some people say. Try and catch him out!"

"We shall catch him out," Bogoslovsky said resolutely.

"Really?" Ganichev said surprised.

"Sooner or later."

"Oh stop it, Nikolai Yevgenyevich," Postnikov said wearily. "He's not the worst by far. And besides he's eternal. There have been people of his sort in the past, and they still exist today."

"He's eternal so long as all of you quake before him," Bogoslovsky replied grimly and disagreeably. "But once people stop doing his work for him, writing his articles and making diagnoses for him..."

Polunin raised his hand.

"Enough," he said. "It's time to go home, or else there'll be a fight."

"Let's take a little stroll. It's quite early yet," he said when they were out in the street.

Bogoslovsky and Ganichev declined because of the lateness of the hour, but Volodya naturally agreed. It was a cold night, late autumn had come into its own; the ground was filmed with ice, and it crackled under their feet. Polunin pulled his hat well down over his ears and raised the collar of his coat.

## Chapter Eight

### A NOCTURNAL CONVERSATION

"Do you remember the question you asked Postnikov about scientific *initiative* being the sole token of a scientist's abilities? D'you remember or were you too drunk?" Polunin suddenly asked.

"Certainly I remember," Volodya mumbled sulkily.

"And do you know about Mstislav Alexandrovich Novinsky?"

Volodya did not know a thing about Novinsky.

"In that case, come home with me," Polunin commanded sternly. "It's rather chilly. We'll have some hot tea, shall we?"

They walked across Market Square, passed the cathedral, and went down to the river. Polunin lived in a small detached house not far from the river station building. He opened the front door, let Volodya into the warm, dark hall, then switched on the light and pushed open the door into his study. Volodya smoothed his bristling hair and looked about him at the bookshelves, the polished yellow card-index boxes, and the huge desk piled high with manuscripts. With his ear on Polunin's heavy step coming from the inner regions of the quiet house, Volodya stealthily twirled the handle of the yellow Ericsson telephone and picked up the receiver.

"Number please," he heard at the other end.

"Six-three-seven," Volodya answered and, on hearing Varya's sleepy voice, said sharply, "Varya Stepanova, don't go to sleep. I'll be back soon. Or maybe not so soon. Wait up for me. I have to talk to you about something."

Polunin's step came nearer, and a woman's voice said fondly and cosily between yawns:

"The tea's in the left drawer, Prov dear, and the sweets..."

"Sweets, sweets," Polunin grumbled. "It's not twelve yet, and you've gone to bed already. We could have had such a nice chat."

"A nice chat, a nice chat," the woman teased him in a very comic way. "You've been keeping me from my sleep, for twenty-two years, you and your nice chats..."

Polunin returned to the study, made himself comfortable in a deep, old, leather-covered armchair and, indicating the card index with a nod, said:

"Very interesting hobby. The most up-to-date weapon of our times, one that can decide a battle before it's begun. Systematising is of paramount importance. I've invented the system myself, and I'm inordinately proud of it. The stories collected here are highly instructive and absolutely true. Well then, would you like to hear a story about Novinsky? While we're waiting for tea. Very briefly..."

He pulled out a drawer curiously labelled "Sergeant", took out a batch of closely written cards and spread them fanwise on the table.

"Why? Was Novinsky a sergeant?" Volodya asked.

"By no means," Polunin said with a chuckle. "The word sergeant on this box indicates Griboyedov's 'For your Voltaire some sergeant true I'll give Prince Gregory and you,' remember? Didn't you *do* him at school, as they say nowadays? Well then, Novinsky..."

Polunin lay back in his chair, half-closed his eyes, and told the story, flipping the cards but not looking at them.

"In 1877, having conducted a number of experiments on the inoculation of malignant tumours, Novinsky wrote a treatise of importance to the whole world. It was entitled 'On the Problems of Inoculating Malignant Neoplasms (experimental research)'. This work gave the impulse to the development of experimental oncology for many years to come. Cancer was subjected to the first real attack.

"Do you grasp the meaning of this, Ustimenko?"

"I do, Prov Yakovlevich."

"And now, can you imagine that this scientist, who would perhaps have become a very great scientist, a pioneer if ever there was one, was conscripted for service in the Second Don Cossack regiment under the command of General Count Loris-Melikov, and was never able to take up science again?"

"But why?" Volodya asked, frightened by the fury in Polunin's eyes.

"Because!" Polunin shouted. "Because! Didn't Doctor Novinsky have to do his military service according to all their damned rules? Could he afford to pay for the privilege of studying at the Academy of Medical Surgery? No. Well, then, he had to go and serve his tsar and his country. Petitions were sent in, correspondence exchanged, the decent members of society put up a hard fight for Novinsky, but nevertheless he was packed off to the back of beyond. Serve the tsar, ordered the general, that Griboyedov's bassoon, and Russia lost one of her great sons, while oncology was brought to a standstill for many years. His military service done, he had to make some sort of living, take any job available to keep his family alive, so what chance had he of going on with his experimenting?"

Polunin fetched the teapot and some sweets in a box, and poured out for Volodya and himself. Sucking at the cigarette that had gone out and pushing it from one corner of his mouth to the other, he glanced at a card with the corner of his eye and read out:

"'Appointed district veterinary surgeon in St. Petersburg.' It was his duty to examine animals brought into the city for slaughter or stud, horses including, and also to examine all animals leaving the city. That, in effect, is all."

"Is he dead now?" Volodya asked in a hushed voice.

"Oh, naturally! Certainly! And today he's completely forgotten," Polunin replied with bitterness and disgust. "Petrov was still mentioning him in 1910, but a book has just come out by Blumenthal, a foreigner, and our Novinsky is not in it. It's the foreigners again — Hanau and Moro. However, that's not the point, it's something else, something much more serious. One single stroke of a 'sergeant's' pen could bring to a standstill what might have been the greatest era in science, and stifle the thought of a man who would probably have been a great scientist."

Polunin put the cards back into the drawer and pushed it in. He got up and silently walked the length of the room twice.

"It would also make a pretty theme for an article entitled, shall we say, 'Careful, Honoured Generals!'"

"Did you like Bogoslovsky?" he asked abruptly, and without waiting for an answer from Volodya, went on, "A perfectly amazing man. Thinking of him in moments of sadness or anger makes it easier somehow. It's people like Bogoslovsky who will revolutionise the world, set up genuine law and order in it, and put everything in its proper place. I expect you'll have something to do with him sooner or later, so listen to this, it's quite interesting."

Volodya drank his tea. His head now felt quite clear, and it was a pleasure to listen to Polunin's deep steady voice. He was off on his favourite theme, he was telling about a real man, and his anger had given way to admiration.

...Bogoslovsky first came to Chorny Yar as a very young doctor with his wife, Ksenia Nikolayevna, a gynecologist, and their daughter Sashenka. The head physician at the Chorny Yar hospital was a certain Sutugin — a member of the Black Hundred, a pogrom-maker who had once devotedly served the land-owning Voitsekhovskys and the Chorny Yar merchant class, and who had even been sent by that rascally crew to Petrograd with a certain petition to the Duma. Needless to say, the reception he gave Bogoslovsky was hostile. "Ah, so you're a Bolshevik! Well, Comrade Bolshevik, we'll give you a taste of our Chorny Yar hospitality!" Sutugin looked like an English gentleman. He smoked cigars, wore spats, rode, and swam in the icy river. The hospital was crawling with lice, it was cold, foul, and the toilets were out of order. Polunin had been sent there to investigate, and even then it was obvious that Sutugin was an undisguised saboteur. He refused to attend the sick, he performed no operations, had a surgeon called in from town when the need arose, but strictly forbade his medical staff to come anywhere near the patient after the operation. "We didn't operate, so we're not responsible," he used to say. Another pet formula of his was: "The worse the better."

The moment they met, Sutugin asked Bogoslovsky if he was not the son of Father Yevgeny Bogoslovsky, the archpriest at the Kamenka Cathedral. "Yes, I'm his son," Bogoslovsky replied. "And did you join the Communists to weather these godless times?" Sutugin asked. "No, not for that," said Bogoslovsky. "It was to see that scum like you were not allowed within gunshot of public health."

Well, the fat was in the fire.

Bogoslovsky did the work, while Sutugin the would-be English gentleman penned complaints against him. Who didn't he write to! To the Gubernia Committee, the Uyezd Committee, the Military Commissariat, and the military commissar, too. And the better Bogoslovsky did his work the more harassing and numerous were the commissions, investigations, summons, and inquiries he had to cope with.

The complaints were not anonymous, not the kind that could be simply thrown into the fire. They were all signed, and the authors belonged to the former cream of Chorny Yar society, all cronies of Sutugin's.

Bogoslovsky began to show the strain. Accusations and the ensuing inquiries are not, as everyone knows, conducive to fruitful endeavour. He slaved all day and, instead of getting a good night's sleep, spent long wakeful hours thinking his bitter thoughts.

One day the secretary of the Uyezd Committee of the R. C. P. (B.) Comrade Komarets arrived at the hospital. Polunin knew him. He had once been a raftsman on the Uncha, a handsome, brawny red-haired chap, a dare-devil who loved a good song. He was accompanied by a young woman from the Gubernia Committee of the R. C. P. (B.), a certain Aglaya Petrovna Ustimenko. Perhaps she was a relation of Volodya Ustimenko?

"No, none," Volodya muttered the lie glumly. He did not want to be known as the relative of a prominent woman.

"You're lying, you know. However, please yourself," Polunin said, and then he resumed his story.

Komarets got the entire staff of the hospital together and proposed that they should discuss the present needs and the future plans of this institution, which because of its curious architecture was called the "aeroplane" by the local population. Many of the patients who were well enough to walk also attended. In the course of discussion it transpired that Bogoslovsky had done a great deal of good. The young woman from the Gubernia Committee got up and in a steady voice read all Dr. Sutugin's accusations, signed with different names, addressed to Moscow, to the Procurator's Office, to the Militia, to the Workers' and Peasants' Inspection, to the G. P. U. and to the Military Commissariat. She also read the conclusions drawn by all the investigators. The staff and the patients looked gloomy. They were frightened. They had already come to know and love their Bogoslovsky, and the baseness of

Sutugin's action appalled them. As for Sutugin, he went on smiling vaguely, a menacing yet cowardly smile.

"Well then, Sutugin, what would you call it?" Komarets said.

Sutugin was discharged. Komarets and Aglaya Petrovna said many kind things to Bogoslovsky and advised him to forget all this sordidness and carry on with his work with an easy mind. Before leaving, they made the rounds of the hospital once more. The building was in good repair, the steam heating was working, but the equipment could not have been poorer. There was also a shortage of bed linen, blankets and beds. The inflow of patients was on the increase, over 200 operations had been performed at the "aeroplane" that year, an unprecedented number.

"We shall have to do a lot of thinking, but we promise to help," Komarets said.

While he was doing his thinking, Bogoslovsky went to the glass works at Sibirtsy and held a meeting there. The workers unanimously agreed to contribute a day's pay towards the new hospital equipment. The same decision was adopted by the workers of the Rosa Luxemburg Saw Mill, the brick works and the Soldiers of the Revolution Steam Mill. The working class showed thereby how well it appreciated the importance of having a hospital of its own and the need for supporting a doctor like Bogoslovsky.

Having collected 7,447 rubles 9 kopeks, Bogoslovsky wrapped the money in a square of linen, which his wife sewed into his vest with thick, strong thread, and departed for Moscow. In the meantime, Sutugin sent a libellous complaint against Bogoslovsky to the Gubernia Committee. It purported to be from a group of workers requesting protection against Bogoslovsky, a quack and impostor who was extorting money from them. The signatures were legible. Sidilev, the hospital accountant, had very neatly forged the signature of Artyukhov, a sawyer who really existed, and also the electrician's. The book office had yielded other signatures that could well be copied. Sutugin's wife had done a good job of the miller's signature and some others besides. While the accusations contained in this cleverly concocted fake were being checked and rechecked, and until the filth could be completely cleared away, the Moscow authorities were requested in a telegram received from the Gubernia Committee to see that Bogoslovsky made no purchases and remitted the money he had collected to the Uyezd Committee. Bogoslovsky, who had not had time to buy anything yet, mailed the money to Komarets of the Uyezd Committee, and then had everything the hospital needed sent C. O. D. to the same Komarets of the Chorny Yar Uyezd Committee of the R. C. P. (B.). Overripe cucumbers and bread was all Bogoslovsky could afford to eat on the train going back home.

The instruments and fittings arrived in due course. Komarets, who had by then got to the bottom of Sutugin's latest fraud, paid for the order. At last Sutugin was taken into custody, and the hospital became a different place. Men came to Bogoslovsky to have their old hernias repaired, to get badly-knitted fractures reset or shell-splinters lodged in their bodies since the "imperialist war" removed; women came from villages far and near with their "gnawing", "griping", "pinching", "scabs" and other pains and mysterious ailments. It was now considered an honour to serve on the "aeroplane" staff, and Bogoslovsky beamed. Cocking his eye at you in his funny way and chuckling he would say, "If you make use of all the opportunities latent in our Soviet state system, you can accomplish a devil of a lot."

Artyukhov, the sawyer, a reliable, decent sort, headed the trio who made it their job to help the hospital. The business manager of the Sibirtsy glass works, one of trio, supplied the hospital with glassware rejects, while the third member, Kholodkevich, provided it with bran from the mill.

At this point Bogoslovsky displayed another aspect of his gifted personality; the acumen of a good husbandman. He had good practical sense, knew the value of "our daily bread", was no stranger to farming, and actively loved the soil and its blessings. Through the mail he ordered all the latest manuals on livestock raising, pig fattening, kitchen gardening and field-crop cultivation. Bogoslovsky and Plemenchuk, the supplies manager, fitted up a laundry in one of the wings and took in washing from the Chorny Yar population. The small town was baffled by the novelty of the venture at first, but then they decided to give it a try, though fully expecting all their linen to be ruined with Javelle water. The linen came through the ordeal unscathed. Out of the money made by the laundry with the lovely name of "Snow-white", Bogoslovsky bought the hospital's first cow and also called it Snow-white. And so it began. Within three years the hospital owned a whole herd of cows, the patients had all the milk, cream and cottage cheese they wanted, and the staff was allowed to buy dairy products for "private consumption" as well. The short, plump Plemenchuk bought some pigs at a state farm in the neighbouring gubernia. A pig farm was started. In due course they could afford to slaughter a pig a week. Bogoslovsky devoted all his spare time to the management of the farm, working out in the fields, at the dairy, or in the stables. In the summer his face peeled, and by the end of the day his shirt was pungent with sweat. His reading was a mixture of medical journals, articles about calving, siloing and poultry-breeding.

"Wouldn't a cheese dairy be fine!" Plemenchuk would say longingly. "It's not such a tricky business really, and I'm familiar enough with it. We'd make cheese for sale — the best Limburg and Backstein, and soft cheese in boxes. It'd bring in a lot of money. And in due time, we'd be able to build a new, civilised morgue."

"You're too commercial-minded, Plemenchuk. I don't like it," Bogoslovsky would brush the proposition aside.

Not long afterwards Plemenchuk was caught stealing in a big way. His lawyer, a man from another town, defended him fiercely and, with his glassy eyes on Bogoslovsky, hinted to the court that his client was only guilty of obeying the orders of his boss. The judge called the lawyer to order more than once, but Bogoslovsky felt soiled and ashamed. Plemenchuk, making his final defence, said tearfully (he was rather given to weeping) that he would have remained immaculately clean had it not been for the "atmosphere" at the hospital.

The court gave him only three years, but the prosecutor opposed the verdict and had the terms commuted to five.

So far so good, but the farm was now in for some mud slinging. Plemenchuk's dealings and then his defence had left a lasting stain on a praiseworthy and much needed undertaking. His wife, a typist at the uyezd finance department, busily spread all sorts of tales and rumours against which Bogoslovsky was powerless. And now the patients were often heard to say, as they sipped their delicious cold milk, that if *they* were refused none of this then how much must the management be stealing of it, what piles of money it must be making by selling the stuff on the side! And invariably they recalled the half-forgotten Plemenchuk, some calling him the deposed chief surgeon, others the assistant surgeon's wife, and still others the matron. The chairman of the Uyezd Executive Committee, a kind and obliging person, once said to Bogoslovsky:

"Isn't it high time you put your house in order, my good friend? People are saying all sorts of things."

143

"It has been put in order long ago," Bogoslovsky replied wearily. "You can't stop people's mouths, it's too bad."

Auditing commissions descended on the hospital; the bespectacled auditors burrowed in the accounts, drew up statements and uttered the cryptic "hm" of their profession. They wanted to see the circulars which permitted the hospital to set up auxiliary establishments such as farms. They demanded the written approval of the People's Commissar, the republican and the gubernia administrative bodies. They said the price of milk consumed by the patients was arbitrary, and after four more days of work raised it to 29 kopeks.

"You are a surgeon, aren't you," said the chief auditor of the fifth commission that came, a man with a spongy nose and a pendulous lip. "Why do you, a surgeon, want to soil your hands with these trifles? Hand everything over to the May Day State Farm. We'll arrange the transfer, and that will be that. I once read a book about Dr. Haase; he did his great work, you know, without all these beehives, cowsheds, pigs and hens."

Bogoslovsky raised his tired head and shocked the well-bred, highly cultured auditor with a coarse, clearcut and furious roulade. Bogoslovsky had a blasphemous tongue and liked to let himself go occasionally. The auditor's lip dropped even lower and his lumpy, spongy nose turned crimson.

"I happen to be doing my duty!" he said.

"So am I!" Bogoslovsky replied. "Lately, you've all lost sight of the fact, damn and blast you all, that besides the farm I have a hospital on my hands, of which I'm not just the head physician but also the chief surgeon, with all that implies..."

Bogoslovsky reached the end of his tether that spring. His quiet wife secretly got together the trio, headed by old Artyukhov. They composed a letter and had it signed by people whom Bogoslovsky had treated and operated on. After much thought, they addressed it to Aglaya Petrovna Ustimenko personally, for she was well known in the town, in the gubernia, in Sibirtsy and in Chorny Yar. They expected her to come herself, but instead there arrived a short, podgy man in thick-lensed glasses, a correspondent of the *Uncha Worker*. Bogoslovsky rashly took him for another auditor and spoke to him in somewhat rude tones. But Shtub, the podgy department chief of the gubernia newspaper, did not take offence. He put up at the farmers' hostel and calmly and coolly proceeded with his work. The emotional patients' letter left him as unimpressed as the pile denigrating the doctor. He was after the *truth*. And faithful to his own private system, that is, working along the spiral towards the centre, he reconstructed for himself, without bothering Bogoslovsky at all, the life of this country doctor day by day, month by month, and year by year. The work Bogoslovsky had been doing was splendid, humane and courageous in the true Party spirit. He found out, too, that when Bogoslovsky took a different road from his father's, that stern servant of God cursed his only child from the pulpit of Kamenka Church; he also found out that, foregoing his chance to remain on the medical institute staff after graduation, Bogoslovsky had deliberately chosen to work in a small remote village; he found out, among other important details, that Bogoslovsky's family *never* took anything from the farm, "no milk, honey, eggs, cottage cheese or pork". Shtub took the trouble of finding out everything about the patients who now came to the hospital from all over the gubernia and even from towns very far away. A crippled boy had been brought all the way from Astrakhan, and another patient, an elderly land surveyor, had come from Kaluga. Shtub heard much of interest from the staff, from Maria Nikolayevna the scrub nurse, Dr. Smushkevich the black-haired, energetic pediatrician, Uncle Petya the orderly, old Dr. Vinogradov the deputy head physician, Auntie Panya who had charge of the linen, and Rukavishnikov the new supplies manager.

Smart and saucy Dr. Alexandra Petrovykh, a very pretty woman, told Shtub about the mineral spring that had been discovered during the digging of the artesian well. Sutugin had known about the spring. There was a letter from the old swindler himself in the gubernia state archives claiming the water as his own private property on the grounds that his masters, the Voitsekhovskys, had made him a present of it. He had found it himself and had named it "Chernoyarskaya". Shtub only discovered these details, however, after hearing Dr. Petrovykh's story. She also told him that Bogoslovsky had taken a sample of the water to Moscow to get an analysis of it, and afterwards had had a long interview with some dimwit, trying to persuade him to give the order for the building of a small mineral water factory close to the hospital. But the dimwit had replied, fatuously, that mineral springs were becoming a disease, everyone was discovering them; he only wondered who would drink all the water. And then, he had said, the bottles presented some difficulty too. Bogoslovsky being what he was, had probably ended the interview with one of his roulades. He came back in a towering rage. Getting his trio together, they worked out an amazingly cheap method of piping the health-giving water to the wards, the dressing-room, the dining-room for the up-patients, and the kitchen. Rukavishnikov brought some thin metal pipes from town to carry the mineral water to the kitchen garden, and the soil quickly repaid its debt. The yield of vegetables almost doubled. Bogoslovsky then built some hothouses, and his patients had plenty of early greens — onions, parsley, dill and what not, they even had cucumbers before anyone in Chorny Yar could dream of them.

Shtub had his best laugh when he heard from old Artyukhov, who worshipped Bogoslovsky, how he had got the better of "that mean devil", the local priest, Father Yefimy.

The Cathedral of SS Peter and Paul, built in the last century at the expense of Zhukov Bros., the grain merchants, stood in a huge park, the far end of which had gradually been converted into a cemetery for the more eminent citizens of Chorny Yar. The park was still a favourite spot with the townsfolk, but no one was buried in the cemetery any more. It had fallen into neglect, and its magnificent cast-iron railing adorned with crosses was quite useless. The "aeroplane" had no fence at all. Bogoslovsky did not want to have a fence of stakes, and there was never enough money for a better one that would take in the entire hospital grounds, kitchen-gardens, yard, outbuildings and all. The absence of a fence, however, made itself felt quite badly. There was no stopping relatives from bringing patients strolling in the garden such forbidden things as pickled mushrooms, cucumbers and cabbage, with sometimes a half-bottle of vodka slipped in besides.

After thinking the matter over, Bogoslovsky donned his black suit, specially ordered for his Moscow trips, and went to see the local priest, Father Yefimy. He called on the malicious old priest every night until he finally succeeded in getting a meeting called of the church committee of ten. The trio, headed by Artyukhov, accompanied Bogoslovsky to that meeting at which he displayed his thorough knowledge of the Bible, the New Testament, the Book of Psalms, and other holy writings. An argument took place — polite at first, growing more flowery as it wore on and ending with roulades. Basing his claim on some splendidly chosen quotations from the church fathers, Bogoslovsky proved irrefutably to the committee of ten that the cast-iron railing should be handed over to the hospital, because giving succour to the suffering was a much more Christian cause than decorating churches. Father Yefimy argued himself hoarse; the committee of ten, after some vacillation, expressed divergent opinions, but in the end eight of the ten supported Bogoslovsky. The railing of the Cathedral of SS Peter and Paul was delivered to the "aeroplane" in carts belonging to the hospital, and was safely installed there. Soon after that, Bogoslovsky performed a most successful operation on the malicious old priest's hernia, and the old priest, strolling about the hospital kitchen-gardens fenced in with the church railing, sipping mineral water and marvelling at the bumper crops of cucumbers, onions, cabbage and other "blessings", was moved to singing psalms in a thin, husky warble, sighing contentedly, and finally admitting to Bogoslovsky that he regretted his recent rudeness and the "black words" he had used.

Shtub remained in Chorny Yar for about a month. Before he left he stole Bogoslovsky's photograph from the personal record file and made a copy of it. A week after his departure an article appeared in the *Uncha Worker* and the photograph was there. Reading it moved Bogoslovsky's wife to tears, and she said to her daughter:

"You see, Sashenka, your father was right. He's always right no matter how hard it is on him. I do hope you'll grow up to be like him."

Sashenka wept too. She loved her father and had suffered silently when all those auditors came to humiliate him; she had even eavesdropped when he confided his troubles to her mother. And now all that was over. Who was Shtub actually? How did he happen to know everything? Why was all he had written true? Weren't there some wonderful people in the world!

Bogoslovsky came home late that day, he was not his usual self, he seemed embarrassed and a soft laugh escaped him at every word. His wife Ksenia Nikolayevna baked a bilberry pie, and late that evening they had guests: Dr. Vinogradov, Dr. Alexandra Petrovykh, Dr. Smushkevich, who brought a bottle of home-made apple brandy, old Uncle Petya the hospital attendant, Maria Nikolayevna the scrub nurse, who brought some home-made liqueur, and Artyukhov. They sang *Gaudeamus Igitur, I'll Walk Through the Tall Rye, Black Eyes* and *The Seagull* that was "shot down in fun by a man unknown, to die with a flutter of wings in the reeds". Komarets arrived on horseback when they were in the midst of the song; he hugged and kissed Bogoslovsky, made a speech "on behalf of and on instructions from" someone or other, and rode away into the warm, starlit night.

"The press, when it proves equal to its task," said Smushkevich, the thin black-haired physician, "the press, when it has a sense of responsibility and understands its mission..."

"I say, let's dance," Ksenia Nikolayevna suggested. "Both Nikolai and I are good dancers, honestly we are. We can do the mazurka, the polka, the waltz, the Cracovienne and the pas d'Espagne."

Vinogradov was expounding his point of view to Alexandra Petrovykh.

"In my opinion, the results of our argument may be summed up as follows: perform or recommend only such operations as under similar circumstances you would agree to have performed on yourself or on someone you loved."

"How banal," she exclaimed. "That was maintained by Sydenham as far back as the 18th century."

Her cheeks were hot, she wanted to dance, but there was no one to dance with. Smushkevich was still holding forth about the press.

"I was there, too," Polunin sighed in reminiscence, ending his story. "But as a matter of fact, it was more of a consultation than a party. However, I really was an eyewitness to the victory won by Bogoslovsky and Aglaya Petrovna, your relative. It was a good cause well served."

"Have you put it all on record, too?" Volodya asked.

"No. There are only the dead in these small yellow drawers. These are miniature coffins, Ustimenko. I leave the living to you. When you begin to practise medicine, model yourself on people like Bogoslovsky."

The clock in another room struck one and Volodya rose to go. Polunin took him to the gate.

"Reflect on things," he said in parting. "It helps. But don't overdo it. A man lives by his deeds."

It was very late when he reached Varya's house, but after all he did have to relieve his mind of all the thoughts crowding it or didn't he?

"D'you want to talk?" Varya asked, curling up in a chair.

"I do. D'you mind, Ginger?"

No, she did not mind. Did she ever really mind anything he did?

"You're a real friend, and I'm a pig," Volodya said. "But, you know, Ginger, a man lives by his deeds." He added in embarrassment, "It's Polunin who says that, not I."

"All right, tell me everything," Varya ordered. "Only tell it properly. I hate a disjointed story. Well then, you were invited to Postnikov's. You came in. Now go on from there."

"I came in," Volodya went on. "I came in and began to make *pelmeni*..."

## TO THE "AEROPLANE" YOU GO!

The day before Volodya was to leave for his practical training he and Varya came across Polunin in the park. A brass band was blaring out from the white bandstand, the lilac bushes were already in flower, elderly citizens were strolling about in their tussore suits, and the stars glowed warmly in the deep, dark sky. Varya's hand was warm, too.

"Hello, Ustimenko!" Polunin called out.

Volodya squeezed Varya's elbow hard to warn her that something extraordinary and important was about to happen. Varya knew at once that the huge tall man was no other than Volodya's legendary Professor Polunin.

"Act as if you're terribly clever," Volodya told her, and greeted Polunin stiffly: "How d'you do, Professor."

Volodya became more formal and reserved with Polunin and Postnikov the more attached he grew to them, the bigger men he thought them, and the nobler their characters appeared to him. He did not want them to think him an ambitious toady like Misha Shervud or, what was even more intolerable, that he was currying friendship with them.

"Leaving?"

"Yes, I am."

"They say you're going to Chorny Yar, to Bogoslovsky?" Polunin asked, knowing perfectly well that he was.

"Yes, that's right."

"I'm glad. A doctor could learn a great deal from Bogoslovsky, even a doctor of experience, to say nothing of a medical student. However, you know him, don't you?"

Volodya blushed slightly remembering the *pelmeni* party and how quickly he had got drunk there.

"Why don't you introduce me to your friend?" Polunin said, changing the subject.

Varya gave him her rather large and always warm hand and said "Varya". She gazed up at the huge man who was so tall she had to crane her neck.

"Let's sit down and take a breath," Polunin suggested. "It's so stuffy today, there's no getting away from the heat."

His broad chest heaved laboriously, his expression was strained and weary; however, after lighting one of his thick cigarettes and taking a long pull with relish, he said in his usual manner:

"By a strange coincidence I was thinking of your career only this morning and of Bogoslovsky, too, although we did

149

discuss him rather thoroughly once. There's just one thing I want you to do, Ustimenko. While you're getting your training from Bogoslovsky, take good note of such little things as this, for example. It's undeniable that a surgeon proves his worth not so much by the operations he performs as by those *he does not* perform."

"Oh, how clever!" Varya exclaimed.

"I think so too," Polunin nodded. "An operation as such is a question of technique, more or less of course, whereas abstention from it requires mental ability of a high order, self-criticism at its most, exacting and faultless observation."

"I don't understand," Varya said, wrinkling her forehead.

"Shut up," Volodya snapped.

"The second thing you should take note of while working with Bogoslovsky, is the part played by the doctor's personality in dealing with the patient," Polunin continued earnestly. "It's like this, you see. Some patients only believe in their doctor when that doctor is a professor. And yet one can easily be a professor without being any sort of doctor."

"Is it your Zhovtyak he means, Volodya, the one who puts scent on his bald patch?" Varya asked.

Polunin smiled very, very slightly. Volodya nudged Varya with his elbow to stop her from making unwanted comments.

"Yes, without being any sort of doctor," Polunin repeated. "As far as I'm concerned, think what you please of me, but I see nothing heretical in thinking more of our stethoscope- and thermometer-armed country doctor, of his experience, acumen, keenness of observation, lucidity of reasoning, and, above all, his humaneness. Yes, of course, X-rays and laboratories are all very well, but one wants to trust a man more than one trusts machines. Your work and mine is *human* work, you must realise that. And with that in mind, study Bogoslovsky's approach to his work and his methods. He is a high-principled doctor, strong in spirit and tempered in battle. He relies on knowledge and technique, but also, and even more so, on the doctor's personality, on our ordinary and yet wonderful doctors. The best doctors are naturally the ones who combine the three requirements: knowledge, technique and personality. Build up your personality as much as you can while you're there, acquire as much as you can of that sterling pride of ours that once made Schweninger exclaim in a moment of crisis at his patient' bedside, 'You shall never see me at the end of my resources!' I'm inclined to believe that in that particular case it was the exclamation, the strength of spirit, more than the medical resources that brought the patient back to health."

"I agree with you! I agree absolutely," Varya said.

"I'm very glad you do," Polunin acknowledged politely. "Are you also a medical student?"

"Me? No, I personally work in art. That is, I'm still at technical school but I..."

"Study art at home?"

"No, at the studio."

"Oh, really? What is it — sculpture? Or painting, perhaps?"

"No, it's the theatre."

"I see, so you're dedicating yourself to drama?"

"Yes. We're taught by Esther Grigoryevna Meshcheryako-va."

"Her name isn't really Esther, is it? It's Yevdokia, and she has a double surname Meshcheryakova-Prussian."

Varya nodded. For all her devotion to her teacher she always felt a little ashamed for her having a double name and surname.

"It's a curious thing about the old actors, the young ones don't do it," Polunin said. "The old ones simply must have a double name with a beautiful sound. I remember I once had an old actor, Vronsky-Golundo and an ex-thief, an expert safe-breaker, in the same ward. The thief kept teasing Golundo. 'I've six names,' he'd say. 'Shkurin-Borovikov-Zunder-Prent-kovsky-Ivanov-Kassis, but at least they made me a pile.' Well, well... Yes, but what can Meshcheryakova teach you?"

"Why, her technique is amazing!" Varya said.

"But she's a hopeless actress, isn't she? You must forgive me. I'm speaking as a layman, but I should imagine that one can only learn the art of acting from people of talent. A doctor who teaches others must have a certain gift besides a mastery of technique."

"Meshcheryakova has a very subtle, individual talent, you're wrong there," said Varya. "And as for technique, Glama herself praised her for it."

"Ah? Glama?" Polunin drawled with his own peculiar chuckle. "Oh well, if Glama did, then I certainly have no right to argue. But did Glama really praise her, I wonder? And is it praise that matters? Take our Ganichev, Volodya's teacher. He for one has been subjected to harsh, I should even say insulting, abuse very, very frequently; still Ganichev is Ganichev, and there's no getting away from it. There you are..." Turning to Volodya he said, "I'll say once again that I'm very glad you are going to work with Bogoslovsky and not somebody else. Remember me to him and give him my best wishes. When does your boat leave?"

"At three in the morning."

"Well then, I'll see you in the autumn. It's a pity you can't work longer with him. I once read somewhere that before letting a professor teach he should be asked, 'Your highly esteemed learnedness, have you had at least a year's practice as a country doctor?'"

He laughed and shook Volodya's hand.

"See you on September 1st then. Good-bye, our future actress. 'My dear actresskins' — wasn't that how Chekhov wrote to his wife? And, by the way, Chekhov was a really splendid doctor and a 'country doctor' in the loftiest sense of the word."

Volodya and Varya got up to go.

It was not until Varya's letter reached him in Chorny Yar that he learnt that Polunin had died that night on the very bench on which the three of them had sat. His heart was very bad but he had never had it attended to properly, he died suddenly with an unfinished cigarette between his fingers. Perhaps it was the same cigarette he had lighted with such relish when they were there with him, perhaps the band had still been playing that popular waltz, perhaps Volodya and Varya had not gone far and Polunin, feeling an attack coming on, had called out to them. Anything was possible. No one knew exactly how it had been, no one would ever know.

Varya was the only person to see Volodya off. Aunt Aglaya was away on business. Volodya's baggage consisted of a pair of sturdy top-boots, a tarpaulin raincoat that stuck out stiffly, two volumes of Pirogov, and some books tied with string. He also carried a paper bag of salted herring, bought at the insistence of Varya's grandfather, who had assured them that the herring situation was tense in Chorny Yar. Besides these items, Volodya had some underwear, an air cushion, and a batch of envelopes addressed in Varya's hand to herself. He took along with him a small snapshot of Varya and one of his father taken during the Civil War. Yes, there was his dad, looking quite young and terribly plain, posing picturesquely beside his Sopwith with a smile that seemed to say: "Here I am, you people! Look what a fine big chap I am!"

Pych had left already, so had Ogurtsov. Varya was shivering: it was a cool night and she had on her new white, sleeveless dress made specially for the occasion. She wanted Volodya to remember her like that — someone very special and out of the ordinary! But he never even noticed the new dress, he was so engrossed in his thoughts of the morrow.

"Hey you, newlyweds, make way!" a sailor, carrying a huge bale, shouted at them.

There was a hollow rumbling in the bowels of the ship, the gangplank heaved and the ship's side grated against the pier.

"Take me in your arms, I'm cold," Varya said.

"That's silly sentimental stuff," Volodya replied.

Varya slipped under his arm and snuggled up close to him within the warmth of his coat. They had never known such intimacy yet, and Volodya looked with a thrill of amazement into Varya's happy, sly eyes. A lovely, damp freshness from the river clung to her hair, her heart was beating next to his, and her hand was in his own. Volodya closed his eyes, pressed his cheek to her fluffy hair and said huskily:

"Ginger, I do love you."

"That's what you say," she replied through her sudden bitter-sweet tears. "You care for nothing but Pavlov and Sechenov, and what was man born for and Herzen. They'll blow the third whistle now, kiss me."

Volodya kissed her closed mouth, wet with tears.

"Not like that," she said. "You kiss the dead like that. Give me a good hot kiss..."

Angrily, he parted her lips with his teeth and she clung to him with all her young, strong body. Somewhere close above them, the ship's siren blared.

"There was nothing in it," Varya said, twisting free of his strong arms. "I read in some book or other that kisses have a tart taste."

"Idiot," he snapped, hurt.

The gangplank was slipping from under his feet. Volodya jumped aboard, and the ship called *Uncha Hero* began to move slowly into the fairway. He sat on deck all night long murmuring, "Ginger, I love you, love you, love you." With bitter regret he recalled the hours they could have had together but had spent apart or with others, he remembered his stupid jokes at her expense, his taunts, his fatuous high-handed tone, and her eyes that were always wide open to meet his gaze, her readiness to see him at any hour of the day or night, her readiness to be amused, and her patience with him when for hours on end he discoursed on things that interested him but could not possibly interest her. "My darling, my darling, my dearest darling Ginger!" he thought as he paced up and down, stumbling over the sleeping deck passengers, and hearing none of the oaths that followed him. "Darling, I'm a fool, a beast, a worm."

Towards morning sleep overpowered him. On awakening he ate some bread and boiled sausage, and washed it down with lukewarm water from the drinking-water tank on deck; he wanted to go on with his thoughts of Varya, but he did not get a chance. Paddles churning, siren hooting, the ship began to swing in towards Chorny Yar pier.

"Hello, Ustimenko, don't you recognise me?" Bogoslovsky, even more sun-tanned than he had been in the autumn, called out to Volodya.

Bogoslovsky's much-washed cotton shirt was open at the neck, his moleskin trousers were tucked into high boots, and he carried a whip in his hand. The shirt and his cap, which he wore on the back of his head, suited him better than the dark suit and tight collar he had worn at Postnikov's that night.

"Are you going away?" Volodya asked, expecting Bogoslovsky to mount the gangplank and stepping aside to let him pass.

"Not on your life! I'm here to meet you."

People bumped into them with their suitcases, bags and baskets. Many of them knew and greeted Bogoslovsky. Volodya looked at him and marvelled. It was unheard of for a head physician to meet a student. They wouldn't believe him at the institute if he told them.

"I've had the experience of arriving for my first job, too, you know. The only difference between you and me was that I had already qualified," Bogoslovsky said as if in answer to Volodya's thoughts. "No horses had been sent to the station, and the old man who met me, a former S.-R. and, incidentally, a decent doctor, snubbed me good and proper. And, mind you, it took me 48 hours to get to my destination. A feeling of bitterness remained with me for a long time, you know."

The lively, dapple-grey horse pulled the buggy uphill from the quay into town. Bogoslovsky sat beside Volodya on the comfortable spring seat expertly handling the reins and greeting people to left and right.

"My respects to Maria Vladimirovna! Hello Akinfich! How are you, Pyotr my boy! Yelizaveta Nikanorovna, my respects!"

Shifting his thin cigarette from one corner of his mouth to the other, he spoke in his lingo of a countryman:

"We've got you board and lodging at a reasonable price, the landlady is an old Lettish woman, her name's Daune, she's a rare gardener, I've learnt a great deal from her. You'll be getting your milk from the hospital farm. A townsman like you, standing at life's starting point, should drink all the milk you can hold, until it sickens you. We sell it at cost price, 29 kopeks a litre. How d'you do, Anna Semyonovna! That's the Cathedral of SS Peter and Paul, colleague, we'll speak of it later. You are in for a tremendous amount of work, so watch your diet. Semyon Trifonych, good afternoon. You will be subordinate to me alone, colleague, I vote for one-man management, I am its supporter and truest admirer. Democratic centralism is a great thing..."

The horse's croup turned dark with sweat. Bogoslovsky deftly struck down a gadfly with his whip, and began to talk of that year's crop. Volodya stared at Bogoslovsky's hands — was he seeing things, did surgeons ever look and talk like this? His eyes were extraordinarily shrewd as he spoke of the cost price of milk, and he handled the reins like a hereditary coachman. But his hands, oh what hands! They were huge, broad and strong, spattered with freckles. Good God, what couldn't one do with hands like his! And once again, the amazing surgeon must have read Volodya's thoughts or the expression of his eyes.

"Besides I was born left-handed, my dear colleague," he said. "If an inborn defect is turned to good use it yields very fruitful results. My left hand has helped me both in fighting Kolchak and in surgery. It's a pity I can't pass on my experience in that field to anyone. If you happen to have a left-handed student friend be sure to send him to me, I'll make a splendid surgeon of him."

They were driving across fields. Larks were singing their high-pitched song in the hot blue sky. Bogoslovsky's shirt was wet through; a pleasant smell of horses, road dust, leather and tar hung in the air.

"There, you can see our 'aeroplane' now," Bogoslovsky said, squinting in the sun and pointing with his whip handle — a timeless coachman's gesture. "It's the former country seat of the Voitsekhovskys. During the First World War, those fine Russian patriots could think of no better idea than to build a hospital for Austrian officer prisoners of war. An Austrian architect, a baron, designed this crazy structure for them."

Volodya stared down into the valley. The building shaped like an aeroplane with wings, fuselage, tail and all, looked stupid and insolent, sprawling among the tall birches and limes. And suddenly that nocturnal conversation with Polunin about Bogoslovsky came back to Volodya in such vivid detail that it might have taken place only the night before.

"D'you drink?" Bogoslovsky asked suddenly.

"How d'you mean?" Volodya said, turning a painful red.

"Vodka, I mean. When we first met, you know, you got pretty soaked, and the impression you made on me was quite repulsive."

"That was the only time it ever happened to me in my life," Volodya said in crushed tones. "I must have overrated my capacity or didn't take enough to eat."

"Let's leave psychology alone," Bogoslovsky cut him short. "Here, take a look at our farm, you can see it all spread out below. We had a hard job making sense of that idiot baron's flight of imagination."

Checking the horse on the steep descent with sharp commands and skilful use of the reins, Bogoslovsky explained the layout pointing with his whip handle: there was the hospital, the outbuildings, the farm, the dairy, the kitchen-gardens and the village.

They drove into the village past a flock of children playing a noisy, jolly game with a puppy. It was the drowsy after-dinner hour. The passers-by were few, but all of them greeted Bogoslovsky. He drew up beside a neat white cottage with a tin roof, loosened the grey's belly-band, pushed open the gate, which responded with a homely creak, and said to someone pottering at the far end of the garden:

"Here you are, Berta Ernestovna, take good care of him. Vladimir ... and your patronymic?"

"You just call me Volodya."

"Oh no, everyone will call you by your full name *only*." Bogoslovsky said sternly, even harshly. "And if ever our old scrub nurse Maria Nikolayevna calls you simply Volodya, you are to correct her. Understand?"

"I understand."

"Good. And so it's Vladimir..."

"Afanasyevich Ustimenko."

"So your name in full is Vladimir Afanasyevich Ustimenko. Very good. And now let's go and see how they've accommodated you."

The old landlady, a little overawed, took them to Volodya's room. It smelled of freshly scrubbed floors and baked bread; pink morning-glories of an extraordinary size quivered beautifully in the breeze outside the low open windows. A brightly burnished, loudly spluttering, lop-sided old samovar appeared almost at once; next, the landlady brought in a plateful of

156

caraway buns and some jam in a glass bowl — marvellous rhubarb jam.

"How d'you like it?" Bogoslovsky asked sternly.

"It's splendid," Volodya replied.

"You'll pay Berta Ernestovna a month's lodging in advance," Bogoslovsky continued as sternly. "You'll also give her some money for the milk, she'll fetch it for you. There are no bedbugs or other vermin here, I guarantee that. And now, let's sit down and enjoy our tea, I feel rather tired, I operated this morning and didn't get any sleep last night; they called me to the hospital twice."

He sat down, wiped his face and neck with a huge, immaculately clean handkerchief, made the tea and poured Volodya's weak and his own very strong. There was a pensive expression on his sunburnt face, and at that moment it looked very handsome — the face of a Russian peasant, the cheekbones high and the forehead prominent, a man of rare health both physically and morally.

Volodya was silent, too, enjoying the stillness, the breeze, the tea and Bogoslovsky's company. He thought not without pride: "Imagine, that amazing person is sitting here with me, he's not anxious to go either. Does it mean that he likes my company too?"

### ROULADES

After his second cup of tea and more wiping with the handkerchief, Bogoslovsky said somewhat morosely and without looking at Volodya:

"I must warn you on one score, Vladimir Afanasyevich. You're a good-looking lad and young. It's entirely your own business if it's love, or an attachment involving the loftiest ideals and the corresponding emotions, which, in due course, lead us all to the registry offices, or whatever you care to call it. But if you, my dear colleague, imagine that the hospital nurses are there to..."

And here Bogoslovsky let out a roulade of swear-words so lusty and descriptive, albeit in the same morose, even bored voice, that Volodya glanced round to make sure that the old landlady was not within earshot.

"That I shall certainly not stand for," Bogoslovsky resumed his polite manner. "If anything of the kind comes to my notice, and be sure it will, I shall throw you out at once, and I won't even provide a buggy to take you to the ship. It is in this sense precisely that our hospital has become known as the 'Bogoslovsky Monastery'. Will you consider yourself duly warned?"

"I will."

"I had to warn you, you see, because we've had such a precedent. Now then, let's get down to business."

In later years, whenever Dr. Ustimenko, not a timid soul by any means, recalled that two-hour conversation, he always broke out in cold sweat. Sipping his fifth cup of tea and glancing at Volodya with a shrewd, affectionately intent look, Bogoslovsky bombarded him with volley after volley of utterly unexpected questions, probing his knowledge from every angle, attacking him with sudden fury, making him doubt the correctness of his answers, repeating his questions with a little laugh, till Volodya was swamped in the endless flood of his damned "now then, supposing we add this to the given symptoms..." By the end of the second hour of this, poor Volodya turned pale and felt as sick as a spiderman on his first climb or a passenger new to air travel.

"Tired?"

"I feel sort of sick," Volodya confessed.

"It was the bowl of jam you gobbled up while we were talking," Bogoslovsky observed. "There was at least a pound of it. Drink some tea, it'll rinse your insides."

"So it was the jam!" Volodya thought resentfully. "So he's blaming it on the jam, is he! Pretending he's a nice sort. The man's a fiend!"

To Volodya there indeed seemed to be something fiendish in this left-handed surgeon with the high cheekbones, in his contented grunts over the tea, and in the way he glanced at him, sideways like a cock. Nevertheless Volodya won that small battle, he knew it. But this first battle with Bogoslovsky was only a verbal one, he wondered what it would be like at work. He shook his head dizzily at the thought of all the trials fate held in store for him in the person of Comrade Bogoslovsky, head physician of the Chorny Yar hospital.

In the meantime, Bogoslovsky had gone to the window and, perching on the windowsill, was already deep in conversation with the landlady, asking her what she intended to give the young *doctor* for dinner that day, and advising her how best to make the *doctor*, a very good *doctor*, an able *doctor*, though still a young *doctor*, drink as much milk as possible in order to restore the health he had undermined by studying too hard.

"Doctor! It's me he's calling a doctor," Volodya thought to

himself. "I'm not even an intern, yet he calls me a doctor already!"

Once again his self-opinion grew, but not for long, for a very brief moment, in fact.

"See you tomorrow," Bogoslovsky said, and there was ambiguity in his next words: "You'll report to me at eight, and then we shall see."

What did he mean: "We shall see"?

"Thanks for your kindness," Volodya replied dryly. He was no simpleton either, he was too old a bird to be caught with chaff. "You think me useless, but we'll see, we've yet to see!" he said to himself as he paced the creaking floor.

His feelings were strangely mixed: admiration for the man and fury. But there was far more admiration.

"I didn't eat a whole pound of jam either," again Volodya remembered angrily. "There wasn't more than a spoonful in the bowl anyway." He was already hungry for his dinner, the feeling of nausea had gone, and now he felt only a slight twinge of fear at the thought of tomorrow. But it was an exciting sort of fear. "Never mind, we'll live and learn," he thought. "You weren't born a surgeon either, Doctor Bogoslovsky. You were like me, too, once."

After gorging himself on milk soup, cottage cheese dumplings with sour cream, cottage cheese with honey, and then more sour cream with sugar, *Doctor Ustimenko* went out into the garden, put Pirogov's Volume One beside him for the sake of appearances, and after chewing on his pencil for some time began writing a love letter to Varya. A small tow-headed boy ran through the garden blowing on his whistle.

"Quiet, Caesar, quiet, the doctor's working," the landlady hissed at him terribly.

Caesar, who was young enough to run about the garden with practically nothing on, gave Volodya a frightened look and darted into the currant bushes where he could be heard moving about and grunting softly for a long time. Volodya wrote on and on. He had never realised that he loved Varya so much and had loved her so long. In his present elevated frame of mind, however, everything appeared bigger than life-size, more extraordinary and grander than it really was. The garden, the table at which he wrote, the landlady's daughter or was it granddaughter — a tall, strong, broad-shouldered Lett, the warm twilight, and the thought of having to report at the hospital tomorrow, it was all amazing, extraordinary, never known before.

*"We're the Red Cavalrymen"* Volodya hummed, while his pencil raced over the paper.

"You see, Ginger, maybe he'll really throw me out tomorrow, he's a fiend, but I shan't go," Volodya wrote, quite forgetting that the paragraph before was devoted entirely to love. "I've got to work with him and find out where this man's strength comes from. I also want you to know that when a young doctor comes to work with me some time in the future I'll..."

Volodya thought it over and, crossing out the words "young doctor" wrote "student" instead.

"When a fourth-year student comes to work with me, I'll give him the welcome I was given here."

It was amazing what nonsense he wrote all that afternoon. He marvelled for a long time afterwards that Varya had been able to make sense of his jumble of feelings, thoughts, defiance, conceit and fright. Before supper, Dr. Ustimenko hurried to the Yancha, a tributary of the Uncha, took a dip in the bright moonlight, did a few overarm strokes, got out, dressed, chased some strange little beast in the grass, and then took a sedate walk home. His bed was already made, a cricket was chirping in the house somewhere, he wanted to concentrate, to "give himself a full account of everything", as Varya used to say, but he fell asleep the moment his head touched the pillow, and slept like a log till six next morning.

Bogoslovsky took him on his rounds and introduced him to the staff in expressionless tones: "This is Vladimir Afanasyevich Ustimenko, a medical student."

Volodya bowed in a stupid way, blushed terribly and tried to make himself inconspicuous. Making the rounds took two hours. After that Bogoslovsky had a talk with the other doctors. Volodya could not understand what it was all about, but one thing he grasped at once: Bogoslovsky was not a man to be trifled with. The dark and pretty young doctor's tears and promises got her nowhere.

"I shall discharge you," Bogoslovsky said clearly and solemnly. "Moreover, I shall give you the worst possible character. You are free to take your complaints to anyone you please. The chief physician of the Chorny Yar hospital, the petty tyrant, the clergyman's son, the kulak, or whatever else it's customary to accuse me of, will not be intimidated. Add that to your complaint. The matter is now closed. Vladimir Afanasyevich, are you there?"

"Yes, I'm here," Volodya replied in a choked voice.

"To the operating room. You will assist me."

Bogoslovsky stopped to talk to someone in the corridor, and Volodya went in alone. He had already begun to wash his hands when he noticed a seat like a bicycle saddle beside the washstand; pushing it towards him with his knee he sat down.

"Well, well!" someone said behind him. It was the scrub nurse, Maria Nikolayevna, a lean woman with the face of a martyr.

Volodya ignored the "well, well!" He made himself more comfortable still and, whistling a tune, went on scrubbing his hands according to the rules.

"Whistling too!" Bogoslovsky said, coming into the room. "You're a bit young to scrub sitting down, my good man."

Now Volodya understood the irony in the "well, well!" He jumped to his feet, but Bogoslovsky said:

"Finish your scrubbing, now that you've begun."

Pressing on the pedal of the other washstand, Bogoslovsky proceeded to scrub his huge hands, hairy with reddish fluff. He did it with pedantic care. Volodya stole a glance at him: Bogoslovsky was frowning thoughtfully.

They worked in the operating room till two in the afternoon. Volodya felt weak in the knees, he had a splitting headache, and his shirt was stuck damply to his back. Bogoslovsky was as fresh as if he were only starting on his day's work. Scrubbing his hands, he sang softly to himself:

> *My star, my precious little star,*
> *Shine for me in the dark of night,*
> *You are my one and only guiding light,*
> *There'll never be another one...*

No comment at all was made on Volodya's work. Perhaps this surgeon who looked like a wood goblin had forgotten Volodya was there.

Bogoslovsky hung up the towel neatly and turned to Volodya abruptly.

"Do you know who it was we operated on today?"

"You mean the gastrointestinal anastomosis?"

"No, the prolapse. That was Sidilev, the accountant we used to have. It was Sidilev, you know, who helped Sutugin to get all that false evidence against me. They sent in fourteen reports in all to different places. Eventually the old bird was transferred to Zarechye, but fate brought him here again. Sidilev's wife is absolutely convinced that I'll make short work of him on the operating table, she declared it formally to everyone only this morning. Frankly, I felt rotten just before he was given the anaesthetic. There was the old man looking at me, and I saw from his expression that he honestly believed the hour of my bloody vengeance was drawing near. God, isn't it disgusting!"

Bogoslovsky shuddered and a bitter look came into his face.

"But why did he write all those things?" Volodya asked quietly.

"Was he the only one? He's an angel compared with the others. It was an eventful time."

They went through the anteroom, down a curving passage, and came out into what Volodya thought was the tail end of von Staube's, the architect's, flight of fancy. Birches were murmuring gently outside the open bay windows. The nurse on duty got up at Bogoslovsky's approach and he acknowledged it with a short nod. Volodya also nodded with dignity, never thinking that disgrace would soon crash about his poor ears.

Bogoslovsky sat down on a white-painted stool beside the patient, picked up the man's sinewy, yellow and lifelessly heavy hand, and took his pulse. The case history lay on the bedside table. Had Volodya glanced at it with even half an eye, everything would have turned out differently, but his natural decency forbade peeping.

"I say, Yegorov," Bogoslovsky said to the patient.

"It's no use," the nurse said. "He was very far gone when they brought him in."

"Look him over," Bogoslovsky ordered Volodya. "Make the examination and draw your conclusions."

The nurse obligingly helped Volodya to examine what he took for a carbuncle. It was disappointingly clear. Was it really worth Bogoslovsky's while to show him a case so simple?

"Well? What do you think?" Bogoslovsky asked a moment later.

"An incision has to be made," Volodya replied.

"Are you sure? Yegorov works in a workshop that makes felt boots, bear that in mind."

Oh, why did he turn a deaf ear to that remark about felt boots! But the young are hot-headed and touchy. "What have felt boots got to do with it?" A fleeting thought ran through Volodya's mind. "You won't make a fool of me, Dr. Bogoslovsky. Oh no, you won't."

"It is imperative to operate," Volodya declared stiffly. "Take a look at the oedema yourself. The general condition is grave too. There's the localisation on the neck; a carbuncle like that may lead to meningitis."

162

Bogoslovsky's eyes, which had a slight Tatar slant, regarded Volodya with mounting animosity.

"Well? And how will you operate?" he asked.

"I'll make a cross incision through the healthy tissues, liberate the edges of the skin flaps, removing the necrotic tissues naturally, excise the abscess and thoroughly drain the cavity..."

Suddenly the nurse heaved a mournful sigh.

"And you do not consider it necessary to make a bacteriological analysis of the pus?" Bogoslovsky asked in an unpleasantly calm voice. "Eh? A fatal little mistake might occur, you know."

The patient groaned weakly and began to toss about.

"Read his case history, Doctor Ustimenko," Bogoslovsky said with no trace of sarcasm, merely stressing the word doctor.

He sent the nurse on some errand or other. Volodya heard his voice as through a thick fog, but he did realise that Bogoslovsky was sparing his feelings.

### ANTHRAX

The words "*Pustula maligna* — anthrax" leapt at Volodya out of the page. Pinpoints of sweat broke out on his forehead. He noticed that the words about the felt boot workshop in the village of the Razgonye were underlined in red.

"Well?" Bogoslovsky asked again.

Volodya could not bring himself to look at Bogoslovsky, but when he did so at last he noticed that the man's expression was not gloating at all but rather sad and dejected.

"You must be more observant, my lad," Volodya heard as from a distance. "Being observant demands energy, you know. We came here through an anteroom that has a sign over the door: Isolation Ward. We turned down two corridors and again came to a door with a sign above it: Entrance to the Isolation Ward. Besides, I drew your attention to the fact that Yegorov is engaged in making felt boots, in other words, that he handles wool which may be carrying an infection. And still you said operate. Aren't you quick with your scalpel! Any incision is definitely contraindicated."

"I do see it now," Volodya brought out.

"Absolutely contraindicated," Bogoslovsky repeated in a voice of steel that rang with unquestionable authority. "Incisions, probing, tamponing and all the rest are definitely contraindicated," he stressed the last two words again, shaking his finger at Volodya. "Traumatising the focus leads to penetration of what?"

"Of bacilli, of course," Volodya said with a sigh of relief. "It leads to the penetration of bacilli into the blood and to the development of a grave septic condition."

Bogoslovsky smiled.

"Good for you. What is the treatment prescribed?"

Volodya mentioned serum inoculation and intravenous injections of Salvarsan. Bogoslovsky stood thinking of something, absorbedly and gloomily.

The nurse came back, and only then Volodya noticed that you came in through one door and left the room through another. He and Bogoslovsky scrubbed their hands carefully and left their white gowns in the anteroom. They went out into the garden.

—"I'm going to send you on a none too pleasant mission," Bogoslovsky said, sitting down with a sigh of weariness. "This is Saturday; tomorrow there'll be a Sunday fair at Razgonye. The locality must be proclaimed unsafe, all necessary measures must be taken, and with the assistance of the veterinary inspectors that confounded felt-boot establishment must be disinfected. The source of infection must be destroyed, Vladimir Afanasyevich. The thing is that Yegorov is already the third anthrax case from there. We had two lethal cases, one was intestinal and the other pulmonary. Our epidemiologist is gone, I was obliged to part company with her (Volodya recalled the incident that morning), she was a worthless creature, weak, cowardly and quarrelsome. I shan't be able to get away myself, I've several operations scheduled for tomorrow, and anyway I can't leave the hospital just now. Your job is to impose a quarantine on the place, put a veto on the fair, make a detailed investigation on the spot, and deliver the Razgonye villagers from anthrax. Come along, I'll make out the documents, write a memo and compile a list of people who may be of help to you. And there's something else besides."

While Bogoslovsky was busy writing, Volodya searched rather feverishly through the books in the library next door. On the whole, as far as prophylaxis went, he knew everything. He looked up the Ascoli test once more, and now he felt fully prepared.

Out in the yard he found a whiskered attendant putting some tanks, lengths of hose, a few large straw-covered bottles, a couple of axes and, strangely, a boathook, into a buggy.

"You may rely on that man entirely," Bogoslovsky said,

leaning out of the window. "I've worked with him for many a year, I know him and trust him. Do what he advises you to do. I've also got to warn you that there's an official there, Gorshkov by name, a nasty piece of work, venomous, spiteful and thievish. I don't quite understand it all yet, but he's been up to something."

An hour later, Volodya — hungry, tired, cross and proud — got into the buggy. It was drawn by the same dapple-grey that had brought him to Chorny Yar. The day was sultry and still, as if tensed to meet a gathering storm. Uncle Petya the attendant, whose old soldier's face was adorned with a tow-coloured moustache, gathered in the reins unhurriedly and shouted to the gatekeeper, "Hey, Fomochkin, open up!"

The horse moved off at a smooth trot. Volodya opened his newspaper with a rustle. The insurgents were again advancing on Bilbao. "The fascists' air force is committing atrocities with impunity ... mass annihilation of the peaceful population ..." he read. "Junkers planes have already destroyed Guernika, the holy city of the Basques, and are now out to make Bilbao into another, a larger, Guernika."

Volodya clenched his teeth.

"Where are you, Dad? Are you alive? You must be having a very hard time. Out of one battle into the next, back from one flight and off on another? You're not the sort to idle your time away at a café with *that* going on in the world."

Uncle Petya was a talkative soul. He started chatting the moment they drove out of the village and only paused now and then to roll and light another of his fragrant cigarettes that were flavoured with clover.

"Our surgeon is no ordinary man," Uncle Petya's tone challenged any objection that might come from Volodya. "We, the junior medical personnel who've worked with him for some time, respect him above all others and we'll stand by him, we won't let no harm come to him. You're a young doctor, you're here today and gone tomorrow, we've seen plenty of your sort and we can speak our minds if the need arises, but he, now, he belongs to us. Medicine can't do everything easily yet, but what it can do our surgeon knows through and through. You're a young doctor, I often have to take your sort back to the boat..."

"What has my youth got to do with it?" Volodya was stung into interrupting. "And as for going back to the ship, after all I'm not a doctor, I'm only a student, and I have to finish the institute first."

"That's as you please, it's not for us to meddle," Uncle Petya carried on in the same level voice. "But what we do see is young chaps swaggering about the place for a while, learning a bit from our surgeon, and then taking to their heels without so much as a thank you. We, the junior medical personnel, see everything. We say nothing, of course, we're not asked, but you can't stop us from seeing things. We have our say when there's a Party members' meeting. You a Party member?"

"No, I'm still in the Komsomol."

"Non-Party, in other words. We'll leave confidential matters out of this then. But we say what we say at closed Party members' meeting. And it's no one's business."

Volodya sighed with boredom. The trip was a long one and Uncle Petya talked without pausing for breath. The day was unbearably hot and close. Blurred outlines of cottages appeared in a shimmering haze beyond the gullies, a low rumbling was already coming from the west, and a thundercloud was creeping up the sky.

"Is that Razgonye?"

"It is," replied Uncle Petya, fluffing out his tow-coloured moustaches. "There'll be trouble enough with that Matvei man."

"Who's that?"

"Why, Gorshkov, the chairman. What with the fair tomorrow, I bet he's been drunk since dawn."

True enough, Gorshkov was tipsy. They found him sitting outside his cottage teaching tricks to a mangy lop-eared mongrel. His gaze was heavy, leaden.

Hammers were banging away round the corner, where a merry-go-round was being erected in the square. A tousle-haired man with a fat neck was shouting directions in front of a stall on which a signboard bearing the words "Delicatessen, Wine and Other Goods", was being nailed up. A tall, imposing militiaman was lecturing an old woman peddling sunflower seeds out of a basket; she was a representative of the fair's "private enterprise" sector.

A young woman, visibly pregnant, came out of the house and handed Gorshkov a bowl of skim milk. With a long fingernail he fished out a fly, blew on the milk, took a sip, and then turned his stare on Volodya.

"Want to see me?"

"Yes, if you're Gorshkov," Volodya replied with the loathing he always felt for drunks.

"You're from the factory?"

"No. There have been three cases of anthrax among the members of your workshop, that's why I'm here."

"So we're back to where we started," Gorshkov said with a weary sigh. "I sent one goddamned nuisance packing, and now here's another one! Tobik, bite him."

The dog sniffed Volodya's boot and sprawled out on the ground.

"There will be no fair tomorrow," Volodya declared firmly and clearly. "A guard has to be stationed around the village. We shall begin by disinfecting the workshop premises at once, that is, your raw material stocks. After that..."

"Can't be done," said Gorshkov.

"What do you mean?"

"Simple enough. Can't be done and that's that. We've already adopted a decision to burn down the workshops, as being the source of infection. We've already delivered the kerosene, the wood shavings and the water tanks to the site. Hey, Babichev!" he suddenly yelled to the imposing-looking militiaman.

Babichev came up, treading softly in his fine kid boots.

"Are we burning down the workshops?"

"We are," Babichev replied, regarding Volodya with his big liquid eyes.

"And they're forbidding us to hold the fair."

The militiaman laughed, showing his beautiful white teeth.

"The source of infection has to be destroyed at the root," he said. "If carcasses of diseased animals are subject to burning, surely wool and ready product containing bacteria must also be burned? We're not quite ignorant here, you know, we are well informed." He gave Volodya a knowing wink and added, stressing the syllables, "We have consulted..."

"Whom?"

"We know whom to consult."

"Listen Babichev, don't try your double talk on us. I know you, and you know me," Uncle Petya said sharply, coming to the fore.

They measured glances, and Babichev seemed to wilt.

"Whom did you consult?"

"The chairman did, I didn't," Babichev said indicating Gorshkov with a nod.

He retreated a pace or two.

"Wait a bit," Uncle Petya said. "Have you taken an inventory of the stocks as of date? Where's the auditor's statement?"

Volodya gaped at Gorshkov open-mouthed, like a child. The

truth was only just beginning to dawn on him. Gorshov ran his tongue over his lips, started to get up, and sat down again.

"Are you in your right mind, you whiskered devil?" he shouted at Uncle Petya. "How can I let people go in there with those bacterias of yours hopping about all over the place? Supposing the auditor gets bitten, who'll be blamed? Gorshkov again, I suppose? Or supposing you go inside and catch it, who'll be responsible? Me? Oh no. I'm not letting anyone in there. The place has been sealed up in Comrade Babichev's presence and it's got the board's seal on it. A fly couldn't get in!"

Babichev took a few more steps back, retreating towards the square. Uncle Petya watched him go with a calm, almost vacuous, stare.

"All right, we're humble folk, it's not for us to decide," he said in weighty tones with a wink at Volodya. "I'll keep your company in the shade here, give my legs a rest, while Vladimir Afanasyevich goes and gets instructions on how to set about the burning. It can't be done in the ordinary way, it's got to be scientific, not just a burn-up but a comprehensive disinfection *normalis*."

Uncle Petya's scientific parlance had the drunken Gorshkov completely beaten. His discoloured mouth opened and he broke into a raucous song.

"This business means the criminal code and prosecution for misappropriation," Uncle Petya whispered to Volodya. "That's what you come across when you take up medicine. I'm an old bird, I saw what they were up to and bowled the bastard over with that *normalis* stuff."

Thunder crashed in the sky above the broom grove behind the chairman's brand-new, well-built house. It grew unbearably close; an ominous, rainless, dust-raising storm was coming.

"Take the buggy and drive for all you're worth along the old highway, across the bridge, and all the way to the military camp," Uncle Petya whispered to Volodya. "When you see tents on your right and tethering posts, stop. Ask for the army surgeon, Comrade Kudimov, and bring back some cavalrymen. Otherwise they'll burn down the premises with nothing in them, try and catch anthrax by the tail then. Ready product worth thousands will also be as good as gone. You tell them to send someone for the prosecutor or the investigating officer. Get the militia, too, we've some mounted militiamen in Chorny Yar to make the enemy quake!"

"Look out, they might bump you off, Uncle Petya," Volodya whispered.

The merry-go-round in the square was given a trial run. Gorshkov sat bellowing songs at the top of his voice.

The young woman appeared in the doorway again, this time bringing a bottle of vodka, some radishes and salted herring on a plate.

"Hey, docs, steer this way," Gorshkov called out to Uncle Petya. "Let's make a disinfection *normalis*, let's drink when the lightning flashes and guess our fortunes."

Uncle Petya sat down, fluffed out his splendid moustaches, and accepted a glass of vodka from his host. Volodya took another look at him, gathered up the reins awkwardly, and said softly to the old horse:

"Come on you what's your name. Let's get going."

The buggy clattered away across the square.

"I say, Matvei, where's Babichev?" Uncle Petya asked Gorshkov.

"Doing his duty."

"Some duty!" Uncle Petya said, clinking glasses with Gorshkov. "Conniving, that's what his duty is."

"What are you driving at?"

Uncle Petya loved keen-edged conversations and risky situations. And now he had a feeling of levitation as if he were flying up in a swing.

"What, indeed? It's just this, citizen Gorshkov. Everyone knows that the thief is not the one who does the stealing but the person who instigates him to the theft."

Again lightning flashed in a yellow streak straight down the sky somewhere near the bridge. Gorshkov ducked and spilled his vodka.

The dapple-grey, clumsily driven by Volodya, squatted for a moment and suddenly, with ears twitching, changed to a gallop. Volodya nearly fell over backwards, coiled the reins around his hands and shouted, trying to be heard above the crack of thunder.

"Easy, horse, easy, you idiot!"

He wished he knew the dapple-grey's name. What were horses called anyway?

After that everything became a jumble of impressions: finding Kudimov, who was still drowsy from his long after-dinner nap, the lightning crackling like rifle fire, the rousing "To horse!", the thick, yellow cloud of dust on the highway, the cavalrymen riding at a quick trot, the ambulance, mounted Kudimov, the hook-nosed squadron commander with the bluish jowl riding a black pacer, and then Uncle Petya again, drunk

169

but safe and sound. Then there was lightning again with no rain and no crackle, mounted militiamen, cans of kerosene beside the sealed workshops of the felt-boot workshop, and angry yelling crowd of wool-beaters and other workmen, the crowbar with which the militiaman was forcing the sealed padlock, and Gorshkov's threats: "You'll answer for this! You'll answer! You and your disinfection!" Then there was Kudimov again, his eyes narrowed to slits in his laughing face, saying, "Ustimenko, take a look, the place is absolutely empty. They've stolen everything, the scoundrels, taken everything away. Oh, there's some stuff here, but it's no more than ten kilos of wool. And the boots! Where are the boots? The documents say there's a stock of more than four thousand pairs. Right, comrade prosecutor?"

There was not a pair of boots to be found. Gorshkov and Babichev were taken into custody at once. The prosecutor had brought an investigator along, a mystery man with a large revolver on his hip. He had a saddle nose and his eyes saw right through you, Volodya thought, and his talk about footprints and clues took Volodya back to the days when he used to thrill to Conan Doyle's stories.

It was quite dark, everyone carried lanterns, and it was all terribly mysterious and creepy as in childhood.

Volodya turned to the prosecutor, who was a young man in a short grey overcoat and a leather cap.

"We must find out at once where the wool and the boots have gone to," Volodya said. "The spores of the anthrax bacillus are exceptionally viable. It takes ten minutes' boiling to kill them. Dry heat at 120°C kills them only after one or two hours."

"But this son of a gun is drunk, I'll never crack him open now," the prosecutor replied. "He's dead drunk, you can see that yourself."

The men were clamouring for an open trial for their chairman. The ox-eyed Babichev was weeping like a woman, dabbing at his eyes with a dainty handkerchief. Uncle Petya was chatting with the cavalrymen, explaining to them that anthrax was just as dangerous for humans as it was for animals.

Later that night, Gorshkov came out of his drunken stupor and, realising that he was under arrest, admitted everything, stumbling over the words in his haste. The goods had been taken away in lorries the night before last by two old dealers from Zarechensk. The money was intact, the Comrade Prosecutor could take it for the Soviet treasury, the wad was hidden in the old milking pail under the nails that were kept there. The prosecutor sat down at a table, wiped the perspiration off his face, and began to count the money, which was straight from the bank with the wrappers unbroken. He dropped the bundles in his cap, got mixed up in the counting and started all over again. Babichev called out to him from across the room:

"I've another 2,200 at home. I got it for looking the other way. Please note, Comrade Prosecutor, I'm making a voluntary confession."

It was all extremely interesting. Kudimov went to snatch a few hours' sleep and left Volodya to post the quarantine guard. Very politely Volodya explained to all the soldiers in turn that no peasants were to be admitted to the fair under any circumstances, that the place was under quarantine, and that it was no joking matter. The soldiers dozed in their saddles, Volodya's ardent injunctions were a bit too verbose and lengthy, but he did not know it. He no longer remembered the words that had struck him the day before in a pamphlet on anthrax: "Do not overrate the disease." He fancied he was fighting the plague at the very least.

At dawn, two militiamen took the criminals and the money to Chorny Yar; the prosecutor and the investigator got into Uncle Petya's buggy; there was an escort of six cavalrymen. The investigator, finding a good listener in Volodya, told him a lot of tall stories about heinous crimes he claimed to have disclosed. He was a sharp fellow, he loved a joke and took his fun where he could. Volodya's eyes, framed in thick eyelashes, shone with an eager light, he was good to tell stories to, especially when you were feeling sleepy. The prosecutor was snoring away, Uncle Petya was smoking and sighing. More militiamen were expected in Zarechensk.

"I'm not sure there'll be no mess," said the investigator.

"You mean shooting?" Volodya asked warily.

The wool and the felt boots were only run to earth the following day, and not in Zarechensk at all but at a farmstead in Glinishchi. Volodya and Uncle Petya went without sleep for another 48 hours. They quarrelled with the Zarechensk vet, lost their water hose, and did not manage to get back to the Chorny Yar hospital till Tuesday evening both reeking of chlorine. Volodya bathed in the river, put on fresh clothes, combed out his matted hair, and with an air of a conqueror went to Bogoslovsky to make his report.

"Tell me," Bogoslovsky said after carefully hearing him out. "What did you do about the stores of wool and workshop in

Razgonye? Simply abandoned them? No disinfection or anything?"

Volodya had nothing to say: he had simply forgotten all
about those empty barns. Clean forgotten. The chase had been
so exciting, the lightning had flashed so, the mounts of the
escort had snorted so creepily in the night, and it had been so
very important to run to earth the stolen boots and wool that...

"You're only an irresponsible kid, really, I'm not surprised
you forgot to do it. I wasn't relying on you particularly. But
it's a damnable business that Syomochkin, our most experienced
attendant, behaved like a bungling fool!" Bogoslovsky said
harshly, and ordered Uncle Petya to be woken up at once.

"It's all my fault," Volodya began, but Bogoslovsky interrupted him rudely, "Keep quiet."

Some forty minutes later they started back for Razgonye.
The night was starry, hot and still. Uncle Petya kept emitting
long, howling yawns, the young dark bay mare ran at a steady
pace, the springs creaked sleepily. Volodya kept silent for fear
that Uncle Petya would give him what for if he tried to speak
to him. It appeared, however, that Uncle Petya was most peaceably inclined.

"Our surgeon is an extraordinary person, I told you so, Vladimir Afanasyevich. He sees right through everything. But
then, you'll never bungle things again. It was my fault too, of
course. I had one too many with that dirty thief, and slipped
up on my special mission."

He yawned once more, and said pensively:

"In this way our Soviet health protection fights the cursed
survivals of tsarism. Our surgeon's dead right about that."

Chapter Nine

### "MY COLLEAGUE"

And once again no praise was forthcoming. No one even
mentioned Volodya. He was back sitting at his desk behind the
polished yellow cupboard, the sun was shining in his face as
usual, and now it turned out that all the happenings of those
three days — the chase, the search, the cavalrymen, the wonder-
detective, the drunken Gorshkov, and the flashing lightning —
were mere trifles and not worth anyone's notice. Quite naturally, Volodya minded, but what could he do? Get up and tell them
how difficult and even frightening it had been? Tell them that
he and Uncle Petya were fine fellows? No, he couldn't do that.

And before long, he was swept into the rhythm of the hospital world, business-like and measured, and forgot all about the happenings at Razgonye.

That morning Bogoslovsky told him to prepare Roman Chukhnin from ward 5 for his operation. Romka, as that hefty chap was called by the other patients, was scared; plagued by his cowardice, which he concealed both from himself and the hospital staff, he made life miserable for the attendants, the nurse, the patients in his ward, and Nina Sergeyevna, his doctor and a very gentle lady who wore ringlets on her forehead. The most disgusting part of it was that Romka, who had read some popular booklets on medicine, brazenly alleged that all the Chorny Yar doctors were ignoramuses, illiterate small town practitioners, years behind what he called the "achievements of modern medical science". Sweaty, beefy-faced and bad-tempered, he wandered up and down the corridors, prying and nosing things out, and then, garbling the facts, recounted them with relish to the patients.

"Last night they smuggled an old man out of here into the morgue. A mistake in diagnosis, more likely than not. They all ought to be had up, and tried without clemency. They're not doctors, they're just a crew of swindlers. They finished off a young girl too — some air got into her heart by mistake. I saw an oxygen sack taken into ward 3— why? Because the man in there is nearing his end with their help."

He said the food was bad, told the dirtiest stories about Sonya, the young nurse, and assured his fellow patients that if they ever left the hospital it would certainly be feet first.

"You do not apply lysate therapy here at all. That's when urine, pardon the expression, is used in treatment, you know," he once said to Volodya, to the latter's astonishment. "And anyway, comrade nurse, attendant, or whoever you are, my hemoglobin and erythrocyte count is below normal. Something ought to be done about it at once, and instead you want to operate."

"Are you a medical man?" Volodya asked.

"I'm just an ordinary Soviet intellectual," Romka said with a patronising chuckle. "We know a bit about anamnesis, and have an inkling of other things besides."

He looked at Volodya with insolence and scorn. The other patients tittered approvingly. An elderly man, suffering badly from a compound fracture of the hip, offered a suggestion between wheezes and grunts.

"Why don't you give that young rat a kick in the pants?

He's becoming a proper menace. Our patience is wearing thin too. See we don't take the law into our own hands like they do with horse-thieves, it wouldn't be very nice."

"Some state of affairs," Romka said with a sigh. "I wish the People's Commissar of Health could come and see all this." He changed to a whisper: "At least 25 per cent of the patients are shamming, bear that in mind. Now, about my alimentary tract: it's not in order. I can't agree to the operation, and that's that."

Volodya sent a nurse to fetch Bogoslovsky. While she was away looking for him, Romka baited Volodya, jeering at his obvious youth, his thick eyelashes and ready blush. Volodya pretended not to mind, but it was torture.

"Look here, Chukhnin," Bogoslovsky said, taking a stool near Romka's bed. "You came to this hospital of your own free will and asked us to fix your face for you, which, you told us, had been marred in some secret but heroic affair. There was nothing secret about it, I have since found out. It was an ordinary drunken brawl on a Church holiday."

Bogoslovsky spoke in a deliberately loud voice for all the patients to hear.

"Your participation in that brawl was all the more disgusting because you are a more or less well-read man, an accountant. You wear a tie and a felt hat and look down on those who manage without. You got into the fight in an underhand way, and though I'm anything but a champion of fist law, in this particular case I consider that justice was done. Your ear was injured, and your wish to improve your appearance is understandable. But the way you've been behaving here is abominable. We shan't operate today, but on Friday you'll either agree to the operation or be discharged the same day. If you're going to be troublesome again, we'll discharge you today. Come along, Vladimir Afanasyevich."

"Ours is a difficult and ungrateful job, Vladimir Afanasyevich," he said when they were out in the corridor. "When I was on the threshold of my career, so to say, I believed that since we doctors were putting all our skill and strength into the work, and were doing it conscientiously, of course, we were entitled to an equal measure of kind words, hearty handshakes and various other expressions of sentiment that make life jollier to live. There's nothing of the sort, however. Sidilev, who used to intrigue against me and whom you and I rescued from a far from pleasant predicament, has now forgotten his fears of the time—remember, he imagined I'd cut him to pieces while

174

I was at it — and is very angry with me for 'slashing him up more than necessary' as he puts it. And only this morning his good lady screamed at me that I could have done a 'better job on him for old times' sake'. We are forced to listen to it all, because we can't call the militia in to protect us, after all, can we? There's a woman now in the fourth ward, Aza Lyadova, a cultured person who's married to an important executive. I don't want to brag, but we got her out of a real fix. She is suffering pain, needless to say. What's her reaction, do you think? It's calling me and our meekest lamb, Nina Sergeyevna, butchers, sadists and even masochists, and throwing things at the nurses. Her husband, a decent man, a loving husband and a good father, glares at us with a lowering scowl. And he does not just glare either, he says things which we are forced to listen to as well. Oh, that's nothing. The other day a fond mamma attacked our good old Vinogradov with a stick. I am telling you all this because you are about to enter upon your professional career and you must know that you should expect no tears of gratitude from moved relatives, no handshakes, and no posies of wild flowers picked for you by grateful baby fingers. Especially in cases when medicine proves powerless. Be prepared for the worst then. Even summons to the Procurator's Office you must take in your stride, with no rancour. The heart of a loving relative is apt to be extremely vengeful, and you, having done more than man can do with his limited knowledge, will be a criminal, not a convicted criminal perhaps, but still a 'suspect'. It's hard on one, of course. No need to say that there are exceptions to the rule — personal letters of thanks, through the press sometimes, too, it's all very touching and nice, it almost moves you to tears. But the remarkable thing is that more often than not we get thanks where no thanks are due and it was nothing but luck or nature doing the trick. Our grateful patient is not a doctor and has no inkling of what is known to us. Polunin, for instance, my good friend and your teacher, often quotes the words of Gandhi which, to my mind, are very true: 'I know but one tyrant, and that is the quiet voice of conscience.'"

Bogoslovsky sighed, took a sip of soda water from his thick tumbler, and said as if in answer to Volodya's thoughts:

"Incidentally, it's a mistake to ignore such words as conscience, honour and decency, imagining that they don't belong in the language of medical men. They do belong to us and to us particularly, for in the world of moneymaking a surgeon sometimes performs an operation not because an operation is indicated but because the patient is rich and is easily tricked into paying large sums in pounds sterling, French francs or American dollars, as the case may be. After all, their patent medicines are advertised with scientists' names *for money*. We, on the other hand, are working in a world of honour, conscience and decency, and we must wage a struggle against those who stifle within themselves that 'quiet voice of conscience' just as we struggle against all that is inimical to our ideology, take Zhovtyak for instance, who is referred to as 'Professor'..."

At this point Bogoslovsky glanced at Volodya and, remembering that Zhovtyak was after all his teacher, stopped in droll embarrassment, grew flustered, chuckled and said:

"All right, let us go and operate, my colleague, you and I have a busy day ahead."

"My colleague!", "you and I", this man had said it. This thick-set, broad-shouldered, sunburnt, wonderful man. And all the while Bogoslovsky operated and Volodya anaesthetised the patient, gave him a blood transfusion, a saline injection, and took his pulse, the words "you and I" rang in his ears, said as they had been without the least sign of affectation in a rather gruff, rustic voice. It was recognition, he was one of them, and though he was not the chief assistant by a long stretch, he was an assistant nevertheless, one eligible to hear those bitter truths which, it stands to reason, were not confided to anybody and everybody.

The clock in the anteroom struck one when Bogoslovsky at last lit a cigarette, holding it in a pair of tweezers. Volodya scrubbed his hands feeling utterly spent; he was drenched in sweat and his throat was clogged with ether, which he was finding hard to get used to.

"Varicose ulcers on the legs are the damnedest thing going, honestly they are," old Dr.Vinogradov was saying to no one in particular. "I remember a case we had..."

The door opened half-way and there was Rukavishnikov, the supplies manager, a sanguine, energetic man, good-natured and placid.

"I came to tell you that the mower's been assembled and Vakhrameyev and Antoshka are going to give it a try just now. A test-run, so to speak. There she is, isn't she a beauty!"

The brightly painted mower could be seen crawling to and fro on the other side of the hospital fence. Volodya was unimpressed, but Bogoslovsky said angrily:

"I'm surprised you let Antoshka try it. He's always breaking things. Go and tell him to leave the mower alone."

Volodya saw the funny side of it. Bogoslovsky was obviously dying to go and try out his mower himself, but he could not do it because he had to go back to the operating room and perform the hardest and longest operation scheduled for that day. Bobyshev, an elderly stable-man at the Znamya Truda State Farm had been kicked in the stomach by a stallion. He had just been brought in. Bogoslovsky knew him personally and liked him, as he did a great number of hard-working and upright people in their neighbourhood.

"I'm afraid his spleen is ruptured, Vladimir Afanasyevich. Observe this: increasing pallor, blood pressure dropping, the skin turning cold, you'd feel it? And nausea besides, he feels sick all the time. Oh well, let us begin," he said with a grimace of pain, for strange as it may seem, compassion was as strong in him as ever for all his years of practice.

With a strong and graceful stroke Bogoslovsky made the laparotomy, and explained to Volodya in a level voice precisely how the spleen was ruptured. Maria Nikolayevna handed him the instruments in swift succession; the silence was only disturbed by the metallic clang of scissors, tweezers, clamp or scalpel, thrown on the table after use, and the laboured breathing of the patient.

"Pulse?" Bogoslovsky asked from time to time.

Volodya replied in a low voice attuned to the established mode of behaviour in the Chorny Yar hospital operating room. The stocky Dr. Vinogradov was breathing noisily. The clock in the anteroom struck two, then half past. At 3.32 p.m. Bobyshev was rolled away. Bogoslovsky sank down on a stool and after a minute of stony silence said:

"Won't the old man pull through?"

Suddenly his eye caught the new mower going straight at the iron railing.

"Antoshka again!" he cried, turning an angry red. "Antoshka, all by himself! The devils, they'll ruin it, and where will I get another, I ask you!"

He rushed out of doors, angrily flinging off his gown and mask on the way, pulled the gate open, and shouted at the fearless flaxen-headed Antoshka, waving his arms comically and opening his mouth very wide. Watching from the window, Volodya saw Bogoslovsky jump astride his precious mower and start off; Antoshka trotted beside him, while Vakhrameyev, the long-legged attendant, who had suddenly appeared on the scene, stood crossing himself fervently.

"Heavens, what a man, what an amazing man!" said

Nina Sergeyevna, the gentle soul, standing at the window beside Volodya. "He was near collapse just now. Did you notice it, Ustimenko?"

"He's touched enough to be a saint, Lord forgive me," Maria Nikolayevna said fondly. "If you want to know the truth, he spent half the night putting that mower together with Vakhrameyev."

When Volodya left the hospital some twenty minutes later, he found Bogoslovsky in his shirt-sleeves shouting at Vakhrameyev:

"Didn't I tell you the shaft needed tightening? And what did you do?"

The white surgeon's cap was still on his clean-shaven head, but it had slipped over one ear, and gave him a funny, dashing look. His patients, walking in the garden or looking out of the windows, watched him in amusement as he advanced threateningly on the lanky self-styled mechanic and demanded with anguish but no malice:

"Where can we get another flywheel from now? Where? Carve it out of your Antoshka perhaps, eh?"

"Go on and do it," Antoshka said tearfully. "Carve it out of me if it's my fault. You fitted the shaft in the wrong place yourself, and now you're picking on me. It's always Antoshka this and Antoshka that. I might as well hang myself!"

"Just you try!" Bogoslovsky growled.

Two sleek geldings hauled the mower away to the repair shop. Bogoslovsky put on his old jacket and went to the small office in the left wing of the "aeroplane" where some papers wanted signing. Volodya, watching from the window of the room where Bobyshev had been brought after the operation, saw him exchange a few words with the gardener, and shake a finger at Paushkin, a heart patient, who was greedily inhaling from a huge, homemade cigarette, and then disappear inside the building.

### SWEET LIFE!

Bobyshev's daughter, a sweet, shy woman, was weeping softly on the other side of the door.

"Don't lose hope, my girl," the old nurse was saying to her. "Providence guides his hand, it's life-giving. He may be an unbeliever, but no priest could hold a candle to him. Priests just burn incense, but he serves God truly. Think of that, my girl, don't give up hope."

"To serve and not just burn incense! How well said, how amazingly well said," Volodya repeated the words to himself, firmly and delightedly.

The two women fell silent. Bogoslovsky walked in. Volodya stood up, but the older man told him to sit down. His keen, somewhat slanting eyes peered into Bobyshev's white face with long, calm scrutiny.

"This man has a splendid mind — original and witty," he said softly. "A real Russian character. I've spent many a pleasant hour with him. Yes, I want you to realise that there are really a lot of splendid people in our district. But the other day I met one of my old fellow students in town, he's a surgeon too, he's a professor and author of a series of medical essays on rather conventional themes, but a man of eminence and unquestionable authority just the same, and a striking figure besides. Well, he asked me, 'I suppose it's so dull there that you've taken to drinking on the quiet?' Isn't it amazing that after all these years of Soviet power, with so much achieved and such impossible hopes realised, a professor in his right mind should still be judging of your life and mine from what he remembers of Chekhov's *Ward No. 6*, honestly believing that we feel lonely and hit the bottle. Well, that evening I called on my old fellow student, or rather I had the honour of being invited to a *soirée* he was holding, as he put it. And what do you think? They were playing whist."

"What's that?" Volodya asked.

"It's a card game, one of the brainy kind. They gave themselves up to the game passionately, they were absorbed in it completely, oblivious of the world. And not an intelligent word, no sign of thought the whole evening! Oh hell, I thought, why did I ever come here, silly ass. There he was, a professor, a surgeon, a man with several books to his name, if you please! No wonder there's a saying about people who have everything for their own glory, but fall short of making ours. Why did he get his degree then? No, I thought, my judgement is faulty, I am too hasty. And so I tried to engage my fellow student in conversation about surgical endocrinology, and, just imagine it, he patted me on the shoulder like this, in a most patronising way, and said, 'We're giving our minds a rest tonight. But if you like, come to my clinic tomorrow and have a chat on the subject with my assistant.' Naturally, I didn't go near the place."

Bogoslovsky had a quiet, good-natured laugh at the memory, stopped to talk to Bobyshev's daughter in the corridor, and then went on to the outpatient clinic.

Volodya did night duty with Bogoslovsky's wife, Ksenia Nikolayevna. Tall and slim, she looked, a mere girl with her hair piled high under her white cap, a pale flush on her cheeks, and a stern but gentle look in her eyes. She explained things to Volodya as she worked, with none of the superiority of an experienced doctor but just as a fellow student would, a friend who knew more on the subject than he did.

They had a very difficult case. The patient's groans were hoarse, her voice was tortured. It was hot in the delivery room.

"Make an effort, my dear," Ksenia Nikolayevna kept urging her. "It's hard work giving birth to a child, but you'll be so happy afterwards to see the little boy or the little girl you've worked so hard for."

She talked like her husband, and Volodya very much wanted to learn to talk like that too.

"You'll have a little boy."

"I want a girl," the woman sobbed out. "All boys are bad, the other day our neighbour's brat shot an arrow at our cow."

She began to scream again. Ksenia Nikolayevna bent over her whispering endearments, and comforting her. Volodya was torn with pity. First he winced, then he actually bent forward and began straining together with the patient. The old midwife noticed it and embarrassed him by saying with a smile:

"You too, Vladimir Afanasyevich? It's funny the way all medical students try to help by straining. You young people are really a scream!"

Just before daybreak the baby was delivered. The midwife held it up by the legs, slapped its buttocks with a large red hand, listened to its cry for a moment, and pronounced:

"You've got yourself a real naughty. He'll shoot arrows and take sling shots too."

Volodya helped Ksenia Nikolayevna to put in the stitches. There was blood all over the bed, the rubber sheets and the linen. The woman lay motionless, her cheeks and forehead were turning an ominous blue. Volodya picked up her hand to take her pulse — the hand was sticky with sweat.

"Let's start the blood transfusion," Ksenia Nikolayevna said. "Hold the ampule a little higher. That's the way".

They gave her 500 c.c. At daybreak the nurse brought in the apparatus for the saline injection. His mind in a daze,

Volodya did what Ksenia Nikolayevna told him to do. "It's death," he was thinking. "Death. What more can we do? Why don't we call in all the doctors, why don't we send for Bogoslovsky?"

There was a clink of glass striking glass, the pleasantly slim doctor was calmly issuing orders — didn't they understand?

But it was he who did not understand. When morning came, he saw that the woman's face had taken on colour. Her eyes were still glazed, she could not command her wits properly yet, but it was not death, no, it was not the end, it was life, the beginning...

Day had begun. Babies were crying somewhere down the corridor, nurses were busy delivering the tagged baby boys and girls to their respective mothers, and soon this mother too would put her dark nipple, heavy with milk, into her first-born's mouth. She would forget that she had wanted a girl, she would caress her boy, croon him to sleep with a lullaby, and tell everyone how exceptionally clever he was. Volodya had witnessed two miracles that night: a woman, who according to all the canons of ancient midwifery could not have given birth and lived, had given birth and was alive; the child, who according to the same canons could not have been born alive, was alive. It was due to the efforts of people, many people, people who certainly did not waste their evenings playing whist or holding *soirées*, people who did not sweat for their learned degrees merely to be able to live in clover and drink and be merry in the hour of national calamities.

Sechenov, Guborev, Fyodorov, Kadyan, Dyakonov, London, Bogomolets, Spasokukotsky — Volodya had to make an effort to remember their faces. "Why do we know so little about them?" he thought with bitter regret. "Yes, they were all here last night, they fought in the battle, they conquered death, death itself, and yet so little is said about them in textbooks, just a few dull lines. The chapter about them and people like them should be entitled 'Conquerors of Death'."

"What are you muttering about?" Ksenia Nikolayevna asked him. "Why don't you go and get some sleep? You keep muttering and muttering."

"Good-bye," he said.

"Good-bye, Vladimir Afanasyevich," she replied and smiled.

The nurse was holding a towel ready for Ksenia Niko-layevna to wipe her hands on. Still Volodya did not go.

He could not leave like that. The night had been too

long, too much had been revealed to him in those sleepless hours, and an immense feeling of gratitude flooded his entire being.

"Was it very bad?" he asked, indicating the delivery room with a nod.

"It was rather complicated."

"Very?"

"Yes, I suppose so," she said with a wan smile.

"And now?"

"You do know it's all right, don't you?"

It was high time he went. Why stick around any longer? She had already said good-bye to him, so what was he waiting for? Oh hell, why didn't he get going, the fool...

"If ever I can be of service to you, please call me," he mumbled gruffly in embarrassment.

She nodded. He would have loved to kiss her hand, it looked so frail with the tiny blue veins showing, such a slim, lovely hand. But naturally he did not dare. Backing to the door he went out — a long-legged, long-armed boy in battered shoes. He stopped spellbound on the porch. Birds had already broken into song in the hospital garden, the sun had dried the dew but the scent of the flowers was still as strong and heady as at night. A huge, plump bumblebee buzzing good-naturedly smacked into Volodya's face, and flew on to attend to its urgent, bumblebee business.

"Life! Sweet life, hard but real!" Volodya said to himself, feeling tightness in his throat. "You see, I'm helping you. There's very little I can do yet, I'll only be runnig errands for you now, but I will help. I promise I will be like them one day. And you'll come to respect me, sweet life!"

He went to see Bobyshev before going home. The old man looked wonderingly at the pale young doctor, and complained of pain. Volodya took his pulse and sighed. Pain — what a funny word. Why, you're alive, dear old Bobyshev! You're alive, and you'll probably live for a good many years. And yet you were all but dead when they brought you in.

Bobyshev, however, understood none of it. And no wonder! What did he know of the narrow escape he had had. Now he was in pain and angry. To talk him into being glad he was alive would be silly.

Volodya slept until midday. His old landlady made the whole household walk on tiptoe.

"Sh-sh!" she hissed. "Sh-sh, you young devils. Doctor's asleep. I'll take my rolling-pin and kill the lot of you, and then Doctor won't be able to cure you. Hush, Caesar, leave your whistle alone."

"So it's Caesar blowing his whistle," the thought came to Volodya through a fog of sleep. "That's what it is."

### WHAT IS HAPPINESS?

Volodya was eating a huge breakfast when his old landlady brought him a letter from Varya. He began reading it as he ate, and suddenly a piece of cottage-cheese cake stuck in his throat. He coughed and spat. Polunin was dead. Dead! But how could such things be? Why? No, there must be some mistake, it must be someone else with the same name, the whole thing would be cleared up directly.

Dropping his breakfast and forgetting to do up the straps of his sandals, which flapped as he ran, he rushed to the hospital. A copy of the *Uncha Worker* was lying on the desk in the office. The Sechenov Medical Institute regretted the untimely passing of Professor Polunin and offered its condolences to the family of the deceased. There was an obituary with a photograph of Polunin with a *black* surround, a poor likeness. Volodya read it through a mist of tears.

God, how unlike Polunin were these dull, flabby, insipid lines, what a dummy official the obituary made him seem, and what would he himself have said after reading this bombastic, vulgar and colourless rot about himself! And why use words like "sensitive", "warm sympathy", "unforgettable image" — ladylike words, Polunin always thought them. That's what he used to say: "Spare me your ladylike insincerities, and I'll take care of those who frankly curse me."

"He's dead," Volodya said with quivering lips to Bogoslovsky. "Polunin's dead."

"I know. I saw it in this morning's paper."

Bogoslovsky clenched his fist, wincing with grief.

"Foolish, too foolish for words!" he said. "How dared he, what right had he to neglect his health, to spit on it as he did? I told him time and again, Prov, stop playing the fool, what d'you think you're doing? Chain-smoking, eating rich food, working all night long, drinking strong coffee, tea and vodka... You don't know how he used to spend his vacations, do you? He'd take the steamer up the Uncha to the Great Rapids, buy a wretched little boat there and sail down alone. Alone, mind you. I watched him once from the bank, from the Weeping Rock, and believe it or not the sight made my flesh creep. And after that there'd be a fire, fish soup, cigarettes... Always thinking, always searching, such excessive demands upon his own strength, such merciless criticism of himself, he never stopped, never gave himself a second of inner tranquillity. What more could a man want, you'd think? He was a doctor, a professor, they invited him to Moscow, but he just laughed it off and that was that. 'What sort of a professor am I? I'm a raven and not a professor at all. All men are worth exactly as much as they have actually created minus their vanity. A professor, indeed! The history of medicine knows many who were considered dilettantes and could not get a professorship all their lives. And now they're dead, hundreds of professors live by popularising their opinions and making a poor job of it too! And you say professor!'"

Bogoslovsky fell silent.

"We were going to celebrate his fiftieth birthday in style," he continued reminiscently. "That was six years ago. Great heavens above, the row he made! So we just abandoned the plan. 'It's vulgar,' he said, 'to sit enthroned in an armchair and listen to your own funeral oration. They'll start enumerating my works, three-quarters of which are trash, and what then? Would you have me get up from my place of honour and deliver a speech on my mistakes? And how could I help making mistakes when the whole of medicine is a history of human mistakes?' Try and reason with a man like that. And then he threw me down on the carpet and demanded, 'What shall it be — life or death?' And now this..."

Neither spoke. Bogoslovsky cleared his throat painfully and said:

"It's a terrible, irreplaceable loss. He was sincere in everything. Not just with his friends, but with himself as well. A big man, everything about him was big. When I used to reason with him, saying those stupid banal things about taking good care of himself, he answered, 'I find it more fun this way.' And now this — dead instantaneously. But he always wanted to die like that. He wanted it to be sudden — no pills or powders, no doctors."

Bogoslovsky's chin quivered and he burst out:

"But perhaps he was right? Maybe it was more fun to do it his way? Perhaps it was the right way for him? There are people who can't, who won't, who just don't know how to spare themselves."

He lit one of his cheap, thin cigarettes, inhaled deeply

and greedily, brought his fists hard one against the other, and asked:

"What does a man live for?"

Volodya glanced at him in sad amazement and thought: "Can this question still be bothering this man, a surgeon who has done so much in life already and is still doing more?"

"What for?" Bogoslovsky demanded irritably. "Haven't you ever given it a thought?"

"I have..."

"I believe it was Korolenko who said that man is born for happiness," Bogoslovsky continued. "For happiness, as a bird for flight. Pretty, but vague. People interpret and will always interpret this happiness thing differently. Take Polunin and that one-time fellow student of mine who resides so smugly in Moscow now, but I believe I told you about him. Which of the two knew real happiness? Polunin, always ready to take a risk, or the card-playing professor? Polunin, who rejected and destroyed concepts, or the author of papers that are read by no one but himself? Where is happiness — in a game of whist or in a wretched little boat tossed about by our savage rapids? In Polunin's hazardous assumptions or in the chewing over of dogmas that do neither good nor harm? In Polunin's feeling of tragic impotence and his attempts to revolt against it, or in a meek admission of this impotence, an admission so unconditional, mind you, that you're spared any extra thinking at all? People say, and very wisely too, 'alive but not worth a corpse'. Isn't it perfectly true! The strong in spirit in ancient Rome held that there was no misfortune greater than losing the purpose of life for the sake of mere existence. What does it mean? I suppose you can be truly and even sublimely happy lying on a hot beach, say, and listening to the song of the waves or something. But isn't that exactly the sort of happiness experienced by a young calf leaping about the green with its tail in the air? In both cases it's purely the joy of living, and it's taken for happiness by countless so-called people, but then why, may I ask, are people called the kings of nature? For centuries the love of man and woman has been poetically compared to that of doves: cooing doves, billing doves, and all the other trash elevated to poetic heights. But I refuse to think of myself as a cooing dove. Besides being ridiculous for a man my age, it's downright stupid. And for people of Polunin's sort dovelike happiness is insufferable. If you are a real man, you want more than the physical feeling of happiness on the hot sand, you want more than dovelike bliss — and, mind you, all doves are beggars and spongers, which for some reason people find so touching. You want more than all that, you want to go ahead, to fight, to penetrate fields of knowledge no one has explored before you, to feel that you are useful not just to yourself and your children, which is not enough for society, you want to feel that you are doing, creating, contributing to the common cause."

"You mean, happiness lies in struggle?"

"In struggle?" Bogoslovsky thought his answer over. "Yes, I suppose so, yes, of course. If we mean man in the true sense of the word, man the propelling agent and not just the consumer, then of course struggle *is* happiness. But let's go, we ought to be operating by now."

Volodya worked in the outpatient department and the casualty ward all that evening, and no matter what he did the thought haunted him: "There's no Polunin. No Polunin and never will be. He's no more, he's dead, he'll never laugh his rumbling laugh again, never walk into the lecture hall with his long, easy stride, never crease his big, freckled forehead in a frown again. Polunin is dead."

"Another amazing thing", Bogoslovsky said, coming into the casualty ward. "Another amazing thing is that people like Polunin are not ambitious at all. They grudge nothing, they don't put their signature, their trade-mark on anything: made by so and so. If a man like that observes a new symptom, he doesn't start crying from the house-tops: look everyone, this is Polunin's symptom! He doesn't care, he's generous, his resources are enormous. But after personalities like his something always changes in science, and changes with a jolt. It's very curious, isn't it, Vladimir Afanasyevich?"

Volodya only got back to reading the rest of Varya's letter late that night, and once again he marvelled at *his* Varya. How well she understood everything always. There was nothing chatty or gushing in her description of Polunin's funeral. "What else could I do? I didn't tie any ribbon to the flowers or anything, of course, I just whispered when I was laying them on the grave: it's from Volodya, from your pupil, Volodya Ustimenko. But I said it very quietly, of course, no one heard."

He had more work to do every day. It was not long before he became indispensable to everyone, in a human emotional sort of way, because of the alertness in his wide-open eyes, his readiness to be up and doing, the sincerity and deference with which he asked the doctors to explain things to him, his desire to be useful as far as he was able rather than to be conspicuous, and his passion for learning, for accumulating knowledge. Even Maria Nikolayevna, the stern scrub nose, called him in pretty often to teach him that peculiar efficiency with which she managed her complicated and highly responsible job.

"Now here's a set," she would say, clattering her instruments. "I put it into a steriliser and — take note of this — make use of the time by going to the washstand and scrubbing my hands. Watch me carefully, don't miss anything, the time will come when you yourself will have to drill your theatre-nurses. And don't make a face, it is drilling, there's no other way. Now, while I'm putting on my sterile smock, the instruments have been taken out of the steriliser by the assistant nurse. I place them on the left-hand side of the instrument table and cover them with a cloth. Watch carefully, learn how to save time. You've got a tiptop nurse in front of you, quite worthy of assisting a surgeon like Bogoslovsky."

Volodya made a point of attending all autopsies. He accompanied Nina Sergeyevna on her calls to the villages Opolye and Bolshoye Gridnevo. He diagnosed four cases correctly — acute appendicitis, renal colic, chicken pox and atheroma. He treated two of the patients himself. Dr. Vinogradov praised him for it when making the rounds and Bogoslovsky only uttered "hm". Volodya personally excised the cicatrix in front of Romka Chukhnin's ear. This was done under Bogoslovsky's supervision, of course, but it made the nuisance from ward 5 change his tone with Volodya to one of rank flattery. He performed some other minor operations as well. Everyone called him "our Volodya", "Volodya dear" or "Doctor Volodya", disregarding Bogoslovsky's orders. Volodya behaved with dignity, he hardly ever smiled though he often wanted to, and spoke curtly. But sometimes he would say meekly in spite of himself, "May I ask you, please..."

He landed in some embarrassing situations too. Once a peasant woman he had cured of mastitis in the outpatient clinic lay in wait for him outside the hospital and attempted to make him a gift of a basketful of provisions.

"Here's some fresh combhoney for you, Volodya dear, I want you to enjoy it," she said, handing him her neat, new basket. "Your cure was so good, thank you, dear boy, bless you.

I've put some tiny little cucumbers in the basket, too, and a few tomatoes and sweet turnips. It's for you."

"For me?" Volodya asked in bewilderment, holding the basket.

"For you, Vladimir Afanasyevich, for you. It's to thank you for all you've done."

"Are you mad?" Volodya said, turning purple with anger.

The woman waved his objections away and quickly walked to her horse and cart. Volodya stood riveted to the spot for a moment, then he raced after her, his loose battered sandals flapping.

"You won't dare!" he yelled, catching up with her. "I forbid it, I'll take you to court for this."

For a long time afterwards he squirmed at the memory of his stupid yells and threats, and it shamed him to remember the frightened look on the woman's kind face.

Another time, a wily little man with a crooked mouth nicknamed Goatmilker, the caretaker of the hospital wharf stores, asked Volodya to give him six rubles and keep it a secret.

"What d'you want it for?"

"What day is it today?" the man asked.

"Friday."

"What saint's day is it, I'm asking you?"

Volodya did not know. He had no time to stand there chatting, and simply gave the Goatmilker the money. The caretaker got roaring drunk before the day was done. Bogoslovsky made a thorough investigation and the blame fell on Volodya. The Goatmilker swore on his oath that Dr. Ustimenko had given him the money to celebrate his name day. Volodya was severely reprimanded.

"Forgive me, will you," the Goatmilker said to him afterwards. "The chief wouldn't leave me alone and kept asking who gave the money. Everything's open and above-board with me, I'm that sort, and so I admitted it was you, to please the chief."

Volodya always learned something new from Bogoslovsky whether he made the rounds with him, worked with him in the outpatient department or in the casualty ward.

"In his day, Bier the German said some very blunt but true words: 'Frequent operating dulls the mind.' You must first consider how to cure a person rather than what surgical operation to propose. An operation has to be *absolutely indispensable*."

"Look here, why do you seem to be consulting your patients?" Bogoslovsky asked Volodya one day. "You must realise that suffering makes a person weak, frightened and tired.

He wants to be *managed* by his doctor, and you're turning everything into a debating club."

One very hot, stuffy day, Bogoslovsky flew out at Volodya catching him sprawling in a chair in the outpatient department.

"Feeling ill?"

"It's so hot."

"It's so hot, you say?" Bogoslovsky shouted, his brown face reddening with fury. "Go home, if you're quite cocked. A doctor should not look like a piece of overdone beef, he must be a strong, energetic *man* whom it is a pleasure to obey. You must be a pillar of strength morally, a legend, a fabulous giant, and not a jelly-fish. A patient should try and get well for his good doctor. You must use your personality and not merely rely on your scalpel, on physiotherapy, or on pills. Go home, and come back in good condition."

"I can't be a legend, I'm simply Ustimenko," Volodya said sulkily.

"Take a dip in the river and come back. Is that clear?"

"Yes, it is," Volodya said, feeling wronged.

The following day Bogoslovsky asked him if he had ever read the New Testament. Volodya said no, bristling at the catch in the question.

"And I, being a priest's son, have read it naturally enough. There's a bit about you."

"About me?"

"In St. Luke it is said: 'Woe unto you, when all men shall speak well of you.' Understand? And remember another thing: it's much less trouble for me to perform an operation myself than to stand beside you and watch. And don't get huffy over my remarks either, because it's much less trouble not to make them. I hope you are ashamed of yourself for saying that you are not a legend but simply Ustimenko. I want you to become a legend eventually." Saying this, Bogoslovsky walked out of the room.

Volodya drank two glasses of mineral water. "What a mess I've made of things!" he thought. "I can't even tell Varya about it. I could the legend part though."

Volodya was usually on night duty with Vinogradov. At about midnight, the old doctor would make a bed for himself on the sofa in the interns' room, take a shower, and settle down to sleep with grunts and sighs. Volodya would wander about the wards, see that the nurses on duty did not fall asleep, that the patients did not play chess in the corridor after midnight, and did not stay up talking too late disturbing the others. As a rule, he woke Vinogradov up at least two or three times during the night.

"Savchenko's coughing", he woke the doctor up to tell him one night.

"What's that?" the doctor asked crossly.

"Savchenko in ward 3 is coughing. After his operation, I'm afraid it might..."

Vinogradov dressed obediently and, yawning and snorting, shuffled to ward 3. Savchenko's cough was gone, he was asleep. On the way back Vinogradov stopped suddenly in the corridor, listening with a frightened look on his face.

"What's wrong?" Volodya asked in some confusion.

"I'm keeping my ears open."

"Why?"

"What if someone should sneeze?"

Volodya forced a smile.

"Wake me up if anyone sneezes," Vinogradov said, going back to bed. "I'll come and wipe their noses for them. I've got to do it, haven't I?"

Volodya giggled inanely, hating himself.

It was his damned conscientiousness, but what could he do about it?

On the fourth night, Vinogradov forbade Volodya to wake him up unless the action was approved by the nurse.

"I'm anaemic, my boy, sleep is the best thing for me. You'll forgive me, but I kept count last night — you woke me up eleven times quite unnecessarily."

"But supposing..."

"Go to the devil," Vinogradov cut him short with affectionate rudeness. "I'll be sixty soon. Does that mean anything to you?"

He made himself nice and snug on the sofa, chuckling and muttering under his breath — such a cunning, wild old bear he was. Once he was settled, he yawned with relish and said:

"I know what's on your mind just now, I believe you're condemning me. My advice to you, young man, is don't. We old doctors are not bad people, we're essentially honest and straight, and we have been through a great deal. A very great deal."

Volodya listened in silence.

"In the days of tsardom, which fortunately you never experienced, we all had a terrible time, especially the young men with ideas and thoughts in their heads. I don't count the fashionable practitioners with carriages of their own and a greed for acquisition. When the Revolution broke out, I already had over ten years of Zemstvo work behind me and my fill of trouble, believe me. I suppose you're looking at me now and thinking that I'm a selfish person, worrying too much about my precious self. What if I am, old age is knocking on my door. And I want to be about a bit longer. I want to enjoy my present life a little longer — people respect me, I have some prestige, I'm not the smallest pebble on the beach in our parts, but when you come to think of it it's only right. I have worked hard, I'm earning an honest living and everyone knows it. But in the old days, my dear young man, our work was anything but safe. Sixty-seven per cent of the deceased Zemstvo doctors died from infectious diseases. Sixty-seven per cent! Not a small percentage, eh? And we, knowing what we were in for, went to the remotest villages and worked there with no thought for our own safety. We went into wilds such as you'll never find anywhere nowadays, they just don't exist any more... And what about the conditions we had to work in? Professor Sikorsky has established that over ten per cent of the deaths among Zemstvo doctors were self-inflicted. Suicide — over ten per cent. To sum up then. Out of every hundred, 67 died of infection and 10 committed suicide. There, that's a picture of old Russian life for you. A wearing life, to put it mildly. I'm tired, my dear young man, and so I want to get all the sleep I can. Don't judge me harshly."

"But I'm not judging you!"

"Oh yes, you are. But then it's only natural for the young to judge and condemn everyone. We old ones won't let you, though. The way we've lived our lives, we owe you no particular apologies or explanations. Do you understand, my dear young sir? Go in peace then."

Treading softly, Volodya left the room and went up the spiral staircase to the solarium on the flat roof of the "aeroplane". Stars were glimmering with a warm, exciting light in the distant, infinitely distant, black sky. Perhaps the same stars were visible to his father in Spain, to Varya in town, to Aunt Aglaya spending the night in a farmers' hostel somewhere, to Ganichev, Pych, and to Varya's father from the bridge of his ship.

Clasping his knees and staring up into the sky he sat there alone far into the warm summer night. His heart was beating evenly and calmly, his head was amazingly clear, his thoughts were lucid and serene. The people are really fine. It doesn't matter that Yevgeny Stepanov is a swine. And never mind Dodik and Alevtina Andreyevna. They don't count. The people doesn't consist of them. The people that's Bobyshev, Vinogradov, Bogoslovsky, his wife, Uncle Petya, that plucky detective chap, Dad and Varya, Ganichev and Polunin. It's very important to be indispensable, to be needed, to be the sort of man good people can't do without. The rest just doesn't matter much.

From where he was he could hear the front gate bell. It was an emergency case. An urgent operation, most likely. The light went on in the interns' room, which meant that the nurse had woken up Vinogradov. A moment later the large square windows of the operating room were flooded with light.

"It's a difficult case," Vinogradov said, scrubbing his hands.

Though the man's condition was hopeless, Vinogradov went into battle. During the next two hours they tried everything. Vinogradov's gown was soaking wet, sweat poured down Volodya's face under the gauze mask. The nurse had to sterilise a second set of instruments. But there was nothing they could do. They only managed to hold him a little longer at the border line, but death won. He died on the operating table, a handsome young man with a high clear forehead, a powerful body now slowly turning white, firm, tightly compressed lips, and muscular arms.

"All over?" Vinogradov asked.

"Yes," Volodya replied, and laid the hand that was turning cold in his beside the man's body, as if it were a mere thing.

Vinogradov pulled off his mask.

"What chance had we, damn it," he said, still breathing hard. "Four bullets, and the regions they were lodged in too. But what a powerful constitution."

He glanced into the still face with regret and turned to go. The nurse gave him some valerian and convallamarin drops in a glass. He tossed it off as though it were a glass of vodka.

"What's going on anyway," he said angrily. "Shooting at a healthy young man, how d'you like that! He could have lived another fifty years at least."

Once they were back in the interns' room, Volodya asked him how it had happened.

"She didn't love her husband, she loved this man; but the husband loved his wife and killed his rival."

Vinogradov heaved a sigh and opened the window wide. Volodya heard a muffled groan.

"It's the woman," Vinogradov said. "Go and help her, Vladimir Afanasyevich, she's in a bad way."

Volodya went out into the garden. Two nurses were already doing what they could.

"Oh God, oh God, why? Why?" Volodya heard a low, heart-rending cry. "Oh God, why, why? But why? Let me see him. Let me in at once!"

"Let her in," Volodya told the nurses.

He himself helped the woman to get to the ward where the body was laid out. At the door, she fell on her knees and crawled to the man she loved, stretching out her arms to him and whispering, "Forgive me, forgive me, forgive me!" Then she called to him in a whisper, "Igor!" And softer still, "Igor!"

Her face was quivering when she turned to Volodya.

"Nothing? Can nothing be done?"

Volodya made no reply. The dead face was white now. Only the night breeze playing gently with his fair hair created an illusion of life.

"You murdered him here, God damn you," the woman said. "He was alive when I brought him here. You killed him, damn you. Were you practising your hand on him, you dirty young swine? Were you? Practising on a helpless man? Speak up!"

"How can you!" Volodya gasped. "Aren't you ashamed to say it!"

The two nurses and the attendant shielded Volodya from the woman or she would have torn at his face.

"Go away," the nurse told him. "Go away, Vladimir Afanasyevich. There's no good your talking to her."

He left — crushed and miserable. He looked into the interns' room, heard Vinogradov's measured breathing, and went out into the garden. But even there the woman's screams reached him.

"Murderers! God damn you! You killed him, you killed him here!"

In his sleep, too, he saw her face — contorted with grief and hatred, foaming at the mouth. Why such hatred for the doctors? Could they have saved a dead man? Could they have performed a miracle?

He was due to leave the following day. Bogoslovsky gave him a letter in a sealed envelope addressed to the dean, and took him down to the wharf. A fine rain was falling, and dirty-grey clouds were moving low over the domes of the Cathedral of SS Peter and Paul. As on the day of Volodya's arrival, Bogoslovsky kept greeting people in the street, wrinkling his shrewd Tatar eyes in a smile as he talked.

"Don't take it to heart. I read in *Izvestia* a few days ago that in Rybinsk a certain Dr. Nikolsky was not just called names but was actually injured. In Ivanovo-Voznesensk a man called Feoktistov threw some nitric acid at a Dr. Wichman. Dr. Nartsisova barely escaped with her life. Good morning, Sergei Semyonovich. In Kaluga, three morphine addicts robbed the hospital they were attending. How d'you do, Alexei Petrovich. You've got to remember, however, that we have much less of that now than we did before the Revolution. Eight times less, in fact. See? And in time such outrages will be no more, they'll be gone and forgotten like a bad, foul dream."

He shook Volodya's hand and went back to his buggy — a slightly stooped man in an old mackintosh and an old-fashioned leather cap. Half-way there, he turned abruptly and came back.

"Look here, Vladimir Afanasyevich," he said after a moment of silence, giving Volodya one of his sidelong glances. "It's possible that I'll be leaving Chorny Yar for some very distant lands. It will neither be today nor tomorrow. Will you come with me?"

"But what about the hospital here?"

"It'll survive," Bogoslovsky replied with a laugh. "There's no scope for any further action here, I'll say quite frankly. And I love to fight, to storm and batter down walls, to start from scratch. Well, will you come?"

"Yes!" Volodya put resolution, gratitude and joy into that one word. "Forgive me for being a nuisance to you, and thank you for everything."

"Keep it under your hat for the moment. But it's going to be an interesting job, interesting is not the word for it! It'll give us plenty of trouble, God knows."

He went away to his horse and buggy. Volodya liked the way he gathered up the reins with a youthful, smart and experienced gesture, the way he touched the grey with his whip and started off for the hospital without a backward glance, engrossed as usual in his own busy thoughts.

"Good-bye, my good friend," Volodya thought gazing wistfully down the road with the buggy long lost to sight. "Good-bye, my kind friend. I thank you for everything. For your parting words too. I can't be such a hopeless case if he's inviting me to share a difficult job with him. It's very important for your self-esteem to learn from others that you're not just a rotten apology for a man."

### Chapter Ten

## DODIK AND WIFE

A mere six weeks had passed, but he was so greatly changed that Varya did not cry, "Oh, Volodya!" at once when she came face to face with this tall, broad-shouldered man with dark bristly cheeks, hatless, wearing a crumpled tarpaulin raincoat and battered top boots.

"Oh, Volodya!" she said a moment later, surprised and happy.

It was drizzling. Autumn had come early and raw that year. Tiny drops of rain clung to Varya's face; Volodya's raincoat, his hair and his thick eyelashes were dripping. And heavens, how huge he had grown, her Volodya.

"Hell, my books are getting wet," Volodya said.

"Volodya! Hello!" Varya said, pushing away the books tied with string. She wanted to put her hands on Volodya's shoulders, draw him close and kiss him, and the books were in the way. But she had her own way of doing things and she kissed Volodya nevertheless.

"You smell of hospitals," she said. "Judging from your letters you're a proper doctor now, are you? Don't give me that patronising smile, answer me!"

"What can I say?" Volodya replied. "I'm just an ordinary half-baked know-all. In any case, I wouldn't advise you to let me treat you."

"Yevgeny came back home simply bursting with self-importance."

They walked up the long slope of the bank. The fine rain kept falling, and muddy little streams ran alongside the road. Varya talked without a pause. Volodya gave her a puzzled look: she had never been such a chatterbox before. Was something wrong, perhaps?

"Any letters from *over there* lately?" he asked.

"From over there? No," she said. "None for a very long time. Have you seen yesterday's paper? Have you read about that wonderful brigade forcing a crossing over the Ebro? It was the battery named after Ernst Thaelmann."

"Why do you jabber so?"

Varya had her face turned away from him. He gripped her shoulders and made her look at him. He knew it. She was crying, of course.

"Is he wounded?" Volodya asked.

"No. Your father is not wounded and mine is alive," Varya replied firmly.

He missed the strangeness of her reply.

"Then there's nothing to cry about! You've been letting yourself go without me, that's what it is."

"Yes, my nerves have all gone haywire," she agreed.

"What nerves could you have, you're just a kid! That's ridiculous."

Aunt Aglaya was not due back from her business trip until the next day, and so they went to the Stepanovs. Yevgeny was lounging on the sofa. He, too, was just back after his practical training. He seemed depressed, however.

"I'm in the soup, and what soup!" he said the minute Varya left the room. "And there's no one I can go to with this particular trouble. It's just a stupid mess. Of course, I like her both as a woman and a friend, but marriage is a thing that needs thinking about. And there's her papa, he's the dean. If he lets the cat out of the bag I'll be finished, nipped in the bud, so to speak."

Volodya listened with a scowl on his face.

"I'm no adviser in such matters," he said after a while. "But on the whole you're a dirty beast, of course."

"And you're a saint! Just you wait, my dear sister will make a cuckold of you with your saintliness yet, and then you'll have a nice jolt. After all, physiology is physiology."

Volodya simply could not work up enough anger. "It's just like being fair or dark," he thought. "A person can't be blamed for being dark, for instance. It's the same with Yevgeny, there's no helping his crazy, mulish selfishness, the cheapness of his values, or the philosophy of life he has adopted once and for all."

On a small round table — for anyone coming into the room to see — lay a pile of flattering testimonials referring to Yevgeny's work as lecturer. Volodya looked at them — they were all of a different size, some on letter paper, others on pages torn out of exercise-books and some were even scribbled on the back of used printed forms, but they were all properly endorsed with signatures and rubber stamps. Yevgeny's lectures had been thought very highly of. They dealt with different subjects including cancer prevention, personal hygiene, anaerobic infection, erysipelas, and physical training for children.

"The optimistic outlook expressed by the lecturer..." Volodya read in one of the testimonials.

"In short, a lecture a day was it?"

"What did you expect? Sometimes it was two. You'd be surprised how the Soviet people yearn for knowledge. I feel dead beat, old chap, dog tired."

"What did you do at the hospital?"

"Oh, what didn't I do!" Yevgeny said without being explicit. "And besides, mind you, I had to deliver lectures to the junior medical personnel, talk to the patients, and perform my other social duties."

"I see, you were a sort of entertainer there."

It was amazing the way Yevgeny refused to be provoked and let unpleasant remarks go unheard.

"Poor infant, you don't know life at all, my precious," was all he said in his facetious tone.

Sharik, grown fat in Varya's care, came running in joyously from the yard. His coat had a nice sheen on it now, and there was a jolly light in his eyes.

"Earnest, here! Earnest, down!" Varya told him.

The ex-Sharik "played dead", next he fetched Varya's slipper, and then he "gave tongue". Volodya watched her with the tolerance of the aged and thought: "Isn't she still a child!"

"Who's my love? You're good enough to eat!" Varya said and actually bit Sharik's ear.

"It's a madhouse!" Yevgeny moaned.

Walking up and down the room in his flapping slippers, Yevgeny sang the praises of Professor Zhovtyak. Zhovtyak was a "kind old chap", a "nice old chap", a "capable old chap" and "our old chap". He also implied that Volodya was to blame for the unwholesome attitude the class had adopted towards Zhovtyak. One had to respect the good old chap's age, his past, and the kindness and consideration he showed people.

"When did you get to know him so intimately?" Volodya asked.

"He spent the summer where I was. We went fishing together, and what with one thing and another we became fast friends."

"Keep it up, you're doing fine! You're two of a feather," Volodya said laughing.

"That's stupid."

"Why stupid? You'll see, he'll start boosting you. It's awkward for Iraida's father to do it, and after all Zhovtyak must have someone to lean on. You'll pull Misha Shervud up with you, too. He's a clever chap, you know, not like you."

Yevgeny twitched his nose like a rabbit, in a very funny way he had, and agreed with his engaging frankness.

197

"Yes, why not? It's quite an idea. Shervud is a clever chap, gifted I'd even say, and old Zhovtyak can lean on him quite safely."

Grandfather returned from market; he gave them a long-winded account of the prices and grumbled that no calf liver was to be had for love or money. There were heaps of carrots, but who the devil wanted them? "Are we rabbits or what? Here, I've a basketful of them, but no one had any liver to sell."

"Grandpa dear," Yevgeny said. "Tell me, did you often taste meat when you were a peasant in tsarist Russia? I expect it was just Christmas and Easter at best."

The old man looked bewildered.

"I'm glad you see it," Yevgeny said in the tones of a mentor. "We have shortcomings, of course, particularly in trade, but you shouldn't exaggerate. No, that won't do at all. Carrying market gossip smacks of philistinism..."

"Why, it was you I wanted the liver for," said Grandfather. "I don't want any. What do I care for it, but Varya, now, she always makes a hearty meal of liver."

"Leave Grandfather alone," Varya said. "Stop heckling him."

"He's been preaching to everyone since his homecoming yesterday," Varya explained to Volodya.

She sat down close to Volodya, took his hand in hers and looked into his eyes.

"You see, today's the birthday of Mother's Dodik. It sounds silly, but they will mind terribly if we don't show up. They invited us well in advance."

"Yes, do come along," Yevgeny agreed good-naturedly. "Let's suffer together. The food's so-so, and it's a bore, of course, but the mater will always be the mater and there's no getting away from the fact. Wash and change, and then we'll toddle along. We are the young generation, after all, the flowers of life, so let's go and adorn their stagnating society with our presence."

"Your case is beside the bathroom door in the passage," Varya said.

Yevgeny shut the door tight after Volodya.

"You're not going to tell him anything?"

"No, I can't."

"Shall I, perhaps?"

"Keep out of it. No one can tell him except Daddy."

"And if you keep on blubbering, what then?"

"That's none of your business."

Yevgeny shrugged.

"In any case, we must keep him here with us more," he said. "It's always easier with others around. As for the fact as such, being killed in action against fascism, and as heroically as his father..."

"Shut up!"

Volodya opened his suitcase and took out a change of underwear that had been laundered and mended by the old Chorny Yar landlady, Bogoslovsky's letter to the dean in its sealed envelope, a pair of socks, the necktie he never once had occasion to wear there, and a plain grey shirt. He looked with longing at his books, tied together with a string. He had not read a line in Chorny Yar.

Yevgeny came out of the living room, took a look at the envelope and whistled.

"My! The things they must have written about you! Let's open it carefully and afterwards you can tell them the seals just broke. Come on, let's read it, it's fun!"

"Put it back," Volodya snapped.

"Gosh, you do stink of hospital," Yevgeny said. "And you didn't get yourself a single new thing? I got myself an excellent suit length at that local general store, by the way. It was a deal, of course. I gave a talk — free of charge, naturally — on 'Hygiene in Marriage', serving it with a piquant sauce, and everything was in the bag. We're the seniors, you know, we've got to look decent."

Volodya let him talk. He had decided not to argue with Yevgeny any more, it was a waste of breath anyway.

After a shave, he got under the shower and enjoyed the long ritual of washing, his love for which he inherited from his father. It was his father who had taught him to whip up the soap into a lather with a piece of bast, scrub himself down under a small and then a big shower, give his body a "rough" and then a "final" rinsing, and test the cleanliness of his hair by rubbing a strand to hear if it squeaked. In days long past they used to go to the bathhouse together, they would scrub themselves thoroughly, then go into the steam room where they gasped and groaned with the heat, and after a drink of cold kvass begin all over again. His father was sure to have found a bathhouse in Spain. A marble affair, probably, with caryatids and with pink cupids painted on the ceiling.

"Will you be much longer?" Yevgeny asked.

Varya tied Volodya's necktie for him, he was quite helpless

with such things, and plastered his hair down with a brush. Yevgeny sprayed himself with scent. Volodya helped Varya into her overcoat.

"I say, we don't want any dinner today," Yevgeny called to Grandfather in the kitchen.

"That's not my trouble," the old man answered, rustling the pages of *Ogonyok* weekly. He loved looking at the pictures. "I wonder that they'll feed you there. I saw their cook at the market this morning, she says they gave her next to no money and told her to get dinner for a big crowd."

Iraida and some heavily made-up women Volodya did not know were already there, chatting on Valentina Andreyevna's cold, damp veranda. Iraida was decorating the table with yellow oak and maple leaves, a leaf "doily" under each plate and glass.

"Ah, the country doctor has arrived," said Valentina Andreyevna and gave Volodya her hand, held high for a kiss. He only gave it a firm shake, though. "Well, what did you have to do, tend the sick all the time?"

"Yes, all the time," Volodya replied sullenly.

Dodik wasn't home yet, he was sponsoring some motorcycle races. A hunting dog of his was yelping on its chain in the yard. Lucie Mikhailovna, a friend of Yevgeny's mother, was talking with her eyebrows raised superciliously.

"Ah, my dear, please don't argue with me. Early wrinkles appear as a result of our taking too little care of ourselves. Take laughter, for instance. See the way I laugh. I form a circular opening with my lips and emit the sound 'hu-hu'." Lucie Mikhailovna showed how she did it. "The act of laughing is performed, but the muscular system is not enfeebled."

Volodya stared at the woman, and Varya had to nudge him in the ribs to stop him. Yevgeny was pacing the veranda, smoking and quarrelling quietly with Iraida. Makaveyenko, a plump, cheeky little man, was as usual entertaining the ladies with funny stories and, as usual too, breaking into laughter first.

More guests arrived — a married couple Volodya did not know. He had the face of a lion, and she wore such loudly rustling silks that she seemed to be whispering angrily all the time.

"Who are they?" Volodya asked Varya.

"She's the town's best dressmaker," Varya told him. "She is called Madame Lisse in the old-fashioned way. And the man is her husband, she takes him alongto parties with her."

"Science has proved," the sallow and wrinkled Lucie

200

Mikhailovna took up her lecture again, "science has proved that the early appearance of wrinkles is also caused by placing the facial part of the head in an undesirable position during the process of sleep. Early wrinkles may be avoided if one watches oneself during sleep as well."

She saw Volodya staring at her fixedly and "formed a circular opening with her lips" in lieu of a smile.

"Isn't it so, our young doctor?" she asked.

"I don't know, we didn't study the subject," he replied with an insolent inflection. "And how could one watch oneself in sleep anyway?"

"Hu-hu-hu," laughed Lucie Mikhailovna. "Very easily, very. And I must say that we all give much too little thought to self-massage, in other words, to the system whereby creases, wrinkles and flabbiness are patted away."

"She makes me sick," Varya whispered to Volodya. "How horribly she speaks of that patting stuff."

But Lucie Mikhailovna was off and away now.

"Self-massage is my hobby horse, my alpha and omega, my last infatuation," she said. "Now then, with your right hand pat the creases on the right side of your face, and with your left hand pat the creases on the left side. The flabbiness under the eyes must be patted away with the cushions of your finger tips. Now then, to combat submaxillary bagginess and wrinkles, you must pat with the back of the fingers of both hands simultaneously..."

The cook started bringing in the salads, lots of salads in handsome glass bowls, all-vegetable concoctions of potato, carrot, beetroot, lettuce and onion. Makaveyenko sniffed at them and said insolently:

"The newlyweds' inevitable vegetable diet! Green fodder! It's wholesome, cheap, and in their style. I told you beforehand, you know, that I like meat."

Dodik drove up in his car. The first thing he did was start the gramophone which had a foreign trademark on the inside of the lid. He put on one of Vertinsky's records.

> *To your fingers clings a scent of myrrh,*
> *Sorrow slumbers in your eyes...*

"Look here," Yevgeny said to him *sotto voce*. "That's going too far, you simply went and pinched our gramophone. You made Grandfather give it you while I was away."

"Oh, stop it, you hard-boiled man," Dodik said.

They drank vodka, Madeira, port, beer and chartreuse. Valentina Andreyevna sat with her finger tips pressed to her temples.

"Can science really do nothing for an ordinary migraine?" she said to Yevgeny. "It's been killing me for three days. Three whole days!"

Mrs. Gogoleva, the barrister's wife, had always complained of migraine and used to press her fingertips to her temples too.

"Drink some vodka, Mother," Yevgeny said. "The blood vessels will expand and the migraine will slip through."

"Really?" his mother asked, widening her eyes in surprise. After the vodka, she had both beer and Madeira.

"Oh no, no, never," Lucie Mikhailovna was saying at the other end of the table. "There's a world of difference between care for oily skin and care for dry skin. That's elementary. It's just as ignorant as using cold creams and liniments if one has blackheads."

"Volodya, stop goggling," Varya begged in a small voice. "Don't listen, that's all. Don't pick on anything."

"But I'm not picking on anything!"

"Yes, you are!" Varya snapped at him. "Have some vodka instead."

"It's too absurd," Dodik was saying. He sat half-way down the table from Volodya with all the flowers and bottles ranged before him. "It's ridiculous. In rainy weather, a racer is bound to observe certain rules..."

"Three cheers!" yelled the tactless Makaveyenko. "I believe I've found a beef gut in this salad. Madame Lisse, by the way, is enjoying a different fare, served to her alone. There's chicken salad there. Three cheers for the generous newlyweds!"

Madame Lisse playfully slapped Makaveyenko's hand, and the leonine Mr. Lisse poured himself a full tumbler of glutinous liqueur.

"Madame Lisse, is it true that boleros are coming in again?" Iraida asked.

"I only talk shop in my shop, sweet child," Mme. Lisse replied.

"Bravo! Bravo!" Valentina Andreyevna cried, clapping her hands. "Honestly, let's talk shop in the shop. Tonight we'll drink! It's a holiday, a family holiday."

Valentina Andreyevna was happy. The wine had gone to her head and her dinner party seemed exactly like the dinner parties the Gogolevs used to give. There were these nice, respectable people eating and drinking at her table, no one talked of ships, guns, manoeuvres or flying hours, and no husky voice started any songs about Red Cavalrymen.

After the salads, the cook served everyone a cup of beef tea and a small pastry; next, they had some tiny cutlets with green peas, and then a huge, horribly rich, heavily smeared cake.

"Makaveyenko brought it," Varya whispered to Volodya. "He's in charge of the cake-making department. Mother says he'll probably land in jail soon, he steals an awful lot."

Valentina Andreyevna felt sick while dinner was still going on. Yevgeny and Iraida had vanished. Volodya helped Varya to take her mother to the bedroom, which had pots of cactuses on the windowsills and a framed picture of a cactus on the wall.

Dodik watched his wife leave the room, knocked out his pipe against the heel of his shoe and said to Makaveyenko:

"I got caught good and proper. And this is the thing called married bliss. I can't even go out because she'll start screaming that she's ill and I care little enough to want to go philandering."

"Let's have a drink," Makaveyenko suggested.

"Let's."

They were joined by Lucie Mikhailovna and another middle-aged woman called Babe. Babe's hair was bobbed, freshly peroxided and frizzed like a young lamb's. Her dress came down low over her pink shoulders.

"Well, old girls, we'll fight flabbiness yet, shall we?" Makaveyenko said with facile insolence. "I heard somebody say that a pack of rye flour did wonders for beauties the wrong side of fifty. Just smear it over the bags and wrinkles and you've done the trick!"

"How ungentlemanly!" cried Babe. "One should be kind..."

"I make no claims to gentlemanliness, by the way," Makaveyenko told her. "I'm in trade, sweetheart, and trade is ruled by jungle law."

He took a gentle bite at Babe's pink shoulder.

"Yum-yum! Scared?"

Dodik put on a record and asked Cookie, Babe's young sister, for a dance. Makaveyenko invited Babe.

A rich, oily voice crooned:

> *When the wearied sun*
> *Kissed the sea good night,*
> *You told me, darling,*
> *That love was gone...*

Volodya sat in Dodik's study and angrily leafed through the man's books. In the next room, Valentina Andreyevna lay flat on her bed, and holding Varya's hand, confided her troubles to her.

"You can't imagine how complicated it is to be with him, my little girl. He insists that I have interests of my own, and he actually forced me — he's strong-willed, you've seen his huge jaw — well, he actually forced me to take a course in sewing. And it's not just to keep me interested, it's money. He's a madman, he wants to create a world of beauty around me, he wants me to enjoy all life's comforts always. 'Little one,' he says to me — he likes to call me 'little one' or 'honey' or 'baby' — he says, 'little one, you have fine taste, you could become the town's most popular dressmaker.' Not in the sense that I'll *make* the dresses, I'll only give orders to others... Take our so-called close-fitting dresses, for instance, why, they're hideous! No line at all. They've not the slightest notion of how to take the hip measurements. And what about the tuck just below the armpit? Babe and I are taking a course with Madame Lisse..."

"Varya, come," Volodya called sulkily from the study.

"I'm coming," Varya called back.

"Is that Volodya?" the mother asked.

Varya nodded.

"He's a crude fellow, I must say," her mother said. "He's so surly, there's no charm in him at all. And charm is everything in a man. I'm reading Dostoyevsky just now. Prince Myshkin is an idiot, and yet what charm..."

"Mummy, please don't talk about things you don't understand," Varya said plaintively.

"Now, what do you mean by that?"

"Don't talk about Prince Myshkin, please!"

"You're rude to me, my little girl, you're rude to your mummy."

"Don't talk about Prince Myshkin, don't you dare!" Varya cried out and ran out of the room.

"Varya, come back! You're insolent! Varya!"

"Let's get out of here," Varya whispered to Volodya.

The husband of Mme. Lisse got drunk and fell asleep at the table, his leonine face pillowed in his huge, hairy paws. Madame Lisse was dancing with Dodik. The plushy voice was still crooning about the wearied sun. Dodik's white dog, stirred by these strange goings on, rattled his chain and howled in response to the song's lament. Makaveyenko, perched on the edge of the table, was delivering a speech addressed to Babe's sister Cookie.

"Yes, the purpose of life is to get all you can out of it without putting off the gratification of your desires for a minute, for a second! I'm a materialist and I don't believe in heavenly bliss after death. Come here, young man," he invited, catching sight of Volodya in the doorway. "You don't agree with my idea, I see. He doesn't agree with me, Cookie darling, does he? I take whatever I wish from life because I'm not an idealist like some others I know."

"Come on, Volodya," Varya said.

"Why ever did you bring me here?"

## FATHER IS DEAD

It was still drizzling.

Holding hands, they went to the cinema. The newsreel was about events in Spain. Germans in the Thaelmann battalion singing the *Carmagnole,* the insurgents' tanks advancing on Jaram, a chatter of fire from AA guns, volunteers coming into the Segovia bridge region. Huge, black Junkers dropped load after load of bombs on beautiful old Madrid.

"Stop crying, for heaven's sake," Volodya said rudely.

"I can't, I can't, I can't," Varya gasped between sobs.

They did not stay to see the feature film to the end, the love story was all too mushy and smooth from the very beginning. The music, too, had something of the "wearied sun" in it, and the hero looked like Dodik, dimpled chin, short straight pipe and everything. The only difference was that he wasn't called Dodik but comrade director.

"Everything's suddenly got so very difficult," Varya said.

"But why?"

She gripped his hand and said nothing.

When they got home they found Yevgeny and Iraida sitting on the sofa in the dark except for a small, thickly-shaded lamp. They both looked disgruntled.

"You may congratulate us," Yevgeny said with a sneer. For some unknown reason, he always spoke with a sneer now in Iraida's presence. "We are to be congratulated."

"On what?" Varya asked.

"On our decision to make our relations formal at the registry office."

"Yes," Iraida confirmed with a jangle of chains and trinkets. "In the language of officialdom: a favourable solution to the problem has been found." And she laughed, not too happily.

"We wish the same to you," Yevgeny said, walking up and down the room. "Before it's too late. It's more elegant that way."

"What on earth do you mean?" Varya asked, baffled.

"I mean, my dear little sister, that I like marriage to be a free choice and not a conventional necessity. We two, for instance, have breezed into necessity."

"You fool, you idiot, you beast, you cheap, worthless thing!"

"Varya, don't swear," Yevgeny begged her. "It's easy enough for you to swear, but think what Iraida and I must be feeling. You'd better tell me how the mater is. Is it true that she wants to become a great dressmaker?"

Varya told him.

"Good dressmakers make pots of money as a rule," he said. "Since we don't live with her it's not our worry even if the tax inspector does catch her red-handed. But personally I expect to get a little something out of that deal."

"Good God!" Varya exclaimed. "I've never seen a scoundrel as pure and unalloyed!"

"But why d'you call me a scoundrel?" Yevgeny asked in genuine bewilderment. "Do I eat children or what? I'm on splendid terms with everyone, I have no enemies, but surely I've got to think of myself? Or will your Volodya do the worrying for me? Or maybe *you* are planning to support your married brother? Or will Father lavish millions on me? Granted, the parent of my future wife, our good dean, will slip us something, but it won't be so very much either. There'll be my student grant and Iraida's student grant. So far so good. But the baby? The nurse, the pram, the nappies and one thing and another, what of that? And then it's not just for a year, have you thought of that? She and I have been sitting here and working things out. How much will I be getting immediately after graduation? How much in terms of hard cash?"

He took off his coat, draped it on the back of a chair, and picked up the piece of paper with their calculations on it.

"What do we have to start with?"

"I'll be going, Varya," Volodya said, getting to his feet.

"Go then," she said in a tired voice.

What a long, difficult, unclean sort of day it had been! And now, after all she had suffered, she divined accusation in Volodya's eyes, she was to be blamed on top of everything else! He was such a beast, he never helped her, he just withdrew squeamishly, as much as to say, leave me out of it, I've nothing to do with your sordid squabbles.

Without a look at Varya, he put on his raincoat and picked up his suitcase and books. It was amazing how he never turned and looked at you! Surely he would have liked to take one more look at her, surely he could feel how miserable and lonely she was just then, yet he slammed the door shut without so much as a nod! He always remained his own aloof self, that man. And now, of course, he wouldn't come back for a long time.

At dawn, Aunt Aglaya came home wearing high boots, a belted tarpaulin raincoat, and a kerchief on her head. It seemed to Volodya that she too, like Varya, knew something and was concealing it from him. She had grown thin in the six weeks he was away, he thought there were tiny lines of bitterness at the corners of her still red mouth; there was misery in her eyes, and she had a new habit of moving things restlessly about the table. She picked up a box of matches, a teaspoon, the salt cellar and put them back again, and then she suddenly got up and went to straighten a photograph on the wall. She looked more strikingly handsome than ever, though. It was a wonder men didn't go crazy about her.

"You're terribly restless, you won't keep still for a minute," Volodya said. "Is it because you're a big boss now?"

"That's silly," she said absently.

"And you're more good-looking than ever. You're jolly beautiful, my darling auntie."

"What good does my beauty do? Come on, tell me about yourself, stop this silly nonsense. Tell me about Bogoslovsky, the hospital, everything. Did you operate?"

Volodya rushed into his story but something brought him up short—his aunt was not listening.

"What's wrong?" he asked.

"Carry on, it's nothing. I'm tired, that's all."

"It's enough to drive a person crazy," Volodya said resentfully. "Varya says her nerves have gone haywire, you're too tired to listen, and none of you act like yourselves!"

But that remark, too, his aunt missed. She was busy with her own thoughts; Volodya might not have been there at all. He saw that her lips were moving soundlessly. Now he understood everything, but he could not muster the courage to ask the question, it was so frightening. At last he asked with pale lips:

"Is Father dead?"

Aglaya nodded silently.

"Killed?" Volodya cried, springing to his feet.

"Yes, he is dead," Aglaya replied softly and steadily. His plane caught fire in an air battle over Madrid."

"And Daddy ... he died?"

"Yes, Volodya, your daddy had died."

"Did he die of burns?"

"I don't know, Volodya dear, but Afanasy is dead and buried."

"Is it known for certain? Quite certain?" he asked in a whisper, leaning across the table to his aunt. "Is it true?"

His aunt's lips formed "yes" but made no sound. Tears poured down her face unchecked. Volodya stood motionless. Only that day he had pictured his father looking for a bath-house decorated with caryatids and winged cupids. And his father had already been dead then. He had been dead when he was reading the news about Spain.

"Where have they buried him? Over there? In Spain?"

"He died fighting for their freedom. So they buried him in their land," Aunt Aglaya answered in a low voice. "You see..."

She could not go on, she vainly tried to pull herself together, biting at the fringe of the shawl she had let slip down on her shoulders and tossing her head to stop crying, but the tears just poured down her cheeks. Suddenly she began to gasp for breath. Volodya quickly lighted a spirit lamp, sterilised his syringe, and gave her a camphor injection.

"You must be..." she did not finish. She was going to say to him that he must try to be like his father, but then she realised that there was no need to say it, that he was a man now and understood everything himself. All she said was: "Volodya dear," and pressed her face to his shoulder.

He was incomparably the stronger in those hours. He stroked her black hair and gazed, in silence, at the greying window. Nothing more was said between them on that foggy, damp, ghastly morning. Why torment one another with words that were superfluous?

"You're leaving?" Aunt Aglaya asked, startled by the ringing of the alarm-clock set the night before, and watching Volodya put on his coat.

"Yes, I'm going to the institute," he replied without turning around.

His aunt was perhaps the only person in the world who could understand without being told just why he was going to the institute. She understood everything. She understood that from now on Volodya's life would be different, that the old life was over, that outwardly it would remain the same, but deep inside all would be changed. He had to carry on the work his father had left off. Aglaýa repeated the words in a whisper to herself again and again in the days that followed: he must carry on where his father had left off. The son of a Kharkov drayman, pilot Afanasy Ustimenko, a Ukrainian, could not die fighting for the freedom of the Spanish people without someone carrying on the fight. It could not be.

Not weeping now, she watched Volodya getting ready to go. Perhaps she had better go too. They left the house together, carrying between them the burden of their common grief, too new and raw to share with others.

"My father has died," was what Volodya had to say in case anyone asked.

Died. Simply died! After all, people do die of diseases. A man lives, then he takes to his bed and dies, mourned by his family, his friends and relations.

### THE RIGORIST AND TORMENTOR

"Hello, old bird, how's life treating you?" Yevgeny said, coming across Volodya in the institute. There was sympathy in Yevgeny's eyes.

Volodya said nothing. He peered into Yevgeny's pink, round and good-natured face in an effort to understand. The day before this fellow, knowing what had happened to Volodya's father, had been worrying about money matters and talking about his and Iraida's budget.

"Why the glare?" Yevgeny asked.

Pych pressed Volodya's hand warmly. Yevgeny must have told everyone, because they all looked rather peculiarly at Volodya. And every one of them tried to say something particularly heartening to Volodya, all except Pych. He spoke only of his practical training. He had been in luck, the hospital was small but very soundly run. He even recounted some amusing experiences of his, and Volodya smiled. He did not look pale, preoccupied or tragic, as befitted the son of a fallen hero, and this, Alla Shershneva, a fellow student of Volodya's, remarked upon to her girl friends.

"He's not a very emotional sort anyway," said Nyussia, the girl Ganichev had once advised to drop medicine and take up shorthand. "There's a sort of hardness in him."

"He's too conceited," Svetlana said with a curl of her painted lip. "We'll have plenty of trouble with him yet."

The three girls did not know how wisely Svetlana had spoken, what insight her words had shown, insight so utterly out of proportion to her trivial mind.

"He is a rigorist and a tormentor," Misha Shervud said, summing up. "Forgive the vernacular, but he is what is popularly known as a stinking bore. Wouldn't I hate to find myself subordinate to him one day, wouldn't I hate it!"

Volodya no longer made fun of the lazy and the idle, he did not call Svetlana a fashion doll, he did not turn a blind eye to Yevgeny's shabby tricks. It never occurred to him now to feel sorry for students who failed their exams, no matter what excuse the poor souls offered.

"Kick them out," Volodya demanded at Komsomol meetings. "Kick them out before they get a chance to disgrace the medical profession and the title of doctor which they expect to be conferred on them. There must be no half-measures, no edifying talks, no propping up. Out! To the devil with them, we've played wet nurses to these spoiled mother's darlings long enough. It's their sort, the passengers we're paddling so hard for in this boat, who eventually form legions of those who won't work in the provinces. It's their sort who make their way by devious routes to the Deputy People's Commissar with notes certifying their ill health. It's their sort who wear out their trousers in the pseudo research institutes, instead of getting down to real work!"

He spoke from the rostrum in the assembly hall — a skinny young man with boyishly tousled hair and eyes blazing wrathfully from under his drawn eyebrows. And there was nothing to retaliate with. He was now the pride of the institute, he was spoken of as the future luminary, there was no biting back at him with anything like: "Look who's talking!" His thin face had grown more haggard in that difficult autumn. The look in his eyes had become harder and sharper, and when he derided someone's failing there was more venom in it. He spent more time than ever with Ganichev in the dissecting room, anxious to catch up on what he did not know, to digest anything that still puzzled him, in order to enter the battle armed to the teeth with knowledge.

"The students are not overfond of you, Volodya, you know," Ganichev said to him one day.

"It's a sad fact but people still like the happy-go-lucky sort best. The kindly sort," Volodya replied after a moment's thought during which he sharpened his scalpel on the whetstone. "My belief, however, is that they are rather noxious insects on the whole. They start by taking a drink and singing old student songs, and then to keep themselves in drink and song they begin to strike bargains with their conscience and end up by developing into a malignant tumour in the organism of mankind."

"You're becoming quite eloquent, and rather vicious, too," Ganichev said.

"I'm getting more vicious and you're getting more kind-hearted," Volodya said, dissecting the fascia on the corpse's hip. "My opinion is that the kindly sort are of little help to our country in the difficulties it has to surmount. Tell me, for instance, why did you give a good mark to Yevgeny Stepanov, a person you despise? Did Zhovtyak want it so or was it the dean? You're being kind-hearted, that's all very well, but in the long run, your kindness benefits you alone. This kindness of yours breeds contempt for the institute, for science and for justice in some students. But then you don't want to cross the dean or Zhovtyak. I'm not a child, I understand perfectly."

"Look here, young man, doesn't it occur to you that I'm your professor?" Ganichev asked irritably, and thought: "The crazy young cucumber, he's quite right and he's not afraid to speak up, the devil. Why isn't he afraid, I wonder?"

They went on working for a long time in silence. Ganichev felt ill at ease, Volodya continued to scowl. At last the silence became more than Ganichev could bear.

"You've been attacking Stepanov here, but I'm sure you say nothing of the sort to his face. Does that make you a good friend, from your point of view?" Ganichev asked, looking down at Volodya's bent head, his large, clever and already capable hands.

"That's not fair," Volodya replied, taking his time. "You said yourself a moment ago that the fellows were not overfond of me. That vile attitude to study — as though they're doing it for someone else's good and not their own — is still alive in us. I mean cribbing and all the other dirty tricks. And you talk of friendship! Why, certainly they're not overfond of me. But then what would it make me if a chap like Stepanov, for instance, regarded me as one of his sort? Why, I'd rather hang myself. I always oppose him openly and he knows it and reciprocates by hating me. I think that's the only way to act, or else you simply slide downhill to hell. As for disliking me, not everyone does. There's Ogurtsov for one, Pych, and some others, too, they're my friends."

There was a note of wistfulness in Volodya's tone, and so Ganichev decided to change the subject.

"Will you stay on as my assistant after graduation?" he asked.

Volodya's look provided the answer.

"What for?"

"What do you mean — what for?" Ganichev was honestly bewildered. "Why, my chair..."

"No, I won't stay. The security of your chair is not what I want. You know that. I want to be a doctor. The way everyone started — like the late Polunin, like Postnikov, Vinogradov, Bogoslovsky... That's the way I want to start."

Ganichev was disturbed and stung. He wanted Volodya to think well of him.

"Not everyone started out the same way," he said. "I, for one, began quite differently. Let's go outside, I'll tell you about it if you like."

Volodya covered the corpse with a sheet. Ganichev put away his instruments, stretched and yawned.

"My way of starting was rather amusing," he said. "I dropped philology when I was in my fourth year, can you imagine that..."

They went out into the garden and sat down on a bench. Ganichev took out a cigarette and kneaded it with his fat fingers before lighting up.

No, Volodya would never have thought that Ganichev had once been a student of philology writing poetry and rhythmic prose, that he had next enrolled at a school of painting and sculpture, and then at the Conservatoire.

"And when did you first take up medicine?"

"When I was twenty-nine, my dear boy. I dropped everything: sculpture, composing fugues, writing thrashy verses, cosmic in style and lulling in impact, and I even dropped my ladylove who believed in my titanic gifts. It all happened because of a certain fireman, Orest Leonardovich Skripnyuk his name was. During the Civil War, as you very well know, my dearly beloved Kiev kept changing hands disastrously and was invaded by all those Skoropadskys, Petluras, Whiteguards, Germans, and so on and so forth. All the conquerors, naturally shelled the city. Yes, they shelled and set fire to our wonderful Kiev. I ought to mention that at the time I had lodgings close to a small fire brigade, and it fascinated me to watch our firemen, made up exclusively of old fellows, start out to fight one of those huge, blazing fires, in their squeaky old carts drawn by old nags. Firing or no firing, my heroic greybeards headed by Skripnyuk — a great one for swearing, I must say, and fond of his drink too — would come galloping along, looking very picturesque in their gleaming brass helmets. All hell was breaking loose, the end of the world was coming, but still they galloped on, and not on anyone's orders, mind you, because in those hours, anarchy ruled the town. It made me think. And this is the way Skripnyuk explained it to me. 'Supposing there's a baby perishing in the flames and the fools can't rescue it, or supposing there's a cripple in the house or something and they don't have the brains to get him down. We're not doing much good, of course, but it is *doing good* all the same and not just *passing the time.*'"

There was a queer break in Ganichev's voice. Volodya thought he heard a sob in it.

"A burning rafter killed my friend Skripnyuk," Ganichev said very quietly. "The old Russian intelligentsia of unblest memory had an amazing tradition of putting a stamp of ridicule on various honest professions. A fireman was inevitably rhymed with lady's man, and the lady had to be a cook and none other. In his youth, Skripnyuk, too, favoured the cooks, he was quite a Don Juan, but then think what truly human passion there must have been in his heart if it made me, a grown man, spoilt by my wealthy parents, who refused me nothing, start my whole life anew. I was always to remember the difference between doing good and merely passing the time, a simple truth proved to me by his example."

"There, you see!" Volodya said glumly with a veiled implication in his tone.

"What must I see?" Ganichev demanded testily.

"Why, that thing about doing good and merely passing the time. You didn't remember it for all time apparently..."

"Listen, Ustimenko," Ganichev said, controlling his temper. "You are always passing judgement on me, why? You are making perfectly exorbitant demands on me, you think you have the right because you know I like you. After all, Stepanov did know his subject fairly well and..."

"I'm not judging anyone," Volodya interrupted him with anguish. "I keep thinking about it all the time, you see, and I've come to the conclusion that one must live like Bogoslovsky and like Polunin, in many ways if not in all. There can be no half-measures in anything, or else you'll be finished. Please don't be angry with me, I'm not too happy about it either, but then why did you say that Stepanov knew his subject *fairly*

213

well? What is your own attitude to your subject, to science, if *fairly well* is good enough for you?"

"D'you know what?" Ganichev cried furiously. "You make me sick! I refuse to be lectured by an unlicked cub. Good night."

## I'M SICK AND TIRED OF YOU

Ganichev got up and stalked away, and Volodya went in search of Varya to tell her how he hated himself. They seldom saw each other now. The tension at which he was living, the sternness in his voice and his malicious jibes at her art studies and Mme. Esther-Yevdokia Meshcheryakova-Prussian made Varya shrink from him a little. Surely she could not go on for ever feeling guilty because Volodya's father was dead, and yet Volodya seemed to hold it against her that she was alive, had fun, laughed, rehearsed plays, went swimming and skating.

What did he want of her?

What did the stern look in his eyes, as dear to her as ever, demand of her?

Why should work alone command respect?

She was at home when Volodya called, but was getting ready to go to a rehearsal.

"How are things?" Yevgeny said.

"I've just spoken to Ganichev about you," Volodya said. "I spent hours trying to prove to him that giving you 'fair' for pathoanatomy was wrong."

"Of course, it was wrong," Yevgeny nodded. "I deserved 'excellent' the way I crammed."

"You don't know your pathoanatomy," Volodya said. "He ought to have failed you instead of letting Zhovtyak and others influence him."

"Have you gone mad?" Yevgeny asked.

Out in the street Varya said to Volodya that he was becoming a terribly difficult person to know, like one of those religious sectarians who burnt themselves alive. Yevgeny was right, she said, his conversation with Ganichev proved what a poor friend he was.

Volodya felt no hurt — just surprise.

"What are you talking about, Varya?" he said sternly. "Is it bad to be exacting? I didn't deserve the sectarian, and one that burns himself alive at that."

"Oh, you're just a tormentor then."

"That's Yevgeny's point of view."

"Not only Yevgeny's!"

"So much the worse for you," Volodya said spitefully. "You're *all* looking at things the same way now. Remember that fat Makaveyenko preaching on the purpose of life at your mother's birthday party? He expressed the point of view you all share. It must be hoped that in due course a touching union will be formed — Yevgeny, you, Dodik the shady broker, and their lady friend who's so good at self-massage. You all belong to the same gang."

"What! Are you in your right mind?" Varya cried out.

"I am," Volodya replied harshly. "All the vileness in this world begins with tiny little compromises. Wee little ones, as you used to say when you were a kid. And after that you take the ascending or the descending line, whichever suits you best — you, then Yevgeny, Ganichev, your mamma, Dodik..."

He no longer knew what he was saying. He was carried away. Varya's help, her support, was something he needed badly that night, and there she was siding with the others, with his enemies!

"Listen, I'm sick and tired of you," Varya said when she had had enough. "Very tired. I'm also sick of your rudeness. And of preaching too. I've been to school and I know that the Volga flows into the Caspian Sea. As for you, Volodya my pet, you're a bit too virtuous to be true. Go your way, be a beacon to others and burn yourself out, and I'll trudge along my own little path. Good luck to you."

She sniffled in pity for herself and pity for Volodya — he simply did not seem to understand what she was talking about. She herself had not sorted out her feelings properly yet, all she knew was that she was hurt and he had to beg her forgiveness instead of standing there, blinking his stupid thick eyelashes and saying nothing. But he shut up like a clam, as only he could, and then turned and strode off towards the library without once looking back.

"You wait and see! You'll come back crawling!" Varya thought viciously.

Her face hurt in the icy wind, but she stood waiting — surely he would turn? What was it all about anyway? Did he love her or not? Or had he already forgotten writing her that crazy letter from the Chorny Yar hospital? He looked at her with the eyes of a stranger now, he never asked her about anything, and when she went to his place he was either studying hard with Pych, or he was out, or else he was asleep, book in hand. What did it all mean anyway?

"If he turns around, we'll be happy," she made the wish with a sense of hopelessness. "And if he doesn't, what then?"

He did not.

He strode on uphill towards the library. The wind tore at his old threadbare coat. One of the earflaps, with the string undone, dangled from his fur cap.

The person she loved best in the world, her dearest friend, was leaving her because of a quarrel about compromises or something. What compromises?

Should she call him back?

Run after him?

She must stop him at all costs and explain to him what so many people fail to understand: there is no room for petty quarrels when love is already there, no room for anger or sulks. People lose one another because of trifling hurts, and then these trifles gather into an avalanche against which mortal man is helpless.

She must stop him at once, this very minute, she must call him back!

But she could not do it.

"Volodya, you daren't go away," she said almost inaudibly.

He did not hear her.

And then, throwing back her shoulders defiantly and proudly, Varya started for her art school to rehearse her new spy part. Lately she had been getting nothing but the spy parts — elderly, short-breathed, evil women. Meshcheryakova-Prussian, speaking in her monotonous and inevitably weary manner and cracking the joints of her long fingers, dismissed all Varya's objections to the part, which the girl assured her she could not do.

"Ah, my dear, surely you do understand that to develop one's talent one must train, train, and train again!"

"All right, let's train," Varya thought indifferently as she stepped from behind a prop that was supposed to be a weeping willow and said her piece.

Well then, Comrade Platonov, or rather Mister Platonov, if you squeal you'll be done for. If, on the other hand, you agree to blow up the power station, you'll have all the money you want. The night life of Montmartre, roulette at Monte Carlo, a well-deserved holiday in the Alps, love..."

"Stepanova, what's the meaning of your tears?" asked Meshcheryakova-Prussian.

"No meaning," Varya replied. "Just as there's no meaning to your second name — Prussian. Why Prussian anyway? Why not Belgian, French or American? Why Prussian? I don't care, you can lump it, I'm leaving. To hell with everything."

Varya jumped down from the platform that was rather small and low, and holding her head proudly walked unhurriedly to the door. She had almost reached it when Meshcheryakova-Prussian at last found voice and yelled like a fishwife:

"Get out! You're impudent! I'm expelling you. Get out and stay out!"

"Must you yell like that?" Boris Gubin spoke up. "What d'you think this is — a private company under capitalism? It's a united students' art school, and we shan't let anyone..."

He rushed after Varya.

"Never mind, she'll change her stick-and-carrot methods now," he said. "We're not children after all. We've stood enough."

Varya said nothing.

"Are you in trouble or what?" Boris asked.

Varya did not reply. Boris walked beside her in silence a few steps, then he said good-bye but did not turn down his own street. He had for long been hopelessly in love with Varya, ever since the day they had come upon the bleeding shepherd boy on the tracks and Volodya had applied the tourniquet to his stump. Boris had always realised that Volodya was the bigger and better man, and had never tried to cut in. But just then he felt strangely bold.

"Have you quarrelled with Volodya?" he asked.

"And that, I'll have you know, is none of your business," Varya said. "You've said good-bye already, so hobble off on your way. I need no escorts."

She said the meanest things sometimes. "Hobble off on your way!" But why?

## Chapter Eleven

### THE TRUMPET SOUNDETH

They were having supper in the kitchen. The table was laid with a pink, fringed table-cloth in honour of Rodion's home-coming. There were also napkins, starched to the stiffness of tin. They discussed the napkins. Grandfather admitted with a grief-laden sigh that he simply could not master the starching part, because one kind of starch made them overdone, and another — underdone.

"Oh drop it, Father," Rodion said. "What the devil do we want starched napkins for?"

"We must keep up with other people," Grandfather said, holding up his gnarled forefinger in admonition. "Your ex-wife eats off starched napkins, and you must be no worse. Or else she'll start wagging her tongue that her poor old husband is neglected. What do we want that for?"

The old man had taken a glass or two of vodka early that morning, and now he was adding drop by drop to the "old leavening". He liked to go on the spree, as Varya put it, once or twice a year. He was wearing the new three-piece suit Rodion had bought for him in Leningrad, and leaned far across the table as he ate, his neck craned forward. He was not taking any chances — supposing he missed his mouth and ruined the new suit?

"Enjoying yourselves?" Yevgeny asked, coming into the kitchen.

"We're relaxing," Rodion replied. "Why don't you call Iraida and join us?"

"Can't be done, Dad. We're invited to a certain house where we can't be late."

Yevgeny stealthily studied his stepfather as, lost in thought, he twirled his empty vodka glass in his fingers. Rodion had had plenty of drink that day but he was perfectly sober, except that sometimes he sighed or suddenly began to whistle some march or other. It was queer seeing him there in his striped sailor's vest, surely his first night at home at least he could have worn his dress tunic adorned with the two new glittering medals! But no, not him, he just sat there twirling his glass.

"How's your mother?" he suddenly asked.

"Fairly well, I suppose," Yevgeny replied. "At the moment she's the best dressmaker in town. Dodik has actually made her take a job at the theatre. She has studied the history of costume and now she's busy dressing up all the Louis and Ferdinands and what have you."

"What is it, a sort of private enterprise?"

Yevgeny stifled a yawn.

"Why private? I have already told you that she's working at the theatre, and everyone thinks highly of her there. Dodik is no fool, you know. If it were a private enterprise there'd be trouble at once over the licence and taxes and everything."

"Clear enough," Rodion nodded. He always nodded and said "clear enough" when a thing was particularly obscure to him. "Well, and how are tricks with you?"

Indolently, Yevgeny replied that he was almost a full-fledged doctor, that he had no complaints about his marriage to Iraida, that on the whole life was running its normal course, and that Iraida's father had given him a guarantee, more or less, that he would stay on at the institute.

"So you've blossomed out as a scientist, eh?"

"Maybe not a scientist exactly, but we did have a students' scientific circle and worked on certain themes. We had one small paper published in our news bulletin too."

"Who's we?"

"The members of our circle."

"How many are you?"

"Sixteen."

"A collective effort, in other words," Rodion said. "Clear enough. Before, it used to be Zinger, say, or Kiselev, say, or Mendeleyev, on their own, and now it takes sixteen of you. Did Volodya sweat with you chaps, too?"

Yevgeny dropped his eyes to hide the fury in them. What did this tiresome prosecutor want of him? What was he after? Why the jeering undertone? All right, he's back from Spain, he fought there and lost his friends, so what? It was his job, his duty. Had they sent Yevgeny, he would have gone too. Any one of the students would have gone. They were Soviet men, weren't they?·

"In short, everything's shipshape?"

"Perfectly shipshape," Yevgeny replied somewhat defiantly.

"Oh well, that's fine."

"I think so too. I've chosen my speciality, I'm going into administration. Pirogov used to say that in wartime a surgeon has to be a good administrator, first and foremost. In this particular field, Dad, matters leave much to be desired."

"The administrators' field, you mean? That's just where we were doing swimmingly, I thought. We're short of workers, but administrators now..."

Yevgeny took a slice of cheese from the table and munched it.

"It's not that simple," he said with a sigh.

Luckily the telephone rang and he could get away. Rodion and his father remained alone.

"That man will drive me crazy," Yevgeny said to Iraida out in the corridor. "He still wallows in his 1920s, but times have changed. Different times, different songs. And all the rest of it..." Yevgeny dismissed the whole thing with a wave.

"Still, he does look run down," Iraida said. "We ought to arrange a consultation, call in Daddy and Professor Zhovtyak." Suddenly she flared up on seeing Sharik come out of the kitchen. "Good God, I honestly don't know what to do about that dog! It's too ridiculous — a baby in the house and there's that mongrel always sniffing around!"

"All right, get dressed or we'll be late," Yevgeny cut her short. "And do your hair properly. That shaggy mop is anything but becoming. I wish you'd wear less jewelry. Why be so conspicuous? We're ordinary Soviet students, but every time we go out you insist on being an eyesore."

"Do stop nagging," Iraida moaned.

The two in the kitchen heard the front door bang. The cultured nanny, Pauline Hugovna von Hertz, who had been taken on because her name was *von* Hertz, was singing a German lullaby to Rodion Stepanov's little grandson in the nursery. The old lady promised more than once that she was going to leave all her marvellous wealth to the dear little baby, a small part of which was kept under lock and key in a huge trunk of hers that stood in the corridor.

"How d'you get on with her, Dad?" Rodion asked, helping himself to a piece of pie.

"Nothing much to it. It's the way these things go," his father replied. "She calls me a country bumpkin, an old dog, and a nobody, and I come back with dirty old hag or, say, what we called bitches like her back in the village..."

"In full?"

"Sure, why should I stand anything from her?"

"You're not finding things dull then?"

The old man thought a moment and gave a comprehensive reply.

"How could things be dull? I've got to get Varya her meals, clean the house, cook, do the shopping and see that there's plenty of firewood. All that Hugovna woman does is jabber, jabber, you get no work out of her. Then there's Yevgeny and Iraida, they come home hungry. Who'll give them some nice hot soup if not their grandfather? Shall we have another one?"

"Let's."

Rodion poured out the chilled vodka. The old man lovingly picked up his glass, and fondled it for a moment in his calloused hand.

"What makes it taste so good, blast it?" he said in a

voice that had grown strangely gentle. "Eh, Mefodyevich?"

He now called his son by his patronymic, he thought it more fitting. His eyes twinkled merrily, he had drunk his fill, eaten a hearty meal, and now he sat back well-pleased with himself, proud of the dinner he was giving his son. He looked at the pies, baked according to Aglaya's recipe, at the roast beef, and the sausages sizzling in the frying-pan. The pickled cucumbers couldn't have been better, and the purple sauerkraut looked pretty, too, among the other dishes. Everything was "right and proper", as the old man liked to say after a few drinks.

"You've come home with a decoration, I see," he said, wiping his moustache and beard. "With government medals, with signs of honour. My congratulations, naturally. But tell me, where have you been, my dearly beloved son?"

"Where I've been, I'm no more."

"You're hurting me, Mefodyevich, I can keep a secret."

"You can, but what about gabbing in the market-place. The whole of our street knows your secrets."

Flustered, the old man hurried to the stove ostensibly to take off a Polish dish called *bigos*, which, he said, was getting overdone. He took the casserole out of the oven and asked from where he was:

"I say, Mefodyevich, you and I have to get down to accounts. There's quite a bit of your housekeeping money left over, when d'you want to have it?"

Rodion said never. Staring at the wall facing him, he broke off small pieces of pie and ate them with an absent look.

"'Never!' What sort of talk is that?" the old man said, feeling wronged. He had been saving long and carefully, haggling at the market, buying firewood where it was cheapest, and washing the bed sheets and towels himself rather than pay the laundry. He even scrubbed the floors if Varya was too busy. And all the thanks he got was this "never".

"Oh, no, Mefodyevich, nothing doing," he said angrily. "I'm no drain on your housekeeping money. I try my best for you, I get Varya to make out a written account for you every blessed day, and you say never!"

"As punishment for your fussy accounting, take the balance and buy yourself a new winter overcoat," Rodion said sternly. "We'll go shopping tomorrow and get you a fur-lined coat and a fur cap."

"Can't be done," the old man answered on thinking it over. "Hugovna will have a stroke."

"If she does, we'll stand her a funeral."

"No, it can't be done," the old man persisted. "If that's the way you feel, let's get Varya a fur coat instead. I saw a grand-looking fur coat in the shop down the street."

"We'll buy for Varya without your money, but you're going to have your coat just the same."

"I don't care for a new coat. It's Varya who really needs some new things. The wench is in full flower, she's old enough to marry. We could get things ready for that, buy pillows and quilts, and all that's right and proper..."

Rodion made a wry face. The thought that one day Varya would marry was always a disagreeable one.

"All right, enough of that," he said. "Let's have a drink instead in old Afanasy's memory."

The front-door bell gave a long peal. Hugovna was nearer the door but she did not go and open it. Rodion released the catch on the lock, took one look at Volodya and hugged him right there on the landing. Behind Volodya stood Aglaya and Varya.

"I dragged him out of the lab, Dad. Don't let it surprise you that he smells so funny," Varya said.

Rodion kissed Aglaya too.

Grandfather got busy getting clean plates and glasses on the table and filling the decanters with different vodkas — one flavoured with galingale, another with currant buds, and one more with red pepper.

"Let us drink to Afanasy's memory first, and then I'll tell you everything," Rodion said.

He raised a glass of vodka in his hand, exposing a tattooed design running up his forearm, held it aloft for a moment and said in a low voice:

"Let us drink to the memory of a Communist, a Ukrainian, to your father, Volodya, your brother, Aglaya, and my best friend — to Afanasy Ustimenko, who died a hero's death fighting for the freedom of the Spanish people. May he rest in peace in the soil of Madrid."

Grandfather crossed himself. Everyone drank in silence. Volodya ate the pie, choking back his tears. In the nursery, Hugovna took up her lullaby again. Rodion lit a cigarette, and his look became lowering and hard.

"I'll tell you briefly," he said. "There were seven Junkers approaching Madrid in V-formation, I saw that myself. The rest I didn't see, I heard it from others. The Junkers are heavy, three-engined planes, and the pilots were Germans, nazis.

222

Afanasy went in alone. He must have had a very hard time until the rest of his flight managed to take off, something had gone wrong with the planes. The Junkers dropped no bombs on Madrid that time. Afanasy shot down two of them, both crashed. And then..."

Rodion inhaled deeply, and continued in a low, clear voice:

"And then his plane caught fire. He tried to fight the flames but they got him. Our Afanasy was burnt to death over Madrid. They buried him there, in Madrid. Thousands of people, I don't know how many, attended the funeral; mothers carried their children in their arms, flyers, tank and infantry men, all escorted him on his last journey. He was a Russian, everyone realised that. The coffin was borne not the way it's done with us, but upright, without the lid. It made you think that Afanasy himself was striding along with all those Spaniards. The fire hadn't injured his face much, only his hair... They sang the *Internationale*. They also sang some Spanish songs and the *Varsovienne*, they gave three salvoes at the cemetery. A white stone was placed on the grave..."

Volodya stared at him unblinking. Aglaya was weeping quietly, Varya had turned away to the window and was wiping her tears with her fingers. Grandfather listened with a gloomy frown.

"I had some photos, but I had to destroy them," Rodion continued. "There were some notes too, and a letter your father wrote you just in case ... but there's nothing left. I'll tell you what I know, Volodya. Afanasy often said to the Spaniards, 'If you're tired, give yourself a shake; if you're weakening, pull yourself together; if you've forgotten, remember: the revolution is not finished.' In our spare time we two used to read Lord George Gordon Byron, he appealed to us particularly over there because of what he had done for Greece. Afanasy often repeated some of the lines, with a laugh as if it were a joke, but it was no joke at all, of course. I remember a little:

> *The dead have awakened — shall I sleep?*
> *The world's at war with tyrants — shall I crouch?*
> *The harvest's ripe — and shall I pause to reap?*
> *I slumber not: the thorn is in my couch;*
> *Each day a trumpet soundeth in mine ear.*
> *Its echo in my heart...*

"That's what he used to say, he'd ask me, 'Hear the trumpet, Rodion?' And I'd say, 'I certainly do. Especially after your treats of green olives, of cuttlefish in its own inky juice, or some other Spanish delicacy you've discovered.' That's all. There's nothing more for me to tell."

Rodion lit another cigarette with absorbed attention and fell into one of his long habitual silences, ignoring his guests completely. Perhaps he was thinking of the graves he had left there, the living who were still kept behind barbed wire in French camps, or perhaps he was remembering those women in severe black who lay in the dusty square of the small village of Rambla in the province of Cordova, clutching their dead babies to their breasts. Together with Afanasy he had seen those wives of antifascists, stoned to death. He and Afanasy had looked at one another then and understood that something new, something unprecedented in cruelty was descending on the merrily dancing world. That something as yet opaquely vague and blurred, as yet lurking behind a thick mist, had to be repelled at once and at all costs, or else the world, frivolously living in the present, singing songs and laughing at all the funny little jokes about its presidents and ministers, the world clamouring for its "bread and circuses," would soon, too soon, be reduced to smoking ruins with huge, swastika-painted bombers roaring triumphantly overhead. "It's begun," Rodion had said then. "Yes — full blast," Afanasy had agreed.

"There's another thing I want to tell you about," Rodion said, looking hard at Volodya with his keen, chilly eyes. "Your father and I were driving through the village of Rambla one day. In that village all the wives of anti-fascists had been driven to the square together with their children and even babies, and, in broad daylight, had been stoned to death. Those women, they stood huddled together, with their arms round one another, and had those great big stones flung at them.

"Could a half-hearted effort get the better of *that?* Even Afanasy and I, no great statesmen, God knows, realised that it would not blow over, that it had begun, it was going at full blast. And the turn it's taking is this. They don't want two worlds or two systems any more, they want just one system, and they reckon to get it by conquering. They staged a rehearsal there, just to see how the old world would face up to it, was it for them or against them. If the world didn't come to an agreement, they'd get good and ready and start in earnest, because if the world couldn't come to an agreement there it would never agree anywhere. And all he, Hitler, wants is for no one to come to an agreement anywhere, so he can knock everyone out one by one. Do you understand?"

"I do," Volodya replied.

"Have a drink. My first day home has been rather a screwy one, I've been drinking vodka since I arrived. It's amazing, honestly, all the time I was out there, I never managed to catch up on my sleep."

He looked about him with an anxious glance, and everyone noticed how run down he was, this tough, self-possessed, brawny man, who took what was coming with a smile, a true sailor salted through and through by the briny sea breezes, "the glory of the Baltic" as he called himself with a laugh, recalling the clumsy verses composed during the Civil War.

"You're not running a temperature, are you, Dad?" Varya asked him very softly.

Rodion hugged her with one arm, and drew her close.

"I'm fine, daughter, perfectly fine," he said with bitterness. "I'm just tired, and the thoughts that are worrying me are none too cheerful. For instance, we all imagine that fascism will sort of pass us by like a thundercloud. But it can't pass us by, I'd been thinking and watching events even before Spain. Take this: why did the German aviation man, Hugo Eckener, have to arrive in the USA in his DR-3 Friedrichshafen? To bring moral pressure to bear on the Americans, see how strong we're getting sort of thing. Why did the *Bremen* win the Blue Ribbon on the way to New York and not on its way home? Once again, to give them a shock. Take their flyers, their boxers, their films — German strength demonstrated everywhere, German victory, German superiority, the German fist. And the damned fools in Europe and across the ocean just dance and dance. Thaelmann is in prison — what does it imply? The 'Thousand-Year Empire' — what does that imply? The German delegation has left Geneva — why? Now they've founded an Anglo-German corporation in London, they're spreading Hitler's ideas among the English people, Lord Mount-Temple has been made chairman and he's a big shot in the British chemical industry... Chamberlain is a sap, he's either in their pay or he's a plain fool. And so, the way I see it, our good old planet has no one but us to rely on."

"You mean there'll be war?" Varya asked.

"Something big's going to happen," Rodion said, turning to face Aglaya. "Our task at the moment is to make sure that our people, and our young people especially, are ready to be called up at a moment's notice. You are a big noise in education, Aglaya, so bear it in mind. Our military registration and enlistment offices won't be able to cope with the thing unless we ourselves make our young people staunch and unassailable ideologically. We're cocksure and flippant about it still, but now that I've been around I know that we're in for quite a lot of trouble. Maybe we ought to drink to this, to ultimate victory over what I have seen and what you have, fortunately, never known yet."

"Victory over what, I wonder?" Grandfather asked blinking rapidly.

"Over the enemy, Father," Rodion answered, unsmiling.

"Well, if you're drinking to it, I will too," the old man said. Varya's presence always embarrassed him when he was on one of his sprees. "Do you add dried sweetbrier to your tea?" he turned to Aglaya. "It's good idea. Makes the tea cheaper and the smell is pure hay."

"Tea shouldn't smell of hay, Dad," Rodion put in. "If you're so keen on economy, just brew pure hay and be done with it."

"Hay, brew hay, all the street knows my secrets," the old man mimicked his son. "I have my wits about me too. You've been to Spain, Mefodyevich, that's where you've been. There's a land called Spain. They're always talking about it on the radio. There's even a verse about it, Varya's always muttering it. That's right, isn't it?"

He ran a triumphant eye over the gathering and suddenly broke into song, in a toneless, old woman's chant:

> *A girl I was*
> *And never knew*
> *How bitterly*
> *I'd marriage rue...*

He believed that if there were people sitting at his table, eating and drinking, it was up to him, the host, to keep the fun going and be the first to start up a song. The cultured nanny, however, banged on the wall with her bony fist, and the singing had to be given up.

"Their kid is terribly high-strung," Varya said. "Professor Persianinov looks after him, and he simply can't make out why the boy should be so nervous."

"They call themselves professors too!" Grandfather sneered. "He comes in and starts kissing the kid on the buttocks right away. Ah, you beautiful child, and ah, you lovely little boy! He gets a whole fifty roubles for that, why, I'd do even more for half a hundred myself."

"How can you, Grandfather!" Varya said. "Professor Persianinov is a big specialist, he lectures at your institute, doesn't he, Volodya?"

"He used to, but he doesn't now," Volodya replied. "And he's not a big specialist at all, he's just popular with the mothers because he tells everyone of them that their child is unique."

"Meaning the child has quality?" Rodion asked.

"But he's so dignified, so cheerful, he's so full of fun..." Varya said wistfully.

Volodya did not seem to hear, he was so busy with his own thoughts. All that long and far from easy evening he kept forgetting where he was, then coming back to reality and asking in embarrassment, "What? Were you speaking to me?"

Rodion walked Volodya and Aglaya home. Varya stayed behind to do the dishes with Grandfather. Her father looked questioningly at her, then at Volodya, but said nothing. On the staircase they met Boris Gubin on his way up. He was a huge, handsome chap in a smart overcoat, casually worn, and a felt hat.

"Hello, is Varya in?" Boris asked, addressing Volodya for some reason.

"She's in," Volodya replied indifferently, and Varya's father again looked at him sharply.

"Who's that chap?"

"That's Boris Gubin. Didn't you recognise him? He's the town's celebrity now, he writes poetry and reviews, and when you're walking down the street with him you often hear people say, 'Look, that's Gubin. A good chap, and very clever.' Varya thinks the world of him, she says he's an easy-going man, not a tormentor like some others she knows."

"The tormentor, I take it, is you?"

"I suppose so," Volodya answered vaguely.

He walked ahead, preoccupied and glum, his hands thrust deep into the pockets of his overcoat. Aglaya and Rodion came behind, talking in muted voices.

## CERTAIN CHANGES

After that Rodion came to see Volodya — or so Volodya thought at first — practically every night. But then it dawned on him to his disappointment and surprise that it was not himself but his Aunt Aglaya whom Rodion came to see. He spent long hours with her, telling things to her alone. She sat listening, her beautiful face cupped in her hands, her gaze on their an-

cient desklamp with the embroidered cotton shade. Rodion, looking handsome in his uniform with the gold chevrons, his face
tanned a dark red, offsetting his greying temples and black
tufty eyebrows, paced the length of Aunt Aglaya's room,
talking, laughing, and asking her no questions. Volodya knew
well enough how easy and jolly it was to tell her things.
And one night, for the first time in his life, he heard his
aunt singing for someone, for a man. The bang of the front
door when he came in must have gone unheard for them.
Volodya sat on the edge of the bathtub and listened, spellbound,
clutching a towel in his hands. Aglaya sang low, with all the
artlessness and sincerity of someone confessing her deepest feelings to a friend; she sang as only Russian women can sing.

> *Ah, you gloomy night,*
> *Autumn night so dark!*
> *Why so deep a frown?*
> *Not a star looks down...*

When the song died away, Volodya jerked the tap and the
water rushed noisily into the tub. He was not quick enough to
close the door, however. Aunt Aglaya came in. She was wearing
a new dress and her eyes were glowing with happiness.

"Have you been home long?" she asked.

"I heard you singing," he answered sulkily.

"Don't judge me, don't judge me, dear," she begged.

Volodya looked at her in wonder. He had never seen her like
this before. People said that his aunt was good-looking, he had
noticed it, too, but he never imagined that she could be so
beautiful, so glowing, so graceful and so young.

The bluish bathtub was fast filling with the noisily gurgl-
ing water. Volodya stood beside it in his shorts, a skinny
boy with jutting collarbones, while his aunt held his arm with
a warm hand and whispered to him rapidly and tenderly:

"I've been in love with him for years, for many, many
years, but it couldn't be, there were difficulties in his way
and mine. But now I'm happy, my dear, I'm completely happy.
Just think — Grisha was killed in 1921, and you will leave me
sooner or later. He is lonely, too, so why should we lose one
another now? I see condemnation in your eyes, but why?"

"I'm not condemning you," Volodya said, looking into his
aunt's shining eyes. "It's just that ... you're all deserting
me... Varya, and you, and Pych. Don't desert me, you at least,"
he asked humbly. "How shall I live all alone? It's miserable,
you know."

The water ran over the edge of the tub. Volodya slipped on the tiled floor just as Rodion came out of Aglaya's room and called plaintively:

"Everyone deserted me, it's heart-breaking!"

"Hear that?" Aglaya said to Volodya. "What am I to do now?"

At supper, Volodya crossexamined them and they confessed everything gladly.

"So you wrote to one another, too?" Volodya questioned them.

"Of course we did," Aglaya replied. "Look, you can't butter your bread with that, it's cheese, here's the butter."

"And did you see him when you went to Leningrad?"

"We met, yes," Rodion replied. "We went to the Hermitage, to the Russian Museum, and climbed the belfry of St. Isaac's Cathedral."

"At your age!"

"That's cheek!" Aglaya said.

"Did you know about Spain as well?"

"I didn't know, I guessed," Aglaya said, pouring out more tea for Rodion. "It wasn't too wise of Rodion to keep it a secret from me."

"I didn't want you to worry too much."

"What's going to happen now?" Volodya wanted to know. "I personally vote against your moving out."

"What's the trouble between you and Varya?" Rodion asked.

"No trouble. I suppose it really is true that I'm difficult, that's all. If I believe a thing is stupid and of no importance in life, I just say so frankly. And that makes me a tyrant. She actually calls me a despot. However, she's younger than I am, and all her values are different of course. I'm not judging her, I simply can't take things the way she does."

"That's a lie! You *are* judging her," Rodion said. "You shouldn't, you know. You won't find another like her if you lose her. I'm not trying to make a match between you, I ... how shall I put it ... I respect you or something, and that's why I want to tell you one thing. Ask a lot from people but only what's humanly reasonable."

"I demand of everyone that they be like my late father," Volodya said, all colour suddenly leaving his face. "I demand it of myself first of all. Of everyone else too. Nothing less than that suits me."

Rodion glanced at Aglaya and then turned to Volodya again.

"Have you gone off your rocker?"

229

"No, I haven't gone off my rocker, Rodion Mefodyevich, not at all. But I do consider," Volodya suddenly heard himself speaking exactly like Polunin, "I have the boldness to consider that the purpose of human existence lies in meeting the highest demands made upon oneself, just as my father did when he flew out alone against seven Junkers. He wasn't longing for self-sacrifice, was he? Nor was he merely performing his duty. In those seconds he took the whole responsibility for the fate of the world revolution..."

"Easy, Volodya, don't get so excited, you're terribly pale," Aglaya said.

"I'm not getting excited. I always think that if everyone was like my dad there'd be no more wars, and we'd be curing cancer as easily as a cold or heartburn, say, and we'd have forgotten TB ever existed. Because the way it is now, most people think of their own personal welfare alone, refusing to understand that it is society's welfare that will bring them theirs, and on a grander scale than anything those individuals ever fancied in their dreams."

He gulped down what remained of his cold tea.

"Please forgive me for letting off steam, but at times I find it terribly hard," Volodya said. "A swine called me traitor today because I refused to ask Ganichev to let a certain chap try for his exam again. It hurts... I refused because I know for a fact that this fine chap will definitely stay on in town and will rule the roost, too, with his scraps of knowledge, his feeble brain, and warped little notions."

"Is it Yevgeny?" Rodion asked.

"I'm going to bed," Volodya said, ignoring the question. "I've been feeling the strain lately."

He shut the door tight behind him, and rang up Pych at the hostel. Pych sounded ill-tempered.

"How does it feel to be a married man?" Volodya asked.

"Go to hell," Pych came back.

"Get this, you happy newlywed, that if you fail to turn up tomorrow again, we'll be through for good. Ogurtsov has given me a hint, more or less, that he'd like to take your place."

"That's up to you."

"Coming tomorrow?"

"Yes," Pych said, and added after a short pause, "You really are a difficult fellow, Volodya."

"Such is our stand!" Volodya quoted cheerfully.

While Volodya was on the phone, Rodion talked about him to Aglaya, pacing up and down the room with a cigarette in his fingers. Volodya was right, of course, but he was over-shooting the mark, it was a phase he was going through.

"His sort have been known to blow their brains out," Aglaya said despondently.

"His sort — never!" Rodion replied with calm conviction.

When he left, she took off her new dress, put on something warmer, listened for a moment to Volodya's steady breathing, and stole out of the house. The buses were still running. En-grossed in her recollections, she rode as far as the square near·the railway station.

...In those days cabbies used to park there in a row, the droshky smelled of old leather and tar, and over there, beyond the flower garden, there used to be a market-place where they sold the roast tripe, fish, homemade sausages, pickled cu-cumbers and yellish home-brew. There it was — the square, the stone mansion once occupied by Knyazev the mayor, and the small timber cottage with the veranda, the small wing, the shut-ters and the birch tree beside the gate. The tree was so tall and beautiful now, and the leaf-buds were already filling out even though spring was so late and cold. Wasn't it nice that the tree was still there!

All at once Aglaya felt tears gathering in her eyes. It was there, beside the birch in front of the small cottage with the veranda, that Grisha Kondratyev, chairman of the Gubernia Cheka, had told her that he was going to Moscow for a few days and when he came back there would be a "quiet wedding whether she liked it or not". The words "quiet wedding" sounded queer, and reluctantly he explained:

"I mean you'll move in with me for good. To hell with in-viting a crowd. You're my wife, so who cares? Will you move in?"

She nodded.

"You *will* move in! You will move in and a new life will begin. It will be a life based on new, communist ethics. And, mind you, none of those rotten prejudices of the past. Marriage is love and without love there's no marriage, it's just a sham, just bourgeois hypocrisy, as bad as being in a house of ill re-pute, as they're called."

"What are they?" Aglaya, a young girl then, had asked.

"That I'll explain to you when I come back," he replied stiffly. "I have more to say. Listen. If you stop loving me, don't be scared. Begin life anew with another comrade. It won't be too jolly for me, of course. But our new society won't tol-erate inequality in love. And it won't tolerate pity in marriage either. That's what I myself think, and that's what Comrade Kholodilin, a *Politprosvet* lecturer, said. Did you hear him speak?"

"No, we had machine-gun practice that night," Aglaya said defensively.

"As soon as I get back I'll give your military instructor a piece of my mind. He's always wrecking *Politprosvet* undertakings. Now then, to go on..."

They stood beside the birch tree for a long, long time —he, with a leather jacket on his arm and a Mauser pistol in a yellow leather holster on his hip, and she — in a frock made of cheesecloth. It was her best, her prettiest dress. She had dyed the cheesecloth a bright blue, starched it and trimmed the dress with a small white collar. It looked so wonderful, it actually made her feel overdressed, it must have been the best in town. And Grisha stared at her, stunned and happy.

"Well, well, well! What's the stuff called?" he said shaking his head in wonder.

His train left, and the day Grisha was due back Aglaya took a long bathe in the warm Uncha. She swam about and thought: "Your carefree youth is over, Aglaya, you've had your fun, and now you'll be a wife for the rest of your days. A citizen in your own rights, of course, but still a wife."

That evening — an airless evening with a storm gathering in the sky — Aglaya collected her belongings and came to this cottage here. Grisha, tightly belted in his soldier's tunic, stood waiting for her in the middle of the room. It was clean and tidy. There was Karl Marx gazing from the wall into the distance, there were some books neatly stacked on the table beside the narrow bed, and a candle was spluttering on an inlaid card table. Grisha's eyes were wide-open, and all their short life together he looked at Aglaya wide-eyed, as at a miracle. When he was killed she did not see his body, she had been down with typhus then, and so she always remembered him like that — gentle and shy, standing and looking at her, while the thunder rolled and rumbled in the sky, mustering its strength for a crash and failing in the attempt.

"Now listen, I want to say something about our future life together," he said, turning away a little not to be distracted by Aglaya's childishly artless expression. "I'm doing a rugged job, and all sorts of characters are trying to buy me in order to wreck our strict revolutionary law and order. Never accept anything from anyone, Aglaya, never accept any presents, not one, remember that. Another thing: the Gubernia

232

Cheka owns a two-horse phaeton for official business only. The horses are not bad, we feed them well to give them a decent look. We don't use the phaeton for private needs, it's there for urgent business exclusively. If I ever catch you driving about in that phaeton, I'll disgrace you publicly wherever it may be." Without a pause he asked, "Got anything to eat with you by any chance?"

On their "quiet wedding" night, they ate Aglaya's dry bread and drank some milk. About six months later, the office phaeton called for Grisha, and he went with the other Cheka men to catch the former Baron Tadde, a criminal wanted for rape, murder and robbery. Grisha never returned. In the final clinch, Tadde's adjutant blew up himself and Grisha with a hand grenade.

When Aglaya recovered from her typhus, she found herself a widow. She was given Grisha's engraved Mauser to remember him by and was sent to Moscow to study. She left the cottage with the birch tree by the gate and had never revisited it since.

"What shall I do, tell me," she whispered, leaning against the tree.

She saw two faces — Grisha's and Rodion's — in her mind's eye. Her past short-lived happiness was also tangled somehow with the present. Was she being untrue to Grisha? Who could tell her? Who?

She rang up Rodion from the railway station. He seemed to be expecting the call because he answered at once.

"Stepanov speaking," his voice sounded rather husky.

"We'll leave whenever you say," she said softly. "I can take my vacation beginning Saturday if you like."

"Good. I'll make all the arrangements," he said gravely.

He hung up and went back to the dining-room where Varya was learning something by heart with an angry scowl. He lit a cigarette, walked the length of the room and then made his announcement:

"Varya, I'm leaving."

Varya made a vague, inarticulate sound.

"I'm not going alone."

"Going with Aglaya Petrovna?" she asked without looking up from her book.

"Yes, with her."

Varya closed her book, went up to her father and locking her arms round his neck, gave him three hard kisses on the cheek. And on Saturday, all of them — Varya, Volodya, Yevgeny, Iraida and Boris Gubin — saw Rodion and Aglaya off to Sochi. There was spring in the air that night, it was warm, damp and dark. The window of their de luxe compartment was raised; there were some bright yellow mimosas in a little vase and a bottle of champagne on the small table, covered with a stiffly starched napkin.

"The only way to travel, if you travel at all, is the de luxe express," Yevgeny said, looking up into the window with eager curiosity. "Just look how sensibly and conveniently the space has been utilised. Yes, the rich certainly knew how to enjoy life."

Rodion, who seemed to have shed years, immaculate in his well-fitting navy blue tunic with gold chevrons, a white kid glove on his left hand, joined the others on the platform. Aglaya was giving last-minute instructions from the window of what was, in fact, a small room, gay with carpets, covers, brass and crystal.

"Be sure to eat a whole meal every day, d'you hear, Volodya? Do take the trouble, you've got to understand that you really need it, you're so skinny, you don't sleep enough, you're so run down and nervous, and then the graduation exams are coming on. Listen, it's bad enough that you're studying so hard, you're always coaching someone besides. You've got to eat soup, you hear me? Our neighbour will do all the marketing and cooking for you, don't forget your hot meals and don't stuff yourself with bread. You hear me?"

"Varya, I wish you'd look after him," her father whispered.

"Volodya, you can come and have dinner with us regularly," Boris Gubin said genially. "Mother's an excellent manager as far as creature comforts go."

"Why, he can come and eat with us," Yevgeny offered magnanimously. "He'll pay his share and that will be that."

Varya stood biting her lips, saying nothing. She came third with him, no, even fifth. Science came first, then the institute, then his thoughts, ideas, books and anything else there was, and only then, when his time was really free, came her turn, in his spare time, for lack of anything better to do or when there was no one else to listen to his discourses.

Boris Gubin took her arm and she did not pull it away —let Volodya see. But even this he failed to notice. He had again removed himself from his surroundings, he may have been there alone. What could he be thinking about? Intestines, tumours, or what?

"We can still make the pictures," Boris whispered.

"All right," she nodded.

"Well, it's time we said our good-byes," Rodion said in a

strained voice. "I'll be going straight on to the Baltic from the Black Sea."

The train moved off slowly on its long journey. Volodya started for the exit without waiting for the others.

"I'm not going to the pictures," Varya said.

"Where shall we go then?" Boris asked, always ready to fall in with her wishes.

"I'm not going anywhere, I'm tired."

"Maybe we could go and have some tea at your place?"

"We're not going to drink tea at my place. I told you I'm tired."

In the meantime, Yevgeny was saying to Iraida:

"If one were clever at combining the personal and the social, and were not a poor fish with lofty principles, if one knew how to size up a situation quickly, never miss one's chances, mope or whine, one could make as much a routine of travelling in smart cars and de luxe carriages and frequenting all those palm beaches and Black Seas, as we are making of our porridge for breakfast, don't you agree, sweetheart? By the way, don't you think you're losing a bit of your *savoir faire*? After all, you could smile when necessary and show more life. Your clothes, too, could be more elegant. Go and see the mater, flatter her a bit and she'll gladly alter your summer coat into one of those long jackets. They're the rage just now."

"I have a headache," Iraida said.

"You always have a pain somewhere, sweetheart," Yevgeny said, his voice, though caressing and low, was loaded with hatred. "But actually you're nice and fit, you're eating plenty like a good little girl, and everything is normal. You mustn't let yourself slide, that's all."

The train sped on. Standing in the passage, Rodion took off his cap and rubbed his forehead hard with a handkerchief. The train attendant was making their beds for the night.

"Would you like to change compartments? There's another lady next door," Rodion heard the woman say to Aglaya.

"No, she will stay here with her husband," he said firmly, without a smile. "The lady in the next compartment can travel alone."

She looked up, saw his mocking eyes, the medals on his tunic and the gold on his sleeves, and appeared flustered.

· "What about bringing us some tea then?" Rodion asked gently.

Aglaya was sitting on a chair in the corner of the compartment, her smiling and very pale face cupped in her hand, the way she always sat at home. A warm, damp wind blew in at the window and stirred the yellow mimosas on the table; it came from the fields and brought with it a smell of early spring and acrid engine smoke.

"Sandwiches, pies, wine and soft drinks!" a business-like voice called down the corridor.

"Here we are," Rodion said, sitting on the edge of the couch and gazing deeply, lovingly and reverently into Aglaya's dark eyes.

"Is that all you have to say?" she asked.

He remained silent.

"Here we are, there we are," she teased him. "Stop being shy of your own self. Don't be afraid of words. There's a word — love. You love me, I know that. We're no longer young, we know the value of words. Tell me you love me."

"Love me," Rodion repeated spellbound, in his husky voice.

"Say I love you."

"I love you, Aglaya," he said. "I didn't know until now what it meant. But even when I was in Spain, it was you I always talked about whenever I saw Afanasy. He guessed. He said to me: marry her, Rodion, you'll never marry anyone else now."

"And did you marry me?" Aglaya asked with a little laugh.

"How do you mean?"

"Did you ever say you wanted to marry me?"

"Didn't I?"

"Rodion, I'll tell you exactly what you did say. You said, 'Aglaya, I'm going to Sochi. Let's go together, shall we?' The first I heard about it was when you told the train attendant that you were my husband."

She got up gracefully, sat down beside him, thrust her hand under his arm and pressed her face to his shoulder.

"You're no good at words."

"No good at all," he said. "Aglaya, don't be angry. It's not that I'm afraid of people who are good at words, but it's tricky to be with them. That was another good thing about Afanasy: he knew how to be silent. It's a great thing, this being able to avoid a lot of words you don't need popping out at the wrong moments. You have it too."

"Are we going to live our life together in silence?"

"No, we'll live our life the right way, the way people should live," he said with calm determination, yet his voice held a caress. "You'll see."

Aglaya pressed his arm closer.

236

"What are you thinking about?" he asked abruptly.

"I'm happy, only it frightens me a little," she said humbly. "You'll go off to sea and I..."

"And you'll move to Kronstadt or Oranienbaum."

"I won't. I'm needed here. There I'd have to take a new job. It won't work, Rodion. I'll be here, waiting for you. Always. Do you know what it means to have someone always waiting for you?"

"No, I don't."

"Now you will."

She grew pensive. He asked her what was troubling her. "It's Volodya," she said. "How will he manage all alone?"

## YOU PEOPLE ARE AMAZING!

But Volodya was not all alone. He had Pych and Ogurtsov with him, both of them depressed and sad. An hour before Dr. Mikeshin had passed away, the doctor with whom Volodya had gone out on calls in the horse-drawn ambulance two summers ago. Pych and Ogurtsov were on duty at the hospital when Mikeshin was brought in. He was still conscious, he recognised both students and even joked with them about his condition. He grew worse when he was settled in bed; he became restless, his mind began to wander, and when twilight gathered the kindly old doctor died. Pych and Ogurtsov had also worked with Mikeshin, and they simply could not take it in — it was all over so quickly the whole thing was crazy, unreal.

"We've got to put a notice in the paper," Volodya said. "The whole town knew him, he helped so many. Right, Pych?"

Putting in a notice proved less simple than they thought. To begin with, it was late and the section in charge of notices was already closed for the day. The secretary of the *Uncha Worker* editorial office — a man in a long belted blouse with a strangely jovial manner — told the students, waving a huge pair of scissors, that a regional newspaper could not announce all the deaths any more than it could gladden its readers' hearts with news of all the little citizens born into the world. Saying this he laughed.

"Must you joke about it?" Pych said darkly. "We didn't come all this way for a laugh."

"I'm a born optimist," replied the man. "And besides I know we're all mortal. Well, dear friends, there's nothing I can do for you."

They decided to wait for the editor. The secretary chatted on the phone, went in and out of the room, read damp galley-proofs, drank tea and ate sandwiches. Pych, Ogurtsov and Volodya sat on a small hard sofa and did not utter a word. At long last the editor arrived — the editor in person, whose name Volodya saw daily in the paper — M. S. Kushelev, Editor-in-Chief.

The three students lined up in front of Kushelev's vast desk and stated their business.

"There's nothing I can do for you," Kushelev said, shaking his shaggy head. "I am very sorry but I do not know the late Dr. Mikeshin. In fact, I never knew him."

"Mikeshin saved hundreds, perhaps thousands of lives," Volodya thundered. "The whole town knows Mikeshin, and it's too bad that you, the editor of our newspaper, did not know him. But that's your own affair, what we want is the notice to appear."

"There will be no notice," replied Kushelev and turned his entire attention to the reading of a damp galley-proof, which looked like the one the secretary had been reading earlier that evening. "And please give me a chance to concentrate, this is important material."

The only thing to do was to collect signatures to the obituary notice. They drove to the dean's, then to the clinic to see Postnikov, and after that they travelled from one professor's flat to the next, and finally came to Zhovtyak's. The professor was sitting alone in his large dining-room, helping himself to something that smelled delicious from a German silver dish, drinking mineral water and reading a foreign magazine. On the dinner table, at a distance from the food, stood some dusty figurines, a chipped little jug, an ill-shaped plate and a cup; they had apparently just been unpacked.

"Ah, our successors!" Zhovtyak exclaimed. "I'm very glad, very glad indeed, welcome, my young friends, sit down, my dear guests, sit down."

He covered the dish with a gleaming lid, pulled his napkin out of its ring and wiped his lips.

"You've caught me enjoying a rare hour of leisure," he said in his smugly benevolent, high-pitched voice. "Like the rest of us I, too, your professor, am pray to certain little passions. This has been a lucky day for me, I came across something worthwhile and hauled it to my lair. I collect old china and pottery."

"What do you do?" Pych asked. He was rather obtuse in such matters.

238

"What all collectors do, colleague. I'm a collector pure and simple. Some people collect stamps or match boxes, others go in for paintings, bronzes, money."

"Hoarders, you mean?" Pych put in again.

"Oh no, my dear young man, it's quite an innocent passion, noble and platonic. People don't collect money, they collect monetary units. Now I collect china and pottery because I admire the art, the ingenuousness of the old masters, the beauty and elegance of form. Take this piece for instance."

With his plump fingers Zhovtyak picked up a small, dusty and long unwashed statuette, blew on it and, feasting his eyes on it, said:

"Meissen porcelain, mid-eighteenth century. You see? Two cupids are holding a candlestick. One little cupid has his hand chipped a bit, but it doesn't matter, it really doesn't. But what lovely poses, eh? What ingenuousness! See the ingenuousness of it?"

"I see the ingenuousness," Ogurtsov answered with an effort.

"Now take a look at this little perfume bottle. See the design of the forget-me-nots, it's unique."

Zhovtyak would have gone on exclaiming over his acquisitions for hours if Pych had not thrust the obituary notice at him. Zhovtyak turned sour at once and chewed his lip in doubt.

"Why so grandiloquent, come to think of it?" he asked. "Wouldn't a simple notice be better? Mikeshin ... let me see, Mikeshin..." the words trailed off as he tried vainly to remember who Mikeshin was. "Where do you want me to sign? Shall I make mine last? After the assistant professors?"

"You can be the first if you like," Pych said sternly. "Here, there's room enough for your signature above the dean's. Only make it very small, it won't matter in print, all the signatures will be in the same type anyway."

"True enough," Zhovtyak agreed, and squeezed in his signature at the top of the list. He put in the word professor too.

While Zhovtyak was busy reading and writing, Volodya, Pych and Ogurtsov looked about the dining-room with its bronzes and crystal, its glass cabinets big and small, in which the objects of Zhovtyak's "innocent little passion" were displayed: plates, dinner services, shepherds and shepherdesses, old vases of old porcelain, dishes, bowls, cups in gold, pink and blue. The chairs and sofas, placed between the cabinets, were covered with old brocade, the walls were hung with oil paintings in heavy gold frames — fat naked women, a red-faced monk, angels flitting across a blue sky...

"Well, that's that," Zhovtyak said. "I've crossed out the word 'irreplaceable', simply 'loss' will be more dignified."

Pych nodded. He only let off steam when they were out in the street.

"Not bad for an innocent little passion," he said angrily. "That junk he's hauled in is worth a good many thousand. I remember dispossessing one diehard *kulak*, he owned sixteen cows and his wife tried to tell me that he simply adored keeping cows as pets. Calls himself a doctor, too!"

"You're all wrong, Pych," Ogurtsov said. "He's doing a job in life that's not really his. I saw a shop in Moscow, a curio shop it was. Well, that's where he should work, it would suit him down to the ground."

"For the good of the state, perhaps?" Pych asked. "You're an innocent, that's what you are. His kind of passion in mainly for feathering his own nest, believe me. He's saving up for a rainy day because he feels insecure. The place he's grabbed doesn't belong to him, so naturally he's worried."

The impressive signatures made the obituary notice acceptable to the editor of the newspaper.

The funeral took place on a warm, summerlike morning. Thirty, or at most forty, people attended, but by the time the procession reached the graveyard the number had dwindled down to less than a dozen. Misha Shervud, Svetlana, Alla and Nyussia only stayed for the first part of the ceremony. Yevgeny walked half-way to the graveyard, then took a tram back to town. There was a gentle, steady breeze, the old white hearse creaked monotonously, the horses, too, were old and almost lame. Snimshchikov, the bearded driver of the ambulance carriage, marched beside Volodya.

"I'm in Cart Transport now," he told Volodya gruffly. "Our first aid has switched over to motorcars exclusively. They travel fast, of course, but they get stuck pretty fast, too. The way I figure it, if our dear departed had kept to the carriage he'd have lived to a ripe old age. The air's full of poison inside a car, and that's how Dr. Mikeshin came to his last stop."

Volodya was not listening, he was looking at Mikeshin's widow, a slim woman with short greying hair. She followed the hearse without weeping; she held herself erect and her expression was almost stern. At the grave she suddenly weakened, her legs gave way, and she fell face down on the damp mound of earth, silently, without a moan. The students rushed forward to help her up, but Postnikov held them back.

"Don't. She wants to be left alone," he said sharply.

Ogurtsov looked away, breathing hard; the rough voices of the grave-diggers could be heard exchanging remarks as they collected their spades and ropes, their job done.

"Give us a bit extra, this soil sure takes digging," one of them said.

Once again there was silence, and only high up in a birch-tree a bird, hidden in the newborn leaves, trilled its gay and cheeky song.

"All right, I'll be wishing you all the best", said Snimshchikov. "Fun is fun, as they say, but there's the job waiting. I'll go and drink one to the memory of the deceased and then off to work."

Later, when the widow at last agreed to be put into a cab, Postnikov, Volodya, Pych and Ogurtsov took a walk through the graveyard. There was a heavy granite stone on Polunin's grave now, and a tall slender poplar at the foot. There was also a bench there on which the three students sat down, worn out emotionally and physically. Postnikov went to his wife's grave.

"It doesn't say he was a professor," Pych said, staring at the stone. "Remember, Ustimenko, how it made him laugh that in Germany they have a rank of a privy medical councillor?"

"I remember," Volodya said. "I remember everything about him. I remember him flaring up once and saying that though a person may be a professor he may be anything but a doctor."

Some time later, Postnikov came back, sorrowful and silent. He mopped his forehead and moustache with his handkerchief and sat down next to Volodya.

"What's the reason? Why didn't anyone come to the funeral?" Volodya asked. "We all know what a fine doctor he was, how useful his work had been."

Postnikov put a cigarette into an amber holder and lit it before answering.

"Emergency cases hardly ever bother to find out the doctor's name unless they want to put in a complaint against him, which does sometimes happen on this planet of ours," he spoke slowly and pensively. "But if things go well, if everything is all right, why should they want to know the name of the man who injected them with something, gave them some drops, or even 'cut something out' — for heaven's sake, why? Everyone knows Genghis Khan, for instance; Dr. Guillotin, the scholar who invented the guillotine, is also well known, and so is Dr. Antoine Louis, who experimented with corpses to work out the best method of beheading the people condemned to death. People know Talleyrand, the greatest swindler of all times and nations, they know Fouché and Rasputin, they are curious about the Rothschilds of this world, about kings and princelings, about Azef the provocateur, but Mikeshin... Now, who's Mikeshin?.. Oh yes, there was someone of that name, he wore glasses, but he's dead now."

Looking sternly into Volodya's eyes, he added with a sigh, "That's how it is, Ustimenko."

"No, it is not!" Pych spoke up in a hard voice. "I disagree with you. It has been that way, of course, but it must be no more. It wasn't to let all this rot poison people's minds that we took power in our own hands, that we have those wonderful words about the dictatorship of the proletariat, that we Bolsheviks took command over the press. You may believe it or not, but I give you my word that the time will come and very soon too, it's almost here, it is here, when people like Mikeshin will be national heroes. Not everyone understands it yet, but they will, we'll make them understand, so don't let it worry you."

He broke off as abruptly as he had begun, and coughed once or twice in sudden embarrassment. Volodya and Ogurtsov remained silent.

"Ah, you Bolsheviks, you Bolsheviks!" Postnikov's voice had an unusually joyous ring. "You people are amazing! You will certainly achieve all things that matter."

"We are achieving them," Pych said sullenly. "We have achieved a great deal. And what's ahead will be so staggering, it'll beat anyone's wildest fancies."

"It's hard work," Postnikov said.

"We're not complaining. It would help, though, if the intelligentsia itself would expel from its ranks such professors as your Zhovtyak, for instance. It would be a great help."

Pych tugged at the tops of his boots, rusty-black with age, and gave Postnikov a sidelong look.

"I wasn't personal. You're not angry?"

### Chapter Twelve

## THE OATH

Graduation came as a strange anticlimax. The rector was called away and delegated his duties of chairman to the dean. It was then that Professor Zhovtyak took the floor. He spoke long and bombastically, drawing his pet comparison between the year 1911 and the present, then he enumerated all the "alumni of the institute" who had become prominent scientists, mentioned all the teaching staff, and forgot to name Polunin.

"What about Polunin?" someone shouted from the audience.

"Name Polunin!"

"Let's stand up!"

"I only named the living," said Zhovtyak. "As for Professor Polunin, I gladly propose that we should honour his memory by standing up."

The "gladly" sounded ambiguous, and the audience reacted with a low rumble of protest. Zhovtyak remained standing for the required number of minutes, his expression befitting the occasion.

"Please be seated," he said in an adequately sad voice when the time was up.

They did. Zhovtyak continued with his interrupted speech for another ten minutes or so, and left amid thin applause. The dean — Iraida's father — mumbled something to the effect that it was time to bring matters to a close. There was still no sign of the rector. He was a man of intelligence and nothing of the sort would have happened if he had been there, of course. The dean even bungled the ceremony of handing the diplomas, showing undue haste, getting the names mixed up and cracking little jokes, although it was one of those moments in life when jokes were quite out of place. Even Yevgeny found this face-tiousness revolting. But then of course he had a private bone to pick with Iraida's father.

"Allow me to declare the ceremony over," the dean said, slurring his syllables. "You're off into the world now. Good luck, young people!"

"Well, well," said Ogurtsov, rubbing the back of his head pensively. "Peter the Great knew what he was talking about. 'Serve without slurring,' he said, 'but if you must slur, don't serve.' Well, is that all there is to it?"

"No, that's only the beginning," Volodya replied glumly.

The assembly hall grew empty. The charwoman began to mop the floor, pushing the chairs about with a clatter. Pych sat on the windowsill and leafed through an old, dog-eared notebook.

"Here it is," he said. "Since they've chosen to treat us so shabbily, we'll pledge our oath ourselves."

Nyussia took fright at once. She was a careful little prude with a strong dislike for unfamiliar words, point-blank statements and spontaneous actions.

"The idea! What oath?" she asked arching her eyebrows.

Pych looked at her and sighed.

"Does that give you the jitters too? Do you think we're Masons or something?" he asked.

For safety's sake Nyussia decided not to commit herself, and turned to leave the hall. Her high heels clicked smartly as she walked to the door, leaving behind her a trail of expensive perfume. Nyussia withdrew, pleased for being her own clever little self.

"I copied it down ages ago," Pych said. "Let's do it ourselves, since our betters haven't thought of it. In a way it's outdated, of course. Still, there's something in it."

He jumped down from the windowsill and said sternly, an army commander ordering his men.

"Repeat after me. This, my dear colleagues, happens to be the old 'medical faculty oath' which, so they say, was approved by old Hippocrates himself. Repeat after me: Accepting with deep gratitude the rights of a doctor granted me by science and fully understanding the importance of the obligations imposed upon me by this title..."

"This title," echoed the six young doctors in ringing voices.

"I promise that as long as I live I shall never in any way disgrace the profession which I am today entering."

Pych, Pych the Old Man, Pych the toughest chap in the class, suddenly choked and gave a thin squeak. Brushing away a tear, he handed the notebook to Ogurtsov. In the meantime, the charwoman, who was notorious for her hatred of students, had already reached their part of the room.

"Out you go, must you always be asked twice!" she muttered angrily, shoving the mop at their feet.

"Scram!" Pych roared at her savagely.

The mood was broken, no one felt like reading the oath of Hippocrates now.

"All right, finished!" Pych said. "Let's call the incident closed. When I grow up to be a big boy I'll make them all remember the exciting and touching ceremony of our graduation. If Polunin were here, he'd show them."

"Shoving that mop at our feet too," Pych grumbled. "I'm no puppy dog's tail, I'm a doctor with a diploma, would you like to see it?"

By the time they reached the stairs they had begun to see the funny side of the whole thing.

Volodya went into the garden all by himself. It was not to say good-bye to the medical blocks there, for he was anything but sentimental; he simply wanted to find a bench and relax. The last weeks had really been a strain. He turned down a maple walk and ran straight into Ganichev. Volodya was in no mood for conversation, especially since he knew exactly what the professor would talk about, but it was too late to avoid him.

"Have you got your diploma?"

"I have."

"Was the ceremony beautiful?"

"A dream," Volodya said mournfully.

"They're good at that! Spitting into the soul of a young man on the brightest day of his life — they're experts at that."

"And you?" Volodya asked rudely.

"What about me?"

"Why weren't you there? You're both feared and respected. No one would go spitting into people's souls with you there. Why are you here then, sitting on a garden bench?"

"Look here, Ustimenko, do you know what you're saying?" Ganichev cried furiously. "I'm an old man, I'm tired, it's stuffy inside..."

"Polunin with his weak heart would have certainly been there," Volodya cut him short. "I'm sorry, but I find this talk of old age and weariness unpleasant. Remember Polunin saying that the worst enemy of science, progress, civilisation, and the medical profession is apathy. And now you, a friend of Polunin's, are preaching just that. Oh, what's the use!"

"All right, you win," Ganichev's tone was both injured and apologetic. "The young know no pity."

"Is it pity you want? Isn't it too early for that?"

Their glances met and held.

"I don't suppose Skripnyuk, the old fireman whose story you made so moving, ever begged for pity." And then Volodya said with anguish, "Oh, it's not that, believe me, it's something else that worries me, and please don't be angry. Why do so many people prefer to do their condemning and resenting in the privacy of a garden bench instead of getting up and fighting against the things they resent and condemn? Can you tell me?"

Ganichev flinched and dropped his eyes before the earnest, sorrowful look in Volodya's.

"On the whole, you're right. Not in everything, naturally, but on some points," Ganichev said softly. "However, I did not stop to talk to you because I wanted your opinion of my own person. I must have your final answer: are you going to stay on and work with me or not?"

"Of course not!"

"Splendid! And now supposing Polunin were here, would you have stayed on with him?"

"No, I wouldn't have stayed on with him either," Volodya replied after a moment's consideration. "Perhaps I'd have come back to him in about five years' time."

"You'd have done him the honour?"

"I would."

"But why won't you stay?"

"Because both you and Polunin taught us other things."

"Us!" Ganichev exclaimed. "That is you in a broad sense, and not you personally."

"Spasokukotsky was a country doctor in his day, and you yourself told us about him," Volodya said angrily biting off the words. "And you yourself used to say that the deep practical side of his research, which dated back to his days as a country doctor, was sending up shoots even in our time. It was you who told us about the scope of Spasokukotsky's scientific interests, of his power to get to the heart of a problem. Oh, but what's the good of my repeating your own words to you!"

"Science, you see..." Ganichev began tediously, but Volodya did not listen. He understood that though Ganichev wished him well, he also wanted him for his pupil. But Volodya did not want to be anybody's pupil, he wanted to get down to real work.

He did not listen, he simply let Ganichev have his say while he enjoyed the silence about them, the relief of having nowhere to rush that day, the almost fragrant loveliness of the bright splashes of sunlight, and the fun of watching a funny, bald-headed, pugnacious sparrow pitching into a whole flock of his brethren with little sidewise hops.

"And all that just to be able to pump you for a good dissertation theme afterwards?" Volodya asked when Ganichev had finished speaking.

"You wouldn't pump me, you'd find a theme yourself.

"Why should I take the trouble if I have no inner urge to find one at all? For his skeleton stretching, Spasokukotsky with his own hands built a cramp with screws taken from a pair of skates and some old piano strings. I don't know if you'd call that scientific work, but he needed it urgently for his research and not just for the sake of getting a degree. It was the same with his washing his hands with ammonia, or those groove clamps for gastric operations, or, finally, the problems of blood transfusion. And whatever was done under his guidance was always dictated by the vital needs of the clinic, and with Spasokukotsky the clinic was always associated with his youth, with the Zemstvo hospital. Am I not right? Or again take Pirogov. Everyone knows how hard he was on theses that had nothing new to say and scientists with pygmy minds. Rudnev, on the other hand, was easy-going with them. I personally side with Pirogov. There's no sense in breeding erzats scientists. It's expensive, harmful to science and no help in the work. That's what I personally believe and think."

"And who are you to believe or disbelieve, to think or not to think?" Ganichev demanded, thoroughly angered and upset. "Just who are you, tell me that?"

"A doctor with a diploma."

"That's immodest, Ustimenko."

"Why should I think modesty the best thing in my particular job? I can see myself arriving in some remote hole, in the backwoods, and in my great modesty begging the air ambulance service to fly in a consultant on every single case! Will that suit you?"

Ganichev stretched, yawned, and groaned, "O Lord!"

"Have I tired you?" Volodya asked solicitously.

"No, I'm not tired, but it's all so incredibly stupid. You're a gifted man, you know."

"I do know it!" Volodya exclaimed. "I never doubted it for a moment, otherwise I'd have abandoned my studies long ago, because you and Polunin and Postnikov always told us that a doctor had to be gifted and not merely capable. And I do want to be a doctor."

"All right, let's drop it," Ganichev said. "But I'll get at you through the Komsomol anyway."

And he did, in fact, try to get him.


### THE FIRST JOB

It was only after days of stubborn fighting that Volodya managed at last to get an appointment to Zatirukhi, a village two hundred kilometres from the nearest railway.

"You'll have to ferry across the river too," Ganichev gloated.

"Don't worry, I'll survive," Volodya replied.

It rather pleased him, actually that there had been such a rumpus at the institute because of him. Pych had also got an assignment to a remote village and Ogurtsov had left for Kamenka. Many of the graduates were still there, angling for easy jobs, pestering the institute authorities, or busily securing letters from people who mattered to go to Moscow and try there.

Volodya did not find Zatirukhi on the map of the region.

He was due to leave in a week. Aunt Aglaya showed no enthusiasm when Volodya painted the picture of his future life for her.

"You're set on going just the same?" she asked.

"I am."

"But there's no hospital there."

"There is a dispensary. I'll build the hospital."

"Yourself?"

"Myself."

"Did they teach you how to build?"

"Did they teach you, a former laundress, to manage the country?"

"But I don't manage the country."

"Well, I shan't have to build the hospital with my own hands either. I'll direct the work and issue instructions."

Aunt Aglaya merely sighed. There was a hard look in Volodya's eyes and arguing would get them nowhere, she knew.

"So much for all the talk about today's youth being made of different stuff!" she thought, sighed again, and went out to buy Volodya a sheepskin coat, a fur cap, and two pairs of boots, felt and leather ones.

Volodya was suddenly struck by a sobering thought: "No Varya? What shall I do without her? And just now, too, when I shall want to talk to her every minute of the day, when life is starting right from the beginning! What shall I do?" He felt so lost and miserable that he could not settle down to anything.

He hurried to the Stepanovs.

"Come in, Herr Professor, I've some lovely news to tell you," Yevgeny said, admitting Volodya.

The day being hot, Yevgeny was wearing a pair of shorts made of some special stuff by his mother. His hair was, as usual, set under a hairnet. Nowadays he smoked a pipe, a present from Dodik. After a series of major rows they had estab-

248

lished a friendship of sorts, with more irony than sincerity in it.

Varya was also at home. Sprawling on the couch she was reading poetry. The word "Anthology" was inscribed in gold on the cover. Grandfather was in the kitchen making kvass soup.

"Just in time for dinner as usual," he said. "You'll have some of our kvass soup."

"Why d'you look so upset?" Volodya asked Varya.

"Wouldn't you like to know!" she said bitingly and flounced out of the room.

"See how it is, my friend? I'd have gone crazy if my precious wife hadn't deserted me and gone to the country for the offspring's sake," Yevgeny said, slapping his thighs and looking at Volodya with an expression that invited questions.

"All right, let's hear your news," Volodya said bleakly.

"It's our news — yours and mine, Herr Doktor."

Yevgeny simply oozed satisfaction with himself, with his new shorts, his chubby short legs, his muscles which, though rather flabby, were muscles just the same, his excellent health, his prospects, and the kvass soup he was soon to enjoy.

"You're not going to Zatirukhi!"

"How come?"

"You're simply not going! The Health Department of this town has sent in a request for two young specialists, not just *any* specialists but you and me. You're getting an internship at the First Town Hospital, and I, being a sanitary inspector, am joining the staff of the local Health Department. Not bad, eh?"

Volodya remained glumly silent.

The door opened with a squeak, and there was Varya, wearing a different dress, her white one.

"'And not a shadow of emotion disturbed his lofty brow's repose,'" Yevgeny quoted from Lermontov's *Demon*. "I even seem to see displeasure crease the future intern's brow! Or perhaps you think it right that the son of a hero who laid down his life for Spanish freedom should go to Zatirukhi, and people like Nyussia, Svetlana, Alla, and our astute Misha Shervud should get all the soft jobs in town?"

Volodya sat with drooping head, not looking at Yevgeny, who had become quite incensed and was actually raising his voice.

"I don't particularly like discussing this in Varya's presence," Yevgeny said. "In fact, it's not even decent, but then it can't be helped with people like you. Think, you poor innocent, or something worse in this case, just think — there isn't even a club in Zatirukhi, now is there?"

"No club," Volodya agreed.

"And no House of Culture, of course, no drama circle, no shows. Is there anything like that there, or is your precious dispensary all the place has to offer?"

"I don't suppose he even bothered to find out," Varya shouted. "How could such trifles interest the great man?"

"Look what you're doing to her," Yevgeny said, placing his hand on Varya's shoulder. "Take a good look. No, nothing will move your stony heart, you don't give a damn, you're concerned with yourself alone, with your 'inner world', as Varya likes to gush in your defence, but you can't fool me! If *you* have a job of work to do in the world and a calling for it, she, too, has both a job and a calling. Egoism is a sacred thing but only so long as the egoist doesn't start walking over dead bodies. And you, from what I know, are not as simple as you'd have us believe. You're probably the shrewdest in the class, you only look like a lamb. And your high-principled insistence on going to Zatirukhi is nothing but career-making. Yes it is, don't glare, it's nothing but a start for your great 'country doctor' career. You want to start from the bottom, without wasting time fixing yourself up nicely in town; you'll do a term of two years there, but then you'll come back a somebody and will start climbing fast. But the two years in the wilds with you will ruin Varya. She'll..."

"Don't go on," Varya begged him.

"Her talent will die!" Yevgeny cried with fine emotion. "And who'll be responsible? Surely you must see what a crime you're committing for the sake of your selfish, calculating ambition, surely..."

"All right, enough," Volodya said, getting to his feet and staring hard at Varya with a crooked imitation of a smile. "I told you long ago that you were all one family — your mother, Dodik, Yevgeny and you. Another thing that makes your Yevgeny a scoundrel is that he suspects everyone else of being a scoundrel at heart. He's just called me a career-maker. I leave that to his conscience, but you, Varya, why didn't you say anything?"

His lips quivered like a child's, but he pulled himself together at once and continued in a soft, strangely calm voice:

"I'll tell you why. You made no answer to your dear brother for the simple reason that deep down you've been thinking the same things yourself. But if so, what do you want me for? Me —

a scoundrel and time-server, who has mapped out his entire future guided only by ambition? Do you want to share a scoundrel's lot with me? Do you want to share a scoundrel's sufferings? But I'm not like that, Varya, and you must know it. You do know it, but Yevgeny is stronger, your mother is stronger than you. And though you do believe and understand me now — I can see that — a little later they'll explain it all to you from their own point of view and, on the surface, it will sound very much like truth, only it won't be about me and others like me, it will be about Yevgeny, but all of you seem to think the world is peopled with your Yevgenys. That's not true! Varya, don't cry, there's no sense in it any more, I'm not saying this to hurt you, I'm simply telling you what I think. After all, you two have got to know what I think since this is, naturally, going to be our last conversation. But perhaps you needn't. In fact I'm sure now you needn't. It's a lot of rot anyway talking about oneself, explaining and trying to prove something. One thing is clear, Varya, one thing I repeat, and that is: since you agreed with him and said nothing..."

"I didn't agree with him," Varya said. "Only in..."

"Even 'only in something' is too much for me," Volodya cut in. "You've lost interest in geology, you're only a student in name. In other words you're letting your life slide, believing what these imbeciles tell you about your supposed talent. But there is no talent in you, Varya, you do have certain aping abilities, but that's not the real thing — it's fun for a party, it's not work though."

"I can't understand you, Varya, why need you listen to this drivel?" Yevgeny asked, lighting his pipe. "It's insulting, really."

"It's all very sad," Volodya said, coming close to Varya and dropping his voice to almost a whisper. "It's very sad, and I don't think I've ever known a fouler day in my life, but there's no helping it. Good-bye, Varya."

"Good-bye," she said, looking up into his face. Volodya refused to meet her gaze because it hurt him to see grief in Varya's still childishly innocent eyes.

Grandfather shouted from the kitchen that they should lay the table.

"Oh well, cheerio," Yevgeny called out after Volodya.

"You swine," Varya hissed at her brother with set teeth.

She overtook Volodya when he was just getting into the tram.

He did not seem surprised to hear her voice. The tram jolted and shook at every stop and turning. Volodya stared vacantly past Varya's small ear with the blue earring.

"You'll go to Moscow or some other big town, maybe you'll enroll in a drama school, and then the footlights will flare up, there'll be flowers, and all the rest. To everyone's joy I'll have been wrong. But if so, and especially if so, what will you care for Zatirukhi then? The thing that matters is that you and I look upon life differently; there was a time when you seemed to understand me, but the truth is that you did not understand me at all, far from it, you were just a child playing at understanding. Isn't it true?"

"Oh, Volodya!"

"Good-bye, Varya, good-bye. Write if you have the time to spare. I'll answer. There's no sense in our dragging out this sad business any longer."

He jumped off, ran beside the moving tram for a few steps, then turned away abruptly. He was like that — turning away even when he was in the wrong.

"The obvious thing in my case is to get roaring drunk now, I suppose," Volodya thought on seeing a beer poster. "Or start smoking." But these thoughts fled before the dull grief that bore down on him.


### GOOD-BYE, VARYA

He went nowhere for several days, just lay in his den thinking, and at night he could not sleep. Twice he picked up the phone to ring up Varya, but put it down both times. One sultry day, at noon the postman brought him a heavily sealed envelope. It was from Moscow, from the People's Commissariat of Public Health. Volodya had to sign the receipt in two places — in ink, not pencil.

The envelope contained a large sheet of paper which said that Vladimir Afanasyevich Ustimenko was to leave for Moscow at once and report to Comrade Usoltsev of the People's Commissariat of Public Health. A copy of a note from Bogoslovsky was enclosed. It said that "acting on their understanding" he was recommending Volodya to Comrade Usoltsev for that responsible, important and interesting job he and Volodya had talked about on the Chorny Yar wharf. The note was dated May 9th.

Late in the afternoon, Postnikov and Ganichev came to see Volodya. Aunt Aglaya was busy packing his bag, while Volodya rummaged through his books.

"Where is he off to, I wonder?" Ganichev asked with a sly look in his eyes.

"I got this thing by post," Volodya said, showing them the envelope. "And it has me completely baffled."

"It's plain enough, it means going abroad," Postnikov said.

"What's this I hear about going abroad?" Aunt Aglaya cried. "He's still a kid with no experience and they're..."

"He may have no experience, but he has brains," Postnikov said, stroking his moustache. "And he's reliable, too. That's why he was recommended by three men: Bogoslovsky, who's already working there, Professor Ganichev, who wanted to make a pathoanatomist of him, and myself who sees the makings of a decent practising surgeon in your nephew, in time of course. Usoltsev, who signed this letter, was once a pupil of ours and, on occasion, he still seeks our advice. All clear now, I hope?"

"Going abroad where?" Volodya asked.

"It's not Paris anyway," Ganichev replied. "I imagine it's Asia, and Asia where it's difficult. Does that suit you?"

They had champagne. Volodya was sad and abstracted. Postnikov did not speak at all. At parting, Ganichev said to Volodya:

"The best of luck to you! Write to us when you get there. Believe me, dear boy, I'm sorry, I'm really sorry you wouldn't stay on with me."

Aunt Aglaya went into the train compartment with Volodya.

"Get all the sleep you can on the train," she said gently. "You poor, tired dear, you look more like a saint in an icon than a mortal."

Volodya slept for more than 24 hours. He got up, and ate all the sandwiches Aunt Aglaya had made for him, a bun and four hard-boiled eggs. After that he went back to sleep. He was making up for all his lost sleep; no dreams troubled him but neither did he feel any joy when he finally woke up. Something very precious, something terribly important and big in his life was over for ever.

When the train got in, he had a shave and a haircut at the station barber's, then he had a shoe-shine and bought a packet of cigarettes, just in case. Comrade Usoltsev received him at once. This former pupil of Ganichev's was a thickset man of about thirty-five, with the plain, rugged face of a soldier, and closely cropped hair. He wore a shirt of unbleached linen.

"We are thinking sending you abroad, to the republic of

X. We hope you will justify the trust placed in you, and do all you can to make yourself gratefully remembered there afterwards. By that I mean personally and consequently the country that educated you and moulded your character as a citizen," Usoltsev said, searching Volodya's face with a quick look that had no affability in it.

It was a stiffly worded speech, but his voice did not sound formal, and suddenly a twinkle came into his eyes.

"Can you give me a cigarette?" he asked.

Volodya remembered buying the cigarettes, but said he did not smoke. He had not bought the cigarettes to get into the chief's good books. It was a disgusting thought.

"The place you're going to is quite unlike our accepted idea of 'abroad'. You'll find no cocktail bars there and I doubt if there's a cinema, but there'll be plenty of witch-doctors and all sorts of international scum. Living there will be very hard, and the work anything but easy. You won't get any local help, that is junior medical personnel, until you have proved that your cure is better than the witch-doctors', after which the local people may offer to help you, when they've learned enough from you to be of any help."

He looked at Volodya intently, and waited.

"Have you made your decision?" he asked.

"I have."

"And what is it?"

"I am going."

"You won't get cold feet? No writing to Mummy and Daddy to come and take you home? Think well, you're very young, you know."

"I have no Mummy or Daddy," Volodya replied coldly. "I may be young but I'm a doctor, and that's all that matters."

"Good. Fill in the application form then. It's a three-year contract."

The formalities took quite a long time, but getting himself adequately equipped took much longer and required a great deal of energy. When at last he had all he needed in surgical instruments, medicines, books and clothes, his small room at the new Moskva Hotel was so cluttered with parcels he could hardly move about in it.

Aunt Aglaya came to see Volodya off, and Rodion as if by a strange coincidence arrived quite unexpectedly from Kronstadt. He had been promoted to captain and cheerfully complained that he was kept busy day and night. He begged Volodya to talk his obstinate aunt into moving to Leningrad, the loveliest of cities, or to Oranienbaum, if living on an island frightened her. Aglaya laughed happily and Volodya saw her furtively kissing her husband on his greying temple. Rodion brought Volodya a present — a wireless set with some spare dry batteries, in case there was no electricity where he was going.

"You'll certainly need it there," Rodion said, showing Volodya how to use the set. "This thing will come in very handy when you're so far away from everything."

Volodya felt a little sad and a bit sorry for himself, but both his sadness and self-pity dwindled to insignificance before the tremendous and extraordinary feeling of responsibility that overwhelmed him when he saw himself crossing the border and starting work abroad — something vague and blurred, but certain to be very difficult. He shuddered at the thought of his loneliness there, abroad, but he drove away all those fears — after all, Bogoslovsky trusted him, so why should he not trust himself?

"Why don't you go out for a walk?" Volodya suggested to Aunt Aglaya and Rodion in the tones of a kind old man. "Why sit moping here with me?"

But they did not go. Rodion drank a bottle of mineral water, took off his smart tunic with the broad gold stripes, examined Volodya's "kit" and began to pack, after first sorting everything out with amazing competence. He worked in his singlet, although it embarrassed him to display his tattooed arms with their blue serpents, tigers, broken chains and slogans. As soon as he was through with the piece of luggage — packing case, bag or bale — Aunt Aglaya took over and sewed it up in sacking. Husband and wife sang a very amusing song Volodya had never heard before as they worked, and he realised that they had an intimate world of their own to which he was already a stranger. Rodion sang the couplets in a high, cheery voice:

> *Outside the village — something rare!*
> *You'd never, never guess what's there.*
> *All of a sudden from the trees*
> *A bugle call comes on the breeze!*

And Aunt Aglaya joined in the refrain, her head thrown back and laughter in her shining eyes:

> *Tum-tum-tum, tum-tum-tum,*
> *Tum-tum-tum, oh, tum-tum-tum!*

255

She pitched her voice comically low and there was something sweetly interrogative in the way she ended her lines, but Rodion sang high, as Grandfather did when he was on the spree:

> *Oh what chatter, oh what noise!*
> *At the sight of those Hussar boys.*
> *Handsome and moustachio'ed,*
> *Right in front the buglers rode.*

Aunt Aglaya bit off the thread with her sharp, small teeth, and came in with:

> *Tum-tum-tum, oh, tum-tum-tum!*
> *Tum-tum-tum, oh, tum-tum-tum!*

Rodion sang the next verse:

> *There were billets for the officers,*
> *The soldiers had the sty,*
> *The buglers got the hay-shed*
> *And not a light to see it by.*

Volodya listened smiling.

> *Tu-tum-tum, tum-tum-tum,*
> *Tu-tum-tum, tum-tum-tum.*

"Not bad, eh?" Rodion asked.

"Where did you learn such teamwork?"

"Where there's a life of ease, plenty and happiness for all," Aunt Aglaya recited, blushing. "We just learned it by ourselves."

They went down to the big new restaurant for dinner. Though he had only a few customers to serve, the waiter was nevertheless a long time taking their order and Rodion was beginning to fume. The headwaiter, who had an amazingly insolent face and several double chins propped up by a starched collar, informed them that a large group of foreign tourists had arrived that day and that 1) — he folded back the plump forefinger of his left hand — the kitchen had more work than it could cope with, and 2) — he folded back the second finger, as plump as its brother — that it was the foreign tourists who came first at the restaurant. Saying this, he made a bow before a massive tweed-coated back.

"Why don't you put up a notice saying Soviet citizens come second here?." Rodion said.

Aglaya covered his sunburnt hand with hers; he blinked away his anger and cheered up at once.

"Have you ever stopped to think what ingrained servility

is?" Rodion asked his wife, and they started talking as though Volodya were not there at all. And Volodya ate his soup and thought of Varya, of how the two of them could have been sitting here and talking just as intimately of different things, and then gone on together on that difficult, fascinating and mysterious job that was awaiting him. Some bored-looking musicians stepped on to the stage, moved their chairs about noisily and the leader blew his nose thoroughly and loudly, with an authoritative trumpeting.

"Another brandy, please," the tweed-coated foreigner called out.

"I suppose that's all, Rodion," Volodya heard his aunt's voice as from a great distance. "By the way, you're terribly unfair when you're cross."

Volodya finished his cutlet, yawned deliberately and said:

"Incidentally, I'm here, too. You both came here from different towns for the express purpose of seeing me off, and now you've forgotten all about me. It's not nice, you know."

They remained with him until the train moved off. Aunt Aglaya was wearing a white raincoat, her silk kerchief had slipped down on her shoulders and there was an outlandish, beautifully sparkling comb stuck in her dark hair — she liked a Gypsy touch occasionally. Rodion stood very erect, and when the train began to move he raised his hand in a smart ceremonial salute. Aunt Aglaya ran beside the train, pushing through the crowd, and waving. The glaring platform lights shone on her brown upraised face and her eyes, bright with tears.

And then he lost sight of her in the crowd, the wind tore into the train and jerked back the curtains. The lights of Moscow were running away, Moscow — the city that was sending Volodya, Vladimir Afanasyevich Ustimenko, Dr. Ustimenko to work abroad.

### ABROAD

Volodya had a bristly beard at the end of the six days' journey. His travelling companion, an elderly officer with a round bald patch on his head, offered to lend him a razor if Volodya did not have his own. He let the beard grow on purpose, though, to appear older at the border.

At the border, however, Volodya's appearance aroused little interest in anyone. The border guards checked his documents and the customs officers glanced through his luggage.

257

It was a raw, windy night. A mountain stream howled and roared not far away. Volodya sat drinking strong tea out of his thick glass. The train was still there, and its bright yellow windows glowed with cosiness and warmth. A short Japanese with horn-rimmed glasses on his clever, wizened face, some tall red-haired Englishmen and with them a beautiful, heavily made-up woman were strolling about the restaurant.

The bell clanged twice, it clanged for the third time and then the chief guard gave a long whistle. The earth shuddered as the heavy train moved off into the dark rainy night, towards the arch that divided the two countries. Volodya finished his tea, and paid with the last of his Soviet money. A little later four men came in, they bowed low to Volodya and loaded his luggage into a lorry. The language they spoke was not Russian, they already belonged to "abroad". When everything had been loaded, covered with a tarpaulin and secured with ropes, the lieutenant of the Soviet border guard shook Volodya's hand and said in broad Ryazan Russian:

"Well, good luck go with you, doctor!"

"All the best to you," Volodya replied, as Rodion sometimes said in farewell.

The lorry slowly rolled away only to pull up some fifteen minutes later. Men carrying paraffin lamps and wearing oilcloth capes and caps with long peaks checked Volodya's papers with scrupulous care. They were the border guards of the other side. Customs officers went through Volodya's luggage, turning everything inside out while Volodya sat and dozed. The mountain stream seemed to be roaring directly overhead. It was some time before the officer of the frontier guard saluted Volodya with two fingers, quite differently from any Soviet officer, peered curiously into the Soviet doctor's face and, baring his tobacco-stained wide-set yellow teeth in a broad grin, swung the lantern twice. The driver switched on the headlights, and the heavy toll-bar went up, creaking in the damp night. Groaning in every one of its elderly joints, the lorry crawled reluctantly uphill into the raw starless darkness. The day dawned cold, but by evening it had grown warmer. Volodya's travelling companions slept in the back of the lorry, on awakening they played a game Volodya had never heard about, and at the halts ate half-raw mutton, tearing at it with their teeth. On the second day Volodya saw an eagle. It looked almost as big as an aeroplane, soaring majestically high up in the sky above the winding road. In the middle of the night, the lorry crawled across a dried-up riverbed and got stuck in the mud. Volodya pushed together with the others, laid down boards, dug in the mud, and shoved at the snub-nosed radiator. He also learnt to shout the equivalents of "push", "easy" and "pull", in the manner of those he was travelling with.

At daybreak they drove past a large nomad camp. Smoke was curling up from the *yurtas*, and horses with fiery eyes, their luxuriant manes and long tails streaming in the wind, ran in front of the lorry for a long way. At the next camp Volodya ate a strange, salty but very tasty broth with bits of mutton fat floating in it, and at the third camp they came to he drank tea. His broad-faced hosts studied him carefully, some even fingered and praised his sturdy Russian boots. Volodya did not smile at anyone, bow, pat the children on the head or utter those few words he had already learnt. Nothing was more humiliating, he thought, than trying to make a good impression by kowtowing. He was his own usual self, even a little sterner. He listened and watched intently, memorising the way one ate, drank, and said hello and thank you here. He wanted to discover for himself the people's character, its main distinguishing features, the traits for which this country and her people deserved respect. So far it was difficult if not impossible, but one thing was clear to him already. All that condescending, missionary-like talk about their being "just big children" was a tissue of lies. These reserved, stern but hospitable people had to be treated as equals, one had to be dignified and respectful with them.

On the evening of the third day of driving, when Volodya was resting on a felt mat outside a *yurta*, he saw his first shamans. They were standing close by, looking over the Russian doctor and talking to one another. The evening breeze blowing in from the steppe played with the attributes of their witch-doctor's trade hanging from their belts: woodpeckers' skins, dried roots, bears' paws and the talons of golden eagles. One of the tiny bells in the older shaman's grimy and greasy tambourine tinkled melodiously and sweetly all the time.

"My enemies. They are the ones I'll have to fight," Volodya said to himself.

"Py-ra-mi-don!" the younger of the shamans said all of a sudden and bowed to Volodya.

"What's that?" Volodya asked; the word sounded so queer in this nomad steppe.

"Py-ra-mi-don," the shaman repeated and, with a grimace of suffering, pressed his palm to the side of his head. "Py-ra-mi-don."

Volodya nodded and went to the lorry. It was quite a job finding and pulling free the zink-coated box in which the pills were packed. He put a few in a small chemist's envelope and, standing in the wind, which carried the mournful howling of a mangy dog, wrote on it in Latin: *Pyramidoni 0.3*. The shaman made a low bow, put two pills in his mouth, and turned to the driver, to whom he explained something at great length. The driver afterwards told Volodya that the shaman's advice to him was not to sit on felt mats, for only small shamans sat on felt mats while a big shaman, the elder, could not sit on anything but a white mare's hide. "He who sits on a white hide makes much more money than he who stoops to a felt mat." The shaman offered this piece of advice to repay Volodya for the pyramidon.

They stopped for the night in the steppe, on the bank of the Djyrla-Hao. When day broke, Volodya saw huge herds of sheep, the smoke of shepherds' fires, and in the distance — the faint outline of a mountain range, wrapped in mist.

A little later they turned on to an extraordinary road, paved with flat, cracked stones. At the side of the road a solitary grey stone dwarf with long ears, lipless mouth and sunken slanting eyes, seemed to be dozing.

"Genghiz Khan!" said the driver.

By signs and gestures he explained that the road, too, had been built by Genghiz Khan's men long ago, not in our time.

Volodya nodded and suddenly thought of Postnikov saying how long mankind remembers all sorts of Genghiz Khans.

Mountain spurs, tall, majestic and sheer, came speeding toward them. Smoky clouds floated above the snow-caps. Volodya knew they would cross the range that day and reach the capital.

### Chapter Thirteen

### THE ROAD TO KHARA

He spent the night in a hotel; his room had a private bath, a large window and a ceiling fan. On awakening he did not at once remember where he was, in what town, or why he was there.

At the Public Health Department he was received by a frail-looking official in gold-rimmed spectacles. The look in his small, beady black eyes was attentive, intelligent and unpleasant. The official spoke in flowing phrases, the interpreter — a corpulent man wearing a native robe over European clothes — translated in a curt, abrupt manner.

"The chief of the department is sorry. The Russian doctor will have a difficult trip and difficult work. Very difficult. Our regret is boundless. Four hundred kilometres on horseback, or wait for the snow and drive along river in a sleigh. Very severe frost. Bad. In summertime can ride through taiga and hunters' pass."

The official made a bow. His slim, large-jointed fingers swiftly counted the beads of a milky-white rosary.

"Spring and autumn no travel," said the interpreter. "Rivers flood, marshes impassable. Yes, no? Hunters' pass cannot go, Khara remote place, yes? Khara had no doctor ever. Plenty of work for Russian doctor."

The official took up his softly flowing narrative again, moving his parchment lips rapidly, but the interpreter had no chance to translate the speech. The door was pushed open with an imperious gesture, and a man of thirty or so dressed in a roomy sweater and wading boots strode into the room. The expression on his lined, mirthless face was hard.

Flipping cigarette ash on the floor and completely ignoring the obsequious bows of the official and the interpreter, he sat down and addressed Volodya in a low and pleasantly husky voice:

"Glad to meet you, comrade. I suppose they're trying to frighten you, eh? Don't you be afraid, comrade. I went to study in the great city of Moscow and I know that this won't scare you, comrade."

He repeated the word comrade with obvious pleasure and now and again lightly touched Volodya's arm.

"Difficult yes, and complicated yes, but not frightening. A little frightening, too, perhaps, only not for people who have carried through a great revolution like yours."

The interpreter coughed discreetly, and the newcomer turned on him in sudden anger.

"Go away, I don't need you, and the inspector will just sit here and look on. You needn't come back."

The interpreter made a low bow, pressed his hands to his chest and stayed. The frail-looking official remained standing. The sun burst in a brilliant cluster of rays through the large wide-open window; from the street outside came the lazy shuffling of camels' feet, the shrill guttural shouts of the drivers, and the melodious jingle of the camels' bells. The man in the sweater stared straight into the blazing cluster of rays, his thick eyebrows drawn together.

"At first we had just one doctor in our capital, just one for the whole country. Later, we bought the services of a doctor with a three-year medical school training. He used to be in the Foreign Legion, a shady character, of course, a spy and a scoundrel. Yes, comrade. He rode about with his servants and bodyguards armed with rifles, and sold medicines for sable and squirrel skins. Vaccination cost one sable skin. His men seized and stole whatever took their fancy, and that, comrade, they also called collecting a fee. In Moscow, they told us about the medicine of shamans and the medicine of lamas, but in Russia they knew nothing about this type of medicine, comrade. Our people did, though. That man, Morrison, peddled opium and morphine too, while his assistants told everybody that the great medicine man was selling happy dreams. One happy dream cost three sables. Yes, comrade, it did, and if you wanted two happy dreams you paid five sables. Morrison was more terrible than a shaman, more terrible than the most terrible lama. Morrison used to say he was a healer, but he was our people's murderer, that's what he was, comrade, yes. He made it so that our people now go to the shamans and lamas for treatment and to the Russian doctors for happy dreams. But the Russian doctors refuse to give them any happy dreams, that's good, isn't it? They take neither sables nor squirrels, they take nothing. Our mighty neighbour alone renders us disinterested aid, your people are like that and they teach us to be the same, and every one of you who comes here teaches us how to build our future, isn't that so, comrade? Our great neighbour is helping us to combat ignorance, superstition and disease, comrade. And we..."

He lit another cigarette and fell silent, losing the thread of his thought it seemed. Then he went on:

"We ourselves are making it difficult, you understand?" he said, getting so angry that his yellow skin became blotched with red. "We don't all think alike here; you must be able to see that at once, comrade. As yet, not all are looking where they ought to look. Some are looking in the direction taken by that Foreign Legion scoundrel, that is, the money-makers. But, comrade, the more good our people see you bringing us the more they turn their gaze in your direction. There, I've told you very little, but you have understood me, comrade, haven't you?"

"Yes, I have understood," Volodya replied.

"There's another thing: the lamas' medicine and the shamans' witchcraft is not so easy to overcome, but it is not so hopelessly difficult either, comrade. It will probably take you a long, long time, but it has to be done. There may be danger sometimes, but you must not let yourself get frightened, comrade, because if you do the lamas and shamans and others will rejoice, see, comrade? Have you understood this, too?"

"I have," Volodya answered firmly. "Where can I see Doctor Bogoslovsky?" he asked.

"Oh, Doctor Bogoslovsky!" the man repeated the name and smiled for the first time, a big, happy smile. "Why, he's known throughout the country, he's known in every *yurta*, to every man, but he never comes to this office. No, he is always working, he is always going from place to place and doing his work. He calls on all the doctors, he helps everyone and helps a great deal. We'll come and see you too, not so soon, but we shall come one day, yes?"

"Yes, do! And another thing: who do I deliver the medicines to?"

"An official of the Health Department will take delivery. If there's anything you need write to me at this address. Tod-Jin's my name. Write in Russian about anything you may need. Tod-Jin is the name, remember?"

He gave Volodya his strong, thin, very dry and hot hand. The official bowed thrice and much lower than he need have done. The interpreter, backing to the door, flung it open for Volodya.

Handing over the medicines took till late at night, and at daybreak he was called. With loud swearing and bickering, the guides were already loading their short sturdy horses in the hotel yard. A mangy camel stood in the middle of the yard dribbling unconcernedly, some grimy men with shaven heads were squatting in a circle shooting dice, and a little old man whispered an offer of gold bars to Volodya. It really was like a strange dream.

The caravan was ready to start when suddenly Tod-Jin appeared. He was wearing an old leather jacket and carried a pistol at his hip. At the sight of him the guides became reverently motionless. The cold sun had only begun to rise and the air was transparent and fresh. In the silence, Tod-Jin addressed a short speech to the guides, indicating Volodya with the nod ever so often, at which they all turned and looked at him too.

"Well, good-bye, comrade," Tod-Jin said when Volodya was getting into his saddle.

He looked up into Volodya's eyes with a hard, bright glance that was as bracing as a drink of spring water. The caravan slowly moved past Tod-Jin, and for some reason it made Volodya think of a May Day parade of armed forces.

They covered four hundred kilometres in six days. The second day of riding found Volodya sitting sideways in the saddle, and the third — lying face down on his stomach. "Difficult yes, but not frightening," he remembered Tod-Jin's words. The guides laughed at him without malice, offered him advice that he could not understand, and called halts more frequently than was strictly necessary. On top of everything else, the damned mosquitoes were driving him insane. He refused to have his face swathed in mosquito net because it suffocated him, and he chose the wrong side of the fire at night, he simply could not sit where the smoke from the damp branches was coming. As a result, his face grew horribly swollen from countless bites. It sickened him to eat the half-raw meat, and so he kept taking drinks of water out of his flask and swearing under his breath.

Going through the mountain pass, one of the horses lost its footing and fell into a chasm. Volodya realised with horror that his autoclave was gone and with it all means of sterilising his instruments. Several large bottles of liquid ammonia and a splendid folding operating table were also gone.

### THE GREAT DOCTOR

Towards the end of the six days' ride, Volodya sighted the *yurtas* and houses of Khara, where he was to set up a dispensary and a hospital. He felt strangely timid. Would he manage? The first doctor there! With a vague sensation of alarm he peered at the low huts crouching far apart beneath the ponderous rainclouds, listened to the ferocious barking of the scraggy dogs, and looked at the people who, in their turn, stared with deferential amazement at the Russian doctor's long caravan, whose arrival was loudly announced by the guides riding ahead.

"You see before you the greatest medicine man and healer!" they cried out in different keys, their voices tired but spirited.

"People rejoice!"

"Rejoice and look at him!"

"Look at all the fine medicines he has brought along!

264

He's going to give all these medicines to the suffering, forgetting no one and sharing fairly with all!"

"Come, all the sick, to the great doctor!"

"All the crippled!"

"All the deaf!"

"All the blind!"

"There is no illness that the great doctor cannot cure!"

Volodya, who was so sore he could scarcely sit in his saddle, did not know what the guides were saying. Oh, God, if he only knew! But how could he? He could not have known that these men had come to like him for his good heart, simplicity and courage after sharing food, sleep, toil and silence with him for six days, just as he could not have known that Tod-Jin had ordered his arrival to be properly announced. The guides were naturally doing their best, for Tod-Jin was not the sort of man whose orders were carried out half-heartedly. Advertise in a big way, if advertise at all! And so the guides announced Volodya with all the pomp due to a celebrated lama.

It was raining. Dusk was falling.

The caravan, moving through a dense curious crowd, reached the square.

They halted. Volodya's stallion took loving little bites at the withers of the chief guide's mare. Around them the crowd stood motionless, shivering in the cold rain. The people stared at Volodya, his padded coat, his boots, rifle, saddle, bridle, stallion, and everything, with appraising, baffling expressions.

"Welcome to Khara!" said a Gypsy-looking bearded man with a curly shock of hair, dressed in a *poddyovka*, as he pushed his way through the crowd with a huge, powerful shoulder, beckoning to Volodya with a merry twinkle in his eyes. "Follow me, doctor, and taste of our bread and salt, our dear and very welcome guest. Don't look so suspicious, Markelov's my name, we belong to the Old Faith, we don't leave the country because of you people. It was because of the tsar, the devil's spawn."

Volodya kicked the steaming sides of his horse, and the caravan moved on. A handsome, statuesque young woman with large, dreamy eyes welcomed Volodya at Markelov's house. With a low bow, she handed him a dish covered with an embroidered towel on which lay a round loaf of bread with a salt cellar placed on top. Blinking his thick eyelashes in confusion and smiling inanely, he kept mumbling:

"Oh, you shouldn't... Why, honestly..."

Standing behind him, Markelov urged:

"Take it, you can't refuse, take it and kiss my daughter."

Volodya kissed Pelageya Markelova on her firm cheek, and with a "you shouldn't have bothered" to his host, turned to see where his guides were. They were still in their saddles, tired but smiling.

"I'm not alone, Comrade Markelov, I have friends with me."

"It's all right, there's food enough for everyone," Markelov said. "Don't misunderstand me, my dear sir, but they're heathens, they're natives, so I shan't let them into the house."

In the confusion of being helped off with his top clothes in the front hall of the huge, prosperous house, embarrassed by the bows and ceremony, shrinking from the need to sit down with dignity after his six days in the saddle, and managing at last to lower himself sideways into a chair at the table spread with pickles and preserves, roasts and pies, vodka and brandies, Volodya did not at first understand what Markelov had meant by "heathens". He drank his first glass of White Horse whiskey, burning his throat, and only then it struck him as strange that the only people sitting at the table were Markelov, his obese wife, his daughter, and a cowed-looking clerk or someone.

"We're feeding them, don't worry," Markelov said kindly, reading Volodya's questioning look. "Mother, see the good neighbour God has sent us — his heart goes out to the guides, too, even though they're natives."

An elegant Petersburg-made paraffin lamp was burning brightly and hotly in the centre of the table amid the dishes. (Volodya saw the words St. Petersburg on the metal stand.) The food was too rich, yet everyone took more butter, poured fried fat and cracklings over everything, and dumped spoonfuls of sour cream on top of that. There were curtains at the windows — silk or brocade, Volodya did not know which. There were rugs on the walls and family photographs on them, and in the very middle of the best, the gaudiest rug, hung a crudely coloured copy of Levitan's *Volga Waters* in a gilt frame.

"We're not complaining, we manage," said the host sweating from too much food, working hard with his powerful jaws, now lusting after a piece of pie, now after some fried fish, now after a plump, rosy pancake. "Our grandfathers and our fathers had no complaints either. We're a bit homesick for Russia naturally, but we've got used to living with the natives here, we are kind fathers to them and they treat us with filial respect. It would be a sin to complain. This is a small place,

but even in the capital everyone knows us, we are their benefactors, they benefit greatly through us, through our class,
our capital. We pay our taxes without cheating, because to
live by cheating is a sin of course."

Volodya ate in silence, his ears and eyes open. It had never
occurred to him before that such homes really existed with
all these curtains, rugs, the antiquated gramophone, and the
ancient rifles hung on the walls. He saw a Zeiss camera of the
latest make lying on a small table covered with a lace cloth;
beside the ancient rifles hung a splendid, brand-new Sauer
rifle, and there were two automatic rifles above the sofa,
hanging immediately under an opulently framed portrait of a
venerable old man whose lascivious expression resembled
Rasputin's.

"What business are you in?" Volodya asked at last.

"Who, we? We are in trade, my dear guest, in the fur business. Our house, formerly called Markelov & Sons, is known
everywhere, even across the ocean in the United States of
America. We trade with Great Britain, too, and with the
Japanese fur dealers, all straight and above board, it's a big
business we've built up. The other day, we had the senior
buyer of Guritsu Bros. here. He stayed with us, we went out
hunting once or twice, steamed ourselves in my bathhouse, and
he took back with him a fine batch of sable skins."

Pelageya sat staring raptly at Volodya and tugging at the
fringe of her rich shawl. She ate nothing at all, and only took
sips of the cold, frothy kvass, putting her teeth to the rim of
the cup.

After dinner, Markelov said a short prayer, wiped his
face with a towel, took his cap off a nail, lighted a lantern,
and took Volodya to see where the hospital and dispensary was
going to be. Volodya, utterly bewildered by the strangeness of
"life abroad", meekly followed. In the wet gloom of Markelov's
yard, the guides thronged to them and together they made
their way through the squelching mud to a flimsy clap-board
barn. The doors swung back with a heartrending screech,
and large, fat rats scurried, squealing, into the darkness.
Markelov raised the lantern high.

"Here you are! It's too good for these natives anyway.
They're not worth the trouble or the work. When it turns cold,
I'll give you an iron stove I have. It's not new, of course, but
it'll do for them. You'll stay with us, and eat with us too.
You'll get fat on our food, you've seen it. It's good Russian
food, no comparison with what these beggars eat."

The guides were saying something, talking rapidly and defiantly. The thinnest of them, whom Volodya thought of as Yura, came forward and spoke excitedly, tugging Markelov's sleeve and addressing Volodya, too, obviously trying to explain something of great urgency to all of them.

"Leave me alone, you ape," Markelov brushed off his hand with a smile which Volodya thought rather nervous.

"What is he saying?" Volodya asked.

"Some nonsense or other, there's no making it out," Markelov replied, anxious to dismiss the matter.

But now the guides all began to speak at once, loudly and angrily. The man he mentally called Yura grabbed Volodya by the hem of his padded coat and pulled him to the door, out into the squelching darkness. The wind blew in gusts and the rain poured down with a hollow roar. Markelov tried to silence the guides with a hoarse shout, but they went on talking, and Volodya heard the name Tod-Jin repeated again and again. Apparently, they knew something connected with Tod-Jin which Volodya was completely ignorant of, and which Markelov, for reasons of his own, refused to acknowledge.

Volodya obediently followed Yura, lighting his way with a flashlight and taking no notice of Markelov's cries of warning. The guides, in a crowd, caught up with them; behind came Markelov, angrily splashing through the mud.

Suddenly, the whole thing became clear to Volodya. The guides brought him to a building that seemed to be made for a small hospital and dispensary. It was a long, sturdily built house with large windows, a front and a back door, a kitchen wing and two barns.

"Tod-Jin!" Yura said with a stern and triumphant look at Markelov and Volodya. "Tod-Jin!"

"They're talking nonsense, they're savages, apes they really are," Markelov said, trying to be his bland self. "Heavenly Father, it's a sin to listen to them, fancy making over a trading post into a hospital, and for whom, I ask you?"

"Is this a trading post?" Volodya asked.

"It used to be, it belonged to another furrier but I choked his wheeze." Markelov's manner had nothing bland in it now, he spoke quickly with a fiendish look in his blood-shot, Gypsy eyes. "He was one of *them*, pushing in where he wasn't asked, getting so high and mighty that he built himself this place. Now he's gone back to eat his vomit like the dog he is. Back to his birchbark hut."

"Who does the trading post belong to now?" Volodya asked grimly.

"No one so far, but it will be mine," Markelov replied with a challenge. "I've marked it for my own, and we, Markelovs, take what we mark for our own. Maybe I've made a down payment on it, who knows."

"But Tod-Jin said the hospital was to be in this particular building, didn't he?"

"Let him take possession if he has a title deed to it."

"What shall I do then?"

"Do what I advise you to do, my dear guest, and set up your hospital in that nice old barn. I told you I'd help. The trading post is definitely out, my dear sir, I won't give it up. Private property hasn't been abolished here yet, thank the Lord."

"I don't know," Volodya said, frowning. "I don't know. Your right of ownership has nothing to do with me, but I suppose the Public Health Department will reimburse you if you've really made a down payment. However, it's up to you to settle it with whoever's concerned. I'm only a doctor, nothing but a doctor, and that's why I'm here. So we'll just unload now, and the rest is your own affair."

"In other words, you've no sooner arrived than you're going against me?"

"I don't need you, I need a hospital building."

"Hospital, you say? Why, my good young sir, does anything ever get properly done here without Markelov? Why, maybe I'd give the whole trading post to you for a gift if you asked me nicely? I'm that kind of man. Maybe I've been wanting to do a good deed for a long time? And maybe you'd be getting a salary from me besides for treating my family?"

"D'you know what? Leave me alone, *Mister* Markelov. I'm not interested in your good deeds or your stupid salary. Please go away. Thank you for the meal. Oh, how much do I owe you?"

Thrusting his hand into the pocket of his trousers, spattered with dried clots of mud, Volodya pulled out the wallet he had bought in Moscow.

"How much do I owe you?"

"You are real touchy and flare up like fire," Markelov said with a low chuckle. "Real fire! Touch you off and you're blazing! But I like that sort. Make yourself at home in my trading post, use it. Maybe Markelov himself will come for a cure to you one day. Don't lose hope!"

He slapped Volodya's shoulder hard, pulled Yura's nose, kicked another guide in the seat of his pants and went away in a good mood.

The house grew still.

Still and dark.

Volodya switched on his flashlight again, looked about him, listened to the rain drumming on the roof, and told the guides with signs to bring the packs into the trading post building. A couple of days later, carpenters were already busy filling in the space under the floor for warmth, repairing old and laying new floors; a man was building a brick stove, and a lame old craftsman was fixing the door hinges and locks and the oven in the kitchen. The barns were being stocked with firewood, plenty of firewood, because the winters here were bitterly cold with heavy snow. Volodya, his face and clothes daubed with paint, was painting little figures on a sheet of tin with a child's ineptitude. They were meant to represent patients going into the hospital: one was leaning on a stick, another had his arm in a splint, and one more was slumped across a horse. Volodya put himself in the picture too. Dressed in a white smock he stood on the porch and beamed. He did not know how to make a smile look natural, so the result was a crescent-shaped mouth extending from ear to ear. While he painted no one worked — they just gaped and marvelled.

Nevertheless, he did not venture to put up the sign over the front door of his dispensary and hospital.

Once or twice Markelov appeared with a huge shaggy dog. He would stop and look, raise his cap if he saw Volodya and, whistling, continue on his way.

Under Volodya's direction the repairs and the fitting up of his first real dispensary and hospital with an operating room, a small room for himself, a kitchen, pantry, and other service premises, were completed just before November 7th. He now had an interpreter — a local man, resourceful and quick, with an equably cheerful disposition, Mady-Danzy by name; he had a cook — a very old and terribly shy Chinese woman whom unknown circumstances had brought to these parts before the turn of the century, and whom Danzy in all seriousness called madam cook; he also had a male nurse — that selfsame Danzy.

On the eve of the anniversary of the October Revolution, Volodya invited his entire "staff" to the well-heated kitchen, opened a bottle of Massandra port, told the cook to lay the table nicely, and poured the wine into glasses. The clock on the wall, also brought from Moscow, was ticking loudly.

"At this time, many years ago, the workers and peasants in our country, led by Lenin, overthrew the rule of capitalists and landowners for all time," Volodya said. "Let us drink to the working people who did it."

Danzy translated, and suddenly madam cook burst into tears.

"What's the matter with her?" Volodya asked, gently taking the old woman's wrinkled, claw-like little hand. Madam cook cried the harder.

"How we know why she cry?" said Danzy. "Maybe she remember something, yes? Maybe she also young one time, she have husband, babies? Now she alone, and if you not listen to me and hire her she die, yes, no? She wants workers' peasants' rule, that's why."

"And you?" Volodya asked, suddenly feeling anxious because his question might be considered propaganda and agitation.

The old woman continued to weep. Tod-Jin had said that it wasn't so frightening here as complicated. "So this is what he meant by complicated," Volodya thought, twirling his glass on the table before him. Never mind! He would show them the worth of a man sent by the land of workers and peasants. They'd see. The people would see — all those courageous and reserved taiga hunters, those nomads with the sunburnt faces, those fishermen with frost-bitten hands, they would all see. And then they would understand what the Markelovs and others like them really were. If they hadn't done so already.

In the morning, Danzy came into his room and told him that a lama was sitting on the porch and would remain there all day to see that no patient went into the hospital.

It snowed all day in large wet flakes, but the lama remained seated on the porch without stirring. At dinner time madam cook — a compassionate soul — gave him some hot food. Volodya got furious and shouted at his "staff". The lama was sitting there eating hospital broth and chatting with Markelov, who stood a few steps away, leaning on a heavy stick, his unholy Gypsy eyes ogling the former trading post building. This was a hell of a business when you came to think of it.

When twilight fell, Danzy told Volodya, rather shyly, that the lama wanted to come in for a polite talk, that the lama was a good man and a sick man besides. Volodya decided to let the lama come into the so-called "casualty ward".

Danzy bowed very low to the lama, who ignored him and bowed to Volodya. A candle was burning on a small table covered with a white oilcloth. The wooden, unpainted cupboards contained drugs. Guessing this the lama ran an avid eye over the locked doors, sniffed at the absorbent cotton kept in a glass jar, fingered the wooden scoops, and heaved a long, envious sigh.

"Well?" Volodya asked.

Danzy scratched his bare led with the bare heel of his other leg, and, speaking very quickly, asked the lama questions, which he answered as quickly, in a squeaky voice. The lama's business was short and plain: if Volodya would pay him a monthly salary he, the lama, would not persuade the sick against going to Volodya's hospital. That was all. The salary he named was small, but it had to be paid regularly. And what was more, the lama was willing to let Volodya have all his and the other lamas' surplus patients besides.

Volodya listened grimly and thought of what Bogoslovsky had once told him about the number of suicides among Zemstvo doctors. He raised his eyes and looked into the lama's effeminately hairless, stupid but perfectly serious face. Danzy went on speaking a little longer, and suddenly Volodya saw the funny side of it all.

"Let him clear out," Volodya said. He slammed the door hard as he walked out, slammed the next door, and locked himself in his small room with its narrow bed by the wall, a small table in front of the window, and his photographs of Varya, his father and Aunt Aglaya...

And so the difficult, stupid, anxious winter began.

### THINGS ARE BAD FOR THE GREAT DOCTOR

The temperature dropped to 30° below that night, a silvery rime appeared in the corners of the rooms, the beams of the old trading post crepitated in the frost, and the outdoor thermometer showed a further drop.

Reluctantly, Danzy got all the huge hospital stoves going.

It took him a long time, there were seven stoves in all and Danzy was tired; in the dark wards, the empty beds with their immaculate sheets, towels and spreads, stood out in dismal white blurs.

"No need more heat, no?" Danzy asked.

"Yes, more."

"No more."

"You do what I say, Mady-Danzy, or else I'll get rid of you," Volodya said sharply. "I'm nobody's fool, remember that."

"Sick men come tomorrow?" Danzy asked. "Many sick men? For them I heat all stoves, yes?"

"Man was given a tongue to conceal his thoughts," Volodya remembered somebody's saying, and went back into his own room.

The next day the temperature dropped to 33° below. There was not a single patient.

"Again heat stoves?" Danzy asked.

"Yes, again."

"All stoves?"

"Yes, all of them."

"Sick men come?"

Volodya made no reply.

Madam cook was told to make enough food for three patients every day. But there were not even three. Nobody came to the hospital, this well-equipped, warm, clean hospital. In the mornings Volodya put on his white smock and paced up and down the casualty ward for about two hours, waiting. After all, they had to come eventually.

But no, they did not come.

They lay sick in their *yurtas*, their mud or birchbark huts. They died there to the sound of the shamans' wailings, the jangling and jingling of their tambourines, the soft murmurings of the crazy lamas, and the lamentations of their wives and children. They lay dying of diseases Volodya could easily have cured, while he — young, eager and strong — paced about this room. Why?

Mady-Danzy told him the local news with a superior smile.

"Yesterday Sagan-ohl he not come our hospital, no? I said I go fetch Russian doctor, Russian doctor make you well. Sagan-ohl cannot speak, shaman Sarma answer for him: 'Let your doctor's soul depart his body.' Sagan-ohl died today, I went to see. Sarma he sit beside dead man, he put down bowl of boiled butter, he put down tobacco, millet, also cup of milk vodka, and ordered, 'You dead! Take your offerings, go!' Stupid people, such stupid people, they understand nothing, yes, no?"

Volodya listened with a scowl: they not only refused to call him in, they wouldn't let him in if he went there himself. Who was behind it all? What was the purpose? But the people were dying, they were dying!

Danzy went on with his mockingly cheerful story.

"They brought in the coffin, a whole log. They tied Sagan-ohl to it with a good rope, strong rope made of horsehair, dead man must not get untied. They raised *yurta* flap at the back and carried dead man out, not through the door, no, door no can, dead man must not know where the door is or he come back very bad, and they take him to the mountains on horseback, not straight but this way, that way."

He described the zigzag course uphill with his hand, showed with a gesture how they abandoned him there and came back, careful to cover their tracks.

"Never use road back, no," Danzy said. "If use road, Sagan-ohl come back, very bad, so they do this way, and you sitting here, Doctor Volodya... Maybe it's your fault, why you talk so angry with lama? Very soon now they kick us out, all of us, you and madam cook and me. Madam cook, she die like dog, she very old, you go far away and get plenty to eat, and me? No job here, no salary, what I eat?"

Danzy felt so sorry for himself, he actually whimpered.

Volodya began doing exercises first thing in the morning, he made it ten minutes at first and then added another five. Before breakfast he went out into the yard in his old sweater and mittens and chopped wood. The frozen logs flew apart with a crack. When he struck an old resinous snag he would tackle it angrily, driving in wedges, hitting again and again, working himself up into a frenzy, swearing and gasping, but always getting the better of it. His breakfast finished, he sat on at the table for a long time. The thick logs burned with a homely crackle in the stove's greedy maw. Gazing into the smouldering red coals, Volodya mentally performed one operation after another, amazing in their technique and daring, no matter what the conditions, just as Bogoslovsky and Postnikov used to teach them. He had done a tremendous lot of reading in those months. Theoretically he probably knew and could do anything. But no patients came, the hospital remained empty, and with every day Volodya found it more frightening to live in this enforced idleness, alone with his thoughts, working in futility, operating in imagination, curing in dreams.

"The man is no surgeon, he's a trick rider," Volodya once read about a certain surgeon who was too eager with the knife. Oh, how careful Volodya would be, how thoughtful and prudent, if only that longed-for patient came! The care he'd take of the man who trusted him with his life! No, he for one would not be a trick rider in the operating room. Not he.

To make things worse, everyone wrote to him — Postnikov, Ganichev, Pych and Ogurtsov.

Postnikov recollected amusing incidents from his experience as a village doctor, Pych boasted of being run off his feet with work, Ogurtsov wrote a lot about doubting his abilities, and Ganichev warned Volodya against generalising his experience earlier than he should. "It has become a contagious disease with us," he wrote. "One writes a book to tell the world he has made a discovery, another to establish his priority, a third to remind mankind that the first man to comment on the subject resides in such and such a town, and a fourth — and this kind are particularly numerous — to have a record in research work."

Volodya's replies were brief, cool and mysterious: let them think what they liked!

Markelov invited him for Christmas dinner. Volodya refused, making the silly excuse of being too busy. Markelov came to fetch him himself.

He wore a starched shirt, his shock of hair was brilliantined, he exuded perfume, gaiety tinged with mockery, and even good will.

"You certainly are a busy man, my lad," Markelov said, looking into the empty wards. "The crowds that throng to you for treatment! You *are* a hard-working man! The place is nice and warm, the beds made, there's dinner cooking in the kitchen, yet our natives refuse to come. And don't you imagine they ever will, doctor, don't expect them to, dear heart, they'll never come, you poor innocent. They have their own medicine, and it suits them fine."

He sat down as if he owned the place, stretched out his long legs before him, and said peevishly:

"There, you see where our tax money goes, money earned with the sweat of the brow, honestly made and saved. To keep you windbags, that's where it goes. We do the toiling, tramping through the tundra, the taiga, and all the other God-forsaken places, we bring trade and civilisation here, and what do we get for it? A fig. But idlers, spongers and other natives get nice warm hospital rooms made for them. It isn't right, no, it isn't."

Markelov sat there talking for a long time, then he leafed through Volodya's books, poked his mattress with a fist and said:

"It's hard. Shall I give you a feather bed, doctor? What d'you say?"

Mady-Danzy stood in the doorway, tittering happily, rubbing his hands and bowing.

"So you're not coming?" Markelov asked. "All right, have it your own way. I meant well, but please yourself."

Left by himself, Volodya sat down to write to Bogoslovsky. With clenched teeth he wrote till one in the morning, drinking mug after mug of cold water in long draughts. All his resentment, wounded pride, distress and frustration went into that letter. Why had Bogoslovsky sent for him? Because he wanted to do him a kindness? He had no use for anyone's kindness, he was a man in his own rights and, incidentally, a man who refused to have the people's money wasted on the maintenance of his staff, on fuel and food. Was it perhaps sabotage on the part of those Right-wing elements, those relatives of the bais who still had a say in the government? Or was he, Ustimenko, perhaps needed here for the sake of statistics, so the bureaucrats could report that a hospital has been opened in Khara and a dispensary was working at full swing? Incidentally, the monthly reports he sent in regularly on his so-called work interested no one, absolutely no one. The long and short of it was that he flatly refused to sponge on his government any longer, to sit here twiddling his thumbs and going to seed. He demanded that he be recalled. And if this letter lacked diplomacy and tact he begged to be forgiven and remained Bogoslovsky's sincerely.

The letter was four pages long and Volodya decided not to read it over. Come what may. Matters could not go on like this any longer.

In February he received a New Year card from good old Yevgeny Stepanov. The note was breezy and gay, written in a pally I-have-no-enemies-in-the-world sort of style. "So you proved the smartest of us all, you country doctor, serving lofty ideals," Yevgeny wrote. "Your Zatirukhi turned into a job abroad. Don't mind, it's the voice of envy: all those caravanserais, muezzins, oriental spices, veiled beauties and so forth are an experience, after all, they have their own exotic charm, say what you like. I suppose, as soon as darkness falls you all put on your tails and trip along to one of those night clubs, you old rake?"

What could Volodya reply to that?

Geography had never been Yevgeny's strong point.

He hated to think that Varya, too, believed he was the smartest of them all, and that he tripped to a night club every night in tails.

Volodya seldom listened to the radio. He felt strangely ashamed of himself when he heard the level voice of the announcer coming from thousands of kilometres away: "This is Radio Moscow." It was as if Moscow was asking him: and what are you doing there, dear friend? Are you warm and comfortable, no draughts bothering you? We sent you out to do a job of work, you know, and what have you to say for yourself? You have difficulties, you say? Objective difficulties, comrade doctor?

## Chapter Fourteen

### HOW ARE YOUR HERDS?

He spent his evenings reading.

The things he read left him more bewildered than angry. It was strange and almost embarrassing to read about a man who went on vacillating through page after page, first at a winter resort in the Alps, then in Petrograd during the Revolution, in the Don country, serving in Kaledin's army, and finally in Moscow, unable to make up his mind whether Soviet power was good or bad and whether it suited him or not. The man fell in love, fell out of love, mused in rain and shine (all the weathers and scents were given a detailed and faithful description: hay really smelled exactly like that after rain, and the sun shone exactly like that through a short summer shower), he used his gun, fled, went into hiding, rode in trains, sailed on ships, and finally — again sniffing the various scents about him with a fine sense of smell, distinguishing the many shades of colour in the sky, and admiring landscapes that struck him as unusual — he accepted Soviet power, but with limitations.

"Well!" Volodya marvelled, closing the bulky volume with the promising words on the last page that it was only the end of part two. The author of the next novel he read preferred to hint at things. The hero was for Soviet power, but he, too, spent most of his time looking on and noting the various birthmarks of capitalism in people. He spoke of this wittily and not without venom, but he did nothing at all, not even senseless heroics like Pierre Bezukhov staying behind in French-occupied Moscow because of his idea. No, this particular hero did nothing but observe, arriving now and then at the conclusion that life was not such a simple thing after all. And everything was indeed so far from simple that Volodya gave up trying to understand the novel and put it aside for the time being. The third novel — and this was the last straw — was a lurid tale of a well-known thief in post-revolutionary Petrograd, told in great detail. The thief robbed people and carried on an endless discourse, all the characters discoursed stupidly and lengthily in the extreme; finally, the thief hanged himself, but not quite, and at that Volodya stopped reading novels altogether and again picked up the book he had left unfinished on "mistakes and dangers attending surgical operations".

As a matter of fact, he was reading this book when the thing that radically changed his life in Khara occurred.

Mady-Danzy flew into his room with eyes popping, slippers flapping, and the strings of his underpants dangling (Volodya saw at once that the pants belonged to the hospital because of the tab), and squealed, rather than shouted:

"Sick men! Two men! Quick, yes, no?"

Volodya counted to ten to still his excitement and not behave too much like a fool, put on his smock and cap, and came out into the hall. There were two strange, frozen figures standing silently just inside the door, wearing icicle-hung short fur-lined jackets on top of their fur coats, and fur boots covered with ice. The small paraffin lamp trembling in Danzy's hand shed a miserable light. Volodya told the patients to take off their coats and come into the casualty ward. In answer he heard suppressed laughter. It reminded him of someone, but the resemblance was gone before he could identify it.

"Allow me..." Volodya said.

"What's the difference if I allow you or not," the rollicking, cheerful, rustic voice belonged to Bogoslovsky, he knew it at once without a shadow of doubt, it was Bogoslovsky climbing out of his icicle-hung fur clothes and dragging off his thick fur cap. "What's the difference if I allow you or not," he said again, shaking Volodya's hand and then, stepping back a pace or two, looked him over fondly and gravely. "You'd better try and recognise Comrade Tod-Jin, you couldn't have forgotten him, you saw him not so very long ago. Give us some vodka, Volodya, we blundered into an unfrozen patch. What a steeple-chase across ice, water and the devil knows what else, and damn those expert guides..."

The words came tumbling out very, very quickly, and Volodya fancied that he was back in Chorny Yar, that he had never left it, and that everything was going to be fine now. Bogoslovsky was already looking into the empty wards, shaking his head, rubbing his hands hard, and commenting regretfully on the emptiness to Tod-Jin.

Madam cook emerged from the kitchen only to throw up her arms in surprise and run back with her tiny steps to start a gala dinner at once. In the meantime Danzy brought the guests a change of clothes — flannel dressing gowns, underwear, socks and slippers. He bowed before Volodya again and again, because the way Tod-Jin greeted Doctor Volodya was enough to tell Danzy that the hospital would not be closed down, that he would not be dismissed and would continue to get his salary.

"I hope you have got some vodka?" Bogoslovsky asked.

"Alcohol, not vodka," Volodya replied apologetically.

"That's better still. Does that Chinese woman cook for you? Fine. Alcohol must be taken straight with a water chaser. What? Too strong, you say? Sure it's strong. But then you are an excellent, experienced drinker, you can take any amount and never get drunk, remember that *pelmeni* party at Postnikov's?"

"Yes, I do," Volodya replied, blinking happily. "I remember everything. So you did get my letter?"

"The letter and business will keep till tomorrow. Tonight we're just your guests, and guests, moreover, who got drenched and frozen through and through and are terribly tired. Please have beds made for us, and turn in yourself too; first thing tomorrow morning we'll get down to work."

"Then you didn't mind the things I said in the letter?"

"Not where I personally came in. But I did mind about you. A slightly womanish letter it was, my dear boy, a wee bit hysterical. But tomorrow..."

"Why womanish?"

Bogoslovsky moved up his cup of tea and pondered over his reply.

"Very well, I'll say a few words tonight," he said. "You see, my dear young man, there have always been quite a few doctors in our Party, our Bolshevik Party, even in the days before the Revolution. Have you ever stopped to think precisely what made a doctor join the party in those difficult years? Have you? I personally think that it was the sense of frustration, of the utter senselessness of doing medical work in Russia unless there was a revolutionary explosion, a change of system, and complete abolition of the rule of capitalists, landowners and kulaks. Every thinking doctor realised that his personal efforts and the efforts of hundreds of honest men and women would only be wasted under the existing monarchical system of the empire. We are all convinced, and have been for a long time, that the future of medicine belongs to prophylaxis, to preventive medicine. But what chance did prophylaxis have in those days when even Pirogov with his unsurpassed organising abilities could do nothing or next to nothing about it? Therefore, the fault lay with the system. Now, you've found yourself in a country where the conditions are quite unlike the Soviet state of workers and peasants, and you — coming from our close-knit family united by the Party — lost your bearings, shall I say. You were too young and inexperienced to notice that the beginnings of progress were already in evidence here, and too proud to write to Comrade Tod-Jin at once."

"Yes, you had to write me at once. I would have understood and come," Tod-Jin said somewhat crisply.

"And you only wrote to me when your temper got the better of you, when you had lost all sense of proportion, all understanding of the situation, of the country you are in and the social structure of a society in which a doctor is an unknown phenomenon."

"Not quite unknown," Tod-Jin corrected harshly. "That doctor, for instance, who came to us not from the Soviet Union but from..."

"So much the worse. The situation is not simple, for even at the Public Health Department there are opposing forces. Did you imagine that it would be exactly the way it is at home? At the slightest hitch you'd go to the Party district secretary or the sanitary inspector, and if that didn't help you'd approach the regional authorities. Is that what you expected? You ought to know, my dear boy, that these methods are only practised in our country where the government not only promotes public health but is also responsible for the life and health of each one of its citizens, because ours is a government of working people and not people who exploit the labour of others for their own ends as in a capitalist state. However, let's turn in, you've got to get some sleep because as from tomorrow your vacationing will be over for good."

Volodya went into his room, sat down on the bed and took off his shoes. To put it in a nutshell, Bogoslovsky had just read him the riot act. Had he really deserved it?

"He's a good man," Tod-Jin said to Bogoslovsky then. "A pure soul, or how do you say it?"

"Like glass?"

"No, better. There's that..."

"Crystal, you mean?"

"Yes, crystal. It was hard on him, Comrade Bogoslovsky. I should have come earlier. At once."

"He's a good boy," Bogoslovsky said thoughtfully. "But he is only a boy after all, you know. He hasn't been hardened in battle yet, he doesn't know what the word battle means. Come on, let's take a look at his hospital."

Mady-Danzy went ahead with the lamp, and madam cook brought up the rear.

"He had the seams between the logs plugged with mud, that's clever of him," Bogoslovsky said. "Stopped the grooves up with wool and smeared mud over — see, no cold comes through at all. He used his brains in arranging the beds too. Ah, the poor chap! The bedside tables are exactly like the ones I had in Chorny Yar, with the shelf; it took an observant eye to remember that. He must have made a drawing of them. Now let's take a look at the operating room... Why, who'd ever have thought of it, see the contraption he's got in place of an autoclave? Ordinary galvanized iron pails, double lids, that's right, it's all perfectly sensible and quite ingenious too. See, the opening in the inside lid does not correspond to the one outside. Well, it's all plain enough. You put it on the stove to boil and then cool it for six hours, do you see?"

"Not quite," Tod-Jin said.

"Time six hours," Danzy volunteered the information. "Six hours is the time it takes for germs to get born again from spores not killed first time boil, yes, no?"

"Did he teach you that?" Bogoslovsky asked Danzy sternly.

"Yes, every day two hours," Danzy said, and added hastily, "must boil half hour with addition of carbon dioxide in proportion one zero to one three zero water, that's right, no? But no sick man come," he said bleakly. "I can tell more..."

"Never mind. Good chap," Bogoslovsky said.

"So he did well?" Tod-Jin asked.

"We're going to bed," Bogoslovsky said flatly.

When Volodya woke up he found Tod-Jin gone. Bogoslovsky was having tea at a small table in the spacious corridor. Mady-Danzy stood leaning against the wall, gazing at Bogoslovsky with servile affection — he always gazed like that at those he believed to be in authority.

"Find it hard to get to sleep last night?" Bogoslovsky asked.

His guess was as good as ever.

"Quite hard."

"You were angry with me?"

"No, but..."

"There you see, you start with a 'but' right away. And yet you never moved a finger to make the people come to you. In this business, colleague, you've got to be a public leader, a fighter, a campaigner, and not a sort of Chosen One, idly waiting for blessings to come tumbling down into your lap. Take Mongush, for instance, for all the lamas and shamans there the patients come storming the hospital. In Badan we're adding a wing to the hospital because Melnikov who's there was quick to grasp the political importance of his work and not just the humaneness of it, as we are fond of saying. Doing a good deed is not all this job involves. You've got to make the people believe in the doctor, and that's a big, a huge thing."

He took a sip of tea and lit a cigarette.

"There's been enough damage done to the profession in this country by all sorts of international scum. Do you know that?"

"I know a little."

"Wholesale dealers, retail merchants, fences and bastards of every make and description, highway robbers all of them, nosed it out with their blasted noses that the local reindeer breeders, cattle herders, fishermen, farmers, and other toiling folk, were firm believers in vaccination, and had been for a long time for some reason. The history of it goes far back, perhaps it was epidemics killing off their people in thousands, or maybe it was something else that can't be traced now. But anyway, believe they did. Well then, this international pack of swindlers decided to make good out of this faith: they brought in a supply of vaccine and charged a 'Godly price' — one sheep per shot, no more nor less. Anybody could act the doctor, of course, and the freshness of the vaccine worried no one, but you can well imagine how overdue it was by the time it got here from Europe. With a boom like that in the business, their stocks of vaccine, useless though it was, soon ran out. They diluted it with glycerine or simply used pure glycerine. A day's work and a bottle or two of glycerine made one of those misters, monsieurs or whoever they were, the richer by a flock of sheep of some three hundred head. But the most interesting part is that the lancet with which the incision was made was never sterilised, just think of it — *never*! Consequently, syphilis was spread so prodigiously by means of this fraudulent vaccination that it was impossible to record it."

"Is that really true?" Volodya asked with a grimace.

"It *is* true, that's the trouble. Those colonialist swine care only for their god — be they Catholics, Protestants or Buddhists — their own god, their idol, hereinafter referred to as Cash. And the local people are just heathens, savages, and natives as far as the colonialists are concerned, made for their enrichment only. What you and I are doing here, strange as it may seem, is straightening out the criminal mess made by the wandering knights of Cash, and it is up to us to make the local people recognise us for what we really are. Our task, yours and mine, is difficult, of course, but it's honourable. Soviet means decent, Soviet means kind, Soviet means solicitous, Soviet means fair, Soviet means disinterested — all these concepts must become synonyms of Soviet through your efforts here. Am I making myself clear?"

Never had Volodya seen Bogoslovsky so excited, seething with such wonderful wholesome anger. And again, as in Chorny Yar, he was filled with envy for Bogoslovsky, he envied him his inner moral substance, the sweep and yet precision of his thinking, and the way he lived — in the name of his cause and by his cause, with nothing morbidly self-sacrificial about it, but rather with a cheerful delighted dedication of his entire self to his work. Why had he, a wonderful surgeon, all but given up operating? Why? Because he was busy with more urgent work, work of primary importance, and the urgency and importance of that work for society was, in fact, the recompense he was getting for the temporary loss of his beloved surgery.

They were still having tea when Tod-Jin returned. He was in high spirits and there was a sly look in his eyes. He took off his fur coat, white with hoarfrost, sat down facing the window so that the sun shone straight into his face, and became engrossed in his thoughts, the cup of tea he was holding forgotten and turning cold.

"I know now!" the thought startled Volodya. "I know. He has the eyes of an eagle, he's looking straight at the sun!"

"Well then?" Bogoslovsky asked him.

"We'll go now, in another minute," Tod-Jin replied. "Let Mady-Danzy come too. A lot of them are afraid that they'll be deprived of their age in this hospital, that's what they call dying, and the lamas and shamans are keeping this fear alive in them, but we've got to prove that far from depriving them of their age we'll cure them of their ailments here, is it not so? And let this young comrade," he turned to Volodya, "start doing his job."

Tod-Jin went back to his thoughts, gazing at the cold, white sparkling sun. That morning Volodya did not go out and chop wood, do his morning exercises, or pace the casualty ward. That cold, windy morning, he went uninvited into the town to induce the sick to come to him for treatment. With him went Bogoslovsky, Tod-Jin and three local acquaintances of Tod-Jin's. The snow crunched under their feet. The biting wind stung Volodya's face and in the *yurtas* they visited it swept the pungent smoke of fires that gave no heat across the beaten mud floors. The freezing goats and sheep bleated in their sheds beside the timber huts and mud hovels buried in drifts of snow. Volodya's enemies, the lamas and shamans, kept out of Tod-Jin's sight, watching through a screen of whirling snow. Ferocious, hungry village dogs snarled and wheezed. Darkness had already fallen when Markelov's eyes, glowing like a wolf's, flashed before them. He came striding down the street towards them wrapped in a huge fur coat and leaning on a club. He greeted the doctors and Tod-Jin affably, and said in a hoarse voice that he would be glad to entertain them at his house. Tod-Jin stopped to exchange a few polite words with him, as the custom demanded.

"How are your herds, are they in good health?" he asked. That was the accepted opening phrase of any conversation here.

"My herds are well," Markelov replied. "Are your herds well?"

"Mine are well, thank you, yes," said Tod-Jin. "Are you and your family well?"

The ceremony over, Tod-Jin looked with his eagle eyes straight into Markelov's unholy, wolf's eyes, and said distinctly:

"You will not get the trading post building, the hospital is housed there. It's not yours, you are a thief, with your permission, yes, you are, you wanted to steal it, but you have no title deed to it."

"We pay taxes, we bring civilisation," Markelov broke into a growl, but Tod-Jin cut him short.

"Everything will be precisely as I say," he said. "You

will get it in writing. And now, may I wish your herds a good winter and good fodder."

"Yours too," Markelov grunted, turning his back on Tod-Jin.

Volodya could not help chuckling. Tod-Jin gave him a stern look.

They went into the next *yurta* with bows and ceremony as required. The smoke stung their eyes; they began by inquiring after the health of the herds, and then of their hosts. The last question was superfluous, though. The bright beams of their flashlights showed up a hideous syphilitic lesion spreading over the lower lip and chin of their host — a short, broad-shouldered, and evidently very strong man.

"*Innocentium syphilis*, yes?" Tod-Jin asked.

"I think so," Bogoslovsky replied.

Tod-Jin addressed the host in his own language. The man's wife sank slowly to the felt-carpeted floor, wringing her hands and weeping loudly. Tod-Jin took no notice of her. The man looked intently at Tod-Jin, while his wife crawled up to Volodya on her knees, pressed his hand to her face, and sobbed louder still. Tod-Jin went on speaking, now and then indicating Volodya and Bogoslovsky with a jerk of his chin.

"Kol-Zal and the woman are coming to the hospital," Tod-Jin said to Volodya. "You'll cure them, yes?"

Volodya nodded. He knew how to cure syphilis at this, its second stage.

"How soon?" Tod-Jin asked.

"Say two months, to be on the safe side."

"There will be no lesion?"

"None. But they'll have to undergo treatment for quite a long time afterwards."

"If the lesion disappears, you'll have no better advertisement, comrade."

Tod-Jin addressed the man and woman again. She did not weep now, she listened. In a low voice Danzy translated the conversation for Volodya. They were worried about their livestock, but Tod-Jin promised to get the neighbours to tend it for them.

The owner of the next *yurta* they went to knew Mady-Danzy. Sain-Belek was an elderly man with sunken eyes and an ashen, tortured face. He had been too sick to move for a long time, and the fee charged by lama Yui — the most expensive local healer — had ruined him completely. The shamans had treated him as well, but this was a secret because lama Yui was quick to take offence. Sain-Belek thought very highly of the treatment they were giving him, lama Yui's especially. He drank holy bear bile every day and applied a decoction of ants to the swelling. If it had not been for the skill of lama Yui, the wisest of the wise, he would certainly have been deprived of his age long before this.

Tod-Jin switched on his powerful flashlight, Bogoslovsky sat down beside the sick man, and his clever fingers instantly located what the lama called a "devil's curse" and an accumulation of "angry foam".

"It's inguinal hernia. Surgery indicated," Bogoslovsky said in a business-like tone.

"Will he die?" Tod-Jin asked.

"I hope not."

Sain-Belek was put on a stretcher and carried to the hospital, accompanied by the wails of his entire family. Danzy ran on ahead to get a hot bath ready, and also to warn madam cook that the hospital was going to turn into a real hospital, in case the shock were too much for her. As a matter of fact, Danzy himself was rather frightened by the events bearing down on them. Keeping the stoves going was not the same thing as curing diseases, and besides there was mention of "surgery" — a creepy word.

Tod-Jin's eyes were absolutely impenetrable when he ordered one or another of the villagers to go to the hospital for treatment. People obeyed him. There was no disobeying him. He would brook no argument. The look in his eyes was stern and direct.

In one of the *yurtas* they found a badly scared old man who was all but stone deaf. Bogoslovsky smiled knowingly and promised to restore his hearing the next day or the day after. Volodya guessed at once what was wrong with old Abatai, but kept his silence. He was having a jolly time, jolly exactly described it; it was the sort of thing he had loved as a boy. True, the tricks they were pulling off that day — he, Bogoslovsky and Tod-Jin — were not too dignified really, but it was a beginning, a marvellous beginning, and success was a certainty, a sure bet. Old Abatai got into his fur coat and went to the hospital. Tod-Jin told them, smiling, that Abatai's daughter-in-law would not let him call in even the cheapest of the shamans, and now he was promised a complete cure in a day or two for nothing.

That night Volodya made his first rounds. The patients had had their baths and now lay in their clean beds, frightened and cross.

Madam cook placed a saucer of sweetened condensed milk beside each one, but no one tasted it. Lama Yui had been wily enough to intercept old Abatai on the way and shout in his ear that he knew for certain they were all going to be poisoned at the hospital that very night with the horrible poison *mgnu*. Old Abatai had asked him why.

"Because they need some fresh human flesh," the lama had yelled without batting an eye. "They heal their own wounds by applying good human flesh to them. And they also jerk human flesh!"

Old Abatai had started back for his *yurta* but had unfortunately run into Tod-Jin and the doctors. Like a good friend, he had naturally shared the lama's "wise counsel" with the other patients, and now they all felt ill at ease.

But then they witnessed a miracle. Was there anyone in Khara who did not know good old Opai? And was there anyone who did not know that she was to "lose her age" any day because she could not breathe? She would turn blue in her face, claw the ground with her fingers, and her eyes would start out of her face. The lama Yui gave her a wide berth, because he had taken the old woman's four horses and given her no help at all. And here they had helped her at once. They stabbed her with a needle and the fit was over. She had almost "lost her age" when she was being brought in, but the young doctor came up to her with a glass thing with a needle sticking out of it and pricked kind old Opai with it. She squealed just in case, and then she smiled. Her smile spread wider and wider, and when she had expressed as much joy as she could by smiling and taken all the breath she needed she made a speech. Neither Bogoslovsky nor Volodya understood a word, but one thing was clear to them — from now on everything was going to be different in the hospital.

"After all, it does smack of quackery," Volodya said to Bogoslovsky. "I know it's bronchial asthma, this adrenalin injection is all very well, but still..."

"Keep quiet," Bogoslovsky told him.

Something curious was going on. Talking volubly, the old woman rose to her feet and snatched up Abatai's saucer of condensed milk. Her face was very angry. The patients watched her, terrified. She licked the saucer clean with her tongue and, with a triumphant look at them, turned and walked out. Madam cook brought old Abatai another saucer filled to the brim with condensed milk, because he all but wept when Tod-Jin began rebuking him for spreading that human flesh and poison scare.

"We'll perform a few more miracles tomorrow," Bogoslovsky said, chuckling contentedly, "But afterwards you'll have to work without miracles, my dear boy. You'll have plenty of work, I guarantee that."

Tod-Jin stood smoking by the dark frozen window in the corridor. He faced about abruptly and spoke to Bogoslovsky in his guttural voice, which now sounded strained and harsh.

"I want to thank you, comrade, yes, to thank you for bringing gladness and for being glad. The gratitude does not come from me personally, it comes from our people. Yes, they are thanking you, though they do not understand it yet, but they will. And you, too, comrade," he turned to Volodya who was astonished and moved by the sight of tears in the eagle eyes. "And you, too, because you understand, because you will do more, you will..."

Tod-Jin broke off and walked away to the farthest end of the corridor, leaving Volodya and Bogoslovsky to a long silence.

"All right, let's see what the morning brings," Bogoslovsky said at last. "Tell your Sancho Panza to get busy with the steriliser, we'll start operating early in the morning."

"Who'll be first?"

"Well ... I think we'll do the hernia first."

"Wouldn't it be a good idea for me to start washing out the wax that's plugging old Abatai's ears before we do any surgery? He'll hear better at once and it'll give heart to the other patients."

"Go ahead, I don't mind," Bogoslovsky said, grinning.

At seven next morning Volodya called Abatai into the casualty ward. Bogoslovsky was still asleep. Danzy, grey-faced after his busy night with the steriliser, cut an impressive figure in his white smock and cap — just another surgeon, wouldn't everyone think? On a small table two spirit lamps were burning with a blue flame. At first Abatai hardly dared to look at Volodya — the Russian doctor was so magnificent in his white clothes, with the round, shiny, incredibly beautiful mirror fixed to his head in old Abatai's honour. If his daughter-in-law could have seen him now, wouldn't she change her tune!

"How are your herds?" Abatai opened the conversation politely.

Shouting hard, Danzy translated Volodya's reply that his herds were fine and how were Abatai's?

Abatai did not know what to say. It was dangerous to say that his herds were in good shape, for the Russian doctor might be tricking him into the admission to demand payment like any lama or shaman, but what did he have to pay with? On the other hand, it was too mortifying to admit for all to hear that he owned no herds at all. Therefore he replied with a polite little cough. He was not going to walk into a trap, not he! No one could say now that old Abatai owned any livestock.

"Very well, let us begin," Volodya said.

Abatai sat down on a stool and had a napkin tied round his neck. With a pair of pincers the great Russian doctor very deftly picked up a wonder-working tube out of a shiny saucepan, and very soon Abatai's ear felt very nice and warm inside, so nice, in fact, that he even closed his eyes. And then his other ear felt nice and warm inside, too. The spirit lamps went on burning, this was like a sacrificial fire, only more beautiful, and the Highest of High Russian shamans flashed and flashed with his mirror, probably driving away the evil spirits *aza* and *kai-bin-ku* from Abatai.

The only fly in the ointment was that nobody was there to see the Russian doctor putting the charm on him. No lama, no shaman could do it so well! If only the Russian doctor would jump and stamp a bit and jingle the tambourine, then perhaps the other patients would wake up and come in to see it.

"And the tambourine?" Abatai asked Danzy.

"Be quiet. Don't talk," Danzy said sternly.

"Could you jingle the tambourine just a little?" Abatai begged tearfully. "Only a bit. I'll shoot a squirrel. I promise."

"You're bothering the doctor."

"I'll bring a sable."

"I'm telling you don't jabber."

All at once Abatai realised that his hearing was much better. Danzy was not shouting, he was simply speaking and not very loudly either, yet he could hear every word.

"Hey, I can hear!" he cried.

Volodya was doing something to his other ear, slowly and carefully. When he took out the cotton and spoke, Abatai heard him distinctly. Danzy translated Volodya's words for him with great dignity. The gist was this:

"Tomorrow, after Comrade Russian doctor and I have given

you some more treatment, your hearing will be as good as a healthy child's. And now go. Go and lie down."

Volodya removed his beautiful mirror, and old Abatai's pride swelled: so he really had worn that mirror for him alone! And there was Danzy blowing out the spirit lamps — so they, too, had been burning for Abatai. My, my! Naturally, treatment as wonderful as this could not be had free of charge, and Abatai felt obliged to warn them that he was a poor man.

"We don't want anything from you," Danzy said importantly.

"But I cannot repay your kindness."

"You can bow to the doctor, that's all."

Grunting, Abatai bowed low, and then he began to bow faster and faster, lower and lower, until the room went spinning around him — it wouldn't hurt him to do the thing properly. Volodya gripped him by the shoulder and shouted at him to make him stop. Abatai sighed, looking into Volodya's angry red face. He was probably going to demand a horse, several young reindeer or sheep in payment, after all. And he would probably kick him out too. No, they didn't kick him out. What was more, they brought him a dish of marvellous porridge, some pancakes with something sticky and sweet poured over them, and a cup of tea with milk. The other patients, awake now, plied him with questions in low voices, and he took his time answering. No use spilling it all out at once, he'd keep them on tenterhooks a little longer.

At nine, Bogoslovsky began the ritual of scrubbing his hands. All three of them — Bogoslovsky, Volodya and Danzy, wore long oilcloth coats of Volodya's invention and madam cook's making, with damp gowns on top. With Volodya's method of sterilisation, all gowns and everything required for an operation were perforce damp.

"You will operate," Bogoslovsky said. "I'll be your assistant and instrument nurse today."

Sain-Belek lay on the operating table switching his nostrils like a frightened rabbit, grumbling and complaining to Danzy.

"Why didn't the doctor fix the round mirror to his head? Why didn't you light the green fire for me? Am I not worthier than old Abatai? Old Abatai is a pauper, he's practically a beggar, and I can give these doctors many sheep if I like. Let them screw the mirrors on to their heads, you tell them!"

It was a huge bilateral hernia, and a truss would do no

good, of course. Volodya stood thinking, while Bogoslovsky injected the local anaesthetic.

"What's the verdict?"

"The Spasokukotsky method."

"That goes without saying," Bogoslovsky said with a smile. "There is no god but Allah, and Mahomet is his prophet."

"What's wrong with that?" Volodya replied with a challenge. "I consider Spasokukotsky a phenomenon, as a clinicist, as a surgeon, and as a practitioner too."

He took the scalpel held out by Bogoslovsky and made an incision half an inch above the groin fold. The aponeurosis of the outer, oblique stomach muscle came into view. At the sight of blood, Danzy gasped faintly and started backing towards the door.

"Come back to your place," Bogoslovsky ordered. "D'you hear me?"

Volodya cut the hypodermic tissue and Cooper's fascia. Bogoslovsky assisted in silence, watching intently but giving no directions. He cleared the blood away quickly, with a deftness that was extraordinary. Sain-Belek moaned from time to time or broke into speech but soon lost his trend of thought.

"I still remember one sentence out of a textbook on this," Bogoslovsky said. "It stated: place the edge over the central flap of the aponeurosis as if it were a coat lapel and sew it on."

"And sew it on," Volodya repeated, carefully drawing the ligature. He felt that the operation had been well done and was pleasantly excited. But that was only more reason for "keeping his shirt on", as Varya used to say. In the presence of a surgeon like Bogoslovsky it was ridiculous imagining you were an expert. Some praise was forthcoming, nevertheless.

"You're doing fine," Bogoslovsky said when they were scrubbing their hands before the next operation.

"With you here, I'm not afraid," Volodya replied truthfully.

"It's not a matter of being afraid," Bogoslovsky grumbled.

Their next patient was a not very old woman called Kuk-Bosta. Her stomach was swollen terribly, she had for long been unable to walk, and lama Yui had told her that she would "lose her age" very soon. Bogoslovsky thought she had a giant cyst. Volodya cut the peritoneum to the symphysis pubis and with a thick trocar punctured the containing wall of the cyst. And immediately fluid began to pour into the enamel pail placed there in readiness; there were litres of it. In spite of all precautionary measures, however, Kuk-Bosta nearly died from shock.

While Bogoslovsky was doing all that had to be done in such cases, Danzy slipped out of the room and told everyone that Kuk-Bosta had "lost her age".

In the meantime, Volodya exposed the cyst through the cut in the peritoneal wall and removed it. Bogoslovsky handed him the needle. Volodya sewed the wound up with catgut. Kuk-Bosta's breathing became even, deep and calm.

"Well done!" Bogoslovsky said.

"You taught me," Volodya replied.

Together, they carried Kuk-Bosta into the ward and placed her on the bed. They had to double for orderlies as well, in those days of toil and triumph.

The patients were chattering excitedly in the corridor: Danzy had lied to them, there was Kuk-Bosta as good as new, she was breathing, and her stomach no longer stuck out. No, the great Soviet doctors had not deprived her of her age either.

When they had washed themselves clean, thinking that their day's work was over, Bogoslovsky lit one of his thin cigarettes and said:

"One far from stupid doctor insists that women are much braver than men. Men are brave on the battlefield, of course, but then not every bullet finds its mark, some hit the bushes. In the operating room there's no getting away from the knife, it's unavoidable."

Danzy came in bringing some tea on a tray.

"Here's another brave for you," Bogoslovsky said, chuckling. "He is a man you can fully rely on, I understand?"

Danzy smiled and bowed.

"If it happens again you will have to kick him out," Bogoslovsky said deliberately and loudly. "It's disgusting to see a healthy man turn coward. Slipping out of the operating room and telling everyone Kuk-Bosta was dead."

"She *was* dead!" Danzy objected with some justification.

"And now she's alive," Bogoslovsky said, drawing on his cigarette which had gone out. "Anyway see that it doesn't happen again."

Before he could finish his cigarette in peace, Tod-Jin appeared with an apologetic experession on his face. He had brought in two more patients: Tush, a young widow six months pregnant, with acute appendicitis, and another woman suffering from mastitis. Tush's condition was very grave, and Bogoslovsky with an oblique glance at Volodya, performed the operation himself. Tush was delirious. She was little more than a child herself, this sixteen-year-old widow. Bogoslovsky was fighting for two lives in this case, and the battle was grim. The appendix was buried behind thick commissures and when he did locate it he found it was perforated. He shook his head and sighed. A miscarriage was inevitable, everything pointed to it, and the girl's resistance was so poor she did not stand much of a chance against peritonitis.

"Are we going to lose this Tush girl?" Bogoslovsky said as he and Volodya washed their hands. "It's a bloody shame, but what can we do? What?"

They put her in a room by herself and told Danzy to look after her. Bogoslovsky and Volodya arranged to do night duty between them.

When they were having dinner with Tod-Jin in Volodya's room old Abatai came in and said something looking at Tod-Jin. In lieu of payment for his treatment, the old man was offering his services. He would take care of the stoves. Mady-Danzy was a big man now, a doctor (Tod-Jin smiled faintly), he was busy all the time, but the stoves had to be kept going just the same, didn't they? And didn't the place have to be swept? True, old Abatai had never swept a floor in his life, but with his intelligence, smartness and clever hands he would certainly master the art eventually. He could also help in the kitchen; there wasn't a worker like him in the whole of Khara, the modest old man assured them, they didn't know how clever he was. Never mind that he was not so young. He knew lots of wonderful stories that he would entertain the patients with. For instance, he knew one about the clever bird Shish-kish, who got the better of a fox, and another one about old Techikei, who wound a money bag the size of a camel's neck, or that one about the sly, mean bear who...

"Good. I'll talk it over with the doctor," Tod-Jin said.

"We'll do what you think best," Volodya said when Tod-Jin repeated the conversation to him. "But I shall need more people, you know."

Tod-Jin turned to Abatai.

"Am I staying?" the old man asked.

"Yes, you are."

"Who'll I be?"

"You'll be a big man. You'll have many difficult and honourable duties," Tod-Jin pronounced solemnly.

"I'll be an official?" Abatai asked. Nothing could surprise him after that morning's experience.

"No, you'll be the caretaker."

"That's not less honourable, I hope?"

"No, it's much more honourable than being an official," Tod-Jin replied without a smile.

Abatai went away after wishing good health to the animals and families of the men who had been so kind to him. Back in the ward he lay down on his bed and, rubbing his sunken belly, told everyone that soon he, old Abatai, would get so fat they'd all gasp with admiration and wonder. The Russians and Tod-Jin himself had implored him to stay on and work at the hospital. And the job they were giving him was a good deal harder than any official's.

"Tell us more stories," Sain-Belek said with a groan. "Who wants poor beggars like you anyway? If there's anyone fit to be an official, that's me."

At midnight Tush had a miscarriage. Volodya called Bogoslovsky, and the battle for her life began. "She's all alone in the world," Tod-Jin said. "If you could save her it would be fine. She's only sixteen."

But Tush had not even enough strength to suffer.

And yet, she lived. It was a difficult, a fantastically difficult night for Volodya, and the following day was very difficult, too, with two more extremely grave operations to be performed, and after that there was another night, still without proper sleep. He dozed in snatches. And only at daybreak, a very cold daybreak on the third day, did her condition show some improvement. They had dragged her back from beyond the threshold she had already crossed. The saline injections, the glucose, the hot-water bottles Volodya kept refilling and the very tenderness with which he and Bogoslovsky had supported that almost weightless body in a half-sitting position all the time had helped to save Tush from death. On the fourth day, she was actually strong enough to have a good cry over her dead child, after which she drank some milk and fell asleep. Volodya stood over her and watched her breathing. Beside him, touching his shoulder, stood Tod-Jin and also watched. He looked at her with his hard, fearless and motionless gaze, with eagle eyes that did not flinch from the sun.

"She'll stay and work at the hospital, comrade," he said. "She's clever and light on her feet, yes. I knew her husband, a good husband, he died because you were not here, comrade. He was taken a long way on horseback, and died, but the post-mortem showed that he could have been cured very easily. He was a member of our party here, the first one."

When Tush awoke she saw Tod-Jin sitting by her bed, alone. She looked at him, surprised.

"They have preserved your age for you in this hospital, Tush," he said in a low voice. "You are alone now, Tush. But if you will remain here you will not be alone. A person must do good. You will do it here. Later, if you prove worthy of the great honour, we shall send you to Moscow, to that city of cities, to study. You are very young, you may yet learn to be a surgeon, a person who grants people their age. Your husband hoped to go away with you and study. You must carry out his wish."

"Yes," said Tush.

"Have you understood all?"

"Yes."

"Then why are you crying?"

"I'm crying because my husband and my first-born are dead, Tod-Jin."

"Don't, Tush. They died because we are still living a savage and ignorant life. You had appendicitis. The illness started long ago, as long ago as last winter when I came here. Had there been a surgeon in Khara then, you would not have lost your husband and your child. Have you understood me?"

"Yes."

"Good-bye, Tush."

"Good-bye, Tod-Jin."

Bogoslovsky and Tod-Jin left Khara that day.

"Good-bye, Vladimir Afanasyevich," Bogoslovsky said, shaking Volodya's hand. "It was good to see you. I expect we'll meet again. In any case, wherever I may be I'll have you join me, if you have no objections of course."

He thought for a moment and added gruffly:

"I think you're a reliable sort."

Volodya's face was purple. He couldn't be such a bad doctor if Bogoslovsky said things like this to him.

"Trust Tush, trust her completely. She will help you well," Tod-Jin said. "And that old woman Opai, she can be of some use to you, too. There are many who will help if only the right approach is found. Yes?"

"Yes," Volodya agreed.

They went away and Volodya was left alone with his hospital and his patients. There was also his budding fame.

How scared he felt that night!

## ALONE AGAIN

Old Abatai's hearing was indeed as good as in his youth, and the community of Khara could not stop marvelling at this small miracle. All the deaf came streaming to Volodya from faraway nomad camps, not to mention Khara itself. The incurable refused to believe this verdict and offered him reindeer, sheep or horses in payment. One ancient widower went so far as to promise Volodya a "perfectly good" camel if he cured him; he was contemplating marriage and a stone-deaf bridegroom was not quite the thing. Abatai, whose faith in Volodya's healing powers was unshakeable, told the widower that he ought to beg harder, beg properly, weep and bow to the ground, because Volodya was a *Great Shaman*.

Volodya had all kinds of trouble with the deaf.

But then Kuk-Bosta, with three pails of fluid, pumped out of her by Bogoslovsky and himself, the good, fat Opai and the light-footed Tush, all were loud in their praises of the Soviet doctor Volodya, the Russian hospital and the new Russians, who were not *that* sort of people. Not that sort meant not Markelov's sort. Markelov was hated and feared by the local population, but Volodya did not exactly know why.

He often came across Markelov when he went out on calls to the *yurtas* at the other end of the village. Markelov would look at him intently, greet him politely, and then follow him for a long time with unfriendliness in his unholy Gypsy eyes. Once it seemed to Volodya that there was something the man wanted to say to him and he stopped to hear it, but Markelov walked away, leaning on his heavy stick and dragging his leg.

Business was very bad for lama Yui and shaman Ogu now that people had started calling Volodya in. Lama Yui was the sharper of the two, and left Khara while the going was good. Ogu stayed. He walked about the village flaunting his full shamanic garb to look more impressive and terrifying. Things began to look really bad for the shaman when old Abatai spread abroad the lie that the most highly honoured Russian doctors had told him Ogu had been putting the blight on many out of spite, particularly Kuk-Bosta for paying him short one sheep. Ogu was no longer regarded as a healer, but simply as a sorcerer capable of doing evil. People had not much use for that type of sorcerer unless they wanted the blight put on someone, but that did not bring in enough to feed a sparrow and Ogu liked his drink and could not do without meat for dinner.

296

"Things look very bad for that damned Ogu," Abatai would say with a sanctimonious sigh.

Even the children called out all sorts of indecencies at the shaman when he shambled past their *yurtas* beating his tambourine. He wore a tall hat on which a hideous human face was embroidered with gut, and carried his beribboned staff with the three small bags hanging from it — in one there was a "celestial stone", in the other a "terrestrial stone" and in the third there was food for these "living" stones.

"Give us back our sheep, you dirty dog," one urchin shouted.

"Don't you dare walk past our *yurta* again," another piped.

"We're not afraid of you!" called out a third, but that was a flagrant lie. They were all afraid of him, and how!

It was enough for shaman Ogu to turn his bony face on them, make a horrible grimace and shake his beribboned staff, for all the braves to scatter with loud howls and hide in their *yurtas*, shaking with fright and muttering incantations against the horrid shaman's evil eye, because if he wanted to he could make your stomach bulge out with three pails of water in it like Kuk-Bosta's and you'd have to have it cut open and pumped out, and that hurt, and how!

Volodya had plenty of work and he no longer felt ashamed of himself when he listened to Radio Moscow, for he was doing his job, and passably well he believed. It was a good idea sending *him* here. Both Pych and Ogurtsov would have managed as well perhaps, but as for Svetlana or Nyussia he was not too sure.

One day, after listening to the news broadcast from Moscow, he tuned in to Vienna to hear some music and lay down, closing his eyes to enjoy it. The next moment he sat up with a jolt. Instead of music he was listening to the voice of Schuschnigg, the Austrian Chancellor, just back from Hitler's residence at Berchtesgaden.

Reception was unusually good and Volodya understood every word. At midnight, Seiss-Inguart made the announcement that he had taken over from the former chancellor and had requested Hitler to send his troops to Austria. No waltzes were played, and instead of Schubert's *Unfinished Symphony*, which Volodya had listened to so often before from Vienna, a military brass band broke into a march and ugly voices bawled the nazi song about Horst Wessel. So now it was beginning, the thing his father had warned him of when he had said that wars would hold up science, the thing Varya's father had spoken of as well.

297

Volodya twirled the knob a little longer.

All the stations were broadcasting dance music. "They're dancing!" Volodya thought with bitterness. "Paris is dancing, London is dancing, Rome too. How I wish I could talk to Aunt Aglaya just now, if only for an hour, even half an hour!"

He was settling down to sleep when madam cook knocked on his door and told him that a badly burnt boy had been brought in from the mines.

Nights without any sleep at all were a frequent thing now.

With the first warm winds, shaman Ogu disappeared from Khara. People said that before leaving for the taiga he had stayed a long time in front of the hospital working his magic, and everyone was afraid the building would be swallowed by the earth, or Doctor Volodya would die, or there would be a great fire. But time went on and nothing happened.

Kol-Zal's ugly lesion was almost gone. The villagers were impressed, and now Volodya had more patients than he could attend to. And not just syphilis cases either. He had beds placed in the corridor, in the large hall, and the small passage leading to madam cook's kitchen. The two deaths that occurred did not frighten the people away. Volodya spared no effort to make his patients understand that the two unfortunate ones had come too late, and no science in the world could have helped them.

"You must come to me in good time, and then no one will be deprived of his age," Volodya told them.

It is a true saying that the surgeon dies with each of his patients. Volodya went through that as he made the post-mortem examinations all by himself. He was not to blame for these deaths, but had he done everything to save that young shepherd brought in with a bad case of peritonitis, and that elderly hunter who had been savaged by a bear? They had both died after the operation, therefore their death was a consequence of the operation. True, the hunter had been sick in his *yurta* for eleven days before his family thought of bringing him to the hospital. And again that harrowing phrase: "after" meant "in consequence of"...

As was the custom, the dead men were taken away on horseback into the mountains. Volodya could not face the bereaved families. He thought of his classmates — Svetlana, Yevgeny, Misha Shervud. "You interns, how's life treating you, I wonder? Never mind, we'll meet yet, and then I'll tell you what I think of you, you rotters." He dreamed of that moment, tossing and turning on his narrow bed, through those endless, sleepless nights.

He was working under a terrible strain, he felt so tired towards the end of the day that he could not sleep. He received patients in the dispensary both morning and evening, but there were more than he could attend to. There were also the rounds of the hospital to be made, treatment to be prescribed, and outside calls made. Could he refuse to go when he was called to the sick-bed? Besides, he had two days of surgery a week, with no assistants, no trained nurses, no help. Danzy, that cowardly soul, was worse than useless. The operations were pure torture, the hardest of hard labour, they took so much out of Volodya, they taught him such acrobatics that he would have done well at the best circus now. They also taught him self-control, poise, and how to hold down his screaming nerves, which he suddenly discovered he possessed.

"You'll have a nervous breakdown at this rate, my darling boy," Aunt Aglaya wrote to him. "Ask for leave and let's go to the Black Sea."

Volodya smiled at this sadly. Could people in the Soviet Union know what it was really like here? Even such intelligent people as Aunt Aglaya and Rodion. Who could he trust the hospital to? All that had been created with such pains would collapse if he left just now, distrust would be sown again and all the ground that had been gained would be lost. Rodion understood, for this is what he wrote: "Your father would have been proud of you, believe me when I say that. When you come to think of it, you *are* carrying on where Afanasy left off and are acting the way he acted when we were together over there. Still, take care of yourself, Aglaya's right about that."

Volodya was gradually training Tush, that sweet young widow, as an instrument nurse. The duties of an instrument nurse were not easy to master, but Tush tried so hard, she was so eager to learn, she wept so broken-heartedly when Volodya scolded her, and looked so earnestly into his eyes to read his thoughts and forestall his wishes, that her mistakes no longer annoyed him and he comforted her instead with: "Take it easy, Tush, and everything will go splendidly."

Tush was very bright, she moved lightly and swiftly, her small, clever hands obeyed her eagerly and efficiently if something wanted doing for the patient, for the operation, for the work she was only just learning. The patients were always calling for Tush, she was becoming indispensable, she began and finished the hardest and most unpleasant job as if it were not work at all but a bit of unexpected luck.

She taught Volodya the language of her people. This she also did gladly and cheerfully with an eager light in her dark, gold-fringed eyes and a shy smile on her rosy lips.

By springtime Volodya could more or less understand the hunters, sheep herders and farmers ("the land waterers" they were called because they dug irrigation ditches), and, what was more, he could speak a little, at least, he knew the essential things without which it was difficult to manage. And naturally he learned not to smile when he said his herds were well in answer to the customary greeting, and himself asked the question established by ancient tradition. Modestly dropping her eyes, Tush corrected him whenever he made a mistake.

Danzy hated Tush, but he nursed his hatred in secret, thinking that Volodya simply wanted the woman because she was young and beautiful and Volodya was young and good-looking himself. He saw the adoration in Tush's eyes as she looked at Volodya and also noticed that Volodya blushed red in her presence for no reason at all; the only thing that surprised Danzy was why Tush did not get into bed with the doctor sooner. That did not worry him too much, though. What did, was the fact that Tush had become much more important than himself. Even old Abatai was trying to order him about now. Altogether, Abatai and Tush had got in between himself and the doctor, thwarting his ambition of becoming the most important person in Khara and the doctor's right-hand man.

The two were hard to beat, however.

Madam cook was very fond of Tush, old Abatai sided with them, too, and Danzy could not possibly manage the three of them single-handed. Danzy would have to suffer in silence until *he* came from the capital and then Danzy would tell *him* that all three were Bolsheviks. That's exactly what he would say to him: they are Bolsheviks. Then all three of them would be sacked. That was as far as Danzy's dreams went.

At night, when the hospital quietened down, Volodya indulged in long, bitter-sweet thoughts of Varya. Blood pounded in his temples, his face flamed, he wanted to call out: "Varya, come!" Perhaps she would answer, come close to him and ask as she used to: "What's the matter, Volodya?"

No one came. Volodya would grit his teeth and try to read. But Varya's image refused to be driven away. Then he would give himself a shake, let out a string of abuse, and force himself to think the worst of Varya. Let her do as she pleased. He had his own life to live and she had hers. Everyone chooses his own path. With her it would be footlights, flowers, waltzes, kisses, and then the thing Yevgeny called "physiology". Sweat broke out on Volodya's brow, his hands shook, he felt suffocated. He would open the small window and sit down at his desk again. Forcing himself to register what he had just read cost him a great effort, but read he did, he had to read.

Tod-Jin subscribed to magazines and ordered books in different languages for all his doctors, and that helped Volodya immensely. He could not visit clinics, or attend scientific conferences, all he could do was read — read, work and think.

And also write letters.

He often wrote to Bogoslovsky now and enjoyed doing it. In most of his letters Volodya asked for the older man's advice, but sometimes, feeling the need to set out his thoughts, he wrote letters that were more like speeches, programmes or essays. He told Bogoslovsky, in one of these, how wrong he thought it was to admit young boys and girls just out of school to universities and institutes. "Take all those Svetlanas and Nyussias of ours, for instance," he wrote. "Carrying bed-pans and doing the job of ward nurses in a hospital for three, four or five years, would certainly decide those fastidious young ladies if they really wanted to enter the profession or if they simply wanted a higher education at the state's expense. Am I not right?"

Bogoslovsky answered every one of his letters, debating a point sometimes, but never preaching. He did not agree with Volodya about "all those Svetlanas and Nyussias", the same yardstick could not be applied to everyone, he thought. "Take yourself, for example," he wrote. "You had your values right all along, so it would have been senseless your wasting your best years working as an orderly. And I dare say there was no need for me to spend several years as a male nurse either."

Varya's letter found him in the midst of deep and burdensome reflections on his work, when he was in a state of exhaustion and extreme irritation, brooding resentfully on lickspittles and hangers-on in general. The tone of Varya's letter, the expensive, faintly perfumed paper, the thick envelope, and her little jokes, Volodya took as a direct insult. Varya said that she was finished with her "horrid" geological school at last, after just scraping through the exams, that she was a free agent now and, although her father did not approve exactly, she was definitely set on becoming an actress. That autumn, if not earlier, she was going to move to Moscow and enrol at a studio school there, the name of the theatre Volodya could not make out. She also said that they would probably meet again when they were old and grey, when Volodya was a shining light in some Moscow clinic, for he could not spend his entire life travelling abroad and all outstanding professors eventually came back home. And so, when he did, she hoped he would look for her — a third-rate little actress in one of Moscow's theatres — and they would talk of their silly young days, if he was not above that, of course...

Volodya read the letter through twice, and sat down to write the answer.

He had never written a letter so long, so cruel and so overbearing in his life. He was cruel in spite of himself. The description of his life was a rebuke to her and all those like her. Yes, he said, all of you — all you Yevgenys, Svetlanas, Nyussias and Varyas. So you imagine that I deck myself out in tails every night, do you? All right, I'll tell you how I really live. It was cruelty born of pride, he did not cavil, he simply demanded similar devotion to work from everyone, he vented his rage on the renegades, he jeered at them and called them the worst names. He also told Varya about Tush, his future instrument nurse, he said that Varya and the rest of them put together were not worth her little finger. He wrote about the operations he had to perform all by himself, about the blizzards and the shamans, the frosts of 50° below zero, about Tod-Jin, about his loneliness and despair when no patients came to him at first, and he also said that he was *perfectly, completely* happy although she had *betrayed* him.

"You have betrayed me, I am not afraid to use the word. You could have come here with me and stood by me to help in my job, not glamorous perhaps but important. You would have been my anaesthetist and assistant, you would have been my wife and companion, but you chose your idiotic dream of footlights and flowers. That dream is utterly and completely hollow. Believe me, the only thing that matters is knowledge of duty well done. Who are you now? A geologist? No, you're not. An actress? No, even less so. How can you live with an easy mind and joke about it, you, a member of the Komsomol? Resign from the Komsomol then, if you are like that."

It was an abominable letter, he knew, but he did not read it over. His life and his job were particularly trying just then for all his brave assurances of being perfectly happy.

Too long were the nights of deliberation preceding a day of surgery, too great and all but unendurable was the responsibility he carried for the human lives placed in his hands, too painful were his reflections of duty, free will, man's earthly purpose, and his own right to "sit it out" when the Red Army was storming the Mannerheim line.

Twice he wrote to Bogoslovsky demanding that he be sent into the army in the field, and both times Bogoslovsky replied with formal dryness that while appreciating Volodya's feelings he was not in a position to close down the hospital in Khara.

Evenings in spring tormented Volodya with homesickness; he wanted terribly to go to the theatre, a big, beautiful theatre, to go with Varya, it had to be Varya. He wanted to hear her talk her precious nonsense and be able to say: "Stop talking rubbish." He wanted there to be no smell of hospital, he wanted to walk down a wide, rain-washed street, with the opaque globes of light reflected in the puddles, he wanted not to have to jump up at night when Tush knocked on the door and said: "A very bad case, he'll lose his age right now, yes, no?" His homesickness too he mastered; it was no easy battle, but he won. He ordered himself not to think of things he ought not to think of.


### Chapter Fifteen

### THE SORCERER

In March, when the worst of the winter was over, when the days grew more sunny and the cold less severe, a young doctor arrived from Leningrad to help Volodya out. He was a nice, chubby-faced chap called Vasya Belov. Like Bogoslovsky and Tod-Jin before him, he arrived drenched through; he had also seen a pack of hungry wolves on the way to Khara. He brought with him a good rifle, "Dad's, you know", an impressive supply of cartridge-cases, gunpowder, shot, fishing-line, hooks, wads and handbooks on medicine. He also had a flask of brandy, a photograph of "just a friend, a childhood friend one might say", and a pipe which he smoked "just for the fun of it, you know". Vasya looked up to Volodya, he treated the patients with reverence and said of Tush that in her he saw the "awakening national dignity of millions of fine people". Volodya spoke to him in the damping tone of a wordly-wise old man. He could not treat the chubby-faced young doctor differently.

Vasya kept popping questions at Volodya.

"Are there any tigers in these parts, I wonder?"

"Personally, I've never had the honour of meeting any."

"And what about skunks?"

"Why don't you ask old Abatai about it?"

"Are there any poisonous snakes? If so I'd like to know what kind exactly, and tell me, what do you use against snake bites?"

"I've never heard anything about snakes either, Vasya," Volodya said, but remembering Bogoslovsky corrected himself:

"I beg your pardon, Vasily..."

"Ivanovich," Vasya said, blushing.

"Vasily Ivanovich, then. No, I don't know if there are any snakes here, and I've never had to treat snake bites yet."

"Pity. I specially brought along a monograph entitled *Poisonous Snakes*."

"There's nothing I can do to help."

"Never mind. Tell me, did you have any extraordinary cases at all?"

"Everything is extraordinary here, Vasily Ivanovich."

"I don't mean in that sense. You see, I have a journalist's card from our youth newspaper, and I'd like to send in something occasionally, that is, if you have no objection. Articles or short stories, you know, just to throw some light on our life here."

"Go ahead, throw all the light you please. Only mind it doesn't interfere with your immediate duties, there's plenty of hard work to be done."

They shared a room. Vasya spent his evenings either mulling over his first and only article entitled "Everyday Life at X Hospital", or writing mile-long letters. One day Volodya came across a page covered with Vasya's writing, and read it: "...derful, tremendous personality. I won't go wrong, I think, my faraway love, if I take Ustimenko, with his iron will, scientific foresight, devotion to work and uprightness, as my model of perfection..."

Volodya did not read on. He suddenly felt ashamed, as if he had been deluding Vasya. He certainly had not intended to.

Vasya got on very well with Abatai. The old man could speak a little Russian now. Tush interpreted for both of them, and Vasya listened for hours to Abatai's naive and very funny stories, some of which he actually took down for his future "pamphlet" on the hospital in Khara.

There was as much work as ever, but with Vasya there it

was much easier to manage, and Volodya said so to him almost every day.

"Oh no, honestly ... I'll get a swelled head... If it wasn't for you..." Vasya would protest, blushing and scratching his chin very comically.

And he would work even harder, more energetically than ever. He thrived on praise, whereas a rebuke, even if very mild, made him mope and sulk and snuffed out the light in his usually merry eyes.

Volodya was now able to leave the hospital sometimes if he had to. He went on horseback to the Urchun mines and examined everyone there, sick or healthy; it was a long, painstaking job but it needed doing. He also visited the fishermen on the Ostyu-Be River and called at many nomad camps in the Djishi district. Danzy went with him, as a rule, and they took along a good supply of medicines, some surgical instruments, a tent and two sleeping bags. It was good to ride his sure-footed horse along a faint path in the taiga, or along the edge of a drop with the Taa-Hao roaring over the rapids below the sun shining down on his face with a gentle, steady warmth. It was good to see an entire camp get noisily excited at his approach, with crowds of children dashing forward to meet him, their dignified fathers and grandfathers following sedately, and the women bowing to him in welcome. It was good to have each *yurta* owner invite him to dinner or supper, or just for a chat at *his* place; to ask the customary question about the well-being of the herds and hear the same question in reply, a humorous gleam in the eyes of his hosts because the Russian doctor was known to have no herds, but how else could one start a conversation anyway?

To be sure, he encountered lice, trachoma and syphilis in those *yurtas*, in the miners' huts and at fishermen's camps. Some cases were so ghastly that Volodya, for all his experience, turned sick in the stomach. Still, rolling up his sleeves and washing his hands, he did all he could on the spot, after which he sent the patient, with a note for Vasya, to his hospital on a stretcher tied to two horses one on each side. The hospital was always full to capacity. As a rule, people left it fully recovered, and talk that there was a marvellous, wonderful doctor in Khara spread from one nomad camp to the next. People believed less and less in the healing powers of lamas and shamans, who slunk away into the wilds of the taiga and the tundra. And there, far from Khara, their resentment against Volodya, his hospital, the new doctor Vasya, Tush, who worked with those Russians, and even old Abatai, swelled in volume and intensity.

Volodya was neither relieved nor troubled, he simply did not care. The lamas and the shamans no longer bothered him, so he forgot about them as completely as he had forgotten about Markelov. He was too busy, he worked too hard and too devotedly to give thought to anyone who was not at the moment in his line of vision.

It was already autumn. He was roused at dawn one September morning. All he could make out from the incoherent story of the boy who came for him was that something disastrous had happened, that he had to go and help some people who were far away from Khara. How far, the terrified, exhausted boy could not explain.

Danzy harnessed the horses and saw to the packs. It was a chilly morning. Volodya shivered and yawned, he could not make himself fully awake. By noon they still had more than a hundred kilometres to go, but how much more the boy did not know; he also confessed that there was not one but three men wounded. One of them, the boy thought, must have lost his age by now, and the other two would perhaps last until they arrived.

It was hard going. At first they rode along the river, Volodya knew the path, and then they made a short cut through the taiga. Branches lashed at their faces and tore their clothes. The horses wheezed and their flanks twitched. In a glade near the village of Djem-Chu, where Volodya had been before, they met a group of ten riders or so, with ribbons plaited into their horses' manes and tails, which told Volodya that the wounded men had already been attended to by the shaman. Danzy spoke excitedly to an old man who looked at Volodya with enmity. The wounded, it appeared, were being ministered to by shaman Ogu who had fled from Khara. No one had told the boy to go for the doctor, it had been his own idea, and now the old man was threatening to punish him severely for it.

It was twilight when Volodya, Danzy, and the boy, Lamzy, reached a tall hill, crowned with cedars. The Taa-Hao could be heard roaring near by. Six fires were burning on the lee side of the hill; the dark shapes of men moving about loomed huge against the smoky flames. Some fifty horsemen blocked Volodya's way; they sat very still on their horses, waiting for him to come on. All of them were armed with rifles, even the youngest of them, mere boys. Danzy thought the riders were drunk and suggested going back while the going was good;

"Very drunk, yes, very drunk," Danzy said. "Will be bad, very bad."

Volodya dismounted and threw the reins to Danzy. With determined strides he went straight at the riders. They did not stir to let him pass, and the barrels of their hunting rifles stared sullenly into Volodya's face. Frightened but knowing there was only one course open to him, Volodya pushed aside a horse's muzzle, barged someone's stirrup with his shoulder, cursed, and started uphill. Behind him, squealing from fright and keeping as close to the doctor as he possibly could, came Lamzy — the son of the man who had probably lost his age by now.

Two of the wounded were lying on the ground between the smoking fires, and the third was sitting up with forked props under his arms. His eyes had an anguished, faraway look. Apparently he could no longer see, because he failed to recognise his own son. Shaman Ogu was squatting beside him. The moment Volodya understood what was going on here, his fear vanished.

Everything he might need in that other, "come next" life as Danzy called it, had been put in readiness beside the dying man: tobacco and matches, a bottle of milk vodka, strips of jerked mutton, a new pair of shoes, and a whip. Though still alive, he was already being seen off, and by coming and meddling Volodya had violated the law of death already proclaimed by shaman Ogu. The riders were there, on the shaman's instructions, to see that the law was not violated, for if Lamzy's father recovered, Ogu himself must die, his career as a shaman would be over.

"All is ready for you, all well prepared, nothing has been overlooked. Go then, go, you have no age left," shaman Ogu was entreating the dying man. The branches snapping and crackling in the fire prevented him from hearing Volodya's approach.

"Get out, you dirty sorcerer!" Volodya shouted.

Slowly Ogu turned round, saw Volodya's boots and rose to his feet. This was not the same Ogu who used to shy and slink away from Volodya in Khara, this was another Ogu. In the taiga *he* was the master, and a brazen one at that. He was drunk, and in his hand he held the large knife with which he had been cutting up the mutton for the dying man's long journey. And now the knife, point raised, was poised to strike, to kill the hated Russian doctor with a stab in the belly, a single thrust with a twist at the end. Ogu knew how to kill men, though he did not know how to cure them.

They stood thus, staring at one another with the light of the fires on their faces. The tambourine jingled softly in Ogu's left hand. He was wearing his tall hat with the hideous human likeness embroidered on it in gut. Shaman Ogu was here to enforce the law of death and he was defending death; Volodya had come to bring a man back to life and he was defending life, oblivious of his own safety. He made a lunge, gripped the wrist holding the knife and crushed it so hard that the shaman dropped his weapon and sprang back into the shadows beyond the fires, shrilling and beating his tambourine.

Volodya bent over Lamzy's father.

Death was near, but it was still worth a fight.

Taking off his padded jacket, Volodya got down to work, while the other two hunters told him what had happened, breaking their story with loud groans. Volodya hardly listened, but snatches of their story reached him nevertheless. Hunting had been good but their cartridges had run out, and then the taiga devils Zumbr and Kur, the enemies of hunters, must have crossed the path of Lamzy's father, the best of all hunters. A cartridge exploded when he was recharging it. They had all been squatting close together, but Lamzy's father got the whole charge in his chest.

Suddenly there was a squeal from Lamzy and the next second Volodya heard a sharp click behind him.

He turned round.

Shaman Ogu, deathly pale, stood about ten paces away, holding a double-barreled gun. He had pulled both triggers, but the gun, which belonged to Lamzy's father was not loaded. It was a narrow escape. The taiga men were crack shots and Ogu would have aimed to kill.

Volodya took a belligerent step forward. Ogu dropped the gun, fell on his hands and knees and came crawling to Volodya, crawling and bowing, pressing his face to the ground. He came for protection to the man he had wanted to murder. Volodya alone could save him now from the law of death, save Ogu who had shot at his back. Hugging Volodya's boot he pressed his face to it and begged, whining, screaming and groaning.

"Pick it up, somebody. You hear me? Pick up the gun, load it and stand guard behind me because I've got to work," Volodya shouted. "You take it, Lamzy. Maybe your father won't lose his age after all. But I can't attend to him if someone's shooting at my back. And let the shaman get the hell out of here!"

He was furious, and strangely he remembered Svetlana and Nyussia again.

Lamzy loaded the gun and stood close behind Volodya. The riders dismounted and came up one after the other to get a closer look at the foreigner, who, Ogu had said, could only kill and never cure. He had killed two men at his hospital, and desecrated their bodies by cutting them up in order to steal their splendid, healthy hunters' hearts for his own use.

Volodya did not see them. By the flickering reddish glow of the dying fires, he was busy examining the wound, which reeked of putrefaction. It was on the right side of the sternum, the edges had become necrotic.

"How long has he been with those damned forks propping him up?" Volodya asked.

"Five days," Danzy replied readily. "Yes, five. They don't understand, they are stupid."

Volodya told Danzy to bring the instruments, build the fires high, and get him some water to wash his hands with.

In the meantime Volodya went on with the examination. Shaman Ogu had stuffed bits of fox fur into the wounds; it was supposed to be curative fur soaked in wolf saliva and melted squirrel fat. He had to operate at once, but the man could not breathe if he was laid on his back, and there was no one to give him the anaesthetic.

Volodya poured half a mugful of pure alcohol, diluted it with a little water, and held it up to the man's parched lips.

"Drink, friend," he said loudly and deliberately. "You're alive, you have not been deprived of your age. Drink it down and you'll feel better. You hear me, friend? Don't give in to the illness, resist it, and soon you'll go hunting again."

Slowly, the anguished eyes opened.

"Drink," Volodya said.

Lamzy's father drank, and when he sighed with relief, Volodya gave him a morphine injection.

Now he examined the wound thoroughly in the light of the blazing fires. The hunters stood around him in a motionless circle, walling him in from the whining and wailing shaman. Lamzy's father breathed with a rattling sound, and the boy sobbed at Volodya's shoulder. The wind moaned in the crowns of the cedars, and the turbulent waters of the Taa-Hao roared far below them. The two other wounded hunters sat up and, forgetful of their own sufferings, watched the Russian doctor's quick hands, the flashing instruments, and his tense angry face, in fascination.

The wound was about eleven centimetres deep. Probing it with his finger, Volodya felt several large shot, balls of curative fur, and a felt wad at the bottom. All this he safely extracted.

After a moment's rest, he tamponed the wound and applied a damp dressing.

The man's breathing was steadier, the pulse was still weak but much better than it had been.

It took him at least an hour to undo the shaman's handiwork on the other two hunters. Besides their wounds, they were also suffering from burns.

Volodya got to his feet at last; his heart was pumping, he had a stitch in his side and numbness in his legs. The huge fires went on blazing in the smoke. The circle of riders — hatless, olive-skinned men in short reindeer coats — had not stirred. Volodya faced them abruptly.

"Well? What now? Why did you meet me like an enemy?" he asked them in a language they understood. "What harm have I ever done you? Your shaman Ogu wanted to shoot me, you saw it, yet none of you made a move."

"We didn't dare," one of them answered in a harsh voice. "We are afraid of the shaman. He could have done away with all of us."

"He can do nothing," Volodya said. "He's a cowardly fool. He doesn't work like you people do. He swindles you and yet you're afraid of him."

"No more. We'll kill him now," another man said.

"No, you won't!" Volodya shouted. "You are not to kill him, you hear me? I forbid you."

Towards morning the three wounded men were carried down to the river and placed on the raft that had been rushed there from the nearest camp. Shaman Ogu grovelled at Volodya's feet until he got permission to go on to the raft with them, on condition that he first threw his hat, tambourine and staff, hung with the "living" stones, into the river. Ogu broke into loud wails, and the hunters roared with laughter. Volodya stood on the raft with an implacable expression on his haggard bearded face, his lips drawn into a hard line.

"Forgive me!" Ogu screamed.

"You'll come on my terms or not at all," Volodya said. "Do you understand, Ogu?"

And then Ogu, blubbering and shaking, threw all his shaman paraphernalia into the mighty waters of the Taa-Hao. Strange though it may seem, he really did believe in the magic powers of his hat, his tambourine and his staff. When his hat began to bob on the water, he submitted to the inevitable.

"What am I going to do now? Who will feed me?" he asked Volodya.

"You'll come and chop wood for me at the hospital. You'll get enough to eat."

"But I don't know how to chop wood!" the shaman said, his vanity stung.

Volodya merely shrugged. He did not speak to anyone all the way back to Khara, he felt too bitter and disgusted. For many years to come he was to remember the click of the gun behind his back.

The raft was steered by a local settler; the wounded men talked idly, watching for geese or duck to take flight before the approaching raft. Towards evening a dull roar warned them that they were nearing the rapids. The defrocked shaman and the other two hunters climbed on to a kind of platform, taking Lamzy's father with them; then, leaving Lamzy alone on the platform, they got down again to offer sacrifice to the rapids — coins, bread and salt.

"Hold tight!" the raftsman called out.

The raft heeled over and its stern swung round striking against the rocks. Then a big frothy wave lifted them high, the raft spun to the left, to the right, and the rapids were behind them. Lamzy's father humbly asked if his sacrifice — an old copper cartridge-case — had been thrown into the river.

"You'll make me well, yes, doctor?" he turned to Volodya, breathing hard.

Volodya smiled with a sigh of resignation: why be angry with people who offered sacrifices to the rapids?

In November, Volodya operated on Lamzy's father, removing a sequestrum of his breastbone in which a metal button and two pellets were lodged.

It was later in the same month that Markelov's daughter came to the hospital and asked Volodya to come and see her father, who was very ill.

"What's the matter with him?" Volodya asked.

"Would he tell me?" Pelageya said gloomily. "He only grits his teeth when you ask. And he drinks terribly. There's no flesh left on his bones, he doesn't sleep at all."

"Is it he who wants me to come or you?"

"It's me," Pelageya answered bashfully.

## WHAT IS THE PURPOSE OF LIFE?

That evening, putting a flashlight, a stethoscope and some luminal in his pockets, Volodya went to see Markelov. The ferocious watchdogs chained in the yard snarled and barked at his approach, then Markelov's cowed clerk appeared at the front porch and invited Volodya in.

"Come in, you are expected." His tone was piteous. "Miss Markelova is waiting anxiously, please come in."

The front hall smelt strangely of cypress branches, incense, and something else that was cloyingly sweet. Pelageya was all dressed up for some unknown reason in a rustling silk dress pinned at the throat with a costly brooch, and her fingers were ablaze with diamond rings.

"You go in by yourself, will you? Please, do this for me, pretend you were going past and just dropped in," she spoke in a whisper. "Or pretend you simply called to pay your respects. He's been expecting you to come for a long time. He often talks about you, not of you as a doctor, but just as a person. He mentions you often."

Volodya shrugged, and knocked at the door. There was no answer, so he just went in. The room was huge, low-ceilinged and very warm. Markelov, dressed in a long black *poddyovka*, was pacing up and down, his hands behind his back, his head dropped on his chest, and his grey beard jerking like a goat's. He was muttering under his breath and sighing audibly. He did not see Volodya at once, but when he did he showed no surprise.

"Oh, it's you. To what do I owe the honour, mister comrade doctor?"

Volodya thought the bluster had an artificial sound. True, Markelov's unholy eyes still stared at him insolently, but now there was alarm, weariness and fright in them too.

"Is there anything you want, or is it a good-neighbourly call? What do you want of Markelov?"

"I was just walking past and thought I'd drop in," Volodya replied easily, taking in Markelov's appearance with an experienced eye. "It must be over a year since we last met, so I thought I'd call and see if you were in good health."

"Oh, you'd like Markelov to be your patient? Too great an honour for a suckling like you. Markelov will outlive you all. Yes, all of you!"

Volodya made no reply. Markelov peered anxiously into

the young, chapped face with its firm, stubborn chin, and tried to catch Volodya's eye.

"You just dropped in, you say? No, doctor, that won't wash. It's Pelageya who roped you in, none other. Eh? Nothing to say, eh? I'm glad you came anyway, we'll have a chat and a drink. I've some Marsala — amazing stuff. No, Marsala is for sweet drunks. You and I will have cognac. Will you drink with me?"

"I will."

"And what about my being an exploiter and your class enemy? Why the stare? I know, I know everything, man, I read two of your newspapers nowadays, I subscribe to them."

He strode across the room, pulled aside a blue silk curtain on rings, and revealed a chapel with a lectern in a dimly lighted recess. There were some ancient prayer-books in calfskin bindings lying in a careless heap on the floor, and beside them a stack of magazines and newspapers. Markelov went in, rustled the papers angrily, and emerged with several *Pravdas* and *Izvestias*, which he brandished in Volodya's face.

"There, you see, I read them. So what? Collective farms, you say, five-year plans, state farms, orders conferred on workers for achievements. And how am I to live, I ask you? *With the Internationale the people shall arise*? I know that too. But what am I to do? Go back into the kingdom of darkness to shear sheep?"

"Why shear sheep?"

"That's a figure of speech, it's come down to us from the pillars of our faith. It means squeeze a native, squeeze the juice out of him. They are our providers and we are their benefactors. Got that?"

There was both malice and suffering in Markelov's eyes, the red mouth above the greying beard was twisted and his face quivered as from pain. Flinging the papers away, he walked to the door and shouted for Pelageya.

"Look at this fat cow getting all dressed up," he said with a smirk, eyeing his daughter. "She's never been anything but a sloven, but today she's all silks and jewels. Who for? For the doctor maybe? He won't marry you, he has no use for you, he has a woman waiting for him at home, a *comrade* and not a survival of the old life."

Pelageya turned a slow red, dropping her head low and nervously fingering the fringe of her shawl.

"Bring us a bottle of Martel, there's some in the cellar. Here, take the keys, but don't forget to lock it afterwards or

313

your dear mother will lap it all up," he smirked again and turned to Volodya. "She's our *survival of alcoholism*, she tipples to make life merrier. Pelageya, bring a dish of cucumbers, the dill pickles. Some drink Martel with lemon, but we, in our stupidity, have it with pickles. Bring all the fattest, juiciest joints for our learned guest, see how skinny he is. And get a move on, you've grown too fat, *exploiting the labour of others, you colonialist*," he said with a sidelong glance at Volodya out of his tortured eyes, and snapped at his daughter, "Get going!"

His daughter bowed low according to the old custom, and softly withdrew. Markelov produced a half-empty bottle from behind an old armchair, covered with threadbare carpeting, and took a swig thirstily.

"How shall I live now, tell me that? My ancestors came here, fleeing the persecutions of our father the tsar. They taught me their faith. 'Tell me, brother, who dies but rots not?' And very glibly I answered, 'The Mother of God, she died but rotted not, and was taken alive to heaven.' And there was another bit of dogma they'd ask, 'What creature was not in Noah's Arc?' And I would reply, 'Fish, for even in water it can live and breathe.' Not bad, eh? They also taught me to put myself above the local people, because another newcomer of another nationality might put himself above me and bleed the local people *drier* than I could. My parents taught me to sharpen my fangs, for man, they said, is like wolf to man. And all the while a visiting canoness of the old faith kept mumbling about the divine virtues, humility, understanding, abstinence, charity, brotherliness, concord, and love of your neighbour. What was one to do, how combine those sharpened fangs with brotherliness, for instance? How combine charity and learning to make the sort of vodka for the local native that cost you next to nothing and sent him round in circles? How combine love of your neighbour and your father's teaching to stain sable skins a darker colour, to smoke them so they'd fetch three times the price? Together with abstinence and understanding we were taught how to make a quiet end of a heathen in the taiga if that unbeliever became difficult. Yes, there was that, too. Nothing was forbidden us, we were taught, for we belonged to the old true faith, and would not burn in hell-fire. Some join their five fingers like a hoof to make the sign of the cross, others the thumb and two fingers like a pinch, we know all that but we are baptised by the pillars of our faith, therefore all will be forgiven us. The teaching was not lost on me, though

314

I was chary about much of it, I spilt no native blood myself, it sickened me to, but my late parents were smeared with that blood, plenty of it, and now it is *crying out*. That is why my brains are twisted and all upside down. Is there an illness like that?"

"Not that I've heard of," Volodya replied.

"You will."

Pelageya came in with a tray. Markelov took the bottle, knocked out the cork by hitting the bottom with the palm of his left hand, gave his daughter a glare, but instead of driving her away told her to sit down and listen meekly.

"The more so since you're in silks. Now listen, comrade doctor, I'm getting too clever with my brains twisted and upside down."

Pelageya poured the brandy into thick green tumblers and handed one to Volodya. He sipped it; Markelov tossed his back and began to crunch a pickle.

"Yes, too clever," he repeated. "And one little thing is bothering me. What is the purpose of man's existence?"

Volodya winced. Was Markelov taunting him, jeering not at his own thoughts but Volodya's, dragging them, drunkenly, into the open?

"Is it making money? Let's suppose so. After all our ancestors started it and we've been doing it for generations. Only what's money for? To leave your heiress? All right. But what if she's a silly fool and doesn't care for it? What then? Now suppose for a moment that I'm losing my grip, or, as you say in those newspapers of yours, I'm degenerating. Why should I resist it if there's no sense in anything anyway? All right, I'll put more money in the bank, I'll swindle another heathen or two, swindle those unbelievers neatly, with a laugh even, but what for? I know my speech is not clear, it's clumsy, but you just sit there and listen since you're here."

"I *am* listening."

"That's better. You are a doctor, you ought to understand that there are diseases that are neither in the belly nor in the breast, but much more vicious ones. Try and make this out."

He filled his glass, drank, wiped his lips, and continued in a steady voice:

"My life has been lived in vileness, for I was begotten in prurience, fornication and filth. I have nothing to hold on to, I've lost my way. I am going blind. My wife is a fool, she has flesh and fat, but you can't see the person behind it. Pelageya now, I'm sorry for her, the wench will come to no good."

"Don't, Father, please," she entreated.

"All right, I won't."

Markelov sat thinking and drinking his cognac. Volodya did not break the silence. The glaring light of the shadeless lamp hurt his eyes.

"Have some pie," Pelageya spoke from the far end of the room.

Volodya did.

"Her, yes, I'm sorry for her," Markelov said. "And I spit on all the rest. I haven't much longer to go, I am well advanced in years, and the way I've lost I shall never find now. My roots belong here, in Khara, you know. My graveyard's here, we've a family tomb, we were all made of stubborn clay: we wanted to have *our own* resting place here, so we built the tomb of Russian brick brought from thousands of versts away. Our famous family is known and feared by everyone here, from the oldest heathen to the youngest snivelling brat. Look how much softer I've become, and still they're scared of me. They're *scared* of me, understand? Yourself now, they know but do not fear. They know you for hundreds of versts around and nobody is scared of you at all. You are Russian and I am Russian. Why is it like that then, tell me?"

He emptied another glass, shivered, and said:

"They won't even take presents from me, they're *afraid* to take my presents, they think there's a catch somewhere. They don't believe in my kindness. But maybe I've really grown kind, maybe I have, eh?"

He changed to a whisper, bitter and resentful.

"The shamans wanted to kill you. I know, I've heard about it. You fool, what are you risking your life for? I do it for gold, that's no secret, but you? What royal salary are you getting? What reward will you get for doing hard labour here? What? Take me — I can go to California or to Rome any day I please, today or tomorrow, it's all in my power. And you? You haven't even a woman, you poor fool, and you don't drink. How long have you been here now? A year. I saw something with my own eyes the other day: you were coming up the road and a dog attacked you, and then that woman, Sait-Belek's wife, came at the dog with a stake. But me? Who'll chase a dog off me? Tell me, help me, speak, when do a man's brains get twisted? Answer me, you, comrade,

I'm old but I'm asking you to tell me what does a man live for in this world?"

"To do his job," Volodya replied glumly and all but inaudibly.

"What d'you say?"

"To do his job."

"And what's the job for? Didn't I do my job? Did I sit twiddling my thumbs? What does a pup like you know about the versts we covered tramping the taiga and the perilous swamps hereabouts, the sort of nights we had, the wolves that flew at our throats, the local natives blazing away at my father with buckshot, as though he were a bear. Fighting — isn't that doing a job?"

"No, it isn't. You were just making money, not doing a job."

"From greed, you mean?"

"Yes."

"And there's no saving me from the way my brain got twisted?"

"Are you asking me as a doctor?"

"Curse you and your medicine, it makes me laugh to hear about it. I'm asking you as a Russian."

"You and I are Russians, but we're different Russians," Volodya said, looking hard at Markelov. "I'm a Soviet Russian, and you're only Russian by nationality, a former Russian, Russian by your brick tomb and not by human standards. The Russian today is entirely different from the Russian of before; no working man would shoot at today's Russian as though he were a bear. That's why you're afraid and I'm not."

Apparently Markelov was not listening.

"All right. You have to bow when the incense-burner swings your way, I know all that," he said unpleasantly. "You tell me this: maybe I should donate all I have to the hospital? Maybe that will make me as good as you, mister comrade?"

"What you have is not yours. Donating stolen goods is stupid."

Markelov did not seem surprised, he only came up closer to Volodya and asked:

"And isn't forgiving shaman Ogu stupid? He wanted to kill you and you're feeding him. You ought to have strung him up on a bough right there and singed the bastard's heels over the fire, then they'd know."

"Ogu isn't to blame," Volodya said coldly. "You are."

"Me again? Hear that, Pelageya. I'm to blame for this, too. The doctor's sharp, now isn't he a sharp one! How am I to blame, my dearest friend?"

"You know that as well as I do. For hundreds of years..."

"All right, enough of that drivel," Markelov cut him short. "I did my best for you, I wrote to whoever I had to write, and they'll put your shaman behind good strong bars."

"I won't let them."

"You won't?"

"I certainly won't."

"The Christian spirit?"

"Christianity has nothing to do with it."

"The devil take you then. I'll ask this last question. What job is this job you say a man must live for?"

"Any useful job for the good of the people," Volodya replied sullenly and even angrily. "Any."

"People — they're just cow dung."

"In that case, I don't want to waste my time on you," Volodya said, rising. "I think that only a thoroughly bad person could say that."

"But I am a thoroughly bad person," Markelov replied with a sneer.

"Come and enlighten me in my ignorance sometime," he called out after Volodya.

"No, I shan't," Volodya replied. "It's a strain to be with you and it's useless."

They stood looking at each other for a moment, Markelov in perplexity, Volodya calm and sad.

The clerk was waiting for Volodya on the porch, shivering in the cold drizzle.

"Will it be soon?" he whispered.

"What will?" Volodya asked.

"We've come to the end of our tether, you know. His temper knows no restraint, he's not human any more. It's time for him to pass on, I can't even begin to describe it all to you, doctor..."

Volodya switched on his flashlight and started back for the hospital.

Vasya, lying between clean sheets, himself clean and relaxed, was happily reading some sentimental verses.

"Osh's baby came while you were out," he said. "Only a little while ago. A splendid little chap."

Volodya washed, put on his smock and went to see Osh. She was still dozing, the delivery room was being tidied up, and, in the passing, old Abatai was playing draughts with one of the hunters, squatting in front of the open door of the stove with its brightly burning logs. From ward 4 came the groans of Khem, a ten-year-old boy, who had been operated on that morning. Volodya stayed with him for a few minutes, took his pulse and felt his leg to see if it was warm. It was warm, Khem would not be a cripple. Coming out of the room Volodya saw Tush — the slim, graceful girl with the shining eyes was hurrying towards him.

"Well, what about Moscow? Are you going, Tush?"

"No!" she answered with a joyful lilt, gazing into his face.

"Why not?"

"I'm still very ignorant," she said. "They'll laugh at me there. I'll go later. I'll go when you say: go, Tush, it's time to go. Yes, no?"

He could not look into her eyes because they shone so, and the light in them was so infinitely tender and warm.

### BLACK DEATH

The foundation of the second hospital building was laid that spring. On the day of the ceremony one more doctor arrived from home — a middle-aged, stolid, slow-moving woman called Sofia Ivanovna Soldatenkova. The first thing she did was demand, and in no uncertain terms, that Ogu be forbidden the premises of the hospital.

"It seems very strange that a former priest, or shaman, as they are called here, should be chopping wood for the kitchen stove," she said indignantly. "I saw him doing it myself! It's amazing, really. He chops wood for the wards, too. It's very, very strange."

"But he does no black magic in the hospital," Volodya argued, frowning. "And that man is no longer a shaman. He has neither tambourine nor staff."

"It's very strange. Once a priest always a priest, staff or no staff. And besides, I happen to know that he made a terroristic act against your person."

"A what?"

"A real terroristic act. You displayed spinelessness and misguided kindness when you refused to hand the scoundrel over to the authorities. All sallies of our class enemies should be dealt with ruthlessly, don't you understand?"

"He's not a class enemy, he's a deluded, unfortunate

man," Volodya said harshly. "And it's not for you to teach me what to do, you've only just come and I've been..."

"Oh, so that's your reaction to criticism?" she sneered. "Oh well, I did expect something of the sort: complacency, resting on your laurels, mutual admiration."

It was amazing what a stock of ready phrases that woman had for every occasion. Living in this world presented no problem to her.

"To sum up. Ogu has been working here and is going to go on working here," Volodya said, rising to go. "If it doesn't agree with you, write to Tod-Jin, he knows the whole story. And let us say no more about it. Who else strikes you as an alien class element here?"

"I'll have to make a closer study," she said with a sigh. "Needless to say, there have been certain achievements here as well, there are also people who are loyal to us. It's not all bad."

Sofia Ivanovna did a lot of dull, painstaking work. To her mind the case notes were too brief, and the records generally were handled in a most unsatisfactory manner. She made "radical" changes. Morning, noon and night, she sat writing long, detailed reports, her fingers and even her face were always ink-stained, her forehead wrinkled with anxiety.

"Yes, so much still wants straightening out, so very, very much," she would say with a care-laden sigh. "It is really strange that matters should have been brought into this state of neglect, very strange indeed. So far I've only been looking into things, but when the time comes we'll have a talk, a frank straight-from-the-shoulder talk, with no niceties."

Late one dark night, Pelageya Markelova came to see Volodya. Her eyes were swollen with weeping, she was too overwrought to speak.

"Doctor, let me work here," she forced out at last. "I'm good at any work, you won't regret it."

"How will your father take it?"

"He doesn't have to take it," she said spitefully. "Is he anyone to consider now? He is very far gone, he drinks from morning till night, reads without any sense, and swears."

"He won't let you work, you know."

"I'd live here, in the hospital, in a little corner, anywhere you let me. And then this would be my life. Please, doctor, or else I'll hang myself, honestly I will, and the sin will be on all of you. Please!"

She sank to her knees.

"Stop it!" Volodya shouted at her. "Stop it, you hear? Get up at once."

Sofia Ivanovna came into the room with a paper for Volodya to sign, and asked him the meaning of the strange scene. He told her.

"Ah, you mean Markelov, the local Rockefeller," she said, wrinkling her forehead in anxious thought. "I've heard about him of course, of course."

Volodya turned to Pelageya.

"You will start work tomorrow morning. I'm warning you though, we are very busy, the work here is hard, and we want no shirkers."

With Pelageya gone, and having got rid of Sofia Ivanovna with her duly signed paper, Volodya took a deep breath, walked the length of the room once or twice, stopped to look at the black sky behind the curtainless window, and then switched on his radio. The batteries were running out, he had ordered a new supply a whole month ago but they were slow in coming. There was chaos on the air, he tried but could not get Moscow; twirling the knobs, he happened on some Slav broadcast or other, and suddenly stood stock-still, stunned by what he heard. Hitler had attacked the Soviet Union. This was war, a struggle unequalled in the history of mankind.

Vasya came into the room, rolling up his sleeves and humming a tune. Volodya told him to shut up. Sofia Ivanovna, hearing their voices, came running in, pale and excited. Tush, Danzy and old Abatai stood in the doorway. Understanding came gradually to Volodya. On June 22, at 3.30 a.m., the nazis had launched an attack along the whole length of the huge front stretching from the Black to the Baltic Sea. Field Marshal von Bock, Guderian, Strauss and Both were advancing on the frontier towns, but what towns it was impossible to make out. And then came the strains of a tango and after that nothing but a chaotic jumble of sound.

"Impossible!" Vasya exclaimed. "It's a provocation! Rubbish!"

At daybreak Volodya sent a telegram to Tod-Jin asking to appoint Vasya head physician in his place. The answer came within a couple of hours, and Volodya was now free to go to the Soviet Union, especially since Bogoslovsky too had already flown to Moscow.

Tush came in to tell Volodya sadly that a caravan would

be ready to leave Khara the next day. She offered to help him pack.

"I've nothing to pack. I'll just throw a few things into my rucksack, and that'll be that. Go, Tush, you've enough to do as it is."

Tush left.

Volodya tried to tune in to some news broadcast, but all he heard was the yelping speech of one of Hitler's satellites, which he could not understand. He switched off. "Never mind, suspense won't kill me. In a month at most I'll be at the battle front. I've got to keep a hold on myself, that's all."

And only then he noticed Danzy, who had been standing in the doorway for some time. The man's face was white, his chin trembled and there was a catch in his voice when he tried to speak.

"Speak up, I can't make out a word," Volodya said with angry impatience.

"Black flag over *yurta*," Danzy croaked. "Soon marmot sickness come to Khara. Black death come to Khara. Black death come to Djavan-Ilir already. Go, comrade doctor, go, I not let old man in here, he bring terrible news, he himself must die soon. It will be like many years ago, everyone in Khara die, small babies too, everyone who not run away soon enough, all die."

Marmot sickness or Black Death meant plague. The last and very severe outbreak had been in 1916. Volodya had heard many a story from the older inhabitants about the governor of the province running away, about the people losing their minds from fright, and about the dead in the streets whom no one would touch.

Volodya found a tired, bald-headed old man, with sunken cheeks and toothless mouth, squatting in front of the porch steps, telling Abatai, Ogu, Sofia Ivanovna and Vasya about the marmot sickness. Tush was there, too, interpreting.

That spring, rumour had reached the marmot hunters that buyers at the trading posts were paying five or six times more for a marmot skin than before. The rumour had been brought across the frontier by hunters from Pes-Va, the residence of the governor of the Land of the Sun. Marmot skins, they said, were treated and dyed so expertly now that furriers were making money hand over fist on them. Naturally, the local hunters wanted to make money too. And so they began to catch all the marmots they could, even those who made no sound, though everyone knows that a silent marmot is sick and is not to be touched. A healthy marmot always mutters, "Don't be scared, don't be scared." Everyone knows that too.

The old man drank some water out of a white enamel mug, and lit his pipe.

"Let him tell us what he himself has seen," Volodya said.

But the old man refused to be rushed. It was bad enough killing the sick marmots, but the hunters also ate their meat. The first to fall ill was the younger of the Mung-Wo brothers. Both the older and the younger were very good at setting snares over marmot burrows, and were considered fine marksmen. The younger Mung-Wo fell ill in the steppe and died there. The older buried his body.

"It's bubonic plague," Sofia Ivanovna decided.

"He buried his brother and continued with the hunt, luck was with him. But a few days later people saw him going to his *yurta*, swaying like a drunk. If a man sways like that he is sure to have the marmot sickness, and very soon he must lose his age."

"The elder brother had the pneumonic form," Sofia Ivanovna explained. "In situations such as this, a course of explanatory lectures for the socially active members of the population must be arranged at once."

"Phrases, phrases," Vasya muttered irritably.

The old man went on to say that the elder Mung-Wo did not reach his *yurta*, he only managed to call out that a black rag was to be hoisted on a pole above it. In the steppe people know that a black flag flying over a *yurta* means death. Everyone has to keep away.

"Ask the citizen: has he been in direct contact with the victims?" Sofia Ivanovna ordered Tush.

Tush did not understand the question.

"Did he just see the black flag or has he been inside the *yurta*?" Vasya made it clearer for Tush.

The old man grinned. No, he was too wise to go anywhere near the marmot sickness. That time, those many years ago, all his relatives had died of it, so he well knew what sort of sickness it was.

The following morning, he went on to say, the elder Mung-Wo began to spit blood. And within a few days all the *yurtas* were flying black flags — the marmot sickness had struck Djavan-Ilir. The old man had then harnessed a horse and come here, to the great Soviet shaman. Many fine stories were told about his cures. If the Russian shaman was really as great as people said of him, let him help. But if he was not, he should say so at once and he would not be troubled again.

"It was fun while it lasted, wasn't it," Sofia Ivanovna said nastily to Volodya, and went back to her work.

Volodya asked Tush to tell the old man that he personally could do little to help at the moment, but that he would try to get many doctors to come, a whole army of doctors, who would help, of course. Telling Tush and Vasya to put the old man in quarantine, he went to see Zdaba, the governor of the Khara province.

The governor received Volodya coldly. The boundary line, on the other side of which ruled the governor of the Land of the Sun, was only a stone's throw away. If Hitler devoured Russia, the Land of the Sun would occupy Khara, and then the governor would be sure to hold any kindness Zdaba might show the Soviet doctor against him. Therefore, he did not even offer Volodya a chair. But the moment he learnt about the plague epidemic his manner underwent a quick change. He shouted for tea to be served at once, and ordered his secretary to put an urgent call through to the Public Health Department. No one answered, and Volodya suggested that Zdaba should ring up Tod-Jin at his home.

Fortunately, most fortunately, Tod-Jin himself answered and Volodya told him about the outbreak in Djavan-Ilir. There were outside noises on the line. Tod-Jin said nothing.

"Ask the Epidemics Prevention Department in Moscow to help," Volodya said. "They will help."

"There's a war on," Tod-Jin said.

"They will help anyway. They are sure to," Volodya urged. "I guarantee they will, Comrade Tod-Jin. Those people have sense, they'll understand what a disaster it is for your republic, they are sure to help."

"Very well," Tod-Jin's tone was thoughtful. He then said he wanted to speak to the governor.

A quarter of an hour later, the garrison commander, a slight, grey-haired lieutenant, received orders to put a cordon round the Djavan-Ilir district and let no one in or out. He heard the governor out in silence, responding only with a click of his heels and a salute to the long peak of his white silver-braided cap. Meanwhile, in the governor's backyard, camels, horses and carts were being feverishly loaded with the governor's household belongings, while the ladies of the house — the governor's wife, daughters and daughters-in-law, wept in dread of the mountains and at the thought of abandoning their "palace", which consisted of six rooms, not counting the two winter *yurtas* in the yard.

A telegram arrived for Volodya in the middle of the night, in which Tod-Jin told him that Moscow had helped and aeroplanes bringing drugs, equipment and doctors were already on the way. The expedition was headed by Professor Barinov. Tod-Jin himself was flying to Khara the next day with the Secretary of the Central Committee of the Workers' Party. Barinov's instructions and suggestions, radioed from the plane, followed. Volodya read and re-read the urgent message.

In the next room he heard Sofia Ivanovna teaching Tush how to put on the protective clothing against plague.

"Yes, I know you're bored," Sofia Ivanovna was saying in her flat voice. "Personal prophylaxis, however, is of great importance in our work. There is no glory in contracting the plague and dying through sheer slovenliness. First, you put on the overall, like this, see? The legs must be secured very tightly at the bottom with these strings..."

"Against fleas?" Tush asked in a small voice.

"The fleas of rodents, after the death of their masters, abandon their bodies and the nests they have made in them." Sofia Ivanovna had it all pat, it seemed. "The so-called free fleas readily move to humans. Now look, Comrade Tush, the hood has to be tucked under the collar of the overalls. And, last but not least, we come to the respirator. The space on both sides of the nose has to be filled with absorbent cotton, small clots of cotton."

Volodya came out into the passage and knocked softly on Sofia Ivanovna's door. Sofia Ivanovna and Tush were standing in the middle of the room in full plague-fighting dress.

"What's going on here?" Volodya asked.

"I'm an epidemiologist, you know," Sofia Ivanovna said. "And so I thought it would be a good idea if Tush and I went out there, made an autopsy and studied the situation on the spot. We should render medical assistance where we could. We have the suits, there's a spare microscope, and we have plenty of lysol, carbolic acid and sublimate. You are the head physician, of course, but I should imagine that..."

"I approve, go ahead," Volodya said.

"I expect we'll need credentials and a formal approval from you?"

"No, Sofia Ivanovna, you won't. There'll be nobody there to present them to."

"How preposterous!" she shrugged disdainfully. "It's as bad as the Dark Ages! I was planning to hold a conference with those of the local population who are active in health protection work, and I had a series of undertakings in mind..."

Vasya poked his sleepy head into the room and asked:

"Maybe I should come with you?"

"What on earth for?" Sofia Ivanovna demanded. "We'll manage the interment of the dissected body between us. And besides we only have two suits. We have no right to leave the hospital short-staffed. It is inexpedient generally. One must always do what is expedient, and never act rashly. I shall not come back, of course, until the whole thing is over. You will probably have to look for us in the Mung-Wo district."

When they were ready to go, Sofia Ivanovna gave Volodya an envelope for safe-keeping.

"If something should happen to me, I want you to send this letter to my daughter," she said. "She is all I have. Her father left us, he has a new family now. But that's all right. Marriage must be based on mutual love. If it's not there, it's no marriage. Good-bye, Vladimir Afanasyevich."

They left — the small, slim, black-haired Tush, and the stolid, hefty Sofia Ivanovna. They rode at the head of a string of pack horses loaded with tents, sprayers, shovels, cases of drugs and provisions in hermetically sealed tins.

Sofia Ivanovna's parting words to Volodya were:

"Do look after the paper work, as you like to call it. I have only just managed to put some method into it. And now, with having to leave so urgently..."

The little caravan disappeared from view.

"Some woman, eh?" Volodya said.

"I'd never have expected it of her," Vasya said with feeling.

### THE CAUSE YOU SERVE

Late that afternoon the population of Khara saw their first aeroplane, which was very much like the one Volodya's father had once come home in. There was no airfield in Khara and the pilot circled for a long time deciding where to land; it seemed to Volodya there was an alarmed and interrogative note in the roar of the motor, and the plane almost touched ground several times only to soar up again.

At last, the plane landed.

Three men alighted — a very young, snub-nosed pilot with a bleached forelock, Tod-Jin, and the Secretary of the Central Committee of the Workers' Party — a big man of fifty or so, with closely cropped hair. He did not shake the governor's hand, instead he took him aside and said something to him with fury in his muted voice. The governor squeaked back meekly and bowed.

"The Secretary of the Central Committee will take over personally," Tod-Jin said to Volodya in formal tones. "He is a splendid comrade. Our enemies kept him in a wooden cage, in chains, for many years. Yes. The people know him well, the working people believe in him, and these others fear him. Let them."

The Secretary mounted a horse and rode away with the garrison commander to inspect the cordons. All that day and night the population of Khara worked hard, making a landing field level enough to receive the heavy transport planes coming from Saratov to fight the Black Death.

Pasha, the young pilot with the bleached forelock, eating a breakfast of roast chicken and cold milk at daybreak the following day, asked Volodya to tell him more about the Black Death. "Is it as catching as all that, this plague business? If you ask me, it's not as black as it's painted. It's just a scare, I reckon." Drumstick in hand, he added:

"I just love gnawing bones, I wonder why. Is it a throwback or something, comrade doctor? Has science anything to say about that?"

Volodya asked him for war news.

"They're pressing forward, so far," he said. "Pressing hard too. We've lost certain regions, temporarily, of course. But, do you know, I believe it's like your plague here, no wonder it's called the brown plague. Until we get properly mobilised it will go on taking its toll of us, but once we come out in full force, we'll have it where we want it. The main thing is not to get rattled. After all, the plague can't exterminate mankind. Nor can fascism put an end to Soviet power."

A little later, Tod-Jin came up to them and asked Volodya if it was all right to have a guard of honour to meet the Moscow doctors, was it done, and what did the diplomatic textbooks recommend. Volodya did not know. The pilot did not know either, but in his opinion it would do "no harm". The Secretary of the Central Committee thought the matter over and decided that they would have both a guard of honour and a band playing the *Internationale*.

At 6 a.m. as arranged Volodya rode to the large white stone at the fork in the road where a quarantine post was stationed. The soldiers of the republican army were letting no one through from the Djavan-Ilir district.

Tush was on the other side of the barrier, waiting. Her small horse stood tossing its long mane to drive away the gadflies. The wind was behind Volodya and he did not have to raise his voice at all, but poor Tush had to shout so hard her face turned red with the strain.

"We need lysol," she shouted. "Plenty of lysol. The form is pneumonic. Many dead, many sick, we need food, one or two doctors won't be enough, it's a huge epidemic. We need vaccine, plenty of vaccine."

The wind tousled Tush's black hair, and the soldiers gazed at the brave young woman with admiration and awe.

"Good for you, Tush," Volodya called out. "We'll all be coming to your aid soon. The doctors are already on their way from Russia, plenty of doctors! They're flying, they're coming in planes. Hold out a little longer, Tush, a few hours longer!"

"We will!" she shouted back.

And, with a wave of her whip, she turned and galloped away towards the *yurtas* with the sinister black rags dangling from poles above them.

In the meantime, the first transport plane landed in Khara. The body and wings were marked with red crosses and Soviet identification markings. Twenty-four soldiers of the garrison in white dress tunics and shoulder-straps with silver insignia presented arms. The band leader waved his baton and the band struck up the *Internationale*. Volodya felt a lump in his throat — it must be overwork and sleepless nights, he thought.

To the strains of the *Internationale* the door in the plane was flung open and a metal ladder let down. Tod-Jin and the Secretary of the Central Committee stood at attention, saluting.

> *We hail the mighty tempest raging,*
> *The flash of lightning thru' the gloom —*
> *For us, the dawn of life presaging;*
> *For them, the knell of mortal doom...*

The Russian doctors — ordinary men and women in raincoats or travel-creased suits — lined up beside the plane with their bags, valises and briefcases, and sang. They did not realise that the guard of honour was there to meet *them*. They were truly astonished when the grey-haired garrison commander, marching with a smart goose step, led his soldiers past them. Professor Barinov answered the lieutenant's report courteously with: "Thank you, I'm very glad."

The soldiers marched away. An elderly doctor, Shumilov, with a paunch under his knitted waistcoat, turned to Volodya and asked:

"Tell me, is this the hotbed of infection then?"

"I believe I'm a bit air-sick, you know," another doctor said.

"I'm dying for some hot soup," one of the women, a very young one, said longingly to Vasya. "The last four days in Moscow were such a rush, I never had time for a square meal, and on the plane it was sandwiches mostly. Are they going to feed us soon, d'you know?"

They were. Madam cook had done her best, working all night with old Abatai and shaman Ogu helping her. The tables were laid in the open, near the landing strip. Professor Barinov enjoyed his hot borsch while Volodya talked. And Volodya, looking at Barinov's sharp profile, his old-fashioned goatee, the broken ear-piece of his spectacles and the wrinkles round the eyes was thinking that this slight, very little old man before him had fought in all the plague epidemics of the 20th century. His slim hand had been shaken by Gamaleya in Odessa, by Zabolotny in India and Mongolia; he had known Deminsky, he had treated the plague victims in Manchuria, and had narrowly escaped death during the Astrakhan epidemic. He had worked in the plague laboratory near Kronstadt, he had known Dr. Vyzhnikevich, he had seen him and Dr. Schreiber die. Yet, he had not given up the fight. At seventy he was leading the battle again.

"Yes," Barinov nodded, listening to Volodya. "Yes, I see."

While the doctors, nurses and orderlies were having dinner, one more plane bringing medicines and equipment landed. The population of Khara had turned out in thousands. They stood in a close ring around the landing field talking in whispers with all due respect for their amazing guests, but since they were all whispering together it sounded like the wind sweeping over the crowd in gusts. They were mostly whispering about Volodya. It was all his doing, he was so mighty that at his merest wish all these huge machines came flying to Khara. Shaman Ogu pushed his way through the crowd and whispered in every ear:

"He can do anything, the great Soviet doctor Volodya. That's why I agreed to come and help him. He begged me so long and so hard, I had to agree. Soon I'll learn all the tricks from him, believe me."

The rescue party started out for Djavan-Ilir, the trouble spot, at once. Professor Barinov, Tod-Jin and Volodya rode ahead, followed by a silent procession of doctors, interns, nurses, orderlies, and the disinfection men with their bulky equipment — sprayers, bottles and containers. The sight made Volodya think of an invincible army, well-trained and well-armed, advancing on the enemy, and he felt proud that he, too, was a soldier of that army.

When, at a distance of some three hundred metres they sighted the first *yurtas* flying the black rags — sinister symbols against the roseate evening sky, Barinov gave the command "Dress". And that, too, made Volodya think that they were an army, and the order was "Attack".

They dismounted and began to put on their rubber boots and overalls, helping one another to tie the strings on the back in silence, without any joking. Again, as many times that day, this discipline and calmness made Volodya think of an army.

"Do you know, I never thought I could still ride a horse," Barinov gave a proud little chuckle. "And my coccyx doesn't hurt the way it used to in my young days."

"But I did have too much borsch," he grumbled, leading his horse by the bridle. "The times I promised myself to stay off all rich food!"

The *yurtas* with the fluttering black rags came nearer and nearer; a long-unmilked cow ran beside Volodya, lowing hoarsely, plaintively.

"Go away, cow, we can't milk you anyway," Barinov said. His voice, coming through the respirator, sounded hollow.

Sofia Ivanovna and Tush were waiting for them outside the end *yurta*, a large one. They were so utterly worn out, they could hardly stand. Barinov heard what Sofia Ivanovna had to report, and then ordered her and Tush to go and get some sleep, and again Volodya was struck by this civilian professor's ability to issue commands like a regular army general. Dr. Loboda's "quartermaster corps" was already pitching camp for the medical personnel. They put up tents to live in, laboratories and stores. It was a good location with a lake and the beautiful Kik-Djub crags nearby. The camp was habitable and even the beds were made, but none of the doctors, nurses or orderlies slept that night. Using their flashlights, they examined the dark, dead interiors of the *yurtas*, carried out the dead, cleaned out and disinfected the premises, gave food and drink to the sick, sounded their lungs and hearts, took their pulses, and stood ready for further instructions from Barinov and his second-in-command Shumilov. The whiteclad figures with their weirdly goggled faces moved clumsily but softly in the tall rubber boots they wore. The moans and mutterings of the sick mingled with the soft, muffled voices of the doctors, with the hissing of the sprayer and the dreary patter of rain that had been falling since midnight.

The suits were hot, sticky sweat poured down their faces, backs and arms, their gloved hands could hardly manage a syringe, and even a stethoscope was awkward to use. The blood pounded in Volodya's ears; by morning he was quite dizzy but with Barinov still holding out how could he admit his faintness?

All that endless night long they rode from one camp to the next, isolating the sick from the healthy, taking temperatures, injecting vaccine, turning some *yurtas* into isolation wards, others into kitchens, and still others into quarters for the healthy population. Tod-Jin told these panic-stricken people what they had to do in his stern voice which rang with unquestionable authority, and no one attempted to contradict him.

At the fourth camp they examined that night, Volodya happened to be the first to go into a *yurta* where all lay dead. Bending low, he flashed his light and saw arms twisted from convulsions, the whites of dead eyes, and young, white teeth bared in a grimace of death. And suddenly, in that dead silence, he fancied he heard a baby's very weak cry.

"Quiet," he hissed at the orderlies who were swabbing the floor.

He went towards the sound and stopped: a dead mother was clutching to her breast a child that was still alive. It was struggling and crying weakly in the comfortless grip of the cold dead arms. Volodya, with Tod-Jin helping him, released the baby and handed it to the orderly, telling him to take it to the *yurta* that was fitted up as an isolation ward.

Dawn broke over a damp, unbearably close day. A curtain of rain hung over the steppe. Barinov was sitting under a tarpaulin shed, working on the map of the stricken area. The radio operator was trying to get a call through to Dr. Loboda at Kik-Djub for him. Barinov's respirator hung round his neck, he had taken off his goggles and put them in his pocket and had pushed back the hood of his suit.

"Tired?" he asked Volodya.

"Not a bit," Volodya replied with a swagger.

Tod-Jin joined them.

"So much misfortune," he said. "So much. How put an end to it, comrade professor, once and for all?"

Barinov inhaled deeply, stubbed out his cigarette, and answered reflectively:

"As a doctor I must tell you, dear comrade, that only by reorganising the state system can these terrible disasters be stamped out. In the Soviet Union, plague, smallpox, and many other epidemic diseases are no more. And yet, not so very long ago, in my day, smallpox epidemics carried away forty thousand people a year in Russia, and made cripples of another two hundred thousand — deaf, blind, and generally disabled."

"I'm Stritsyuk! I'm Stritsyuk!" the radio operator yelled. "Comrade Loboda, let us have twenty thermometers, some enamel pails and a gaff, and send us, that, what d'you call it..."

He stared at the paper in front of him moving his lips, then turned to Volodya and said:

"Can't say it, comrade doctor."

"Phonendoscope," Volodya told him, and repeated into the speaking tube, "Phonendoscope!"

They had some cocoa out of thermos flasks and got into the saddles.

"Baby outfit, one set!" the radio operator went on yelling. "Oh no, heavens above, baby I said, baby! We found a baby. The mother was dead, but we got the baby!"

"Stritsyuk, talk business," Barinov told him, and gathered up the reins.

Suddenly they heard machine-gun fire in the distance.

"What's that?" Volodya asked.

Tod-Jin stood up on his stirrups and listened hard. A few more rounds were fired.

"The state boundary runs very near to where we are," Tod-Jin said. "It's the axis — Berlin-Rome-Tokyo. It's fascism. Come on!"

He whipped his horse, and bent low over the pommel.

Before he knew it, the wind was whistling past Volodya's ears and the horses were going at full gallop, as though they were plunging headlong down a steep incline. They raced at this speed for about fifteen minutes, and Volodya kept glancing back at the elderly professor. They stopped on a rise and saw below them the republic's frontier guards in their short capes, they saw also a wall of yellow flame and heard the roar of planes close overhead. The planes had two-coloured rings on the wings and short fuselages; they were attack planes.

"I don't understand, is it a fire?" Barinov said, bewildered by what he saw.

Clenching his fists and holding his breath, Volodya stared down: there, on the other side of the state boundary, beyond the republic's frontier zone, the Emperor's troops were fighting the plague epidemic. Apparently, they had set fire to the village with flame-throwers, and now squads of machine gunners were moving down all those attempting to escape the flames. Volodya could see plenty of machine guns and men, and also the flame-throwers mounted on the side cars of several motorcycles. Higher up on the hill there were some field guns with their muzzles aimed straight at the burning village.

"Impossible! Or is it..." Barinov did not finish.

Several tiny human figures emerged from the flames and ran forward, their arms raised, they had escaped, they were safe.

There was a short burst of machine-gun fire. The small toy-like soldiers in their khaki uniforms and flat sidecaps fired only in short bursts. It was easy enough to kill someone crazed with fear.

Still, one man went on running. He darted to the left, ran on straight, swerved left again. He was making for the boundary line. He knew that once there he could be arrested and put in quarantine, but not killed. He would not be killed there!

But he was.

The machine gun spat out, the man made one more dash, and fell.

A motorcycle with a flame-thrower started with a roar, shattering the dead silence that had fallen for a moment. A sharp, yellow tongue of fire struck at those tiny, prostrate, motionless figures that had already been killed once. Volodya turned away. His teeth were chattering, his eyes misted with tears. The village continued to burn under the drizzling rain, the flames roared and moaned, and thick black columns of smoke hung sagging over the ground, as though ashamed to rise.

"Listen," Barinov turned abruptly to Tod-Jin. "Let them tell the commander of their health service that I wish to speak to him. I am Professor Barinov, an honorary member of their Academy of Sciences, I have attended the same international conferences as their scientists have."

Tod-Jin called an officer of the frontier guard, who then approached the closed barrier and spoke to a captain of the imperial army on the other side. The captain saluted. The republican officer did likewise. The soldiers of the imperial army were wrestling beside their machine guns to get the stiffness out of their legs. Now and then they glanced at the burning village. The planes took off.

A frog-green motorcycle drew up at the barrier with a screech of brakes. A small, elegant medical officer in khaki, wearing thick-lensed glasses, a cap with a tall crown and patent-leather leggings, got out of the side car. Barinov, his mouth a hard line, spurred his horse with his heels. Tod-Jin and Volodya rode after him. The surgeon of the imperial army was finishing a cigarette when they rode up to him. On hearing Barinov's name and all his titles and honours, he saluted, curving the palm of his hand outwards. In this most deferential manner he said that he had the privilege and honour of studying Professor Barinov's works both in Berlin and at home, at the Institute of Experimental Epidemiology. The activities of the special plague-fighting squad just witnessed by the professor were, indeed, a distressing spectacle, but what was to be done if the mortality rate in pneumonic plague was recorded as high as 100 per cent? The most rational and humane method, of course, was to burn out the infected areas, especially since the disease had as yet spread only to an inferior, degenerating and, on the whole, useless national minority. However, this matter, like all orders issued by the high command of the epidemic control centre, was not open for discussion.

The elegant doctor with the line of moustache over his thin upper lip clicked his heels.

"Tell your academy that I no longer wish to be considered one of its honorary members," Barinov said in English, very loudly. "And bear this in mind for your personal good. If I live to see the day when you are tried for this, I shall insist on being the prosecutor. And I shall be speaking in the name of all the doctors who died fighting the plague. I have that right. Understand?"

"I understand," replied the man, turning sallow, but still holding his hand in salute. "But I doubt whether the professor will live to see this hypothetical trial. With such great defeats in the West, with the Führer's armies marching forward so triumphantly!"

He again snapped his heels together and got into the side car.

When they got back on the road, Barinov wiped his rain-splashed face and sighed.

"I wanted to strike him with my whip. Right across the face," he said regretfully. "Never mind, I'll last till that trial."

"You will," Volodya said confidently.

They inspected six more camps that day. In the evening Barinov called a meeting; a bell was rung to bring everyone together. These five-minute meetings, which they now had every day, seemed to Volodya like a council of war or a headquarters conference before a decisive battle.

Reconnaissance data on the enemy's strength were briefly set out, losses were reported, and account was taken of ammunition and weapons available — vaccine, serum, provisions, medical equipment and transport facilities. A map was spread on the table and the General, as Barinov had been nicknamed by his staff, pored over it; the blacked-out plague squares on the map showed where the enemy was. The radio operator, working in the General's tent where the field telephone was installed, took down any messages received and placed them on the table before Barinov. Every day Tod-Jin contacted Khara by direct line and reported on the situation. So far it had always been: "All is well. No cases outside the stricken area."

The Russian doctors and nurses struggled day and night against the spread of the infection, against this loathsome Black Death or "marmot sickness" that threatened to devour the whole of the small republic, all its sheep herders and farmers, its hunters and workers, its old people, youngsters and babies, its very future.

The doctors only saw one another at their daily five-minute meetings. Barinov made it a strict rule that they should sleep a certain number of hours a day, and personally saw to it that his working schedule was adhered to. Sleeping their prescribed hours and eating properly was law; a run-down doctor was liable to make a fatal mistake and contact the disease through "sheer absentmindedness", as Barinov put it.

Pasha, the young pilot with the bleached forelock, fully agreed with him.

"He's absolutely right," he said. "It's just as strict with us in the air force. If you lose two or three hours' sleep, you're asking for trouble. Either you'll fall asleep at the controls or else your senses will get so blunted that you'll stop caring."

Pasha made patrol flights over the stricken area to see if there were any new black rags hoisted on poles above the *yurtas*, to see if the hearths were smoking, to watch for any SOS rockets the doctors might send up, and to make sure that all was well generally. When he came low enough he would have a greeting to the people fighting the marmot sickness. He would return to the camp to refuel, have a shower, eat and take off again. The doctors and nurses worked in shifts round the clock, examining the entire population, taking temperatures, injecting the victims with serum, and vaccinating those who were well. The orderlies buried the dead. A camp kitchen brought hot food to the more remote areas, and it was enjoyed alike by the convalescents, the medical personnel, and those kept in quarantine.

Barinov often flew out with Pasha, when called by radio to help in especially difficult cases.

At one of their five-minute meetings, Barinov made a short speech.

"I want to congratulate you, comrades," he said. "It is obvious now that the epidemic has been localised. It is on the decrease, and we shall be through here in a few days."

All the doctors who were in camp enjoyed their first sound sleep that night and not simply because they were obeying orders. The following morning Volodya was handed a radiogram from Khara. It was a hysterical message from Vasya insisting that he should be called in at once to join them in "the real job".

"Every man must do what he is doing, that's his duty," said Sofia Ivanovna. "And what he is not doing, others are."

Volodya chuckled. Sofia Ivanovna no longer irritated him, he knew her worth now, her real human worth.

On Friday they began to strike tents. Volodya was just back from his rounds and as he dismounted, he suddenly felt sick; he swayed on his feet. Dr. Loboda walked up to him and said warily:

"Got a chill?"

"Maybe," Volodya replied brusquely.

Smiling faintly he went straight to the isolation ward. He had the plague, he was sure now. There was a sharp pain in his side, he swayed drunkenly as he walked, and his tongue was furry.

He was no sooner in bed than Barinov came in, wearing a protection suit but no respirator.

"Dress yourself properly," Volodya said. "Or I'll throw this stool at you."

"Don't you teach me my business," Barinov said angrily.

"You heard me — I'll throw this stool at you. I have the plague."

Barinov went out. Volodya took his temperature, it was 38.6°. Barinov reappeared with Dr. Loboda, both were wearing respirators, and there was Tush hovering behind them. It seemed strange to Volodya to hear their muffled voices while he himself wore no goggles, protecting suit or respirator.

Volodya wrote letters while a laboratory test was being made of his phlegm. He felt dizzy and his mouth was so dry that he drank glass after glass of water.

"Varya, this letter has been disinfected, so don't be afraid," he wrote. "Something stupid had happened. When you get this I shall be dead and buried. I feel rather weak now, I don't want to die, it's too stupid. I love you, Varya, I love you, I never stopped loving you. You see..."

It was Barinov again.

"In my opinion, colleague, you have membranous pneumonia," he said in a loud, cheery voice.

Volodya looked intently into Barinov's eyes behind their protecting goggles.

"You told me yourself that was the usual formula for comforting doctors who've contracted the disease," he said.

"Come on, lie down," Barinov told him.

Tush stood in the doorway. She had brought two letters for Volodya, one was from Varya, the other from Aunt Aglaya. Varya wrote that she was in the navy and again spoke about going on the stage. She also said a few words about the war and how hard it must be on Volodya with his fighting spirit to be cooped up there with "all those bronchitis, appendicities things". Aunt Aglaya, too, wrote about the war.

Volodya coughed. There was no blood in the phlegm. Late in the afternoon Pasha appeared on the outside of the closed window and pressed a note to the pane. "I've got some brandy, want some, doctor?" it said. Volodya made a "nothing doing" gesture and lay back in bed.

The Gram test again showed nothing. The illness had to be given time.

Tush remained on guard outside his door all day, Volodya heard her light step and her whispering. Sofia Ivanovna looked in and spoke to him as if he were a baby.

"And how are we feeling now? Did we like our nice lunch?"

"We want everyone to go to hell with their blasted sympathy," Volodya answered savagely.

He had just taken his temperature. It was 39.6°. And he felt sick, terribly sick.

Dr. Loboda stayed with him half the night. Volodya was delirious. Then the fat Dr. Shumilov took over. Idly, he picked up Volodya's unfinished letter to Aunt Aglaya and read: "It's such a damned pity that I've done nothing yet. If only you could see this great army of epidemiologists, you'd realise what remarkable people all of them are! Take Dr. Shumilov, for example. To look at him he's just a fat log. He tells silly jokes and starts laughing first..."

Shumilov was startled and hurt. Surely I never start laughing first, he thought.

He put the letter back on the table, took Volodya's pulse and, suddenly, noticed a distinct white triangle on his chin and under the nose.

"Tush, quick," he called. "Come and help me."

The two of them turned the delirious Volodya on his back, and Shumilov examined his stomach and chest.

"Rash! See the rash?" he cried happily. "I am a fat log, it's only too true. More than that, I'm a fool. Hurry and rouse Barinov, Tush. At once!"

With his short, thick fingers he undid his respirator, took off his goggles and pushed back the hood of his protecting suit. His plump perspiring face was beaming.

"It's scarlatina," he said to Barinov. "Good old scarlatina! A perfect textbook case for students. So we're not much good, are we. Have we forgotten everything we knew? It was Ustimenko who took the baby out of the dead mother's arms. And the baby girl has scarlet fever. Oh, my Lord, will we ever live it down! Take a look at the rash — an entire field of hyperemia. And the face — he has the scarlatina butterfly, there's no getting away from it. Well, that's that, comrade professor."

"Every man has a fool in his sleeve," Barinov said. "We ought to wake up Pasha, I think, and send him for the serum. We used up all we had on the baby."

Pasha was roused.

"It isn't the plague then, comrade professor, no?" Tush asked very softly.

"No, dear girl, it's scarlatina," Shumilov replied, his whole face radiating joy. "It's dear old scarlatina, darling scarlatina!"

Barinov was still looking at Volodya.

"I've an idea," he suddenly said, turning to Shumilov. "There's some champagne in the dining-room. Let's go and have a bottle. We'll drink it to the young generation of doctors, to chaps like Ustimenko."

Tush remained with Volodya. She listened to his ravings, then she took his large hot hand and kissed it.

In the morning, Professor Barinov's entire rescue party· left for Khara. Three heavy planes took off the same day, and, after circling over the town in farewell, headed for Moscow. The expedition left unexpectedly, in pouring rain, and Tod-Jin alone saw it off.

"Put them in the end *yurta*," Volodya was saying in delirium. "The very end one. And stop anyone from going in or out. Forbid it!"

Volodya was to leave Khara on October 2. That morning he made the rounds of the hospital, said good-bye to the patients and to Abatai, he looked for Tush but did not find her. He came upon Pelageya Markelova cleaning out the operation room.

"Well, how d'you find the work? All right?" he asked offering her his hand.

"It's all right," Pelageya said, dropping her eyes. "I like it, but then Sofia Ivanovna..."

"Sofia Ivanovna is a fine person," Volodya cut her short with a stern look. "And a fine doctor. It's not for you or me to criticise her. That's that. Good-bye."

His parting with Vasya, the newly-appointed head physician, was warm.

"We'll smash the nazis before the New Year is in," Vasya said. "They're terribly short of petrol. And besides we have to expect an explosion inside their country. I've been thinking about that. Have you?"

"Yes, I have, too," Volodya answered smiling.

He always felt like smiling when he was talking to Vasya.

He went out into the yard at about nine. The caravan included seven riders and a number of pack horses. An unexpected autumn heat wave had made it terribly hot. Danzy was holding an open umbrella over Doctor Vasya, the new head physician; he could not care less for Volodya now. Sofia Ivanovna gave

Volodya strict orders to mail her some account forms and files from Moscow. He wanted to kiss her good-bye, but she was very cross about the mess she had found in the quarterly report, and the last thing Volodya heard from her in parting was that something was "really very strange", but what precisely that something was Volodya did not pause to hear.

The patients looked out of the windows, old Abatai was tightening the girths, packs and loads on the horses, directing the show generally and pushing people around. The defrocked shaman stood frowning some distance away. Volodya asked him to come nearer.

"Why did you make me drop my hat, staff and tambourine in the water, in the Taa-Hao?" Ogu demanded in anger. "Now I can't do the proper thing to make your trip good. What can I do now, what?"

"I'll manage without," Volodya smiled. "Don't you dare start that stuff again. I'll tell Tod-Jin when I see him that Ogu is a good man now. Tod-Jin will take you on as an orderly, but Doctor Vasya will sack you at once if you start drinking vodka. Good-bye."

He got into the saddle and only then saw Tush. She was leaning against the hospital gate smiling at Volodya with quivering lips.

"I'll write to you," he said, riding up to her. "I'll write you a long letter. Doctor Vasya will read it for you. All right?"

"Not all right," Tush tossed her black hair defiantly. "When your letter comes I'll be able to read it myself. It won't be soon, yes, no?"

She gripped his stirrup with her slim hand but let go of it at once, because if a woman held a stirrup it signified that the man in the saddle was her lover. But Volodya was not her lover.

"Good-bye, all!" Volodya said.

The caravan moved off. Old Abatai trotted alongside Volodya's horse. As the caravan made its dusty way through the streets of Khara, more and more people came out to see it off. Volodya was offered gifts of sour cheese, which he was known to like, from friends and also people he only knew by sight.

"Take this cheese! Take it, please, you'll eat our cheese at the war."

"Take this bag of dried curds! It won't go bad. It'll last till the end of the war. Then you'll eat it and remember us."

"Take this reindeer cheese, take it, Doctor Volodya. Don't you remember me? You cured me a long time ago, when we were still afraid of your hospital."

Some he knew, others he could not remember. He smiled a hard, fixed smile, and quickly gulped his tears. The clouds of dust grew ever thicker, no one could see that Doctor Volodya was crying. But perhaps he was only sweating; it really was very hot and he was wearing a padded jacket.

"You saved Khara from Black Death! We shall never forget you!" people shouted.

No, it was not he who had saved Khara. The plague could not be conquered single-handed. And these were not sentimental tears that welled up in Volodya's eyes. They were strange tears of pride and happiness that he was a citizen of a great country that was capable of conquering the invincible Black Death, the dread marmot sickness, the plague! And the inhabitants of Khara were not simply seeing off Dr. Ustimenko, they were seeing off a friend and brother, a citizen of a workers' and peasants' state, a country where the working people ruled and good will and common sense reigned.

"We wish you to defeat all your enemies!" the crowd surrounding the caravan shouted.

"We will defeat our enemies," Volodya whispered, as though pledging an oath, and in his mind's eye he saw Barinov, Loboda and Shumilov.

"Let your people be happy because they deserve it!"

"Yes, they do," Volodya repeated, and thought of Pasha, Bogoslovsky and Aunt Aglaya.

"And let all your wounded get well as we got well!"

"They will," Volodya promised himself.

"Come back to us, Doctor Volodya!"

The horses snorted and shied, the crowd was getting bigger and noisier. As they rode out of Khara, Volodya saw Lamzy's father with another fifty mounted hunters or so on a rise. They all held rifles across the pommels. They fired twice in Volodya's honour, and then their splendid little, long-maned horses galloped away, ahead of the caravan, to warn the nomad camps that the Soviet doctor was riding through on his way home.

The nomad camps came out to meet him in full force. Volodya peered into the faces about him in an effort to remember which of them had been to the dispensary for treatment, which he had examined in their *yurtas*, which had been put into the hospital, and which he had operated on.

But he could hardly recognise anyone. They were all smiling now, and when he knew them they had been in pain. They all looked sunburnt and fit now, but they had looked pale and sickly then. Now they were holding back their horses with sure hands, but then they had either been lying in bed, or on stretchers, or leaning on their friends. Who could tell which one of these riders had "kept his age" because of him?

But what did it matter? The thing that mattered was that he had been doing his job, doing it always to the best of his ability. And the people appreciated it. Some of his operations could have been better, but he had done a certain amount of good here.

"A certain amount! Not very much, really," he was thinking. "But then did Professor Barinov's expedition mean so little? And I was a part of it. A tiny part of the whole, of my country."

He gazed ahead, at the mountains in the distance, far beyond which the war was raging. There, too, he would serve the cause to which he had dedicated his life.

## THE END

## REQUEST TO READERS

Raduga Publishers would be glad to have your opinion of this book, its translation and design and any suggestions you may have for future publications.

Please send your comments to 17, Zubovsky Boulevard, Moscow, U.S.S.R.

Перевод сделан по книге:
Ю. Герман. Дело, которому ты служишь.
Изд-во «Молодая гвардия», 1967 г.


Редактор русского текста Р. М. Шубина
Контрольный редактор А. В. Буяновская
Художник И. В. Борисов
Художественный редактор Е. Л. Афанасьева
Технические редакторы Р. В. Никифорова, Н. Н. Должикова

ИБ № 5299

Сдано в набор 5.12.88. Подписано в печать 25.08.89. Формат
84x108/32. Бумага офсетная. Гарнитура Тип Таймс. Печать
офсет. Усл. печ. л. 18,06. Усл. кр.-отт. 18,48. Уч.-изд. л. 22,74.
Тираж 5610 экз. Заказ №0972   Цена 3 р. 20 к. Изд. № 6059.

Издательство "Радуга" В/О Совэкспорткнига Государственного комитета СССР по печати.
119859, Москва, ГСП-3, Зубовский бульвар, 17.

Отпечатано с готовых пленок Можайского полиграфкомби-
ната В/О Совэкспорткнига Государственного комитета СССР
по печати. 143200, Можайск, ул. Мира, 93 в ордена Трудового
Красного Знамени Московской типографии № 7 "Искра рево-
люции" В/О Совэкспорткнига Государственного комитета СССР
по печати. 103001, Москва, Трехпрудный пер., 9.